NATURAL TALENT

"A belt would be useful," she said, folding her body to shield her chest and simultaneously keep her trousers from puddling around her ankles. "Too bad this jungle doesn't have a nice Banana Republic."

"Banana—"

"Never mind. Forget I said that."

They stared at each other.

In a few rapid strides he closed the distance between them and pulled her hard against his body.

She had been kissed before. He was certain of it. She didn't shriek or beat at him or pretend to swoon, any of which acts would have caused him to let her go instantly.

He had nearly half a minute of enjoying her astonished and unguarded compliance before she began to resist. He kept her imprisoned until he had taken full measure of her lips. By then she had gone rigid as a board in his arms, but he'd made his point and satisfied his impulse.

He released her and stepped back, grinning. "I believe you have some natural talent, Mac. Maybe you should attempt to develop it."

She smiled at him broadly. "Maybe I should."

And she pulled back her arm, made a fist, and planted it violently on his chin.

TWICE
A HERO

SUSAN
KRINARD

BANTAM BOOKS

NEW YORK TORONTO LONDON
SYDNEY AUCKLAND

TWICE A HERO

A Bantam Book / June 1997
All rights reserved.
Copyright © 1997 by Susan Krinard
Cover art copyright © 1997 by Franco Accornera
Book design by Laurie Jewell

ISBN 0-553-56918-X

Published simultaneously in the United States and Canada

Bantam Books are published by Bantam Books, a division of Bantam
Doubleday Dell Publishing Group, Inc. Its trademark, consisting of
the words "Bantam Books" and the portrayal of a rooster, is
Registered in U.S. Patent and Trademark Office and in other
countries. Marca Registrada. Bantam Books, 1540 Broadway, New
York, New York 10036.

PRINTED IN THE UNITED STATES OF AMERICA

RAD 10 9 8 7 6 5 4

In memory of
my beloved Granddad,
Hubert Earl Smith

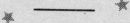

and with special thanks to
Ellie Johnson, Esther Reese,
Casey Mickle, and Callie Goble
for their help with the details.

PART ONE

From a wild weird clime
that lieth, sublime,
Out of Space—out of Time.

—EDGAR ALLAN POE

CHAPTER ONE

★ ───── ★

What's past is prologue.

—WILLIAM SHAKESPEARE

"**Y**OU COME FROM a long line of adventurers,

San Francisco, 1997

MacKenzie Sinclair. Damn it, Brat, I'll haunt you from my grave if you break the family tradition."

Homer Sinclair, his face flushed with passion, subsided back among the pillows. A vein in his forehead throbbed, and his left hand shook; MacKenzie leaned over the bed, stroking his flyaway white hair.

"Come on, Homer. Melodrama doesn't suit you."

"Don't you patronize me," he said, glaring at her. He could still manage a certain ferocity with that stare, even though his withered body had long ago lost its strength. "I'm dead serious, and I'm not going to see you grow old buried in books and moldy pottery, convincing yourself that's all there is to life."

MacKenzie stilled her hand on his forehead. "How many times do we have to go through this?"

"As many times as it takes to get it through that thick skull of yours," he snapped. His glasses slid down his nose; Mac set them carefully back in place, and he batted at her fingers. "I'm not going to have your martyrdom on my conscience—"

"Martyrdom?" Mac unhooked her legs from the chair she'd been straddling and pushed to her feet. "That's a low blow, Homer, and you know it."

"Maybe that's just what you need!"

She hooked her thumbs in the waistband of her loose jeans. No sense in letting him make her angry now; after six years she knew how to handle the brilliant and temperamental man in the bed. "Funny you should mention martyrdom. Of course it doesn't make any difference that *your* academic career got derailed when you were stuck with your widowed daughter-in-law and her two kids—"

"Should I have turned you all out in the street?"

"—and that you raised me and Jason after Mom died, got us an education—"

"An education that'll be wasted on you, Brat, unless you get your nose out of books and make yourself face the real world!"

Mac clamped her lips together and didn't let Homer see that he'd scored a direct hit. *I ought to have humored him,* she thought. But they'd never been anything but honest with each other.

"You want a philosophical discussion on what's real?" she asked wryly. She rested her foot on the chair and blew her bangs from her eyes. "Do you mind if we eat first? This could take all night."

Homer gave a wheezing chuckle. "I should have known I couldn't rattle you, Brat." His chuckle became a cough; he waved off Mac's concern with an irritable flap of his hand. "All right. No more low blows. Come here and sit down."

Something in his tone made her obey without question, as she'd done as a child before she'd lost her awe of him. The high color in his face had drained away, leaving his skin nearly translucent. Fragile, like delicate glass. And that close to shattering.

"I don't have much time left," he said.

The usual protest almost escaped her; a small dishonesty, but one she clung to with stubborn determination.

"You know it, Brat," he said, almost gently. "Your bullheaded denial isn't going to alter the facts." His hand felt for hers; thin fingers tightened with surprising strength. Their hands were much alike, blunt-nailed and sturdy. Or so Homer's had been, once.

"I'm ready to take off on the big adventure, if you'll forgive the tired cliché," he continued. "This old body wants to rest. But I need assurance from you that you're not going to let yourself wither away into an old intellectual prune, holed up with dusty books and artifacts in this house or in the museum because your mother and I robbed you of all the years you should have spent running wild and learning about life."

Mac suppressed a sigh. Homer was like a terrier chasing a rat when he was fixed on his subject. "Running wild isn't what it used to be in your day, Homer. I don't think I was ever cut out for it."

Her grandfather snorted eloquently. "You should have seen yourself when you were small, before your mother became ill. What a hellion you were. Into every scrape, up every tree. Lauren never let your hair grow because it was always full of twigs and gum and God knows what else."

Mac ran her hand through her cropped hair. "Don't remind me."

"You need reminding. You were as rough-and-tumble as any boy. More than Jason ever was. You had the neighborhood bully on the run when you were six, and he was two years older." He grinned. "Never made a lick of difference that you were the first girl to be born in our family for seven generations. You were a Sinclair in every way—"

"Like Dad?" she said softly.

He sobered, but his fingers kept their tenacious grip on hers. "Jake was so much like you." Homer's dark eyes—Sinclair eyes—grew hazy with memory. "He was wild, all right. But he had that stubborn streak of responsibility, same as you. A feeling that things were bigger than himself, that what he wanted didn't matter in the grand scheme of things. He was sure it was his duty to go to Vietnam."

And die, Mac added silently, *saving his platoon from ambush.* That was where his adventuring had taken him. He'd never even seen his daughter.

"Your mother wasn't right after Jake died," Homer muttered. "I was never a damned psychologist. Should have done more instead of spending so much time at Berkeley. . . ."

He was wandering. It happened sometimes—more and more often lately. Mac stroked the loose skin on the back of his hand.

"And then this," Homer said. He pulled his hand away from hers and slapped his sunken chest. "You're stuck waiting hand and foot on me, chained to this mausoleum of a house, thinking you owe it to me." He closed his eyes. "Such a waste."

Mac clasped her hands together between her knees and sucked in a deep breath. "Homer," she pleaded. "Stop this."

He shook his head. She saw the moisture gathered at the corners of his eyes, spilling into the sunken hollows beneath.

Tears. In all her life, Mac had seen him weep only once before. She swallowed and recaptured his hand. "You call it a waste? Without you Jason wouldn't have become the scientist he is. Look what he's already done in cancer research. And me—you gave me more than just reality, Homer. You gave me the world. You gave me a hundred worlds. Ancient Greece and Rome, the empires of China, the Renaissance, the Maya—"

"The past," he countered hoarsely. "Can we ever really escape it?"

"I don't know what you mean."

"Sometimes I wonder if it really is a curse. . . ." Once again his voice had changed, gone strange and distant with all the passion leached out of it. "Bad karma. Maybe that's the right word for it. The downside of wanting to conquer the world . . ."

"Homer, what are you talking about?"

His gaze sharpened. "Crazy old man, huh? Maybe I am. Or maybe things just get clearer."

"You might try making it clearer to me."

He chuckled without humor. "Did you ever wonder, Brat, why the Sinclairs, grand adventurers all, have had such blasted bad luck?"

This was a new train of thought, and not one that Mac liked. "I still don't get you."

"Oh, it doesn't go back very far, really. Only a few generations. But it's left its mark. My father lost in the Himalayas, me in this blasted bed wasting away, Jake and your mother. Maybe you're not so wrong to hide." He tried to sit up, shoving at the pillows with his back and elbows. "But damn it, Brat, maybe you're the one to end this thing."

He was almost incoherent, and Mac struggled to hide her concern. "What 'thing,' Homer?"

He didn't seem to hear. "Yes. A connection . . . I know I'm right." His expression hardened into resolve. "That box I had you get down yesterday. Put it up here. There's something I want you to see."

With a dubious glance Mac complied, retrieving the bulging cardboard box from the floor beside the bed.

The box had been shoved in the back of a closet no one had been into in years—like so much else of the ancient Victorian with its dusty artifacts and closed-up rooms. Mac had never found time for anything but cursory cleaning when she got home from the museum each day, and she and Homer certainly didn't have the money for outside help.

God only knew what Homer had hidden away. A mausoleum, he'd called the house, but he didn't really believe it. He loved this place and everything in it. It was a museum, filled with the artifacts Homer and past Sinclairs had collected. Most of it should be in a real museum, and would be once Homer was gone. . . .

She cut off that line of thought and inelegantly wiped dusty hands on her old T-shirt. The box was no different from countless others—except for the simple, faded label on top. "Sinclair" was all it said. Homer grunted and folded back the dog-eared flaps.

"Ah." He lifted out a wrapped, squarish bundle and set it carefully down beside him on the bed. "I was sure it was in here."

Mac leaned her elbows on her knees. "So what is it?"

"A piece of family history. And perhaps something more perilous." Homer's fingers trembled a little as he unwrapped the top layers of yellowed newspaper to reveal still more layers of ancient tissue. Within were two smaller packages, one a small box and the other a flat envelope.

Homer's reverence for the past was in every careful motion as he peeled the brittle tape from the envelope and opened the top. Carefully he slid out the contents and spread them on the comforter.

A handwritten sheet on old-looking stationery. Newspaper clippings, even more yellowed than the paper they'd been wrapped in. And a photograph, creased at the corner and fragile with age.

Homer turned the photograph toward her and leaned back. "There," he said. "Take a look."

Mac looked. The photograph was of two men, and it was undoubtedly an antique. The men wore clothing that was of a noticeably nineteenth-century cut; one of them even wore a bowler hat set at a jaunty angle.

She picked up the photograph by its edges. The background had an exotic cast to it, and she recognized the setting: ruins. Maya ruins, to be exact. One of the two men—the one with the bowler, dark hair, and a neat mustache—was dressed like a Victorian gentleman on a pleasant stroll into the wilderness. He was smiling.

Mac studied his face with a little shock of realization.

"You recognize him, don't you?"

"He's a Sinclair," Mac murmured. "Who?"

Homer almost grimaced. "Meet your great-great-grandfather, Peregrine Wallace Sinclair."

Peregrine Sinclair. Of course. "I think you mentioned him once before, when I was a kid. The one who was the youngest son of an English viscount, came to San Francisco—"

"And, in spite of his look of great propriety, was one of the Sinclair adventurers," Homer finished. "Note the background."

"Maya jungle," she said. "Lowlands, I'd say." She scratched her chin. "Tikal?"

"Right. Perry was down in the Petén in 1880, after Stephens and Catherwood but before Maudslay took his famous photographs. When the jungle was still a pretty dangerous place." He tapped his finger on the edge of the photo. "Notice the family resemblance?"

She couldn't help but notice. Peregrine Sinclair had the dark hair and eyes, the height, the regular but unremarkable features. And he was lean. All the Sinclairs were lean. On a man it could look quite elegant—as it did in the photos she'd seen of her father, or on Homer before he'd had the accident, or even Jason.

On a woman it streamlined chest and hips and turned into—Mac. Just plain, wiry Mac, who used to be mistaken for a boy.

"Hard not to see it," she quipped.

"Because you're a true Sinclair, just as he was. The same blood beats in your veins, Brat. Even Perry's wife, your great-great-grandmother Caroline, was a Sinclair in everything but blood. She was a reformer against the slave-girl trade in San Francisco and went on to become one of the country's leading suffragettes."

"Good for her. Did they screen her for the proper adventurous spirit before they let her join the family?"

Homer frowned over his glasses, but Mac deliberately turned her attention to the other man in the photo.

He was different from her great-great-grandfather, though at first the differences seemed subtle. Maybe an inch or two taller, a little stronger of build, with a stance that hinted at a greater weight of muscle under his clothes.

The clothes themselves suggested someone less concerned with sartorial dignity than Perry. The man's dirt-scuffed, khaki-colored trousers were tucked into battered boots, and his shirt was rolled up to his forearms and open to mid-chest. His legs were planted apart and his hands rested on his hips in a stance faintly hinting of challenge.

But it was his face that arrested her. A hard face, lacking the subtle refinement of Perry's. Square jaw nicked with a dimple in the chin, high slanted cheekbones, mouth cocked in a twist that indicated a sort of cynical patience. His eyes, under dark straight brows, were pale. Gray, she guessed. His hair was possibly a lightish brown, windblown and just long enough to brush his collar. All things considered, he looked exactly like what he was.

A man from another age. A more romantic age, when a thousand frontiers had yet to be explored. An age when an adventurer would fit right in. And this guy was the perfect specimen. He exuded machismo. It was there in every line of his body.

Funny how that powerful sense of him could transmit itself through an old photo across all these years, when the subject himself was ashes.

"Liam Ignatius O'Shea," Homer supplied.

Mac started as if the man in the photograph had spoken. She shifted in the chair and put the photo down. "Should I know him?"

"Interesting fellow, isn't he? He's quite a story in himself." Homer settled back, folding his hands across his ribs. "Liam O'Shea was Perry's friend and, for a time, his partner in adventure. The two men couldn't have been more different. O'Shea was a self-made man in the true nineteenth-century sense of the word. His family were prosperous landowners in Ireland until they were driven from their farm. They came to New York with almost nothing, and O'Shea lost his mother when he was still a boy. Worked his way across the country with the railroads and right out of poverty to become one of the richest men in San Francisco. They called him 'Lucky Liam.' "

Mac gave Homer a lopsided smile. "I see you can't wait to tell me all about him, and he's not even a Sinclair."

"I've been saving the best for last." But there was a grim sarcasm in Homer's voice. He glanced at the small box he'd left untouched on the comforter. "Go ahead. Open it."

Mac didn't betray the eagerness that had taken unexpected hold of her—just as Homer had undoubtedly intended. Without haste she pried the lid off the box and pushed aside the tissue wrappings.

The ancient chip of rectangular stone inside was evidently part of some larger whole. Three edges were smoothly finished, bordered by decorative symbols; the finely carved glyphs on the stone's gray surface ended abruptly at a clean break on the fourth side. The piece itself was less than two inches across. A small hole had been drilled near the top, and a cracked leather thong was still threaded through it.

A pendant. Mac lifted the piece out and let the thong dangle over her hand.

"Maya," she said, recognizing the glyphs. Maya, like the setting of the photograph. Almost unwillingly she looked at the photo again, her eyes drawn to Liam O'Shea and his timeless charisma.

"Take a closer look," Homer urged.

She saw what she'd missed the first time. Both Liam and her great-great-grandfather were wearing something around their necks—small chips of gray stone on dark, narrow thongs. Perry's rested neatly against his clothing; Liam's was displayed in the impressive vee of bare chest exposed by the open neck of his shirt. No detail was visible, but Mac was ready to bet the pendants matched the one she held in her hand.

"They found those in ruins near Tikal, back in 1880," Homer said.

Mac stroked the raised symbols on the stone. "Then this was Perry's."

"He wrote in his notes from the journey that they found a buried temple in the jungle, not far from the central ruins at Tikal, and did a bit of exploring. A fortuitous discovery put them on to an opening that proved to be, from Perry's account, the entrance to a burial chamber—"

"And," Mac said, "that being a less enlightened age with regard to ancient artifacts, they looted it."

Homer pressed his lips together. "It's true that not every treasure in this house was acquired by modern ethical means. But the only thing Perry and Liam took away that day was a single miniature stone tablet that they broke in two. Each of them took one half—"

"—and made them into pendants," Mac guessed, turning the stone chip over in her hand. "As mementos?"

"Or a sort of . . . gesture of friendship, I suppose. Perry carried his back to San Francisco and passed it down through the family."

"And what about O'Shea?"

"Liam O'Shea vanished in the jungle on a second trip they made to the ruins four years later," he said. "Perry came back alone after a falling out with O'Shea. Liam's death was assumed to be some kind of accident, but—"

Mac felt her stomach knot, almost as if she were learning of the death of someone she'd cared about and not a total stranger whose picture she'd first seen a few minutes ago. "But?"

Homer let the silence hang. She picked up the photo and examined the man who'd lost his life adventuring. The face of Liam O'Shea was utterly unmoved by any knowledge of his fate. He looked as though he'd spit in the eye of Death itself.

"How did it happen?" she prompted.

"That is the question, MacKenzie. The question that has to be laid to rest."

"You mean how he died?"

"Whether it really was an accident, or something else. Something like betrayal."

"Wait a minute." Mac set down the photo. "What is this all about? Curses and bad karma and how Perry's partner died in the jungle—"

He lifted a hand. "I'm getting to that. Maybe you'll understand when you read this letter. Perry's letter." Homer rattled the yellowed, handwritten page he held in his hand. "We don't know to whom he wrote it. Only this page remains, but it's the killer." He gave a dark laugh. "Read it."

She did, scanning the elegant script so unlike her own hasty scrawl. " 'Our quarrel was a terrible one, and I was too angry to consider the consequences of my actions. I left him in the jungle—and I will, until the day of my death, know that I was responsible for *his*. It remains a burden on my soul, a devil's bargain I cannot be rid of. Is Liam cursing me from the unmarked grave he found in that jungle?' "

"Now do you understand?" Homer said wearily.

"You mean—" Mac dropped the letter as if it had burst into flame. "You mean my great-great-grandfather killed his partner?"

"You read the letter. What do you think?"

A thousand times she and Homer had discussed esoteric matters of philosophy and tossed opinions at each other like balls in a tennis match. But this was no mild debate. "Curse," Homer had said. And so had Peregrine Sinclair.

"At a loss, Brat?" Homer said. "I'm not surprised. Didn't know about this skeleton in our family closet, did you? Not a pretty legacy. I don't think those bones were ever buried completely." He sank back on the bed. "One evil deed can echo through the generations."

All at once his meaning was crystal clear. She looked at the photograph again, trying to imagine that peaceful camaraderie rent by violence. "You think that my great-great-grandfather murdered his partner in the jungle and made it look like an accident."

He sighed. "I do, to the shame of all Sinclairs."

"And you think . . . but you couldn't, Homer. You've never been superstitious—"

At least not until you became ill. Mac bit her lip. "You think that somehow what he did so many years ago caused our family bad luck ever since?"

"What causes anything, Brat? Why did your father die in Vietnam and your mother lose her life to mental illness? Why is your brother finding it so hard to get funding for his promising research? Why am I in this blasted bed?"

Odd how Homer's matter-of-fact delivery could make it all sound so reasonable. Homer, who'd always seemed so proud of the Sinclair name and the spirit of adventure it stood for.

Adventure tainted by murder.

Mac shivered. "What was Perry's motive to murder his partner? Didn't you say they were close friends?"

"I don't know. His reasons were lost—"

"Then what other proof do you have that Perry did something so terrible? Did O'Shea leave any descendants to accuse—"

"No."

"But if all you have is that letter—"

"He all but admits he did it."

"Then why haven't I heard about this before? How did he cover such a thing up?"

Homer shrugged. "Who knows? Money can buy secrecy, Brat. Except in one's own heart."

The guilt in the letter. That was what Homer meant. But the way he spoke, the regret in his eyes—it was as if Homer had become Perry and taken that guilt upon himself.

Mac stood up. "All right. It's a terrible thing and I'm very sorry. But you had no part in whatever Peregrine did. None of us were there."

"We didn't have to be. The blood Perry spilled is still on Sinclair hands."

God. Mac looked away. The illness had finally begun to affect Homer's once razor-sharp mind. This morbid delusion wasn't going to help him, not so close to the end. She had to pull him out of it.

"How long have you believed this, Homer?"

"Believed? Not so long." He let out a shuddering sigh. "Certain things have just become clearer to me lately. Clearer and more important."

Mac felt a profound desire to take the blasted photo and tear it into little pieces. She picked it up and held it taut between her hands.

How did you leave this world, Liam O'Shea? Did someone you trust betray you? Did you curse the Sinclairs as you died?

Good grief, she was getting as bad as Homer. "Why are you telling me this now?" she asked. "If you're worried that I'll suffer from this 'curse'—"

"You already have, Brat. I don't want you to come to a bad end like the rest of us."

"Damn it, Homer." She leaned fiercely over the bed. "You're not making any sense."

He pushed up with a burst of strength. "I know why you withdrew from the challenges of life, MacKenzie. Maybe you didn't realize it. You lost too much too early. Couldn't risk losing more, saw what happened to anyone who did. I can't blame you. But now I have to ask you to take a risk. Not only for me and for our family, but for yourself."

A chill ran through Mac, a premonition of sudden and terrifying change. "Homer, I—"

"I have a mission for you, MacKenzie. An old man's last request. And your first quest. Fitting."

"Quest?"

He looked at her squarely, all the old stubborn authority behind a stare that could quell the most rebellious student. "It all happened in that jungle, Mac. And this"—he gathered up the stone Maya pendant in one clawed hand—"this is the symbol of an act that's haunted our family. Haunted me. A Sinclair betrayed O'Shea and left him without anyone to avenge him, to expose the truth. A Sinclair deliberately covered it up. I want to be able to leave this world knowing one Sinclair tried to make amends."

The heavy feeling of anticipation coiled more tightly in Mac's stomach. "Make amends how?"

"By returning this chunk of stone to the place Perry found it. By standing in that jungle, among those ruins, and asking Liam O'Shea's forgiveness."

It was as bad as she thought. "You want me to go to Guatemala?"

He sighed and passed a hand over his eyes. "I wouldn't ask this of you, Brat, if I didn't—"

"Look at me, Homer." She concealed her desperation, all the fear for Homer's sanity and of her own limitations. "I wasn't built for great things or wild adventures or breaking family curses, even if I did once beat up the neighborhood bully." She attempted a smile. "Isn't there something I could do a little closer to home?"

"No." He slapped the bedspread. "No way out of this, Brat. For your own sake. I know in my heart this has to be done. It's not logical. I don't pretend it is. But I ask it of you." His breath grew short and his face flushed with emotion. "I'll even beg if I have to, but you have to go back there and set things right. At the place where it happened."

Mac noted his rapid breathing and high color with alarm. "Homer, lie back. Calm down. You're going to—"

"Die. That's the truth, Brat, no escaping it. But I'm

not leaving until I have your promise. That you'll go down there when I'm gone and do what I ask, no matter how crazy you think it is."

"Homer—"

"Promise me," he wheezed, hands clutched on the bedspread in a stranglehold. "Promise me, Brat."

There was no choice. She would give anything in the world to keep him alive for one more hour.

"I promise," she whispered.

All at once the tension drained from his body, and he slumped boneless against the sheets. "Good. Then I can sleep."

"Homer—"

"Not the big sleep. Not yet. Got to make sure you make all the necessary arrangements," he muttered. But his voice was already fading, his lids heavy. He knocked his glasses from his nose and closed his eyes. "Do it soon, Brat. Don't wait too long. For your own sake."

There was no answer to his obsession. Not now. Perhaps later, when he'd rested . . .

"What about dinner?" she asked.

"Not hungry, Brat. Shriveled old men don't need much." He opened one eye. "Wouldn't hurt you to eat more yourself. You're skin and bones."

You just noticed? she thought as she pulled the comforter up around him and adjusted the pillows. He was already asleep and snoring unevenly when she retrieved the envelope, abandoned letter and his glasses from the bed.

She almost left the envelope and pendant with Homer's glasses on the bedside table. But he'd be upset if he woke to find them there, and she'd promised. Shaking her head, Mac absently looped the pendant's thong over her head and tucked the envelope under her arm as she walked to the kitchen.

No point now in preparing the gourmet microwave

dinner she'd planned for herself and Homer. She fixed herself a sandwich instead, straddled a chair at the tilted kitchen table and idly fingered the pendant as she ate.

Guatemala. It seemed worlds away from the cool, musty rooms of the museum, the safe, almost windowless walls and aisles of antiquities, the silence and solitude and certainty of who she was. The reality of a hot, steamy, primitive jungle was something she could only imagine. Off on a quest to end a curse that surely didn't exist.

Legendary curses had supposedly haunted the robbers of Egyptian tombs. Maybe that extended to Maya tombs as well. Liam and Perry had taken something from a burial chamber, and then Perry had turned inexplicably on his friend and thus sealed his own family's fate. Payback by the angry spirit-owners of those ancient ruins. . . .

Mac groaned and dropped her head in her hands. She definitely didn't believe in curses or bad karma. But Homer did. In the end that was all that mattered. She had given her word. If it meant Homer could go in peace, if she could give him one last gift, it would be worth it.

Resignation was already beginning to set in.

If you did this, Peregrine Sinclair, I think I'm going to add to the curse. I've never had to go searching for a ghost and ask its forgiveness.

If a man like Liam O'Shea would ever forgive. Pretty funny: two deceased men suddenly had her future in their long-decomposed hands.

Talk about morbid, Mac.

But she knew what she was good at, and it wasn't going on a quest or doing anything flamboyant or daring that would mark her out from a thousand other average women.

Hell, she wasn't even much good at being an average woman. Not the way men apparently expected, anyway. She'd just never caught the hang of it, and probably never would.

Without thinking she pulled the old photograph out of the envelope and spread it flat on the table top. *I can guess the kind of woman you'd go for, Liam O'Shea.* And wondered why such a thought even entered her mind.

Because he's on the other side of a century, not to mention dead.

If you're not even a match for a dead guy, you're hopeless, Mac.

She smiled at her own fancy and started on the dishes. No. Except for Homer's troubling and unexpected obsession, it wasn't too likely that some supposed past evil would ever be much of a burden on MacKenzie Sinclair. No more than the slight weight of the pendant hanging around her neck.

✦ ——————— ✦

O! Call back yesterday,
bid time return.

—WILLIAM SHAKESPEARE

T

Guatemala, 1997

HE PAST WAS alive. It panted in great hot exhalations of humid air, rumbled from the very heart of the jungle like the growl of some vast prehistorical beast. More alive than any sculpture or stele or chunk of pottery could ever make it.

It was real, and it was dangerously compelling. In this place you could lose your soul.

Mac stood in the clearing and turned in a slow circle, absorbing the ancient, potent power of the temples that rose on every side. Beyond the ruins of Tikal lay the jungle, a dense wall of brilliant green that hid a thousand other wonders. And, for the first time in her life, she wasn't only seeing it in a book.

You were right, Homer. She crouched on the plaza's neatly trimmed grass and looked up and up until she felt almost dizzy. *I think I'm beginning to understand what it means to be a Sinclair.*

Enough of a Sinclair to be inspired by the magnificence of the monuments an ancient civilization had abandoned so long ago; enough of the adventurer to be grateful she'd come, however crazy the motive.

Absently she reached for the leather thong around her neck, as she'd done so often since she'd boarded the plane in San Francisco. The pendant was her tangible link with Homer; here it almost made her feel as if she'd come to a familiar place rather than one she'd seen only in photographs.

Homer had been gone for over six months, and toward the end he'd been too weak to remind her of her promise to him. Toward the end he'd been content just to have her beside the hospital bed, to have her hold his hand and ease his passage.

But she knew he hadn't forgotten.

Mac swallowed back the lump in her throat. All her links to Homer had dissolved, one by one. The Victorian on Grove Street, far too big for one woman and in need of major repair, had long since been sold. The artifacts that had filled every dusty room had been donated to museums or universities—all but a few minor keepsakes.

And the pendant. The symbol of a curse Mac simply couldn't buy.

She let the stone chip fall back against her shirt and brushed off her khakis. It hadn't been so difficult to come here in the end. Not too much left to tie her to the life she was used to. No one to take care of in the mornings and evenings after work. No vast hulk of a house to try to keep in reasonable order, only a studio apartment in Berkeley. No responsibilities other than her job at the museum. Nothing to stand in the way of a promise.

So here she was, surrounded by a past that refused to die. She glanced skyward. "I hope you're watching, Homer. I'm beginning to wonder if you sent me on a wild-goose chase just to make me spread my wings."

A hint of warm breeze stirred the ends of her bangs under Homer's battered San Francisco Giants baseball cap. She could almost feel Homer with her now; she'd have given a lot to see his expression. Would he be laughing at the grand, final joke he'd played on her?

But he'd been right about her. She'd known it as soon as she'd stepped off the plane in Belize. She'd known it on the short flight to Flores and on the bus to the ruins. She knew it now, surrounded by the magnificent bones of history.

The past was *alive*. And so was she—more alive than she'd felt since childhood. . . .

Hold it, Mac, she chided herself. *Keep your feet on the ground.* She stood and stamped her boot for emphasis. Thinking like that came dangerously close to self-pity. She didn't regret a single moment with Homer. She'd have him back in a second if she could, uncharacteristic superstition and all.

But she couldn't have him back, and no one could ever replace him. Her social life hadn't exactly blossomed since she'd found herself with evenings and weekends free. Freedom wasn't all it was cracked up to be. And when the first pain of grief was past, it had been so easy to slip into the old routine. Spend as much time as possible at the museum, come back to the small Berkeley apartment, pop something in the microwave, read dusty old history books until bedtime.

Until she couldn't ignore the nagging sense that Homer was waiting for her to fulfill her promise and break the "curse."

Mac swore mildly as the toe of her boot connected with old but very solid limestone. She'd wandered to the base of one of the pyramid temples, towering a hundred feet over her head. The narrow steps leading up to the sacrificial platform at the top didn't make very good seats, but she braced herself against the steep incline, knees drawn up to her chest, and shrugged off her backpack. She needed another reminder of her purpose in coming here.

The photograph was carefully sandwiched between two pieces of museum board. She opened the makeshift case and laid the photo across her knees, glancing from faded image to present reality.

This was very close to the right part of Tikal, though the angle was different; you almost wouldn't know it was the same place, so changed was the site from the early 1880s. The temples behind Great-great-grandfather Perry and Liam O'Shea were overgrown and buried under centuries of vines, trees, and undergrowth, as they'd been until the first serious exploration had begun over a decade after their visit.

Now Tikal was a national park. Not much of a risk to visit it these days. But she *was* here, where they had been. She traced Perry's dapper figure with her fingertip and then the shape of the man beside him.

Liam O'Shea. She could still find herself fascinated by that cocky half-smile, that militant macho stance even after she'd looked at the damned photograph well over a thousand times.

Asking herself the same crazy questions. *Did you do it, Peregrine Sinclair? Did you rob this magnificent man of his strength and hope and future? Did you taint the honorable name of Sinclair forever?*

And then she would see Liam O'Shea, and imagine his life, and how he had struggled so far to meet such an end. Alone, with no one to care that he'd died.

Admit it, Mac. You came here as much for him as for Homer.

Pretty crazy, mooning over a guy in a photo. A guy who'd been dead for a century and probably would have been a jerk, judging by that smile. He probably was just the kind to curse someone and make it stick.

But I'm here to make amends. If you'll listen, Liam O'Shea, wherever you are.

She tilted her cap to a defiantly rakish angle. Hardly likely that she'd find Liam's remains. He couldn't have died in Tikal, or they would have found him already, and the old newspaper clippings reporting his death hadn't given any details.

Mac stood and tucked the photo away. No—her symbolic apology to Liam O'Shea would have to be whispered to the jungle itself. Maybe a ritual burial of the pendant near one of the ruins. She wished she'd paid more attention to New Age traditions. Candles and incense and magic circles and chants. Which would probably make Liam O'Shea's ghost laugh his head off.

She snorted. Ghost indeed. No such animal.

She tested her stamina by climbing the precipitous temple stairway to the platform at the top. From this height the other tourists at the site were little more than toy figures, too distant and indifferent to share her minor victory.

She sighed a little wistfully and started back down. The morning mist was lifting. There was still a great deal to see at the site, and even with two days in one of the local hotels she had a lot of ground to cover. During that time she had to decide exactly what to do with the pendant. She hoped that some lightning flash of inspiration would strike.

By early afternoon, following a quick snack of beans, tortillas, and a fortifying Dr Pepper at a *comedor*, she hadn't had a single bright idea. She'd seen two of the main temples and one acropolis, not to mention a number of steles and related exhibits. All of it was fascinating enough. But none of it had given her a clue. She felt as if she were in the wrong place entirely.

As if she'd missed something vitally important.

She wandered close to the dense border of trees surrounding central Tikal, as she'd done time and time again throughout the morning. Out there, perhaps, was what she was searching for—ruins that had yet to be excavated; ancient, overgrown paths untrodden for centuries; the deep green silence of eternal nature.

"That's where Perry and Liam would have gone, isn't it, Homer?" she said. "Liam didn't die in Tikal. You think I should take a shot, however unlikely, at finding him."

A shiver worked up her spine. An image of Liam O'Shea rose in her mind; she didn't even have to pull out the photo. It had long since been memorized.

"Maybe I was premature about dismissing ghosts," she muttered. "I'm beginning to think Lucky Liam is haunting me. Is he up there somewhere egging me on, waiting for me to trip his curse? Is he doomed to wander these ruins for eternity until someone lays his bones to rest?"

"Bones, *señorita*? No bones here. But I show you many things."

The voice was young and masculine and accompanied the teenage boy who stood directly in front of her. Mac was grateful she'd never had much of a blush. The kid probably thought she was nuts, talking to herself.

But he only regarded her with an open, earnest face that bore a remarkable resemblance to the murals and carvings of the Maya of ages past—strong, hooked nose, full lips, and high cheekbones. He was skinny enough to remind her of herself. On his belt, secured by a leather loop, hung a large and imposing machete.

He grinned at her. "You want a guide, *señorita*? Into the jungle? I take you. Only five dollars."

Five dollars. An absolute bargain. *I'm beginning to believe this isn't just a coincidence, Homer.*

More craziness. Maybe the heat was doing funny things to her brain. She made a mental inventory of her supplies. Just enough for a day's wandering: map, small flashlight, repellant, canteen, matches, first-aid supplies, and a few other useful items. "What did you have in mind?" she asked the boy. "I'm not prepared to hike too far out into the jungle today."

The boy's grin widened. "Not far. You want bones? Maybe I know where."

Well, that was too much of an incentive to pass up. *Not Liam's bones,* she reminded herself. *Not human either. I hope.* But she fished in her wallet for a sweat-dampened five-dollar bill and set it on the boy's grimy, outstretched palm. Even if this proved to be a waste of time, five dollars was not exactly a huge investment.

"You won't be sorry, *señorita,*" the boy said, tucking the bill in the pocket of his own threadbare trousers. "I know the best place. *Venga conmigo, por favor.*"

Before she could ask a single question he was off, striding away from the carefully maintained area around the central plaza and toward the border of trees. He set a remarkably rapid pace for someone who must be used to dealing with sedentary *turistas.* The boy hardly waited for her to catch up before he plunged into a seemingly impenetrable mass of green.

At first there was a trail that even Mac could see. On either side the jungle formed a living wall of small trees, palms, ferns, lianas, and a hundred unfamiliar species of flora. Overhead hung the upper canopy of larger trees, with the occasional great ceiba towering fifty feet above the rest.

Only isolated cries of birds or monkeys broke the almost eerie quiet. Mac knew the jungle wasn't as noisy as fiction often painted it, but there was something in the quality of the stillness that made the hair at the nape of her neck stand on end.

It was as if the very jungle were holding its breath.

Mac rolled her eyes as she tripped over a root across the path. *Great. Are you putting these crazy ideas in my head, Homer? I sure as hell don't remember thinking this way before. . . .*

"*Cuidada, señorita.* I cut a path now."

She barely avoided walking into her guide as he deftly pulled the machete from his belt and began to slash at the growth into which their path disappeared. Mac glanced back the way they'd come. One part of her—the familiar, practical part—told her that it wasn't such a good idea to cut through the jungle away from the marked paths.

There was another part of her that snorted in derision at her caution. It was the part that Homer had remembered from her childhood, that had once confronted a neighborhood bully. The part that followed the Sinclair blood. The part that could see a mere photo of Liam O'Shea and respond on a level that made no logical sense.

"This way, *señorita.*"

She blew out her cheeks with an explosive puff of air and followed. The pace was much less rapid now as the boy hacked his way through the tangled mass of greenery, wielding the machete with consummate grace. Mac had more time to consider how hot it was, and notice the black flies that seemed to have suddenly discovered the presence of easy prey. She considered digging out her insect repellant and giving herself another dousing.

But it took concentration to keep up with her guide, who exhibited a preference for scrambling through the roughest and swampiest patches of ground. Mac had been careful to come to Guatemala during the *canícula*—August's two-week "dry" period in the midst of the rainy season—but there was still plenty of mud. And mosquitoes. And plants whipping her in the face.

Any number of things to discourage all but the most intrepid of adventurers.

After almost an hour of walking, Mac was beginning to feel rebellious.

Homer, are you watching? This had better be worth it.

It was. One moment she was floundering in her guide's wake, and the next she walked into a tiny clearing and came face-to-face with a vine-covered ruin.

The place bore little resemblance to the great ruins of central Tikal. A thousand years ago it had been part of the great Maya city-state, which had sprawled over fifty square miles. Now it was a crumbling collection of unexcavated minor buildings. Such places dotted the Petén, Guatemala's lowland jungle, a dime a dozen.

But it had a very peculiar effect on Mac. She stopped and caught her breath, mesmerized. She forgot to slap at flies and mosquitoes, or brush the sodden hair from her eyes. She eased out of her backpack and crouched where she was, taking it all in.

Wild. Ancient. Untamed in a way Tikal proper no longer was. And Mac's heart came alive as it hadn't done in the spectacular but well-trodden Maya city.

This was what Tikal had been like when Perry and Liam O'Shea had come to the Petén. *This* must have been what they felt when they made a discovery, knew they could be the first Americans to see what the jungle had hidden.

Hah. That's not you, Mac. The kid's probably brought plenty of tourists here. But nothing could dampen her strange excitement.

This was exactly the place to enact her little ceremony of contrition for Sinclair transgressions. *This could even be the place where they found the pendant.* Another crazy thought that no longer felt quite so crazy. She wiped sweaty palms on her khakis and reached for the piece of carved stone that hung around her neck.

It was warm. Hell, everything was warm here—but she'd expected stone, at least, to be cool.

She released the pendant and stood. "I never caught your name," she said to the guide, who'd moved off somewhere behind her. "Do you know what this place is called?"

Overhead a macaw shrieked. Mac turned around. The boy wasn't there. She pivoted. No sign of him at all.

"Great," she said. "Hello? *Hola?*"

A mosquito whined next to her ear. She waved it away and started back down the path the boy had cut. Not a single swaying leaf hinted that he'd been there any time recently.

"O . . . kay." She planted her hands on her hips and looked up through the forest canopy at the sky. Still light for several more hours, anyway. At least the kid had made her a trail to return, even if he hadn't considered an escort back to Tikal part of his five-dollar fee.

"I should have paid him ten," she muttered. But this way he wouldn't be witness to what the crazy *gringa* was about to do.

She turned to the ruins once more. Here she was, living an adventure—alone, in the jungle, with a piece of three-dimensional history smack-dab in front of her. Homer would be proud.

And Liam O'Shea was waiting.

The thought sobered her. She walked toward the ruins, picking her way over rubble and low brush. She crouched to examine massive fallen stone steles, patterned by Maya glyphs. Beyond was the first of several buildings, blackened by time, covered by moss and lichen and every kind of tropical vegetation that could gain a foothold.

She walked around the nearest building. From the rear she could see something that hadn't been completely visible before—another, larger structure, and the gaping black maw of an entrance. Temple or palace; she wasn't enough of a Maya scholar to know what the building might be. The narrow-stepped stairway leading to the top of its platform did not rise very high as such buildings went. The rear of the building was butted up against a limestone ridge, and jungle growth had nearly obscured the roof and walls.

The black square of the entrance seemed to lead right into the steep hillside. She knew that the Maya had considered their temples to be artificial sacred caves, their portals gates to the world of the gods. The doorway drew her with its mysterious promise of secrets hidden from daylight.

On impulse she crossed the hundred yards to the building and paused at the entrance. Cooler air brushed her cheeks. She leaned against the stones and peered into darkness. There was no hint of light inside, but obviously the way had been cleared by someone, and not too long ago. That meant anything of value within would have long since been looted.

But there was a feeling deep in her gut that her ritual must be enacted here, a place held sacred so long ago. She had to go in.

Mac squared her shoulders and clasped her pendant. It was no longer merely warm, but almost hot to the touch. The stone must have remarkable properties of heat transference if it could take on her body's temperature so quickly and hold it so well.

She considered removing the pendant to see if it would cool off again, but somehow she felt the need to keep it where it was until she was ready to consign it back to the earth. *Superstition*, she thought. But what if it was? No one was around to know she'd taken the first dangerous step from solid reality into a realm of uncertain fantasy.

The next step was physical. She dug out her flashlight, switched it on, and started into the entrance. She didn't expect to go very far. There would probably be a series of smallish rooms, all dark and damp, where once priests or lords had carried out sacred ceremonies. She shivered a little in spite of the heat, remembering tales of human sacrifice and self-mutilation. Maya lords had routinely drawn their own blood from body parts as gifts to the gods. . . .

"Okay, Homer. You used to love telling me those stories when I was a kid, but they don't scare me anymore." She swung the flashlight beam back and forth, surprised that she still hadn't reached the rear of the building, or even a partition. Instead the walls came closer together the farther inward she advanced, until she was in a long, narrow tunnel.

By now she had to be under the limestone ridge itself. She stopped to run the flashlight beam behind her, along the uneven floor and up and down the walls. Plain and bare, as she'd suspected. Disappointment washed over her.

What did you expect? There wasn't likely to be some fantastic altar conveniently available for her ceremony. Still, the urge to keep going was too strong to resist.

"I know what you'd say, Homer. Get to the end before you turn back." At least the flies and mosquitoes hadn't followed her. She focused the flashlight dead ahead and kept walking. And walking. Something was definitely crazy here. She'd never in her life read about underground tunnels among the Maya ruins. If such a discovery were to be made, it would have been done long since.

She glanced at her watch, grateful for the illuminated dial. Ten minutes she'd been walking, albeit at a very plodding pace. This *was* crazy. If she didn't hit a wall or something in the next few yards, she was going back.

At the requisite few yards, an instant before she turned away, her flashlight beam splashed against a wall. Stone rose in front of her, solid and implacable.

And not plain. No, definitely not plain. The entire surface was crowded with Maya glyphs. Undefaced, unchipped, uncracked, as if time itself had stood still within this strange hallway.

There was no other word for it than awesome. She didn't have an expert's ability to decipher the ancient symbols, but she recognized the glyphs that represented the passage of time, and dates, and the vaster measurements by which the Maya had calculated the march of eons. They had been obsessed with time, those ancient ones—time far before their first civilization, and time to come long after they had vanished.

She stroked the light down the surface of the wall to the more conventional relief carved under the rows of glyphs. It showed a man—a lord—in full-feathered Maya regalia. But though everything else in the scene was perfectly depicted, there was something wrong with the man's figure. It seemed to be cleanly cut off halfway through the body. He was shown walking purposefully, in profile, directly into a wall. And the wall bisected his body, as if half of him had melted into it. She'd never seen anything like that before, not in any book or exhibit or in Tikal itself.

She moved cautiously forward again; her toe brushed something that rattled and rolled under her foot. Instinctively she aimed the flashlight down, expecting rubble, though the floor here was clean of it.

Instead, she found bones.

Human bones.

Mac had never been the flighty sort. She didn't jump back or scream. That kind of stereotypical female behavior had been left out of the mold that had shaped her sturdy, too-rangy body.

So she only looked. That the bones had been here for some time was evident by their condition. There was not a scrap of flesh left on any of them, and only traces of rotted fabric that must once have been clothing.

She followed the loose trail of leg bones to where the torso had collapsed close to the wall. Somehow the rib cage, vertebrae, clavicles, and skull had fallen in almost a straight line. Or perhaps someone had laid them out there.

Morbid curiosity brought her closer. The bones were large; masculine, she guessed. Someone who'd been tall, well built. She winced at the grinning skull. Why did people refer to them as grinning, when there was nothing funny about the end of a once-vital life?

She gripped her pendant again, comforted by its inexplicable heat. *Who were you? A guide like that boy who led me here? A tourist who made a fatal mistake in the jungle?*

She knew there were things that could kill, even so close to a tourist center. Jaguars were too shy, and there were few predators, but nature could set traps for the unwary. And diseases. And violence, for Guatemala was not yet an easy nation.

Mac found herself rapidly losing her enthusiasm for the adventure. Wasn't she here to mourn the death of someone who'd died in a place just like this? Whose bones might be lying, untended, where no one would ever find them—

Her thoughts dwindled to incoherence as the beam of her flashlight came to rest at the base of the skull. Something lay among the vertebrae—something slightly darker, more regular. Familiar. A stone chip, drilled through the top, the remains of a rotted leather cord twisted through it.

Mac dropped into a crouch and leaned closer, careful not to disturb the bones.

And she knew. She knew before she saw the chip close up, before she dared to touch it and lift it to her eyes.

She knew exactly how it would match her own pendant, how it would be the other half of a whole once broken in two. When she pressed the irregular edge of the chip against that of her own, it fit like a hand in a glove.

"Oh, God," she said hoarsely. "It can't be. The world doesn't work this way."

No. Life didn't do things like this—make it so easy, so convenient, giving you a guide to lead you right to where he'd died, so close to Tikal, in a place a hundred others would have seen before you. This could not be Liam O'Shea.

But she knew it was. She knew with a certainty beyond reason.

"Liam," she said, tasting the name. This was all that remained of that handsome, arrogant, *alive* young man she'd seen in the photo.

She'd done what Homer had asked, and more. She'd found Perry's partner. The man he'd murdered.

She felt as if she'd been kicked hard in the solar plexus. Her knees buckled. There, face-to-face with hard reality, she bent her head and mourned. And, in her hands, the two halves of the stone chip burned and burned.

The brief ceremony she'd planned was no longer something simple and far away. It was as real and inescapable as Liam's bones.

What now, Homer? Do I bury him along with the pendant, and hope that will be enough? But she knew it wouldn't be, somehow. Even apologies would never be enough. Now she understood the weight of guilt Homer had felt near the end, as if Peregrine Sinclair's evil act had come to rest on her own shoulders. And only she could set it right.

Mac rose shakily. It was so damned *hard* to think of Liam O'Shea as this pile of bones. She didn't take out the photo, though she wanted to. As if that could bring him to life again.

She forced herself to turn back to the wall. She needed to clear her mind. There was something regular and soothing about the glyphs and ritual figures carved into the limestone surface. Repetitive and patterned, yet elegant and profound. Eternal, as human life was not. She followed each line of glyphs from right to left and back again, trying not to think of Liam O'Shea.

Had he been afraid when he died? Had he cried out for someone to care, someone to hold his hand as Mac had done with Homer?

Had he cursed the Sinclairs with his dying breath?

She laughed a little and leaned her folded hands against the wall, one stone chip still nested in each palm.

"I wish I could undo it, Homer," she said. "His death, the curse, everything. Maybe you'd still be alive. Maybe Dad, and Mom— Oh, this is insane. But if I could go back . . ."

In her right hand, Perry's stone chip flared like a burning brand. In her left, Liam's did the same. A wave of overwhelming nausea caught her by the throat and twisted her innards, propelling her away from the wall. Her fingers spasmed helplessly around the pendants even as they seared her flesh.

A black stab of pain shot into her skull, and she knew she was going to faint. She flailed blindly for the wall again, catching the brim of her cap and knocking it from her head. Her fists struck something solid, and the impact drove the broken edges of the pendants into her palms with enough force to pierce the skin.

The slow welling of blood startled her into a moment of lucidity. She opened her hands. At the precise moment the pendants dropped to the ground, the wall she was leaning on vanished.

She fell. It seemed she traveled toward the ground for a much longer time than distance or gravity could account for. The nausea redoubled, accompanied by a pounding in her skull that drove out anything resembling a coherent thought. When she hit the floor it was as if she landed on something soft rather than unevenly laid stone. A moment later she felt the impact and rolled into a compact ball, waiting for the temple to crash down on top of her.

It didn't. She straightened carefully. The sickness and pain were miraculously gone, but she was in total darkness. Her flashlight had been knocked from her hand; she couldn't tell where the tunnel walls were, or how far she'd fallen. Logic dictated that it couldn't have been more than a few feet. But what in hell had happened to the glyph wall?

"Hidden trap doorways?" she murmured, getting to her hands and knees. "Never heard of those, either." She kept up a steady stream of talk, listening to her one-sided conversation echo back from unseen walls, reminding herself that she'd never really been afraid of the dark. She'd grown up in a big echoing house with a thousand rooms full of mysterious and often scary objects—or so it had felt to a child.

She checked her backpack by feel; okay. Her body was still in one piece. Watch still functioning—she'd been in this place for almost an hour. Next thing was to find the flashlight—and Homer's cap, which she'd been clumsy enough to knock from her own head.

As for the pendants—they, too, were gone, and the ceremony of repentance had yet to be performed.

She groped along the floor, scraping her hands on rough edges where blocks met unevenly. She felt up and to the side and connected with a wall—flat and damp and uncarved. She oriented herself by that and crawled in what she thought was the way she'd come.

No carved glyph-wall met her searching fingers. But the flashlight rolled against her knee, and she grabbed it with a gasp of relief. A quick test showed that it was still working, though it had been switched off sometime in the fall.

She swept the beam ahead of her, pushing to her feet. Sure enough, the walls were there on either side of her, exactly the same as they'd been before. But the glyph wall wasn't there, and neither were Liam's bones nor the pendants. Either she'd gone flying yards into the tunnel, or she'd become totally disoriented in the darkness.

Panic was not a familiar emotion, or one she had any desire to become better acquainted with. Okay—the glyph wall had to be either one way or the other. Once she bumped into it, she'd know where she was.

She played a quick mental game and chose one of the directions. After a minute she knew it couldn't be the right one. She turned around and marched back the other way with a speed that was just a bit reckless in the dark.

When she hit the next firm, hard surface it was definitely not a wall. Her hands came up to steady herself and pressed against warm, damp fabric covering equally warm and unmistakable contours. Hard, sculpted contours. Masculine. Definitely masculine. And they didn't belong to the skinny boy who'd guided her to this place.

The smell of sweat and green and earth and man

filled her nostrils. Deep, harsh breathing gusted past her ear. She dropped her hands and backed away, holding the flashlight low so as not to blind him.

"Am I glad I ran into you," she said. "I've been wandering inside this tunnel for what feels like hours." She heard the rapid patter of her own words and realized how nervous she sounded. She had absolutely no idea who this guy could be. "I . . . seem to have gotten myself turned around. I thought I was alone here."

He gave a low grunt. In the faint illumination radiating from the flashlight, all she could see of him was solid height, light-colored clothing, and a glitter of eyes.

"What are you doing in here, boy?"

She stiffened, every other concern momentarily wiped clean from her mind. The lapse was brief. How many times had this happened to her during childhood? It wasn't such an easy mistake to make now that she'd grown, but in all fairness she knew she contributed to the problem because of her preference for loose, comfortable, practical clothing.

This guy couldn't see her clothing, or much of the rest of her. She knew her voice was husky and low, a little rough now with nervousness. That must account for it. She made herself relax and decided that perhaps it wasn't such a bad idea to let him think she was male. At least for the time being.

A hard, very large hand caught her arm. "You're American. How did you get here?"

She held her arm very still in his grasp. "Yeah, I'm American." *As if it's any of your business, buster.* "I came to see the ruins. I walked. I didn't know this tunnel went so far."

The man felt up the length of her arm. "Just how young are you? Where's your party?" *His* voice was deep, with an edge of roughness—eminently masculine, like his grip and size. She began to feel more than a little annoyed.

"Party? Did I miss the celebration?" she quipped.

He gave a bark of laughter, but in the dim glow she could see his eyes narrow. "Who did you come with? I didn't see anyone else in the jungle. The Indians said no one's been here for months."

No one here for months? She snorted and pulled her arm free. "Look, friend, I don't know who you are or where you've been, but if you go a mile or so south of here you'll run right into Tikal. Which is where I intend to be very shortly." *The minute I've finished what I came here to do, that is.*

"Tikal," he repeated. "I would have known if anyone else was here."

Great. She'd had just the luck to run into a lunatic in a very dark tunnel. She backed away. "Whatever you say. If you don't mind, I have business to take care of."

She calculated how best to slip around him and had gone a few yards when he reappeared beside her. His footfalls were eerily soundless; the hair stood up on her neck.

"I'll join you, lad. My lantern broke, and I'll need your light."

Great. "Well, uh, that would be fine except I have something to do before I leave—"

"Nonsense. This is no place for a child." His hand fastened around her arm again before she could dodge out of the way. The masculine scent of him, as primal as the jungle itself, nearly overpowered her. His strength was irresistible, though Mac had never been weak. Fighting him didn't seem like such a good idea just now.

"You can take me to your camp when we're out of here," he said, steering her along. "I have supplies to replenish, and I want to see who arrived without my knowing about it."

He sounded disgruntled, she thought. What did he expect—to have the entire jungle and its contents to himself? He'd be plenty annoyed when he saw all the tourists at Tikal.

"I can show you the trail back to Tikal," she said. *And you can bet we'll part company the minute I get the chance.*

"Will you, then?" he said, and gave an inelegant snort. "I'll appreciate the help."

She thought better of saying anything more at that point, though she was constantly aware of his presence at her side. He was big and well built, of that much she was certain. If he was crazy, she'd have a hard time throwing him off. Maybe he was some kind of hermit who'd come here to live in solitude. The Petén might be a good place for that, if you didn't mind rain, mud, mosquitoes, and flies and didn't stick too close to the tourist traps at Tikal.

Maybe this guy had been a hermit too long.

Now you're really letting your imagination run away with you. . . .

"There," the man said suddenly. "The entrance."

And sure enough, there was a faint patina of illumination along the tunnel walls. Mac heard a faint hiss that grew louder as the brightness increased.

Rain. Not merely a drizzle, but torrents and buckets of rain, sheeting across the bright square that defined the exit.

Great. She'd deliberately come to Tikal during the August dry period, but apparently she'd cut it too fine. She'd be drenched, and the trail back to Tikal would be a soup of mud.

Her unwanted companion showed no surprise at the

downpour. Before she could turn to examine him in the light, he said something unintelligible and pushed past her.

Mac stopped just inside the shelter of the tunnel. The man had plunged right out into the rain and stood with his back to her, hands on hips and head flung back in defiance of the weather. The rain made short work of plastering his shirt and pants flush to his body, confirming what Mac had already guessed by touch alone.

He was tall. Over six feet, she guessed, and not in the least skinny. Broad shoulders, taut back, firm buttocks. Wavy pale brown hair, just brushing the back of his collar, darkened to a deeper hue as the rain slicked it down. He was very impressive, even from a rear view. Perhaps even especially from a rear view. . . .

Mac felt a jolt of chagrin at the direction of her thoughts. She'd never really let herself admire men in a purely physical sense, not since that one disastrous and very brief relationship in college. She had no use for the male fixation on butts and breasts and beauty, or similar female obsessions; that kind of ritual preening would never be part of her world.

But now she looked. Damn it, why not? This wasn't Berkeley or San Francisco. She wasn't part of the meat market people referred to as dating. She was out in a comparatively safe jungle where no one knew her, where all bets were off and magic waited just behind the next tree.

Maybe that was it, why she studied the man with such fascination. He was . . .

Yes. He was *part* of the magic. He was the opposite of the grim reality of Liam's bones in the tunnel, or curses that echoed down the generations. He was the incarnation of adventure itself, like an ancient idol brought to life. He was an integral part of his surroundings—the ruins, the jungle, even the rain and mud. He owned the place. He *belonged* here.

Mac let herself share in that belonging, experience the feeling of being suspended in time and space, free for the moment of any lingering guilt over a past she'd had no part of.

Slowly she stepped out into the rain. It baptized her with fierce joy, making a close cap of her hair and soaking her clothing in a matter of seconds, bathing face and arms and legs. She felt water trickle under her shirt and between her breasts. A tingle of awareness tightened her nipples.

Primal. Primeval. This was nature in its glory, and somehow it passed a little of that glory on to her. She wasn't plain, ordinary Mac anymore. She was a goddess of the forest, a dauntless heroine ready to meet any challenge. . . .

"I'll be damned. You're a woman!"

The man's deep, husky voice snapped Mac out of her reverie. He had turned around; a retort was already on her lips before she got a good glimpse of his features.

"Gee, thanks for clearing that up. I—" She found herself gazing into eyes that gave new meaning to the hackneyed phrase "steely gray." For a moment all she could do was stand in gaping silence as the man examined her with insulting thoroughness.

"I don't believe it," he said. "What the hell are you doing here?"

But she wasn't really listening. She didn't have time to resent his critical tone or his arrogant questions or the fact that he was acting just as she'd expect a typical male to act when confronted with the unimpressive MacKenzie Rose Sinclair.

All she could hear was the pounding of her own heart and the startled rasp of her own breathing. And all she could see was his strong and powerfully masculine face.

A face she recognized. A face she'd first seen months ago. A face she'd been carrying around in her backpack ever since she'd left the San Francisco International Airport for the wilds of Central America.

The man was the spitting image of Liam O'Shea.

CHAPTER THREE

*The best of prophets of the
future is the past.*

—GEORGE NOEL GORDON,
LORD BYRON

MAC FELT HER mouth go completely dry even as the rain trickled from her nose onto her lips and dripped from her chin.

"I don't believe it," she whispered. "What the hell are *you* doing here?"

She had the vague notion that his lips moved in some kind of reply, but there was a buzzing in her ears that blocked out any sound. All she could do was fight off the impulse to burst into frankly hysterical giggles.

Out of all the things that could have happened to her in this incredible place, nothing could be quite so unbelievable. Or so appropriate. She'd come seeking absolution from Liam O'Shea, and she'd found *him*. First his bones, and then his modern-day clone.

Her discovery stared at her and she stared back, so struck by the absurdity of it all that her shock faded quickly into a curious detachment.

Yes, the likeness was almost flawless. This pseudo-Liam was a little harder, a little more daunting than his photographic counterpart. His hair was a little longer, his eyes paler, his face more weathered with experience. And, if possible, more handsome.

Oh, not in the conventional sense. He was Harrison Ford and Daniel Day-Lewis and Timothy Dalton rolled into one, with perhaps a dash of a young Charlton Heston thrown in. Masculinity personified, with not one iota of boyish softness. His jaw was set, and she could tell he wasn't too happy about something.

Why shouldn't he be happy? Mac was feeling almost giddy, no longer quite tethered to reality. Or to anything else that would normally send her hotfooting in the opposite direction—such as the critical gleam in his eye that surely found her wanting.

"I'll be damned," he said again, this time with a more pronounced drawl of disgust. "Who in hell was idiotic enough to bring an American woman to the jungle?"

"Excuse me?"

His gaze swept the surrounding jungle before fixing on her again, dark with annoyance. "Whoever did it should be horsewhipped. How did you get separated from him?"

"Him," who? The guide? *Horsewhipped?* "I think that might be sort of a severe punishment," she said, "considering I only paid him five dollars to guide me here from Tikal."

He cast her an even more dubious glance, if that were possible. "Then where's the rest of your party?"

"Doing the cha-cha in Tikal, probably."

He was not amused by her lame attempt at humor. "The men you came with. The fools who thought a woman could manage in a place like this."

Mac was in far too strange a mood to be annoyed. With a little effort, she could almost imagine that this was the way the real Liam would have talked. He'd have been a product of his times—in other words, a born male chauvinist. Whoever this guy was, and whatever his problems, he was unwittingly playing the role to a tee.

"Well, la-dee-dah," she said, tapping her cheek. "I came to this big bad jungle all by my little old self. What's getting into women these days?"

The glint of annoyance in his eyes had become something of a disturbance to rival the tropical storm overhead. "By yourself," he repeated with patent disbelief.

"Yup. Amazing but true."

Liam's double took a step forward, crowding her close to the ruin behind her. "Miss—" He looked her up and down again in such a way that his assessment of her person could not have been mistaken. "I presume you *are* a miss? No man in his right mind would let his wife come to the Petén."

No man in his right mind would make such bizarre statements. She returned the favor of examining his nicely revealed physique. The slopes and valleys of his chest and midriff were prominently delineated through the wet fabric of his shirt. Both it and his trousers were a little unusual in cut, as were his mud-splotched boots. He wore a heavy leather belt and some kind of bandoleer hung with small pouches and loops. Expedition wear of the sort you'd see in a '40s safari movie.

Another surge of recklessness moved her mouth before her brain could stop it. "It's Miss," she said. "MacKenzie's the name. But I think it's 'Ms.' to you."

He didn't get it. She could see it went right over his head. Maybe it was time to start asking a few questions of her own. "I didn't catch *your* name, Mr. . . ."

His gaze made another sweep from her boot toes to her dripping hair. "Dressed as you are and in such a state, Miss MacKenzie, I doubt you could catch anything but the grippe."

She guessed what he implied. She knew how she must appear, in waterlogged jeans and camp shirt, not in the least pretty or delicate or curvaceous in the way that seemed to attract the opposite sex. She had no reason to *want* to be attractive to a man like this. She'd thought she was well past caring.

But, oddly enough, she wasn't.

"Charming," she said. "What century did you emerge from, pray tell? The first? Or maybe a little earlier—the Precambrian era, perhaps?"

The creases deepened between his strong brows; Mac saw more puzzlement than anger in his expression. Didn't the guy know when he'd gotten as good as he gave?

But his apparent confusion didn't last long. "I see," he said. "I've heard of your type. Are you one of those female suffragists who think they're the equals of men in all things?"

Female suffragists? Where'd he dig up that label? "I don't just think it, I know it. You have a problem with that?"

For the first time he smiled. It wasn't a particularly nice smile. A spark of some undefined sensation shot the length of her spine. She could be playing with fire here, pursuing her own imaginary game with no thought to who or what this guy really was. She wondered why that edge of danger didn't trouble her any more than the bizarre coincidence of his appearance. The last time she'd felt this way was when she'd been on prescription muscle relaxants for a pulled shoulder.

This is what Homer meant, she thought incoherently. *You can get drunk on adventure. . . .*

"I'm not the one with the problem, Miss MacKenzie," he said. "It's clear you have more than you can handle. Is that why the disguise?"

"What are you talking about?"

"The trousers. The hair." He adjusted his stance to one that practically shouted masculine challenge. "You've done well disguising your gender—"

Mac choked.

"—but not well enough."

His eyes were no longer fixed on hers. Now they were trained on her chest. She was suddenly, terribly aware that the rain had stopped, her shirt was clinging to the unimpressive curves of her breasts, and her nipples were still puckered.

She might as well have been naked. Liam's clone spent a little too long studying that part of her, and his demeanor was no longer quite so pitying. There was a certain distracted quality to it, a slight loosening of his jaw and mellowing of his gaze. Mac was far less familiar with that kind of regard.

The sensation of having a man look at her as if her body were of any interest whatsoever was so novel that she was momentarily incapable of any emotion but surprise.

Until she remembered that this guy might be more than merely eccentric, and it was getting very close to sunset. The almost drunken feeling of invulnerability drained in an adrenaline rush from her body. She took a step away from him, forcing herself to keep from wrapping her arms across her chest.

"Did you consider this masquerade a way of ensuring your safety?" he asked, scowling ominously. "You're fortunate it worked this long."

What *was* this stuff about hiding her sex? He thought she'd come to Tikal disguised as a boy, and that made about as much sense as the rest of the things he'd said.

"I wasn't trying to 'disguise' anything," she retorted,

unable to help herself. "I just decided to leave my high heels and miniskirt at home."

"*You* should have stayed at home, Miss MacKenzie. Your guide could have slit your throat, or worse. You're more a fool than he was."

She tried to imagine that young man slitting her throat and felt an unexpected need to defend him. "No way. Sure, he left without me, but I can make it back just fine on my own."

"Back to where? How long have you been alone?"

Serious warning bells rang in Mac's mind. This time she listened. All at once it seemed like a good idea to let him believe she wasn't alone. For all she knew, *he* might be contemplating slitting her throat.

"Oh, not long," she said airily. "In fact, he's probably right down the trail. I think I should go find him."

Yes, very good idea. The game had gone on long enough. Mac turned cautiously toward the path her erstwhile guide had cut through the jungle.

And realized a moment later that something wasn't right. The ragged clearing that had been there before was—gone. The heavy rain had obscured everything until a few minutes ago, and then she'd been too absorbed by Liam's double to pay attention.

Now she noticed. A few steps away from the temple and she was hitting waist-high foliage—not as dense as in the jungle itself, but thick enough to trip her up at a moment's inattention. She stopped and scanned the area. Yes, she was in the right place. She had to be. The temple and ruins were exactly the way she'd seen them when she'd emerged from the path.

Okay. She must have gotten more confused than she'd thought when she'd been lost in the tunnel. She kicked and batted dripping plants out of her way until she reached the place where a certain crumbling stele had marked the path's end.

The stele was still there. The path wasn't. Mac checked her alignment again. This *was* the right place. The jungle closed in like a wall where the path should have been, solid and impenetrable.

"I know plants grow fast in the jungle," she muttered, "but this is ridiculous. . . ."

"Is something the matter, Miss MacKenzie?"

Mac stiffened. She'd had her back to Liam's improbable twin all this time, and she'd never heard him take a single step. He moved up beside her now, jerking his chin toward the fortress of young trees, vines, and intertwined bushes. "Is that the way you came from Tikal?" he asked. "You said you'd walked here."

"I did," she said. "There's a path, right here."

He brushed past her and examined the area, one brow cocked. "Perhaps you'd point it out to me. My vision isn't as keen as yours."

Mac just managed not to glare at him. She marched forward. Trailing lianas slapped across the nose. Damn it, it *had* to be here. A few broken branches, at least. Something.

The stranger leaned against a convenient tree trunk, arms folded. "Do you need assistance, Miss MacKenzie?"

Definitely patronizing, that was the word for his tone. She ignored him and paced a few yards away, still searching. It wasn't her imagination; the break in the dense vegetation simply wasn't there.

Mac wanted very badly to sit down and swear in the myriad creative ways Homer had taught her, but she'd be damned if she'd let Liam's annoying clone see her defeated. *Great set of priorities, Mac,* she chided herself. But she was coming up blank. She'd have to make a circuit of the ruins, keep searching. . . .

"There is no path."

She whirled to face him in spite of her best intentions. "I didn't fly here," she snapped.

"But he did abandon you."

"The guide? Yes. I mean—no, he cut me the path, and it was right here."

He pushed himself away from the tree. "I know these ruins. The only path is the one I made, on the other side of the temple. It leads to my camp."

Great. Mac lined herself up with the stele and made another attempt at the jungle wall.

"It'll be dark in a few hours," he said behind her. "Whatever suffragist cant you hold dear, Miss Mac-Kenzie, or however you came here, you can't travel through the jungle alone."

She almost shivered at the certainty in his voice. *Better to be alone in the jungle than here with you,* she thought irrationally. But he refused to read her mind. He strolled up beside her, close enough that she could feel the heat of his body even amidst the sweltering humidity.

"And I doubt your unusual lantern will cut you a way through the forest," he said. His gaze dropped to the flashlight hanging from her belt.

It momentarily occurred to her that the flashlight was probably in more danger from this hunky weirdo than she was herself. Hadn't he said he'd broken his lantern?

"Oh, it's not so unusual," she said hastily. "You can probably pick one up in Tikal. In fact"—she backed farther away from his solid, muscular bulk—"I'm sure they have them. Cheap, too."

He cocked his head at her. It was a peculiarly boyish gesture very much at odds with the rest of him. "In Tikal? Interesting. I've never seen one like it. Do you mind if I take a closer look?"

Before she could protest he'd liberated it from her belt and was turning it over in his broad, callused hands. Mac found herself watching his examination with reluctant fascination.

It really was as if he'd never seen a flashlight before. And that was crazy, because he wasn't unkempt enough to be the jungle hermit she'd thought at first he might be. His accent was as American as hers, with a slight lilt that might have been Irish. He spoke too distinctly to be completely wacko.

So, she admitted, she was still curious about him. *Too* curious. Too interested in a total stranger who was almost charismatically attractive but also arrogant and insulting. Not to mention strange.

And as for his resemblance to a certain photograph— could it be possible that he was a descendant of O'Shea's? No. O'Shea had died without children to carry on his name. Mac felt instinctively for the pendant around her neck and remembered that it had been lost in the tunnel, along with Homer's cap.

She was lucky that was all she'd lost.

"If you don't mind," she said, holding out her hand. He ignored it. Her Liam clone had become quite obsessed with switching the flashlight on and off, focusing the beam on the trunk of a tree and then the crumbled stone of a nearby building, drawing patterns with the light.

"How does this work?" he demanded, shaking the flashlight until the batteries rattled. "Electricity?"

Come on. "You know—batteries," she said caustically. "And they're going to be dead before I get back if you keep that up."

He stopped suddenly and studied her with those piercing gray eyes. "Batteries?" he repeated. "This small?" He turned the flashlight upside down and located the little sliding panel to the battery compartment.

"Hey!" Mac made a grab for the flashlight, but he

kept it easily out of reach and tucked it somewhere in the back of his belt.

Mac revised her earlier speculation about Liam's double. Maybe he was an exceptionally *clean* hermit. Or he'd been living in some country where they didn't have flashlights. Or he'd escaped from an asylum somewhere.

"Listen," she said in a low, even tone. "You can keep the flashlight as soon as I'm back in Tikal. I promise. Just let me use it to get there in one piece."

"But you won't be going alone. I'll escort you there myself, and have a word or two with the man who left you."

"Thanks, but I don't need your help, and there is no—"

He fixed her with a look that silenced her instantly. The only person who'd ever been able to do that to her was Homer, and she wasn't about to let this guy have the privilege.

"Excuse me, but—"

"I'm not your fool of a guide, Miss MacKenzie," he said softly. "You have two choices. Come willingly or be carried."

He'd do it, too, of that she was certain. His tone brooked no arguments. Why he was so intent on "helping" her she couldn't figure out, but she knew she wasn't going to get rid of him. She'd simply have to make the best of it.

And there was at least one good thing to be said for the man—he appeared to know about the jungle. Maybe it wouldn't be so terrible to have him with her. Once in Tikal proper she'd be able to get to the hotel and ditch Liam Junior.

"All right," she said. "What do you suggest?"

"You do have some sense. Wait here." He turned on his heel and strode back to the tunnel entrance.

Mac used the time to dig in her backpack for mosquito repellant and a potential weapon. There was a small Swiss Army knife—her father's, sent back from Vietnam—but other than the flashlight, which her new friend had confiscated, that was about it. *So if he attacks me I can give him paper cuts.*

She lost her sense of humor when her would-be escort returned with a canvas bag slung over his shoulder, the unmistakable butt of a gun sticking up from one of the pouches on his belt, and a wicked machete in his hand. A stained Panama hat sat on his damp hair.

"Do you think you can carry my haversack, Miss MacKenzie?" he asked with a frown. "I'll need my hands free for the machete."

The canvas bag didn't seem particularly heavy, but he clearly expected her to refuse. His impression of her was pretty mixed-up, and maybe that wasn't such a bad idea.

"Sure," she said. "No problem."

He hesitated and passed it to her somewhat gingerly. It took a bit of balancing, and she could feel several objects rolling around inside. Another potential weapon if it came to that.

"Are you sure you can manage it?" he asked. "I can't have you losing it."

"It doesn't exactly weigh a ton. I won't drop it, if that's what you're worried about."

He gave her a dubious examination and decided to take her word for it. He lifted the machete; light glinted off the blade, and Mac flinched in spite of herself. He dropped his hand and scowled at her.

"Your prudence comes a little late, Miss MacKenzie, but there's no need to be afraid. *I'm* not going to attack you."

His black expression belied his assurance, but she wasn't about to betray another hint of unease. "I'm not afraid. It so happens I know how to defend myself. And anyway, you won't need the machete once we find the trail."

He muttered something under his breath that sounded suspiciously like "women" and "irrational." "Stay well out of my way," he commanded aloud. She stepped aside as he took a savage swipe at some hapless bush with his machete.

She had an urgent desire to grab the flashlight from his belt and brain him with it instead, but she obeyed. After two more energetic blows—considerably more powerful than those used by her guide earlier in the day, making an impressive display of the muscles in his back—his motions became less choppy and more rhythmic, almost graceful. Mac kept watch for the original path. There was still not the slightest sign that it had ever been there.

The jungle closed in around them like a hungry predator. Almost at once the light faded, turned to false dusk by trees and bushes and every conceivable type of tropical vegetation. Mac reminded herself that any threat from the jungle's scaled and furred inhabitants was likely to be in her own mind. There was no way in hell she'd let her gallant escort, with his strange attitudes about women, know she was even a little bit nervous.

"Tell me, Miss MacKenzie—"

Mac congratulated herself for hiding the way she nearly jumped out of her skin. He'd stopped to rest—not that he was breathing particularly hard, or sweating any more than she was. He was marvelously alive and strong and very . . . virile. Disturbingly so.

"—now that we've established that you didn't come to the jungle alone," he went on, "how did you get to the Petén? You must have come by ship—was it

Champerico or Belize? What expedition of fools did
you dupe into bringing you here?"

That line again. It was beginning to get a bit old.
"Oh," she said, counting on her fingers, "let's see.
There was Allen Quartermain and Indiana Jones and
Professor Challenger. Lord Greystoke couldn't make it
at the last minute."

The quiet lasted long enough to make her wonder if
she'd finally gone too far. She glanced at his face, heavily shadowed in the faint illumination. He certainly
seemed angry enough.

"I don't know them," he said.

He didn't *know* them? Somehow she didn't think it
would help to tell him it was a joke. A little distraction
was probably a better idea. "Uh—where did *you* come
from? Originally, I mean?"

"San Francisco," he said, distracted. "I would have
known if another expedition had arrived."

San Francisco, yet? Curiouser and curiouser. Down-
right scary, in fact. Mac cursed her inability to cut her
own way through this green perdition. It had taken
nearly an hour to reach the mystery ruins from Tikal;
the return journey wasn't likely to be any faster.

At least Liam's double was too preoccupied to question her farther. He pulled a compass from a pouch at
his belt, consulted it, and started off again, as single-
minded and tireless as an automaton. Mac concentrated
on her footing in the mud and swatting mosquitoes
while she balanced the canvas sack over her shoulder.

When she checked her watch again she was startled
by the time that had passed. They'd definitely been
walking an hour; at this very moment they should be
standing in the central plaza of Tikal. Unless he'd taken
her the wrong way. . . .

"Hey," she said, slowing. "I think we—"

Only some last-minute instinct kept her from walking

into Liam Junior. He stood loose-limbed, the machete at his side, head lifted. Mac followed his gaze around a patch of jungle that appeared no different from all the rest.

"Why are we stopping?" she asked.

He looked at her as if she'd said something stupid. "We're there."

Mac went on her guard. It was apparent they weren't in Tikal—a wide, groomed clearing would have marked the main ruins, and there was nothing much like a clearing ahead. Nothing but endless forest on every side.

She gathered her patience. "We must have taken a wrong turn somewhere. This isn't Tikal. Maybe it's a little farther on—"

"I've been to Tikal before, Miss MacKenzie. Maudslay took his photographs *after* my first expedition—"

"Maudslay?" Was *he* joking now? "You were here a pretty long time ago in that case. He took those photos in the 1880s. I think the place has changed a bit since then."

His stillness was as heavy as the humidity. When he spoke again, his voice was eerily gentle.

"Are you mad, Miss MacKenzie, or merely perverse?"

Perverse? He was calling *her* perverse? "Look," she said. "I just want to get back to my hotel—"

"Hotel?" He laughed—a deep, hearty baritone rumble. "Do you ordinarily regard native huts as hotels? Your taste is none too fine. Or perhaps you refer to the . . . accommodations in Flores? You'll have another twenty miles of walking to reach it."

Mac opened her mouth and closed it again. Something very strange was going on here. They were talking at cross-purposes, and nothing he said made sense. "I mean the hotel in Tikal," she said carefully. "Near the park entrance. It so happens I know the ruins pretty well myself, and this is not Tikal."

"I see." Abruptly he turned and strode to a nearly solid mass of vines and trees and bushes a few yards away. "You claim to know the ruins, Miss MacKenzie. You are in the midst of them." He grabbed a handful of vines in his left hand and yanked. Beneath the covering was stone—cracked, massive stone.

They were standing directly next to a Maya temple. It towered above them, almost entirely obscured by leaves and vines, two or three times the height of anything in the ruins they'd left. Bigger than anything outside of Tikal within a fifty-mile radius.

He must have led her north, into the deeper jungle, and not south to the more populated areas near Tikal. But what was his purpose? If he'd meant to hurt her, he could have done it several dozen times since they'd met.

"Where did you bring me?" Mac said, pretending a calm she didn't feel. "What is this place?"

He ignored her question as he might ignore the babbling of a week-old baby. "It seems your party has abandoned you."

"No one abandoned me. It's just that—"

He rounded on her with so much unexpected anger that she backed up a step. "Did you hear me? Your party is no longer here. I see no sign that anyone has been in these ruins. Maybe they found having a woman along more trouble than whatever you paid them was worth."

Mac's resolution to remain calm crumbled like ancient stone. "I didn't pay anyone but the guide. I arrived with a regular tourist group from Flores, to see the ruins like everyone else. So if you'll just give me back my flashlight—"

"And just where do you intend to go?"

That was a good question, but she couldn't let him

know how lost she was. "I think I'll do a little exploring on my own, if you don't mind."

"I don't think so," he said with grim amusement. "Whatever your reasons for being alone, you can't go blundering about in the jungle. I'm not such a black-guard to let even a"—he paused significantly—"woman such as you run loose. I've gone to this much trouble already."

"Thank you so much. And why should I trust *you?*"

There. It was out at last. But he only arched his brow and rested his hand on the butt of his pistol. "You don't have much choice." He noticed the direction of her glance and grunted. "The gun, is it? We and your former companions aren't the only people in the jungle, Miss MacKenzie. There are guerrillas and rebels and petty tyrants in every part of this country. Some are far less scrupulous than I am."

Guerrillas? She'd read about the rebel Maya bands that occasionally ventured out of the Guatemalan highlands and into the Petén, but they weren't any danger to tourists. Her would-be protector saw more potential perils in this jungle than she did.

"I don't think—"

"Obviously not. But have no fear, Miss MacKenzie. Your . . . virtue is completely safe with me. I'm not remotely tempted to test it."

For the second or third time that afternoon Mac was left speechless. How could you argue with a man who kept coming up with such bizarre comments?

How could you even take him seriously? Yes—that was the key. He was out of his gourd and there was absolutely no point in wasting her energy on anger. In any case, she had to admit that he was right about blundering around in the jungle. There must be some alternative.

Liam Junior's wandering gaze and pose of bored indifference gave her the chance to study him surreptitiously. The jungle's deep shadows only made his features seem more sharply cut, more imposingly masculine. Lines radiated out from his eyes and slashed between his brows. His was an outdoorsman's face that had been exposed to the elements: sun and wind and rain. It was a face that hid far more than it revealed.

What would you think of him, Homer? You'd probably have found him interesting, weirdness and all. You'd probably have learned everything important about him by now, too, and have him eating out of your hand.

But she wasn't Homer. Somehow her attempt to exorcise the Sinclair family demon had gotten far out of hand. Liam Junior was right: she didn't have a whole hell of a lot of choice at the moment. She could either follow her insane impulse to murder him, or take what help he could give and put up with the rest.

"All right," she said. "So what do you plan to do?"

"See you safely back with your people, whoever they are."

"We agree on that, anyway. Since we disagree about where we are, the best thing to do is get to a high place and take a good look around."

He grinned, a flash of white teeth brilliant and startling beside his tanned skin. "You do show occasional sense, Miss MacKenzie."

Sense enough to know that the highest scalable point in this part of the jungle was probably the vine-covered ruin right next to them. Mac grimaced. Her clothes were sticky, her feet were blistered, and the last thing she wanted to do was scramble up the crumbling steps of an unrestored temple.

"You don't happen to know the best way up this thing, do you?" she asked.

"Not here. I know a better place."

And he was off again, pausing just long enough to let her glimpse the direction he'd gone. Mac tried out a string of antiquated and colorful imprecations and followed. The sooner she found out where she was, the sooner she could get back to the real world.

She had to give it to him, though—he knew what he was doing. In a matter of minutes he'd cut his way through dense vegetation to another pyramid temple, this one even taller than the first. Familiar, almost. And from the base up the sloping length of the narrow temple steps, someone had worn out a faint path through the growth that coated almost every stone surface.

It was still a very long way up.

"You wait here," Liam's clone ordered. "Don't move an inch from this spot until I come back down."

Oh, yeah. He did have these odd notions of female competence—or incompetence. "Just watch me," she said, and grabbed for the first handhold.

The unrestored steps were hardly steps at all, but they were adequate for the job. No different from climbing trees when she was a kid, really. She'd almost forgotten how much she loved sitting among the branches. . . .

Her foot slipped on crumbling stone. A hard body stopped her backward slide; arms like rock closed around her waist.

"Don't get yourself killed just yet," he said, breath warm against her neck. "The view is more interesting than I'd expected."

It took some effort, but she caught her balance just enough to pull free and start again. Her ears were burning. Just what was he trying to prove?

Jaw set, she scrambled the rest of the way without once backsliding. Feeling him right behind her was motive enough. Her body felt like a single live wire, still singing from that brief contact. What in hell was wrong with her?

That was one of several questions she couldn't answer, but she didn't propose to let him guess how off balance she felt.

When she gained the top of the stairs she knelt on the platform crowning the summit of the pyramid, exhausted but triumphant. Behind her was the temple proper with its gaping entrance and decorative carved comb on top. Below . . .

Below was the jungle. Jungle uncleared, with only a few faint paths visible between the pyramid temples that rose above the green. Temples that were far too impressive not to be well known and explored. Temples that were placed in a pattern identical to that of Tikal.

Mac sat down. She did a quick mental count of the major ruins in the area. Aside from Tikal, the most famous, there were only a few of any size within a day's walk. Uaxactum was north, but it was still a good fifteen miles away and considerably less impressive than Tikal. Its temples were simply not of the size she was seeing right now. El Mirador was even farther away.

Okay. She turned in a circle. To north, south, east, and west the carpet of green was unbroken. No massive clearings by lumber companies eager for the jungle's untapped resources, no smaller patches of settlements or villages. No roads. No airstrip. No sign of habitation.

"It's as I told you, Miss MacKenzie."

Liam Junior settled into an easy crouch beside her, knees spread and big hands dangling between. "I can find no sign that your party has been here within the past week," he continued—without mockery, for a change. He frowned at her. "How long did you say you were alone?"

She wanted to make some wisecrack, but it had managed to get tangled around her tongue. "About an hour after the guide left. Before I ran into you."

"Then where is this guide?"

"I don't know."

"How many were in Tikal?"

"I didn't count the tourists. I didn't come with a tour group. They wouldn't be—" *No, don't tell him no one would be looking for you, Mac. Not a good idea.* "You're still telling me *this* is Tikal?"

He only gave her another of those condescendingly half-pitying, half-contemptuous looks. Her head had begun to ache. A large, warm drop of water hit her on the bridge of her nose and trickled into her eye. More raindrops joined the first in rapid succession.

The square temple entrance provided the only shelter from the cloudburst that followed. Mac retreated just inside. Liam Junior stayed where he was, face upturned.

Mac was grateful for the moment of privacy. A crazy idea was forming in her brain, too ridiculous to think out, let alone speak aloud.

She wiped damp hands on the thighs of her pants, wriggled out of her backpack and unzipped the inner pouch. The photo was as carefully wrapped now as it had been on the day Homer had given it to her. Her fingers were a little unsteady as she pulled it out and held it up to catch the filtered light.

It was almost a shock to see how thoroughly her Liam clone resembled the real thing, even down to his clothing. But it was the ruins behind him and Perry that she examined. The temple framed in the photograph was high and surrounded by jungle, with only a scanty path worn through the greenery that covered the steps to the top. Trees grew on the stairway and on the temple platform, just as they did on the ruin she sat in. The match was almost perfect. . . .

"Where did you get that?"

She flinched. Liam Junior stood over her, his hand already reaching for the photograph. Mac snatched it away before his dripping fingers could take hold.

"Hey! Be careful—that's an antique!"

He shook his head, spraying water from his golden brown hair. "Antique?" he echoed. "How did you get it?" His tone sharpened, and he dropped into a crouch. "Do you know Perry?"

For a moment she wasn't sure she'd heard him correctly. "What?"

He clamped his fingers around her wrist. "Perry. Did he give this to you?"

Mac stared at him. "This is too much. If Homer were alive he might have pulled something like this—"

He shook her, just enough to get her attention. "Perry Sinclair. This photograph was taken the last time we were in Tikal. Perry had it in his rooms."

Mac worked her wrist free of his grasp and tucked the photo behind her. "I don't know what you're talking about," she said carefully. "This photo was given to me by my grandfather. The men in it have been dead for decades—"

"Miss MacKenzie," he said between his teeth, "when Perry left me in this jungle he was very much alive. And I am most assuredly not dead. Did Perry think I was?"

She *had* heard him correctly, but her brain refused to process the information. "Ye—no." She breathed in and out, grateful that her physical functions seemed to be operating normally. "Uh . . . you never did . . . tell me your name."

"Remiss of me. But if you know Perry—"

"I don't. I mean—"

"—you must know my name is Liam O'Shea."

Mac sat very still. Of course his name was Liam O'Shea. He recognized the photograph. He knew about her great-great-grandfather. He came from San Francisco. It all made perfect sense.

Who could have set this up? She didn't have any friends or relatives capable, financially or otherwise, of such an elaborate scheme; Homer was dead, she wasn't close to her uncles, and Jason was too lost in his research to call her more than once a year. No one at the museum would have bothered. Even if they'd known the story behind the photograph . . .

No one would have bothered. No one cared enough or knew enough. But there were only two other explanations she could think of. The most likely one was that she'd managed to hit her head on the wall in that tunnel and was in the middle of some sort of delusion or dream.

Yes. There'd been that feeling of nausea and disorientation right before the wall had disappeared and she'd lost the pendant. She'd never felt anything quite like it before—as if the ground were vanishing beneath her feet. Maybe that had been the last real thing she'd felt before she'd lost consciousness, and the rest was a concoction of all the elements that had been in her mind when the accident had happened.

She pinched herself. That didn't work; she felt it and didn't wake up. This was definitely a new level of dream. Or delirium. Maybe she was even dying. Odd how the idea didn't trouble her.

Maybe because she couldn't quite believe it. But the third possibility . . .

Her giggle turned into a cough. *There is no such thing, Mac. Except in your own possibly delirious mind.*

"Miss MacKenzie!"

She grinned at him. That drunken sense of unreality had come over her again. She braced her hands on her knees to keep from swaying. "I'm . . . fine. Just . . .

let me get this straight. You say your name is Liam O'Shea, and this is Tikal. Correct?"

He regarded her as a jaguar might a particularly succulent deer. "Yes."

"And, uh . . . what year is this?"

Liam-who-claimed-to-be-the-real-thing smiled. "I'll wager you know well enough, Miss MacKenzie. The date is the fourteenth of August, and the year is 1884."

CHAPTER FOUR

They say miracles are past.

—WILLIAM SHAKESPEARE

THE WOMAN WAS evidently an actress of considerable talent. Or she was quite mad.

"1884?" she repeated, her low voice hoarse. "Did you say—*eighteen* eighty-four? But that's not possible."

Liam regarded her stunned expression with suspicious bemusement. Simple insanity did fit hand in glove with the rest of her: thin, wiry, distinctly peculiar with her cap of short hair and bold dark eyes, sharp-tongued, dressed top to toe in men's clothing of an odd cut, and carrying a newfangled electric lantern the likes of which he had never seen in all his travels. And alone here in the jungle, first claiming she'd been with a full party of explorers and then insisting that no man had brought her.

And then there was her odd manner of speech, her absurd assertions of hotels in the jungle and omnibuses from Flores, her reaction to Tikal—as if she'd expected to see something entirely different, though she claimed to know the ruins.

Yes, one could almost be convinced that she was in a state of mental disturbance—if not for the photograph she had so carelessly allowed him to see. The one taken here in these very ruins four years ago.

"What did you expect, Miss MacKenzie?" he asked. "Maybe you *have* been in the jungle too long."

Her dark brows drew down, and her gaze grew unfocused. "Okay, Mac," she muttered. "Time to wake up. This isn't happening."

Was this act a way of protecting herself, avoiding his questions because she'd revealed too much? Liam couldn't forget the shock he'd felt when he'd seen her with the photograph. Until that moment she'd been only an unforeseen burden to dispose of in the nearest safe place, some eccentric suffragist amateur explorer who'd been lost or deliberately abandoned, left for him to save.

After what had happened yesterday, he'd never considered doing otherwise.

The sharp sting of recent memory made the bitterness rise in his throat: Perry's revelation, the knowledge that Liam's trust in his partner had been entirely misplaced; the fight, drinking to drown the rage and loss, waking up this morning to find the bearers, mules, and nearly all the supplies gone. With Perry.

Abandoned. Betrayed by the one man he'd thought he could trust. The man who stood beside him in that damned photograph.

He'd thought the girl in far more desperate straits than himself. She was of the weaker sex, in spite of her ridiculous beliefs to the contrary. But now—now he felt a grinding suspicion in his gut, wild thoughts fully as mad as the woman's incoherent ramblings and disjointed explanations.

Liam scowled at Miss MacKenzie's inward stare. She wasn't the only one with wits gone begging. A woman?

Even Perry wouldn't sink so low. And there hadn't been time. But since yesterday nothing seemed beyond possibility.

And their meeting had seemed more than merely coincidence.

He studied her, chin on fist, allowing himself full rein to his imagination. Perry would never assume that his erstwhile partner would be distracted by a woman like this. She was hardly beautiful. Her hair was short, her jaw too stubborn, her figure too slender. Though she'd proven she was, in fact, female enough when the rain had soaked through her shirt.

He found himself gazing at her chest. More there than he'd first noticed; come to think of it, she couldn't pass for a boy, not unless that loose shirt were completely dry. . . .

You've been without a woman too long, O'Shea. He snorted. *No.* At best Perry would expect him to be delayed further, getting the girl back to civilization. That would neatly fit in with his intentions.

Liam's hand slammed into the wet stone of the temple. Perry knew too damned much about him. He knew Liam wouldn't leave any woman alone in the jungle, no matter what his circumstances—without supplies or bearers or even a single scrawny mule. . . .

Because you trusted him. The rage bubbled up again, and with very little effort he could imagine his fist connecting with Perry's superior, aristocratic face.

By the saints, it wasn't over yet. When Liam got back to San Francisco—

"That's it."

He snapped out of his grim reverie. Miss MacKenzie—"Mac," the name she had called herself and which suited her so well—had apparently recovered her senses. Or ended her game. She was on her feet, looking out over the jungle.

"I'm going back," she announced.

Liam rose casually. The top of her cropped head came almost to his chin; tall for a woman. He hadn't realized that before.

"Back where—*Mac*?" he drawled.

Her stare was no longer unfocused. She looked at him as if she'd like to pitch him over the side of the pyramid. "Only my friends call me Mac," she said, "and you're not my friend. You're a figment of my overheated imagination."

He gave a startled bark of laughter. Whoever and whatever she was, she had the ability to make him hover between laughter and outrage. She was too damned good at keeping him off balance. Was that her purpose—and Perry's?

To hell with that. If there was anything to his suspicions, he'd learn soon enough.

"So," he said, "you don't think I'm real?" He took one long step, closing the gap between them, and felt her shudder as his chest brushed hers. He could feel the little tips of her breasts, hardening through the shirt. He felt an unexpected hardening in his own body. "What proof do you need, eh?"

She tried to step back, but the temple wall was behind her. "You . . . uh . . ." She thrust out her jaw and glared. "Let me by. I'm going back to the ruins."

"If I'm not real, Mac, you should have no difficulty walking through me."

Suddenly she chuckled. "Great idea," she said. With the full force of her slender weight she pushed against him. The assault drove him back a pace. She stepped to the side, strode to the rim of the temple platform, and slid her foot over the edge.

He caught her arm just as an ancient stone step gave way under her foot. "Are you so eager to break your neck?" he snapped. "Or are you more afraid of something else?"

Her eyes were wide and dark and surprisingly large, rimmed with thick lashes he hadn't noticed before. There was a slight trembling to the lids and at the corners of her lips, as if she'd realized how easy it would have been to tumble down that steep incline in her reckless attempt to escape.

Escape *him*. Was that what she was trying to do? Did she have good reason?

He let her go. She shook her arm to work out the numbness. "Can I break my neck if I'm already dead? Maybe it wouldn't hurt."

If this was a game, he couldn't see the point in it. "Dying hurts," he said roughly.

The color drained from her skin. She seemed about ready to say something, and then thought better of it.

"No," she said, as if to herself alone. "If I go back, I'll understand. The answer is there, in the tunnel."

The answer? He'd like more than a few answers himself.

He scrutinized the jungle below them. The rain had stopped, but in a little over two hours it would be dark. He was hungry and wanted coffee, but there was no chance of that. Coffee was not one of the few necessities Perry had seen fit to leave him. At least there was shelter in camp. Best to take the girl with him, and then decide. . . .

Mac had already made her decision. She had turned around and was climbing backward down the cleared path along the crumbling temple stairway, clutching vines and bushes for handholds, her tongue caught between her teeth. Her feet slipped, and she steadied herself and kept going, never once glancing back up at him.

Damned crazy troublemaking female. Suffragist or

not, suspect or not, she needed a keeper—a job no sane man would want. He'd never let Caroline get into a position even remotely like this one. Scrambling down the side of a pyramid, no skirts or corsets or furbelows, drenched with sweat, hair bedraggled. Not a hair on Caroline's golden head would ever be disarranged by any hardship as long as he was alive.

Caroline. He had to get back to San Francisco. Her aunt Amelia was no match for Perry's smooth tongue; he'd be spending every available hour at the Gresham house, using his jaded charm on Caroline, trying to make her believe he loved her. And in less than six weeks she'd be eighteen, in full control of her considerable fortune. . . .

With a pungent oath Liam retrieved his machete, slung his bag over his shoulder, and followed Mac down.

She reached the base of the pyramid unscathed and was already striding back the way they'd come by the time he caught up with her. Her sense of direction was surprisingly good for a woman. She found the path he'd cut with no help from him, and marched through the muck and clouds of mosquitoes without moderating her furious pace.

"Don't feel obligated to come with me," she puffed. "I can find my way just fine now, thank you."

The path wasn't wide enough for two. Liam dogged her heels, restraining an impulse to grab her. "I have no intention of leaving you," he said acidly. "There's still the small matter of Perry's photograph—"

"Yeah. I'll say."

Impossible female. Let her exhaust herself, and then she'd be more tractable. He dodged a palm frond that slapped back into his chest and settled into an easy, ground-eating stride far more efficient than her breakneck rush. Soon enough her breath became ragged, but some stubborn spirit kept her moving.

He could almost admire that. Almost.

They reached the original ruins in just under an hour. Mac—the name was too apt to discard—had half hidden herself behind a cluster of palms. He could see her doubled over, hands on knees, face flushed and hair sodden. That she'd gone on so long was amazing. Liam tipped up his hat and dragged his damp sleeve across his forehead, watching her fumble for her canteen.

She was tired, hot, and thirsty. Good. It would be easier to make her drop her guard.

"What do you propose to do now?" he asked.

She choked on a mouthful of water and glared at him through the lacy curtain of serrated leaves. "Don't concern yourself . . . O'Shea. I've got everything under control. If you'll just return my flashlight now . . ."

"Under control," indeed. "Nothing's changed, Mac. You're not going off alone—"

"I'm not going off anywhere. I just need to take care of something in the tunnel." She clenched her fists. "Please."

It would be simple enough to keep track of her from the tunnel entrance. She couldn't go far. Something had upset her, and he was determined to learn exactly what it was.

He extended the lantern and she snatched it from his hand. Without another word she squared her shoulders and marched straight into the tunnel as if she were about to confront a man-eating dragon.

For all he knew that was exactly what she anticipated. Better a dragon than him—if even a part of his suspicions proved true.

Liam set down his haversack and pitched the brim of his hat low over his eyes. He made himself comfortable under the shade of the temple wall, checked his pistol and let it rest in his lap. He'd give her a half hour, no more. There was little time to waste indulging her freakish starts or devious games—if that was what they were.

He'd left the sack in the tunnel when he and Perry had first arrived, never suspecting the need for emergency supplies would come from such an unpredictable quarter. Along with the additional food Perry had left him, there might be enough to tide two people over for a week, no more.

Two *men*. A woman was another matter entirely. If she were truly alone here . . .

He jerked awake, shoved back his hat and sat up. The long shadows and dim light told him that over an hour had passed. Damn it, he'd slept—an amateur's mistake.

There was still a faint throbbing in his knee where something had struck it. Mac couldn't have come out of the tunnel without tripping over his legs; Liam stood and looked from the tunnel entrance to the faint clearing beside the temple.

She was sitting on a fallen stele, staring into the jungle. Her pack lay at her feet. There was something strange in her bearing, in the way she didn't move as the seconds passed, the way she held her hands out in front of her with a peculiar stiffness.

She turned her head as he came near. Her gaze held his with a vulnerability that stopped his questions before he could voice them.

"Something is . . . very weird here," she said. "I found the wall, but . . . it just ends. There's no way through. It's the same and not the same. I *know* it's the right wall, but the bones . . ." She shuddered. "They aren't there anymore."

He knew the wall she meant; it was the place he and Perry had found the carved plaque of stone from which they'd made their matching pendants. Symbols of a brotherhood that no longer existed.

He shook off his lapse and crouched before Mac. "The wall with the hieroglyphs?" he asked. "It ends the tunnel. There is no way through. What bones are you talking about?"

"I thought they were—" She lifted her hands. For the first time he saw that her palms were raw with bleeding scratches, as if made by ragged stone. "This isn't possible, you know. There isn't any real proof. I—"

Liam caught her hands and held them still. "What in hell did you do to yourself?"

She laughed raggedly. "I was sure there must be something, but—"

Her coherence hadn't improved since she'd gone into the tunnel again, and neither had her rationality. "Be quiet," he commanded. "Just stay there and be quiet." He went back for his sack and dropped it beside the stele, pulling out his own canteen. She remained unnaturally still, watching him as he poured water over her palms and washed away the blood.

"You don't have to do this," she said, smiling with the distracted air of a good-natured lunatic. "I'm okay. Everything will be fine."

He caught her chin in his hand. Her cheek was clammy, and the pulse that beat under the skin at the base of her neck was faint and rapid. She was in a state of shock; he'd seen such conditions before. "I told you to be quiet," he said gruffly. "Sit still and do as you're told."

She blinked and shrugged without protest, proving just how disturbed she must be. Liam used his knife to tear off pieces of mosquito netting from the sack of emergency supplies and made bandages for her hands, knotting them firmly behind her knuckles.

"You know, the Maya were obsessed with time," she

went on. "It would make a weird kind of sense, if it's true. The funny thing is, I know I'm not crazy."

Liam lifted her in his arms and carried her to the shade under the ruined wall. "Of course not," he grunted. Slender as she was, she was no wraith. He eased her down on what remained of the mosquito netting.

"I'm just not the kind of person who has delusions," she said, sliding bonelessly onto the makeshift bed. "Whatever Homer said, I don't have the imagination to come up with so much . . . perfect detail." She flexed her hands in their bandages, counting off on her fingers. "The wall is the same, but the bones aren't there. Neither is Homer's cap. And the first path is gone. And it did look like Tikal, only not the way it did when I left it—the way Maudslay photographed it. And then there's you. . . ." She squinted up at him. "You're just too perfect."

"Thanks."

"And I think I've established that it can't be some sort of practical joke. Just not possible. I'm not dead—"

"It's a wonder," Liam murmured, cursing his lack of a blanket to cover her with. He had only his shirt, and it was too damp and thin to be of much use.

"—so if I'm not crazy," she mumbled, "it must be real. Doesn't that make sense?"

"Perfect sense." God save him.

She tried to sit up, and he pushed her back down. Already her pulse seemed stronger, her skin less pale. He removed the cap of his own canteen, pulled down her lower lip with his thumb, and poured water into her mouth as if she were a child. After the first few swallows she gave a muffled protest and took the canteen herself.

When she'd finished he reached for the canteen, but she stopped him with a touch. Her fingers were trembling as they brushed his hand and pointed at the engraved metal band near the mouthpiece.

"You . . . really are . . . Liam O'Shea," she whispered.

He followed her stare. The engraved, silver-chased canteen had been a gift from Caroline's father the year they'd met, when Liam had been a simple miner and Gresham the mine owner whose life he'd saved. Gresham was dead now, and he'd left Liam a far more precious endowment—a trust Liam was failing at this very moment.

Damn Perry.

"So my sainted mother named me," he said acidly. "Why does that surprise you?"

She inched backward on her elbows and propped herself against the wall. "I don't know," she said. "No. I don't know how . . ."

He took her shoulders between his hands. "Were you expecting to find me here?"

"Here?" She chuckled weakly. "No. Not like—" She closed her eyes, laughter dying. "Can you give me my pack?"

He did as she asked. Her movements were deliberate as she opened the top flap; for the first time he noticed the strange interlocking teeth that held it closed. But when she'd pulled out the photograph she pushed the pack behind her, out of his reach.

"You wanted to know about this photograph?" she said. "It was taken in Tikal in 1880."

Liam restrained his impatience. At last he was getting answers, however jumbled. "I was there," he said.

"Okay. Now look at it closely." She held it up with all the exaggerated pedantry of a professor in a classroom. "Does it look like it's only a few years old?"

He humored her, ignoring the stab of anger that came with the sight of Perry. Indeed, there was something aged about the paper, creased and a bit ragged about the edges, the image faded. He'd seen this photograph in Perry's rooms only a month ago, protected behind glass.

There was no question about it. Perry must have given it to Mac. Their meeting in the tunnel couldn't have been coincidence.

"How long have you had this?" he demanded.

She didn't even flinch at his harshness. "Not long. But it's been around for quite some time. You're seeing a century of wear and tear."

Liam laughed. There was nothing else to do. But she didn't draw back, didn't smile, didn't do anything but gaze at him with a sort of desperate earnestness.

"Don't you see?" she begged. "Of course you don't. You think I'm nuts. I would too, except—I can't even explain it myself. Something happened to me in that tunnel. Before I met you. Oh, damn." She wrapped her arms around her narrow waist and bent over.

If he was right about her she deserved to suffer. And yet . . .

"Lie down," he ordered. "You're ill."

Her head snapped up. "You want answers, O'Shea? You want to know how I got here? I can tell you how I got to Tikal the first time. By airplane and tour bus, with a bunch of other tourists. Does that make any sense to you?"

Sense? Nothing about her made sense. "Airplane," he repeated flatly.

"You know, the metal things that fly in the sky." She nodded at his silence. "You don't know. The Wright brothers haven't done their thing yet. They're only teenagers . . . uh, now. And there were no tour buses in the Petén in the . . . 1880s. . . ." She drifted away again. "This is too fantastic. Homer would never accept this."

Liam's fingers itched, whether to strangle her or merely shake her he didn't know. "Homer?"

"My grandfather. *He* gave me the photograph. It was . . . passed on to him. He never knew Perry. *I* never knew him. But now *he's* actually alive in San Francisco. . . ."

Enough was enough. "What in hell are you trying to say?"

She gave him a whimsical grin. "You said the year is 1884. Well, Mr. Liam Ignatius O'Shea, that wasn't the year I went into that tunnel."

"What?"

"I said—"

He grabbed her shoulders in earnest. "How do you know my middle name?"

"Homer told me. I—"

"No one knows my middle name."

"I can see why you wouldn't want it spread around."

"Even Perry doesn't know. How do you?"

"Actually, Perry did. Does. And I know because he was—is—my—" She stopped herself abruptly and rushed on. "Because you're both in the history books."

Jesus, Mary, and Joseph, give me strength. Was this fantastic story her attempt to divert his suspicion because she knew he'd unmasked Perry's plot? "History books," he repeated.

"The history books we have in the year I went into that tunnel." The look she gave him then was just a little tempered with reasonable caution, as if she'd finally recognized his mood. "The year nineteen hundred and ninety-seven."

★ ★

SOMEHOW SHE HAD to make him believe.

Mac didn't know exactly when the certainty had

come over her. If she could make him believe, she'd know it was all true. Which she already did, more or less. The alternative wasn't acceptable. She wasn't a gullible person. She wasn't lost in a dreamworld. She was practical and had faith in what she could see and touch and feel.

As she could see and touch and feel Liam O'Shea. The real, original Liam O'Shea, in all his potent masculine glory.

And he was very much alive.

That was only beginning to sink in. The pile of bones she'd found in the tunnel was gone, because Liam hadn't died. She didn't have to beg his apology for her ancestor's deed, because it hadn't happened yet. If she could only somehow convince him she wasn't losing her mind, all of this would start making sense.

But convincing him wasn't going to be easy. What little she knew of him and her observations in the past hour didn't suggest a proclivity for trust or belief in the impossible. His expression was thunderous, and she was painfully aware of the pressure of his fingers digging into the hollows above her collarbones. He did, in fact, think she was crazy. And who could blame him?

You've gone about this all wrong, Mac. Homer would be ashamed of you. But she hadn't been thinking coherently since she'd come out of the tunnel again. She'd been in some kind of shock. Maybe it was the shock itself that made it so . . . no, not easy, but *possible* to accept.

Accept that she'd somehow come back in time.

Damn, but that sounded very strange. She choked back a laugh. Laughing was *not* the right approach to take with Mr. O'Shea, who acted as if he'd prefer the company of a poisonous snake to hers.

She cleared her throat. "Uh—I'm sorry, Mr. O'Shea. I haven't been explaining this well. If you could just"—

she wedged her hands upward against his arms, pushing—"just let me go . . ."

He did, if reluctantly. For a moment she let herself just look at him. Before, when she thought him only a coincidental copy of the man in the photograph, she'd been reluctantly impressed. Now—it really *was* him. The guy whose supposed murder had laid a curse on the Sinclairs, or at least Homer had been convinced of it and sent her down here to find his bones, but she'd found *him* instead, and now what in the world was she supposed to . . .

Whoa. Slow down. "Let me start over," she said, as much for her own benefit as for his.

He rocked back on his heels. The gunmetal gray of his eyes was as sharp as his machete blade, and just as capable of cutting. His anger was manifest; she sensed that another wrong word could send him over some dangerous edge. He was sarcastic, cynical, impatient, chauvinistic, and just plain annoying, and none of those qualities were conducive to his accepting what she was about to tell him.

Yet she remembered the way she'd felt, lifted up, light as air, in his powerful arms. And how he'd laid her down so gently and fed her water and hovered over her. She'd felt bodiless then, and more than a little unreal.

But this *was* real. Somehow, incredibly, she of all Sinclairs had been singled out for the most amazing adventure of all. *She,* unremarkable MacKenzie Rose.

"Listen," she said. "I'll spell it out as cogently as I can, but you're going to have to accept that it's not going to sound rational or reasonable."

His lip curled. "Don't be concerned, Mac. I've become accustomed to your insanity."

She winced. "Okay. I really did come to Tikal as a tourist, with a bunch of other tourists. I wasn't part of a group, though. I was exploring the ruins there when an

Indian guide offered to show me something interesting. He cut me a path through the jungle to this place.

"Right after I arrived, my guide disappeared. I decided to explore anyway, and went into the temple, where I found the tunnel. I'd been walking quite a few minutes when I hit the glyph wall, and found . . ." She caught her breath and slowed down again. She wasn't about to bring up the bones, or all the implications of *that* discovery. She wasn't ready to deal with it herself.

"I, uh, ran into the wall and started feeling very dizzy, almost sick. I leaned against the wall, and—" A memory jumped into her mind—of holding her own pendant and Liam's in either hand, pressing her fists against the wall just before it disappeared. The flash of an idea teased her mind and then was gone. "A few seconds later the wall vanished. I was disoriented, and I couldn't find the wall again, so I just started the way I thought was out. And ran into you."

Liam regarded her blankly. "Very interesting, but hardly enlightening."

"Yeah," she said. "But that isn't the punch line. When I went into that tunnel, the date was August 15, 1997. And when I came out, as you told me, it was 1884." She faced him squarely. "In short, I walked through that tunnel and traveled from the future into the past. One hundred and thirteen years. From my time . . . into yours."

His expression went through a series of transformations that were almost alarming. "Let me get this straight. You claim to have come from the next century?"

"I know it sounds weird." She smiled crookedly and clasped her hands, hoping that she seemed both earnest and sane. "It's hard enough for me to accept. I don't blame you for, um, doubting me—"

"Doubting you?" he said with elaborate sarcasm.

"Not at all. But you do intrigue me. You actually traveled . . . through time?"

"Yes."

"Fascinating. 1997, you said? I'd be very interested in seeing this distant time of yours." He showed a flash of white teeth. "Now that we've become . . . comrades, I'm sure you won't object to taking me with you when you return."

This was just as bad as she'd thought. His deep, rough voice was honeyed with mockery. *No time to lose your temper, Mac. . . .*

"But that's the problem," she said. "This all happened by accident—that is, I don't know how it happened. I can't reproduce whatever I did to . . . do it the first time. I can't go back through. It doesn't work. I tried."

He arched a brow. "Then perhaps you can explain to me how this marvelous . . . passage through time functions, and how it came to be here in the middle of the jungle?"

Oh, brother. This was the tricky part. Until now she'd been as sure as any other reasonable person that time travel didn't exist. She was by no means an expert on the theories, though Homer had known some physicists at Berkeley who'd been interested in the subject.

She sifted through memory for examples that would make sense to a man from the 1880s. H.G. Wells's first serialization of *The Time Machine* wouldn't be published for four more years—from the "now" she was in. But she remembered reading somewhere that the notion of time travel had been popular even before Wells.

"*Harper's!*" she said triumphantly. "In 1856 they published an article about time travel, about a guy going into the future. I don't remember much about it, but—"

"Is that where you came up with these ideas?"

Mac refused to be baited. "The concept isn't beyond you, I assume?"

"Miss MacKenzie, you may try my patience, but not my intelligence."

"That's a start." She chewed her lip. "Come to think of it, there are lots of examples from your time and before. Stories about people who went into the future through dreams or suspended animation or even sleeping too long. But that isn't what happened to me. I didn't just stay the same while the world changed. I . . . walked into the past."

"Through a Maya temple." Liam stood abruptly. "I'm returning to my camp. It'll be dark soon, and I don't intend to spend the night here. I haven't got time to search for your people—whoever they are. I'll look again in the morning, and then I'm heading for the coast." His mouth twisted as though he'd tasted something along the lines of an underripe lemon. "As for your 'theories'—"

Mac heaved to her feet, swaying at the weakness that clutched at her body. She batted away his offered support. "All right," she snapped. "I get it. No more theories. You want proof." Ignoring her dizziness, she swooped down for her pack and dug for her flashlight, which she'd dumped inside after her fruitless attempt at getting back through the tunnel. She waved the flashlight at him triumphantly. "You wanted to know about this? This is something from the future. No one's going to invent it until the turn of the century. Or batteries this small." She dumped the AA batteries into her palm and tossed one at him. He caught it, glancing from her to the battery.

"Let's see what else I've got in here," she muttered. She rummaged deeper into her pack. Even before the trip she hadn't completely cleaned it out, and it was full of forgotten odds and ends. Travel toothbrush, maybe—and the first-aid kit in its plastic box. That would be good; no one was using plastic this way yet.

She smoothed out a piece of the mosquito netting and began to lay objects out on it. Old Kleenex, a piece of ancient hard candy, an empty can of Dr Pepper, the bottle of muscle relaxant she'd had prescribed when her shoulder was wrenched while moving boxes, a melted lipstick she'd tried once before giving up all notions of using makeup.

Safety pins—no, he'd know about those. Two battered ballpoint pens; maybe. Tour book; that would be a good way to prove how different things were in her time from the overgrown Tikal he'd shown her. Map, ditto. Wallet—that would have modern money, and credit cards, and her driver's license with the renewal date printed right on it. Pocket calculator—pocket calculator! Now that was going to be way beyond his ken. And her watch as well, with its digital face and waterproof plastic wristband. She unbuckled it and laid it on the netting with the rest.

He had already crouched again and was fingering the items with deliberation. Let him look; it might do some good. She started to unzip the pack's smaller pocket when the obvious occurred to her. The backpack itself was made out of nylon, which she was damned sure hadn't been around in 1884. And the zipper . . . ha!

She held the backpack in front of her, running the zipper back and forth until Liam was following her motions with fascination.

"Bet you haven't seen that before," she said. "It's called a zipper, and it's not going to be invented until—um—the 1890s. Now do you think I'm so crazy?"

He grabbed the backpack from her hand and worked the zipper himself. Then he set it down and picked up the calculator. Mac obliged him by turning it on, and had the satisfaction of watching him jerk, however slightly, at the appearance of the digital readout.

"I'll be damned," he whispered. He punched at the numbers randomly, watching the display.

"It's for calculating," she supplied. "Addition, multiplication, even algebraic equations."

He said nothing, but some of his natural cockiness seemed to have deserted him. He put the calculator back and studied the ballpoint pens, packet of Kleenex, and first-aid kit in turn, saving her watch for last. His sunstreaked hair fell into his eyes, and he slapped it away with all the preoccupation of a little boy examining a particularly interesting bug.

"How did you get all this?" he demanded.

"From my time, where these things are common. I'd like to take credit for being the genius responsible for inventing it all, but . . ."

He was at a loss. She'd never really doubted his intelligence, and she could see it working now as he considered and discarded every easy explanation for objects he had never seen before.

Join the club, my arrogant friend. Now you know how I felt when I realized what had happened. And something tells me you're not the kind of guy who takes well to being at a disadvantage.

"The others with you before," he said. "Did they have these things as well?"

"The other tourists?"

"Challenger, Quartermain—"

Mac had the good grace to wince. "Um—that was a joke. I did come here alone. When I first met you, I thought you were the crazy one. I didn't realize I'd . . . left my own time."

He only stared at her, bouncing her watch in his hand.

"You still don't believe me, do you?" Mac grabbed

the tour book and flipped through the pages until she found a schematic layout of Tikal and its various temples, palaces, plazas, hotels, concessions, and roads. "Take a look at this."

He shifted position to look at the open book, frowning. The legend under the map clearly indicated the name of the place.

"Remember when I said I didn't recognize Tikal?" Mac asked. "This"—she pointed at one of the hotels near the entrance to the park—"is the hotel I was staying in. And this is what the ruins look like in my time; a lot of it is cleared, restored, and opened for tourists."

He said nothing. Mac opened the book to the first page. She tapped at the copyright date with a blunt fingernail. "See? 1996. Date the book was published."

She couldn't read his face. Beneath the tough, handsome exterior, his emotions were hidden like the proverbial currents under still water. Was he in shock, or simply refusing to acknowledge any of the evidence she was presenting?

"I understand," she said awkwardly, "how difficult this must be for you to accept. I had the same problem. I guess I . . . trust myself enough, even if—"

"Prophesy for me, Miss MacKenzie," he demanded suddenly. "If you're from the future, tell me what will happen."

"Well, I . . . I don't know where to start. It's very different from your—this—time. There are ships that fly in the air, even some that go into space. We have ways of sending signals through the air just as your telegraphs do code, but without the wire—"

"No," he interrupted. Though he moved no closer, she felt his focused energy like an unanticipated touch. His eyes had gone from metallic coldness to silvery heat. "You said I'm in your history books. Tell me of *my* future."

CHAPTER FIVE

*If you can look into the
seeds of time,
And say which grain will grow
and which will not,
Speak.*

—WILLIAM SHAKESPEARE

OF COURSE, *OF course* she should have expected this. If he did believe her, it was a natural question. If he didn't, it was a kind of test. And it was the one question she didn't dare answer.

Well, you see, Mr. O'Shea, sometime in the next little while you're going to die and end up a pile of moldering bones in that tunnel over there. . . .

She caught her breath. The image was grotesque. He was here, alive—powerfully alive and compelling as she'd never thought a man could be. The idea that he might, *would* die, and possibly at the hands of her own ancestor—today, tomorrow, a week from now—was incomprehensible. More incomprehensible than her walk into the past.

Unthinkable, impossible—and undeniable.

With shock she remembered his reaction to the photograph, his demands about Perry and her knowledge of him.

"Our quarrel was a terrible one," Perry's letter had said. *"I left him in the jungle. . . ."* Left him how? Dead? Yet Perry wasn't here, and Liam was still alive.

Oh, boy. What have I wandered into?

Not only what, but *why.* Why she had come back to this time and place. Why she was here with Liam O'Shea hours or days before he was destined to die.

She had no way of knowing the answers. Not yet. And until she did, she had to buy time.

"Well, oh Prophetess?" Liam prodded.

"I can't tell you your future."

"Why not?"

"Because . . . because I can't risk changing the future."

Of course. That was the answer. It wasn't merely an excuse, but the truth. And hard on the heels of that realization came another. She'd been so focused on proving to Liam that she wasn't crazy that she'd totally overlooked the possible consequences of each word out of her mouth and every modern gadget she'd revealed.

She'd just finished showing Liam things that wouldn't be invented until well into the next century. She knew very little about him, yet Homer had said he was a self-made man who'd worked his way up from poverty. Just the kind of man who might take an unknown and potentially useful object apart to see if it could be reproduced. . . .

If he survived.

"So you won't predict my fate," he said. She looked up to see him on his feet again, arms crossed. "I must be very important in this future of yours if you're afraid my knowledge of my own destiny will change it." He leaned over her. "Well, Mac? Am I a great man in your history books?"

She swallowed, hastily gathering up the things she'd laid out on the mosquito netting and shoving them back into her pack.

"I'm not much good at this time-travel business" she said. "I don't know what would happen if I interfered with the way things were—are supposed to go. I shouldn't be here."

Babbling, Mac. But she forgot the clumsiness of her rationalizations when she realized her watch wasn't where she'd left it. She felt around, scooting in a circle.

"You promised me the flashlight, but I prefer a different souvenir."

She jumped up. Liam held the watch quite brazenly in one large hand. He was visibly pleased . . . and triumphant and infuriating.

"Give it back," she demanded.

"I don't think so, Mac. This seems more appropriate. I'll keep it as . . . proof of your little story."

"Then you believe me?"

He didn't answer but pocketed the watch, easily avoiding her swipe at his hand.

"Damn it, you can't keep that!"

"How do you propose to get it back?"

She eyed his pocket. There was little chance of distracting him, and none of overpowering him. And he knew it.

"Don't worry," he said. "I won't change your history. My future is very clear to me."

Oh, yeah. She'd never been one for crying, but she felt absurdly like bursting into tears. *Just great.* "You don't know what you're talking about," she snapped.

All at once he was directly in front of her. "Then we do have something in common."

Mac contemplated the pulse beating at the base of his

throat, noted the way the crisp curling hairs of his chest nestled in the open neck of his sweat-darkened shirt. He didn't smell the way she'd expect a man in his condition to smell. He smelled . . . nice. No, that was definitely the wrong word. "Nice" implied something tame. This was not a tame smell, or a tame kind of man. Her own heartbeat picked up speed, and she took a quick step backward.

"I doubt it," she said. For a moment she thought he'd say or do something she wasn't going to like, but he only barked a laugh, turned on his heel, and began to walk away.

She grabbed her pack, snatched up Liam's mosquito netting, and followed. Now what? He had her watch, and she should make an effort to retrieve it. She should try to go back through the tunnel to her own time, but she'd already done that; it emphatically hadn't worked. She was just beginning to realize the full, and frightening, implications of what she had done.

Just by somehow coming back to the past I may have changed the future already. How can I possibly be sure? The longer I'm here, the more risk that I'll mess something up. No one knows the consequences of something like this, and Liam O'Shea definitely isn't the one to share the burden with.

Oh, hell.

"Are you coming?" Liam called. He'd stopped at the opposite border of the ruins, where the real jungle began. Hands on hips, he glared at her as if he'd like nothing better than to charge off without her. He certainly hadn't issued her a formal invitation to accompany him back to his camp. But he *was* waiting, and it was nearly dusk, and he had her watch, and she didn't know what else to do. . . .

"I think I'd rather stay here," she blurted.

He gave an eloquent shrug. "Suit yourself. I don't

doubt that you can repel scorpions, poisonous serpents, jaguars, and hostile guerrillas bare-handed." He tossed his sack over his shoulder and turned on his heel, disappearing among the trees and heavy foliage.

Oh, that was bright, Mac. Reject the only connection you have to reality. And your only protection in this jungle.

She scowled at the cowardly thought. *Protection, my foot. I'm not some sheltered little Victorian female who can't take care of herself. I don't need him.* She threw the mosquito net in a heap beside the temple wall and flung herself down on it, slapping at bugs with more energy than accuracy. Her repellant had decided to give up the ghost.

And it was definitely getting darker. The sun had all but vanished behind the horizon of trees. She looked skyward, listening to the voice of the wilderness. The monkeys and birds were setting up their daily dusk symphony of screeches, howls, and roars. *They* weren't dangerous, but there were the scorpions, snakes, and jaguars Liam had mentioned. None, in all probability, as much of a threat as the man himself.

What was she thinking? *He* wasn't a threat. If there was a threat, it wasn't to her. It was to Liam himself. She wasn't even sure when it was, or where, or how it would happen. Only that he was going to die, and she was sitting here feeling sorry for herself.

Mac dropped her head into her hands. If Homer'd been right and Great-great-grandfather Sinclair had murdered his partner, and she was here where it happened, shouldn't she be doing something about it?

Like what, Mac? Play bodyguard? Wait around until Perry shows up, if he does show up, and fling myself between them? Change history completely without understanding the consequences—if I could do it at all?

Or let it all occur the way it was supposed to, knowing she could have prevented an act of murder.

Her head had begun to ache in earnest. This must be some kind of cosmic joke. Was Homer somewhere up there masterminding the whole thing?

You overestimate me, Homer. I'm not cut out for playing God.

With an explosive breath Mac jumped to her feet. She couldn't just sit here thinking in circles—

"Change your mind yet?"

Mac thought she'd never been so grateful to hear an irksome voice in all her life. Liam sauntered into the dim aura of light, cocking a supercilious brow. "I have a fire going," he said. "You might as well join me. There isn't much food, but you won't starve."

Starve. Mac tried to remember the last time she'd eaten. Her stomach chose that juncture to loudly second Liam's suggestion. She slapped her hand under her ribs to silence it.

"I suggest you make up your mind quickly," he said. "It'll be pitch dark in a few minutes."

Mac glanced at her wrist, remembering belatedly that Liam had commandeered her watch.

Still she hesitated. *You're not afraid of him, are you?*

She didn't like the answer she came up with. The only men she'd been around for the past ten years had been academics and students, most of them buried in studies of one kind or another. Liam O'Shea was utterly different. She'd known that from the photograph. She'd been attracted to that quality while it was safely confined to a printed image.

Now it was almost overwhelming. *Just because he's handsome and sarcastic and thinks you're a female joke . . .*

Forget that. She wasn't going to let any man, from any era, determine her actions. Whatever his motive for offering help, be it curiosity or self-interest or some-thing else entirely, she didn't have a whole lot of choice. The sensible thing to do was follow his advice—for now. Go back to his camp, eat, rest. Tomorrow she could tackle the tunnel again.

She lifted her chin and met Liam's hooded gaze. "All right. I'll, uh . . . be glad of your hospitality. Thanks."

He gave an ironic bow and turned back for the jungle.

She pulled on her backpack and followed him. Sure enough, the last of the sun had vanished save for a faint patina to the west. Even the birds and monkeys were winding down. The mosquitoes, however, had not yet retired for the evening.

"Some things never change," she said.

Liam slowed his pace to match hers, lifting a brow in an unspoken question.

"Mosquitoes," she clarified. "We still haven't figured out how to get rid of them."

He slapped idly at several specimens perched on his bare forearm. "They're nothing to botflies and scorpi-ons. But perhaps you haven't met our other eight-legged neighbors? It should be an interesting introduction."

Mac made a firm resolution not to let him witness her discomfort by so much as a single scratch, and vowed to douse herself with repellant at the first opportunity.

Liam led her along a recently cut path into the jungle, heading away from Tikal. "So, Mac—do the women of your time often travel alone in the wilderness?"

"Some do."

"And their men permit it?"

"It's not a matter of permission. We do what we like and take our own risks."

"Then your men don't even protect their own."

Ah. She kept forgetting the kind of women he was

probably used to dealing with. In 1884, feminism was still waiting to be born.

"In my time," she said, "women aren't owned by men. A lot of women don't need them at all."

"Oh?" In the dimness she could see the angry set of his jaw. "And are you an example, wandering in this jungle alone, like a lamb going to slaughter?"

"I'm—" She choked back her retort. "I admit that things didn't turn out quite as I expected. But—"

"But it's fortunate for you," he said, "that I'm not one of these *men* of yours who leave women to fend for themselves."

"For your information, it's not every day that people walk through a time tunnel into the past. Men or women."

His scathing *"ha"* told her he didn't believe in her time travel. Had she expected it to be easy?

"Don't worry," she said. "You aren't responsible for me. I'm not asking—"

He cast her a look so ferocious that she forgot what she'd been about to say. "Nor am I. You'll do as you're told and be grateful I don't toss you back where I found you."

She hastily considered the best stinging comment to make in reply, but she had no time to put it into effect. One instant Liam was beside her, the next striding ahead to meet a man who'd suddenly materialized on the path before them.

"Fernando!" Liam said, his unexpected grin dazzling in the extreme. It was aimed at the short, dark, lithe man in a pale shirt and loose trousers, who returned the greeting more solemnly in Spanish. He was recognizably Maya Indian, like the guide who had brought her to the ruins.

The two men exchanged a low-voiced conversation in Spanish and halting English. At the end of it Fernando nodded to Liam, glanced with open curiosity at Mac, and retreated the way he had come.

Liam turned to Mac. "Fernando," he said. "One of my muleteers. I didn't expect him to come back, but I underestimated his loyalty."

"Come back?"

"They all left yesterday morning," he said, bitterness twisting his smile. "They must have been paid well. But Fernando preferred me to Perry as an employer."

All left. Paid well. Mac closed her eyes briefly. *I left him in the jungle.* Perry's words. They were burned into her mind.

She summoned up an aspect of mild curiosity. "Someone paid your assistants to leave you alone in the jungle? That's pretty rotten."

"Yes. My partner—my friend—Peregrine Sinclair."

He was watching her. He knew she knew of Perry. She'd let that slip, and she had the photograph.

"I'm sorry to hear that, but I've never met your friend," she said with perfect honesty. "I guess it's not something you expected to happen."

"Not exactly. Ah, I can smell the coffee from here."

Mac could, too, and her stomach continued to give a running commentary on its empty state. Fortunately, Liam was too preoccupied to notice, the set of his lips grim and his attention fixed on the trail.

They reached his camp in less than ten minutes. It was set in a smallish clearing, ringed by tall corozo palms. A pair of palmetto-frond shelters stood at one side, and a medium-sized tent at the other, with a small cooking fire set in front of it. The gray-brown shape of a mule stood tethered close to the tent. It lifted its head and swiveled large ears in their direction.

Fernando was crouched over the fire, stirring the contents of a large dented pot suspended over the low flames. Liam rattled off some command in Spanish and strode toward the tent, leaving Mac to her own devices.

She nodded to Fernando. "*Hola*. Pleased to meet you."

He was unnervingly quiet for some time, studying her with keen concentration. When he spoke it was in musical, rapid Spanish she couldn't follow.

"Sorry—*no comprendo*," she said haltingly. "I don't speak much Spanish."

Fernando nodded and spoke again, more deliberately. Mac wished she'd taken the time to learn more Spanish before she'd come to Guatemala. "*No puedo hablar español—*"

"He asked what you're doing here in the jungle."

Liam appeared faintly amused—at her expense. He squatted beside the fire, a pair of dented tin cups hooked by their handles around his thumb. "Fernando has guessed you're a woman under those clothes."

"Bright man."

Liam inhaled the steam emerging from a second lidded pot. His hard face took on a blissful expression. He wrapped a piece of cloth around the handle and poured himself a cup of dark, fragrant liquid. Almost as an afterthought he tossed Mac the other cup. "Help yourself."

She did, nearly burning her fingers in the process. Apparently Liam had a tongue made of iron. She blew the surface of the scalding coffee, crouching where she was.

"Well, Mac," Liam said, his gray eyes glowing like molten metal in the light of the fire. "Why don't you tell Fernando what you're doing here, just as you told me? He does understand some English."

And wouldn't you find that amusing, she thought. It'd been bad enough trying to explain time travel to

Liam. She smiled politely at Fernando. "I came to see the ruins."

Fernando didn't look like the kind of man who'd give much away, but even Mac could see he was dubious. The corner of Liam's mouth twitched. He spoke to his muleteer in the same fluent Spanish he'd exhibited before. One word stood out among the rest: *loca.*

"What did you tell him?" Mac demanded. "That I'm crazy?"

"It's the simplest explanation. Unless you've another you haven't told me." He polished off the rest of his coffee in one gulp. "And, Mac—try not to display too many of your peculiarities. I wouldn't want Fernando to get the wrong notion of American women."

"I don't think he's the one who needs educating."

"I agree." But his sardonic glance told her exactly who he thought was in the greater need of instruction. "Fernando will have tortillas and meat and beans ready in a few minutes. In the meantime, I suggest you make yourself a place to sleep. There's room for you in the tent."

Mac looked at the canvas tent. Close quarters, indeed.

"Let me reassure you that I have no intention of compromising you, Mac," Liam drawled, setting down his cup.

"Even if you did have 'intentions,' O'Shea, women of my time know how to defend ourselves from guys with testosterone poisoning."

Confusion flickered across his face, but he masked it quickly enough. "You seem to have left your weapons behind. Or do you have . . . skills I haven't seen yet?"

There was something insinuating in the low rumble of his voice. "Plenty," she said. "Things you probably can't imagine."

"You don't know my imagination."

Yes, there was a definite purr in his speech, reminiscent of a large jungle cat playing harmless with potential prey. This was not a side of him she'd seen earlier, and she wasn't sure what to make of it. The open hostility and barely veiled derision had almost been easier to blow off.

And somehow he'd managed to work his way around the fire to her side of it. Mac made the additional discovery that Fernando had disappeared.

"So," he said with a mock-lazy grin, "do the women of . . . what was it? . . . 1997 aspire to be men entirely? A pity. What made them abandon the role nature intended for them?"

"And what role is that, pray tell?"

His gaze drifted to her chest as it had a couple of times earlier that day. "It depends on the woman. For one like you, Mac . . ." The look he gave her made further speech unnecessary.

Good grief. Realization struck her like a thunderbolt out of a clear sky. Was he . . .

Was Liam O'Shea actually making a pass at her?

"Don't tell me," she said coolly, "that you're scared of the idea of women with power, independence, and intelligence who can take care of themselves?"

Ah. She'd got to him, just a little. His shoulders stiffened. "I've never seen such a creature yet. What frightens me, Mac, is that all women of the future might be like *you*."

"And that is?"

"Where should I begin? Perhaps with your distinct lack of feminine charms or delicacy? Or your crude habits of speech—is it the usual practice where you're from to teach young ladies such language?"

"You haven't heard the half of it."

"And your appearance." He gave her another once-over. "Cropped hair. Trousers. A man's shirt—"

"Come to think of it," she said, "I do remember that men of your time preferred women confined in layers of heavy clothing and figure-shaping devices that twisted their bodies and made it impossible for them to move. Wouldn't want them to get above themselves, now would we?"

"You should be writing tracts. Do you dislike men because you haven't had any success with them?"

Mac thought longingly of tossing a few hot coals into his lap. "I don't dislike men. But I can tell you right now that a pair of broad shoulders and a smart mouth don't cut it where I come from. It takes a little more to interest a modern woman."

"And it takes more than a brazen hussy to interest a man. I see we understand each other."

Fat chance of that. But she was spared the necessity of replying by Fernando's return to the fireside. She was grateful for the reprieve; Liam was certainly a product of his time. She'd guessed the first time she saw the photograph what kind of man he'd be: the quintessential nineteenth-century male who'd probably never had his ideas challenged by any woman.

She stood, stretched, switched on the flashlight, and strode for the tent. Mud sucked at her boots, making each footstep awkward and reminding her how desperate she was for a good shower. Preferably a cold one.

"You can have the cartaret," Liam called.

Whatever *that* was—probably some kind of cot. Damned if she'd take any more favors from him, muddy ground or not.

The tent was sturdy and of good quality, though there were many little indications that it wasn't of the modern type. A small portable desk, folding chair, empty crates, and a stack of supplies took up one corner, a hinged cot with a tent of mosquito netting most of the opposite side. There might be enough room for

Mac to stretch out on the ground between, but she wasn't about to risk it.

After a quick look around she found a sheet of canvas folded over the supplies; at least that would keep the wet from her clothes. And she still had the mosquito netting from Liam's bag, somewhat the worse for wear. One of those palmetto huts would provide shelter from the rain. She'd seen modern Maya use them in the jungle.

Her stomach gave a mighty protest. All right—she'd have to throw herself on Liam's hospitality at least as far as a good meal went; she'd need her strength from now on. Damn, what she wouldn't give for a Dr Pepper right now. It might be some time before she could indulge that minor addiction.

Tossing the canvas and netting under the nearer of the shelters, she sauntered back toward the fire, where Fernando was already dishing out tin plates of steaming beans mixed with shredded meat. Hand-shaped tortillas were stacked on a flat stone set beside the fire.

"Eat," Liam commanded, pushing a plate into her hands. "I won't have you swooning for lack of nourishment."

Mac was too hungry to resent his patronizing tone. The food was wonderful; her hunger was no gourmet. Even the mystery meat was tender and delicious.

"What is this?" she asked. "The meat, I mean."

"*Tepeizcuintes*," Liam said. "Also known as agouti."

Mac felt the lump of food stick in her throat. Agoutis were short-eared, long-legged rodents; she'd seen them in nature shows. *No worse than rabbit,* she thought. She smiled at Fernando and held out her plate. "*Gracias.* More?"

When she had finished the second helping she searched for some means of washing her plate.

"Fernando will take care of it," Liam said. Just as he

spoke, large drops of rain began to fall, sizzling in the fire. All too quickly the drops became a downpour. Fernando gathered up the cooking supplies and excess food; Liam got to his feet without haste. "If you want to sleep dry, I suggest you get to shelter."

A little too late for that. Mac slung water from her bangs and considered the dubious haven of the open palmetto-frond huts. Maybe they'd keep most of the rain out, anyway. She trudged through a growing soup of mud and poked her head under the makeshift roof. A small tree served as one part of the support, a sturdy stripped sapling pole another. The ground was unmistakably damp.

Mac sighed and toed the canvas sheeting. Her backpack would make a hard pillow. . . .

"Take this."

She turned at Liam's voice. He held a bulky bundle of fabric and netting in his arms and was already walking past her, bending low to keep from bumping his head on the roof. "One of the men who deserted left his hammock."

She watched as he strung the hammock between the pole and the tree. It looked more like a torture device than something to sleep in, but it would get her off the ground.

"Thanks," she said. "I . . . appreciate it."

"Fernando will be in the other *champas,* should you need anything." he said. "Unless, of course, you'll join me in the tent—"

"This will be fine."

He shrugged and strode from the *champas* into the tent. Fernando was nowhere in sight. Only the stolid mule kept her company, head down and inured to the rain.

Soaked to the skin and hot enough to create her own steam, Mac retreated deeper into the *champas.* For a while she simply stood and stared out at the torrent, struggling to blank her mind. Gradually the rain subsided and stopped, leaving in its wake a syncopated rhythm of runoff from the jungle canopy above. The dusk wildlife chorus had dwindled to the occasional screech or hoot or unidentifiable cry. The world was plunged into a humid, vibrating darkness.

Mac poked her head out of the shelter and saw Liam's tent lit from within like a paper lantern. His silhouette was visible, a shadow-shape rising from the desk against the tent wall. Even as she watched he shrugged out of his shirt, muscular arms flexing, and tossed it aside. His body was formed like a sculpture, its clean lines sharply delineated in profile. His hands moved to his waist, fingers working at buttons.

She turned her back with a soft curse. She had absolutely no interest in watching his unsuspecting striptease. There wasn't any question of changing her own damp, none-too-fragrant clothing; she had no spares, and hadn't thought to ask Liam for any. Not that she'd have wanted to set herself up for his inevitable comments.

There was nothing else to do but try to sleep. Mac spent the next ten minutes making sense of the hammock and getting into it. Twice it nearly dumped her—undoubtedly in league with Liam O'Shea. In the end she defeated it, worked herself and her backpack into a semblance of stability, and closed the mosquito netting as best she could, flashlight in hand.

Something rustled in the palmetto fronds above the hammock. She aimed the beam at the source of the noise; a large white cockroachlike bug with long feelers froze in the light. Mac shut off the flashlight and scrunched deep into the hammock.

Damn Liam O'Shea.

No. That wasn't completely fair. It was Peregrine Sinclair who had set this whole thing in motion.

She brooded silently, trying to ignore the forbidding movements in the vegetation of the roof, until she recognized the absurdity of her anger. In her imagination she could see Homer looking down at her from wherever he was, shaking his head.

For God's sake, Brat. Look what's happened *to you.*

He felt so real that she opened her eyes. The darkness was absolute now, and Homer might have been right there beside her.

"It should have been you here, Homer, not me," she whispered. "I can't even figure out which end is up."

What Homer wouldn't have given for this opportunity. A chance to actually see the living past, as it happened. To learn a thousand details no historical account could pass on. To return to the twentieth century with knowledge no living person possessed. . . .

Bull, Homer's imaginary voice interrupted. *This is your adventure, Brat—yours and no one else's. You were sent here for a reason.*

Mac pinched the skin between her brows. Sent here? That was a very scary idea, and not the first time it had occurred to her, strange as it was. There were patterns here she couldn't begin to understand.

"So what am I supposed to do, Homer?" *What happens if I really* do *something to alter the course of events? What if my even being here is a temporal disaster? No one ever came up with a guidebook for time travel.*

No guidebook, maybe, but there had to be rules. Some way to open the wall again.

And when she found it, she'd have one hell of a choice to make.

The last of her anger drained away. Liam, undoubtedly certain that he had a brilliant future ahead of him. So vibrant, so arrogantly alive.

Stop it, Mac. Just stop it.

But the thought would not go away—no more than the memories of his strong arms lifting her, the handsome and cynical planes of his face, the silhouette of his half-naked body against the tent.

She tossed over in the hammock so hard that it almost capsized. It was a damned good thing that Liam O'Shea was so easy to dislike.

Somehow that thought didn't help.

★ ────── ★

CHAPTER SIX

The time and my intents
are savage-wild,
More fierce and more
inexorable by far
Than empty tigers or
the roaring sea.

—WILLIAM SHAKESPEARE

IT WAS ALL her fault.

Liam tossed in the cartaret, trying for a more comfortable position. There didn't seem to be one. Thanks to Miss Bloody-annoying-crazy MacKenzie, he was being robbed of a good night's rest.

By this time he'd expected her to come creeping to his tent, begging for decent shelter from the jungle's nocturnal terrors. He'd been looking forward to seeing her humbled, even if she spit in his eye while making the request.

But she hadn't come, and he wasn't sleeping, and he

couldn't think of a single imprecation sufficient to the situation.

He sat up on the cot, scowling into the darkness. Damn the baggage. Ever since he'd found her in the tunnel—whether by accident or design—she'd proven to be the most relentlessly annoying female he'd ever encountered, and the most perplexing.

Heaven must be punishing him for past misdeeds, sending a suffragist avenging angel. Except he'd long since stopped believing that Heaven gave a damn about Liam O'Shea, bad or good. And Mac had a far more likely employer.

Perry.

Liam swung his legs over the edge of the cot, not even bothering to check the ground for scorpions. It kept coming back to that same bloody suspicion, and he couldn't let it go.

He'd given her every chance to betray herself, but she'd responded as if she didn't even recognize his suspicions, as if she had nothing to hide.

Liam stood and paced the length of the tent, ignoring the sweat that trickled from his temples and splashed onto his bare shoulders. What in hell was he to make of her? She had the photograph. She knew Perry's name. She'd shown up the same day Perry had abandoned him—alone and with no sign of an accompanying party.

But if Perry had hired her—crazy as the thought still seemed—his former friend had chosen a very poor tool. If Perry's plan had been to slow Liam down, to delay his journey to the coast and back to San Francisco, it wasn't succeeding.

Mac wasn't even making the attempt. If she'd played the lost and helpless female in need of his help, or the wanton willing to warm his bed in exchange for his protection, he could have made sense of it. But Mac?

She rejected his protection as if it were an insult. She told him crazy stories she expected him to accept as truth.

He'd heard of eccentric female travelers who risked their lives and honor in foreign lands, but he'd never imagined them to be anything like Miss MacKenzie.

Where would Perry have found her? Fernando didn't recognize her, and he'd left with the others before returning to Liam's employ. If she'd ever been with Perry in the jungle, Fernando would have known. But if she hadn't been hired by Perry, who or what was she?

Liam paused at the entrance to the tent and lifted the flap. No light spilled from either *champas;* she'd probably be sleeping the sleep of the dead just to spite him. That would be just like a woman.

He knew nothing about her, let alone what she might do next. And yet, for all her strange ways, she was still a woman. And like all women, she was weak, needy, fundamentally flawed.

Like Ma. Like Siobhan.

He knew nothing about Miss MacKenzie, but he would learn.

★ ★

LIAM HAD THE lakeshore to himself for nearly an hour past dawn before Mac turned up.

He paused with his razor against his chin as Mac emerged from the narrow path. Her gaze swept the length of the tiny lake, a blue-brown jewel in a setting of green, and came to rest on him.

He shifted his seat on the folding camp stool and resumed his shaving, watching her out of the corner of his eye. From a distance of several yards he could see her air of uncertainty; she was as easy to read as a babe in arms. Uneasy around him, to be sure—less certain of herself than she pretended.

A very good beginning to the morning.

He smiled injudiciously and earned a nick at the corner of his mouth. Her rumpled clothing, the shirttail that hung almost to her knees, and her mussed hair lent her an almost endearing vulnerability. She suddenly seemed like a lost child, in spite of her sharp tongue and bold behavior. Certainly as incapable of caring for herself in this wilderness as any child would have been.

But he knew, in spite of her outward lack of curves, that she was a woman. He knew it with his body. He'd felt the pressure of her small breasts against his chest, lifted her scant weight in his arms.

He felt it even now.

"Good morning, Mac," he said.

She started, clearly thinking that her arrival had gone unremarked. She patted briefly at her hair as if to tame it into order, tugged at her shirttail, and threw back her shoulders in familiar defiance.

"Fernando told me I could find you here."

He rinsed his razor in the gourd of water on the ground between his feet and toweled his face, dabbing his cuts gingerly. The Maya pendant swung against his bare chest, reminding him of his abrupt decision to put it on this morning. As a reminder—a reminder and a visible pledge. As a symbol of friendship it no longer had any meaning, but as a symbol of betrayal . . .

He stilled the pendant with one hand, noting the way Mac focused on it. Or on his chest, as if she'd never seen a half-naked man before.

"Did you miss my company?" he asked.

She flashed straight white teeth. "Not in the least. I slept like a baby. Amazing how comfortable those hammocks are."

Liam slapped the towel over his shoulder. She was

not a good liar; her dark eyes were deeply shadowed with sleeplessness. "And did Fernando give you breakfast?"

She strolled closer, looking past him at the lake. "He did, thanks." She ran her hands through her hair again and plucked at the cloth of her shirt.

Liam smothered a grin. He knew exactly what she was thinking. The morning mist had lifted, and the day promised to be as hot as any other in the past week. There was not so much as a cloud in the sky to mar the tempting serenity of the water. It provided a perfect place for bathing, formed by a rain-swollen stream and cut off by a shift in the water's course.

"I think you need a bath, Miss MacKenzie," he said.

"How astute of you to notice. As a matter of fact, I—" He noted with interest that it was her bare ears, and not her cheeks, that reddened. "I came down here to wash up. And to ask if you . . ." She choked on her request and finished in a rush. "If you had any spare clothes I could borrow until mine are clean."

So she was finally reduced to asking him for something. Liam stretched his legs and worked the muscles of his shoulders lazily.

"I have no corsets and such with me," he said, watching her. "Nothing, I'm afraid, that would tempt a female."

She shuddered. "I don't need a . . . corset." Her gaze followed the movements of his shoulders almost boldly; maybe she *had* seen a half-naked man before. The thought unaccountably annoyed him.

"If you have any spare pants and shirts—"

"Mine? You'd drown in them."

She cleared her throat. "I don't have a lot of choice, O'Shea."

He gave her request due consideration. Thin as she was, she was tall enough that one of his shirts might not fall much below her knees. The thought of seeing her dressed in his clothes had a peculiar effect on him, and his grin faded. He'd thought her mannish garb outrageous, and yet . . .

"Fernando's would fit better," he said brusquely, "but he hasn't any spares himself. I'll find you something."

"Thanks." Her voice was low and husky, so unlike Caroline's sweet soprano. "If, um, if you're done here, maybe I could use the lake?"

He relaxed and folded his arms. "It doesn't belong to me. Help yourself."

Her small, square jaw tightened. "I'd appreciate some privacy."

"I'm confused. I thought you said that women in your time are the equals of their men, and have left behind such feminine sensibilities."

"Common courtesy still exists—at least most of the time."

"By no means would I be discourteous. But I'm not leaving you here alone. I'll fetch the clothes now, and that should give you enough time to preserve your modesty."

"Really, it's not necess—" She noted his expression and thought better of her protest. "Could you at least stay out of sight?"

"My sight, or yours?"

"You know what I mean."

"You do know how to swim?" he asked.

"Yes."

"Then I'll go fetch the clothes."

"Thanks." She looked at her muddy, booted feet. "I mean it."

Liam grabbed the stool and collapsed it. *I think I've learned one thing about you, Mac,* he thought. *You seldom say anything you don't mean.*

Aloud, he said, "Try not to frighten the water snakes and crocodiles during your bath, Mac."

Her answer was muffled and undoubtedly rude. He knew she didn't move while he was in view, and probably not for some time after he left the lake behind.

Liam slowed, frowning. Damn him for a fool, he was imagining Mac down in the lake. Imagining her clean, fair skin streaked with fresh water rather than sweat; her movements unhurried and easy in solitude. Touching her small, firm breasts with her hands, stroking her thighs clean of mud. . . .

You haven't had a woman in months, he reminded himself. And that restraint had been due to his guardianship of Caroline—and the knowledge that soon he would seal her safety and future by asking her to marry him.

Not that he'd ever expect Caroline to satisfy his needs. She was a lady. She was everything a man could want in a wife, graceful and lovely and feminine. Meant to be cherished and protected.

But as for sharing her bed . . . Liam tried to imagine it, and as always his mind refused to cooperate. He'd known her since she was a child. Desire would surely come in time.

The entire uncomfortable line of thought was neatly severed by another mental image of Mac.

Damn her.

Fernando was nowhere to be seen when he reached camp. Liam went into the tent, tossed his shaving gear on the desk, and rummaged through his trunk of clean clothes. He tugged on a shirt and snagged another from the trunk, one of his older ones. It would do well enough for her. He found a pair of loose cotton trousers and shook them out. They'd go around her twice, and they were of a thinner material than her own. Wet through, they'd leave nothing to the imagination.

Damn it to hell. Why was he thinking of her this way?

He grabbed the shirt and trousers and walked the quarter mile to the lake at a furious pace. As he reached the end of the path he heard splashing and a husky voice raised in some tuneless melody.

She was singing. He stopped and cocked his head, incredulous. Her song was as unmelodious as her overly bold features were lacking in beauty, but there was an artlessness to it, a simple and startling joy, as if she found nothing in the world so wonderful as bathing in a jungle lake.

He couldn't keep himself from stepping out from the path.

She stood waist-deep in the lake, her back to the shore. His first thought was that she had more curves than he had expected, her waist tiny and her hips not nearly as slim as a boy's. He had little more time to contemplate that pleasant discovery before she gave a little hop and dove under the water. She emerged facing him, shaking thick dark hair from her forehead.

She remained oblivious just long enough to allow him an unobstructed view of her breasts. They were hardly large, but they were firm and well shaped, the nipples puckered into buds. Her shoulders and arms suggested a slender strength, and her neck was surprisingly graceful. Her belly was flat, and his gaze drifted lower as she began to wade toward the shore.

Until she saw him. Her eyes widened, and she backpedaled into deeper water, arms flailing. She plunged under the surface and reemerged only to the chin. She tossed her hair with a fierce snap.

"Damn you, O'Shea—I thought you were going to give me some privacy!"

He couldn't help but grin. She looked like a half-drowned cat, dripping wet and hissing with rage.

"I seem to have mistimed my return," he said, displaying the clothes he'd brought. "You did want these?"

Her glance took in the shirt and trousers and shifted to her own, rinsed clean of mud and draped over low branches to dry. "Just leave them there, on the bushes."

Liam did as she asked, bowing low. "Can I get you anything else, Miss MacKenzie?"

The water rippled as she crossed her arms. "You could let me get out."

"Why in such a hurry? You seemed to be enjoying yourself."

"I *was*."

"It is beautiful here," he said lazily. "I'm almost tempted to take a second swim myself."

She bobbed lower in the water. "Don't you dare."

"What are you afraid of? I already promised you'd find me no threat to your honor."

"And what about *your* honor, huh? Can't you at least pretend to be a . . . a gentleman?"

"You'd test any man's gentlemanly conduct to the limit," he said lazily. He squatted where he was, hands dangling between his knees. "In any case, I'm rather curious to see what you have hidden."

She was mute—fuming, no doubt. "At least turn your back."

He sighed. "Very well."

"Give me your word."

So she'd guessed that was the one way to make him do what she wanted. "My word on it," he said. He scooted around until he faced the path, expecting her to take some time about trusting him. But he could hear her scramble out of the water almost the moment his back was turned. Her feet squelched over the muddy bank at a rapid pace. There was a brief pause when all he could hear was her breathing, and then she darted up beside him to snatch the clothing he'd left hanging on the bushes. Pale, bare skin flashed in the corner of his vision.

He kept his promise and let her dress in peace. When he turned, she was enveloped in his clothing, shirt cuffs dangling to her fingertips as she bent to roll up the trouser legs. That accomplished, she straightened, and the waistband of the pants fell to her hips. She grabbed at them and hung on, her ears fiery.

"You need a belt, Mac, or a good length of rope," he commented. "But otherwise . . ."

Otherwise, she looked . . . He frowned. The only words that came to mind were frankly nonsense. Patches of damp shirt clung to her body, including a large portion of one breast and brown nipple. Her legs were invisible, but the very looseness of the trousers was strangely alluring.

"A belt would be useful," she said, folding her body to shield her chest and simultaneously keep her trousers from puddling around her ankles. "Too bad this jungle doesn't have a nice Banana Republic."

"Banana—"

"Never mind. Forget I said that."

They stared at each other. Liam felt something so powerful and unanticipated that he bowed to impulse. In a few rapid strides he closed the distance between them and pulled her hard against his body.

Her lips were unexpectedly sweet. He tested her innocence with a quick thrust of his tongue between them. She opened her mouth on a gasp, allowing him deeper access.

She had been kissed before. He was certain of it. She didn't shriek or beat at him or pretend to swoon, any of which acts would have caused him to let her go instantly. Her astonishment was real, but it was untainted by fear or virginal disgust.

To be sure, the resistance he felt in her body was unfeigned. She was no whore used to being mauled by men. If she were acting now it was beyond his ability to recognize it.

Neither virgin nor whore. Unlike any woman he'd ever known. Astonishingly feminine in his arms, wiry and strong though she was. No fragility, no need to hold back as he embraced her.

And if she didn't fully return his kiss, she sure as hell wasn't hating it.

He had nearly half a minute of enjoying her astonished and unguarded compliance before she began to resist. He kept her imprisoned until he had taken full measure of her lips. By then she had gone rigid as a board in his arms, but he'd made his point and satisfied his impulse.

He released her and stepped back, grinning. "I believe you have some natural talent, Mac. Maybe you should attempt to develop it."

She smiled at him broadly. "Maybe I should."

And she pulled back her arm, made a fist, and planted it violently on his chin.

CHAPTER SEVEN

★ ——— ★

*Enough, if something from
our hands have power
To live, and act, and serve
the future hour.*

—WILLIAM WORDSWORTH

LIAM O'SHEA WAS considerably more solid than the neighborhood bully Mac had supposedly trounced as a child. An explosion of pain shot through her knuckles, she cursed with feeling, and Liam staggered back with a few choice curses of his own.

She shook her throbbing hand and backed away.

"You little hellion!" he rasped. She had a second's satisfaction at his disbelief before he grabbed for her, and then she was concentrating on keeping out of his reach.

Not that it was easy to concentrate on the bizarre little dance they did there on the lakeshore, pursuer and pursued. Liam looked ready to turn her over his knee for real this time. And her lips were humming with the remembered pressure of his, the thrust of his tongue, the wholly overwhelming sensation of being in his arms and feeling the rampant evidence of his desire. However completely astonishing, unbelievable, and outrageous the entire thing was.

"What's the matter, Iggy?" she taunted.

He froze, skin flushed under its tan. "Don't call me that!"

"Can't handle a woman fighting back?"

She darted under his outstretched arm. She'd been angry with him before, but— Damn, but this was almost . . . fun. Her mind tripped on the word. Fun, trading insults with this arrogant jerk who thought he owned the world?

But it seemed as though her newborn twin, the reckless adventurer Mac Sinclair, had possessed her body completely. A body that was keenly aware of Liam's, so ominously close and patently dangerous. A body that had more curves and softness than she'd ever remembered, as wild as a wood nymph and as fearless.

"I can take whatever you dish out," she taunted. "Tell me, how exactly did you get that middle name?"

He choked—she couldn't think of another definition for the sound he made—and lunged toward her. This time she wasn't quite fast enough. His fingers were like clamps as they closed around her arms.

"You think it's funny, you little minx? You think you're a match for me?"

Her heart was hammering. He was close—oh, so close, his scowling mouth a finger's breadth from her own. She fluttered her lashes. "Oh, you're so big and strong. I wouldn't dream of considering myself your equal."

He was startled into laughter. "I could make you say that in earnest."

There was something about his intensity that made the hair stand up on the back of her neck. "We have a name for men like you in the future," she said. "It isn't very nice."

Abruptly he released her and stepped back, the anger gone from his eyes. "And do they have a name for a woman like you?"

"Probably not what you're thinking, O'Shea."

"And what am I thinking?"

"Something insulting, I'm sure."

He turned away. "You're wrong. Unless you know I'm thinking about Peregrine Sinclair and how you happened to turn up the day after he abandoned me in the jungle."

"What?"

The motions of his body were tight and hard, but he made no move toward her. "Did he hire you, Mac? Did he send you to delay me, or to drive me out of my mind?"

A whole array of unconnected facts clicked together in Mac's mind. Good grief. He didn't really think— how could he—how paranoid could anyone— But she had the photograph. She admitted knowing who Perry was. He didn't accept her time-travel story, didn't trust her, had provoked her again and again in ways that hadn't made sense until . . .

She didn't laugh. "You think—you think that I, that Perry left you here and I had something to do with it?"

"Did you?" he asked.

Good grief. She didn't even know the source of the quarrel between Great-great-grandfather Perry and Liam O'Shea. And now Liam thought she might be involved in what could turn out to be something far more fatal than mere abandonment. Suddenly she was glad that she'd omitted to provide him with her last name.

"Damn you," he said softly while she floundered for words. His gaze dropped to her mouth, and the harsh twist of his own lips relaxed. "I ought to—"

A crack of violent sound slammed through the heavy air, echoing like thunder. Mac flinched, and Liam hurled himself toward her, knocking her to the ground and rolling with her to shield her body.

When they came to a stop he released her immediately but continued to crouch over her, scanning the jungle.

"What was that?" she said, catching the breath knocked from her lungs.

He uttered an expletive that almost made her blush. "Gunfire. Guerrillas. I told you there's unrest all through this country."

"Who's fighting whom?"

He was completely focused on the jungle, wary and absorbed. "Get back to camp."

"But if—"

"Go!" he shouted, rounding on her. "Get the hell back and stay there!"

"Where are you going?"

"To find out how likely we are to be caught in the middle." He grabbed her arm and began to drag her. "Get going."

"My boots!" She pulled free, snatched up her boots, and jammed her muddy, sockless feet into them. "I really don't think you should do whatever you're going to do."

He flashed her a wholly unexpected grin. "I don't need any mothering, Mac."

Before she could argue further, he started down the path at a run. Mac knotted her bootlaces with frantic fingers and pursued him at a jog, her mind circling one thought.

Was Liam O'Shea about to die? Maybe this was how it happened, Liam caught in the middle of a skirmish between warring Guatemalan factions . . . a stray bullet . . . He could have dragged himself, dying, into the ruins where she'd found his bones. . . .

She couldn't stand it. She couldn't stand to lose him like this, no matter what the consequences of changing the course of history.

She redoubled her pace, keeping the top of Liam's fair head just barely in view. Leaves and vines caught at her arms as if to hold her back.

But her body had taken over completely, propelling her past the camp and beyond, on Liam's heels, along a trail that was barely wide enough for a deer. When Liam subsided into a cautious stalk, she did the same, keeping a layer of foliage between them.

Voices. Raised voices—a shout in Spanish. Ahead of her, at the edge of an opening in the undergrowth, Liam ducked behind a massive tree trunk and went very still. Not completely suicidal, thank God. She grabbed onto a sapling, knees not quite steady. *Just don't do anything, O'Shea. Be sensible. . . .*

He chose that moment to stand. Mac caught a glimpse of figures in the clearing beyond, the glint of light on metal. Guns. Liam started forward, plainly bent on revealing himself. Mac dove through the vegetation and made a grab for his shirt.

"Don't be an idiot!" she whispered.

He gave her an incredulous glance and pushed her, none too gently, down to the muddy earth. "You little fool—"

But they weren't given time to trade further epithets. Someone shouted a challenge. Footfalls sloshed over soggy ground. Liam pulled his pistol just as a gunshot cracked and a bullet spat through the leaves overhead. He snatched a handful of Mac's shirt collar with his free hand and deposited her bodily behind him.

"*Amigos!*" he called out. "*Soy* Liam O'Shea—"

The muzzle of an ugly-looking rifle pushed into view,

followed by a man whose face was half covered by a filthy bandanna. He barked a terse question, which Liam answered in even Spanish. The man hesitated, nodded, and called over his shoulder to unseen companions.

"It's all right," Liam said. "They're not concerned with us, but stay down."

Thank God. She started to get up; simultaneously a second and third gunshot sounded, so close that Mac was nearly deafened by them. The stranger swung around and darted away. Someone cried out. Liam stood with legs set wide apart, pistol raised, as if he believed himself completely immune to flying bullets.

Mac didn't know what made her move then, what hunch bypassed her rational mind. She flung out her arms, wrapped them around Liam's booted leg, and yanked with all her strength. He toppled like a felled tree, twisting wildly for balance, and hit the ground hard. The portion of the tree trunk directly behind where his chest had been exploded in a shower of bark.

Mac dropped beside him. He wasn't moving. An inconvenient rock had been right in the path of his skull, and blood trickled from his hairline.

"Liam!" He didn't respond. She pushed, heaved, and rolled his unresisting body beneath the broad leaves of a fern and crouched over him, waiting, sick with dread.

There was a crashing in the foliage beyond her sight, and staccato shouts, gradually receding; another gunshot, this one much farther away. The men and whoever they were fighting had taken their battle elsewhere.

She bent to Liam's still face, cradling it between her hands. His blood still beat steadily under his jaw—he couldn't be too badly injured. Unless he'd hit his head hard enough to suffer a concussion.

She pulled her shirttail from the waistband of her pants and used her teeth to tear a strip from it, pressing it against the cut on Liam's scalp and securing it in place with another strip.

"Wake up, O'Shea!" She slapped his taut cheek lightly—the same side of his face she'd slugged before. "Come on. You think I'm going to let you do this?"

He made a sound that might have been a groan.

"That's right. You going to go down without a fight, Lucky Liam? You worked your way up out of poverty and got rich just to die in some sticky jungle? Huh?"

His lids twitched. His left hand flexed almost imperceptibly. She reached for it and laced her fingers through his, squeezing hard. "You're the most arrogant son of a bitch I've ever met, but I took a hell of a risk to save your life. You owe me, O'Shea, and I'm going to collect, one way or another."

"Señorita?"

She looked up, expecting a guerrilla or a rifle aimed at her heart. But it was Fernando, his expression anxious and his attention fixed on Liam.

"Thank God you're here, Fernando. He's been injured. Uh, *el tiene*— We need to get him back to camp. *Campo.* Can you help me?" She pantomimed lifting Liam. *"Ayudeme?"*

Fernando crouched beside her, touching the blood on Liam's forehead. *"Vamos, señorita."*

Even without a common language they understood each other. Mac positioned herself at Liam's feet to help lift him and caught a glimpse of sunlight on metal, dancing at the corner of her gaze.

Not a rifle. Not a weapon at all, but something silvery bright against the foliage, caught on a branch by a metal chain. She reached out and snagged the chain, lifting it free.

A watch. An engraved watch, finely made and definitely of Western origin. But she had no time to examine it. She stuffed it in her pants pocket and took up her place at Liam's feet again. As one, she and Fernando bent to lift him. The jungle had fallen mute again save for the occasional call of a bird or monkey. Mac hoped she'd been right about the guerrillas being gone for good.

With grunts and pants she and Fernando maneuvered Liam's considerable weight along the narrow trail. It felt like far more than a few hundred yards to camp, and Mac was soaking wet by the time they reached the tent. Fernando propped Liam awkwardly while Mac opened the tent flap. Another major effort got him onto the cot.

Mac's reward was to see Liam stirring at last, lifting his hand toward his head. He groaned again. Mac caught his hand to keep it away from the hastily bandaged cut. "Fernando, do you have, uh—medicine? *Medicina?*"

Fernando nodded and turned toward the pile of supplies in the corner of the tent. He came back with a length of soft cloth and a dark bottle and some kind of primitive atomizer. *"Agua,"* he said, left the tent, and returned with a battered pan of water. It wasn't hot, but it was better than nothing.

The contents of the bottle had a very strong odor, and not one that Mac recognized. A little plastic bottle of Bactine would have come in very handy about now.

But Fernando, at least, knew what he was doing. He used a tin cup to pour out a measure of water and mixed it with a little of the contents of the bottle, then filled the atomizer. He gestured to Liam and made motions of unwrapping.

Mac followed his pantomimed instructions and removed the makeshift bandage. The bleeding had stopped. Fernando sprayed the cut and dabbed it with a piece of cloth. Some kind of antiseptic, she guessed; not something that would have been in common use in the

1800s, but damned helpful now. The cut didn't appear deep enough to need stitches, though Liam was going to have a nice goose egg in a few hours.

Liam grunted and twitched as Mac tore more cloth strips and completed bathing the wound. She made better work of the bandage the next time around.

"There," she said, grinning at Fernando. "Finished."

He nodded. *"Bien hecho."* He studied Liam, laying his hand on his chest. *"Estará bien, solo tiene que descansar."*

Mac ran the Spanish words through her mind until she thought she had the gist of them. Liam did need rest. "Someone should watch him. I mean—if he's got a concussion—"

"I'm fine."

Liam was glaring at her, steely gaze perfectly clear. Mac suppressed an urge to do a little jig of relief.

"I see the blow didn't improve your disposition," she said.

"My—" He lifted his head, winced, and subsided back to the pillow. "I told you to stay in camp. You could have been hurt!"

Mac tried to ignore the brief warmth curling around her heart at his real, if angry, concern. "I don't remember agreeing to take your orders. You just about got yourself killed—"

"I don't need a *woman's* protection—"

"—*and* if you had gotten killed, exactly what would I have done out here alone?"

"Are you saying *you* actually need me, Mac?"

Okay. Swallow your pride if it'll make him feel better. "I admit it. At least until I find a way back through the tunnel."

"Oh, yes. Back to the future." He made a sharp movement and froze, the breath hissing through his teeth. "I had everything under control until you came along to distract me."

She bent over him, arms folded. "It's just possible, Lucky Liam, that your luck was about to run out."

"And you improved it? I think it ran out when I met you." Once again he tried to wedge himself up on his elbows; this time he could barely suppress a groan. His face drained of color.

Mac forgot her annoyance. "What's wrong? Are you wounded somewhere else? Is your head—"

"My head's fine," he snapped. "It's my bloody back and shoulder."

She remembered how he'd twisted so awkwardly when she'd pulled him down, in such a way that he'd probably wrenched more than a few ligaments and muscles. Having done the same thing while lifting moving boxes less than six months ago, Mac knew how painful such ostensibly minor injuries could be. Had she even managed to screw up saving his life?

"I guess you'll have to rest, then," she said. "Give the muscles a chance to heal."

"And who's going to run things in camp? You?"

"Fernando seems more than competent."

Liam turned his head with utmost caution and spat a rapid string of words at Fernando. The Maya glanced at Mac and smiled knowingly.

Liam grunted. "I'll be damned if I'm going to lie here like an invalid." He clenched his jaw and heaved himself from the bed in one jerky motion.

He lasted about ten seconds before he sat back on the cot, grimacing in pain. Mac pushed him down the rest of the way with a well-placed hand on his chest. His heart pounded under her palm.

"Now do you get it?" she said. "I know. I've been there. You might as well accept that you're going to be here for a while."

"To hell with that. I have to get to Champerico."

Mac was suddenly exhausted. She felt behind her for the folding camp chair and sat down. "If you're in this much pain, you're not going to make it far in the jungle. You are talking about a pretty rough trip, aren't you?"

"Very rough. No roads, endless walking, steep muddy trails, obstinate mules, scant food, no amenities, insects by the thousands . . ."

"And you're going alone."

"I'll have Fernando." All at once he seemed to dismiss her completely, turning gingerly to his muleteer. He gave a sharp command in Spanish. Fernando pursed his lips and shrugged.

"What did you ask him?" she demanded of Liam.

"Do me a favor, Mac, and leave me in peace." He closed his eyes. *"Hagalo,* Fernando."

Fernando touched Mac's arm. His meaning was clear. Mac let herself be steered as far as the tent flap and dug in her feet.

"You know there's . . . something I might be able to give you for the pain," she offered.

"I said I don't need your help."

She almost left him to his own devices. It was tempting. But for all his high-handed behavior, he didn't deserve to suffer like this. She marched from the tent and went for her backpack, still under the palmetto shelter.

The bottle of muscle relaxant was still at the very bottom of the pack, though her need for the medication had long passed. For once she had reason to be glad of her pack-rat tendencies—inherited from Homer, no doubt.

She nodded in satisfaction and went back to the tent, tossing the plastic bottle in her hand. She waved reassuringly at Fernando, who waited outside the tent, and went inside.

"This should do the trick," she told Liam.

He opened one eye and then the other, looking none too welcoming. She pulled the chair up beside the bed and dropped two pills into the palm of her hand. Not too much, in case he'd really gotten some sort of minor concussion. "Take these, and you're not going to feel much pain for a while, at least."

"What are they?"

"Medication. Muscle relaxants."

"From . . . the future?"

She ignored his barb. "Yes."

"And why should I trust you?"

"You think I plan to drug you or something? That maybe I have evil designs on your body?"

"It depends on what evil designs you mean."

"You're a very sick man, O'Shea. You'd better take these pills."

He hesitated, but only for a moment. And as he took the pills—dry, she noted—he held her gaze without blinking. A challenge and a question. She didn't even know the answers herself.

She rose and pushed the chair back against the desk. "Maybe I can give Fernando a hand. He and I do pretty well, together, all things considered."

"I can only hope he stays in his right mind." Liam folded his arms and made all the appropriate motions of someone preparing to sleep.

A victory, of sorts, in their little skirmish of wills; he'd be out soon enough. She made a strategic retreat. Fernando was still waiting outside. He gestured for her to come near.

"*Señorita,*" he said. "We talk."

It was probably more English than she'd heard him speak to date, but she was willing to give it a try. He walked to the *champas,* well out of earshot of the tent, and she followed.

"Two things I tell you," he said, searching for each

word with grave concentration. "*Uno* . . . The *señor* is *un hombre orgulloso*. He walks alone. He does not . . . like taking help from people. Needing *una mujer*, not good for his pride. Makes him weak. He must be strong. Others need *him*."

Mac listened carefully to his earnest statements, piecing them together. She repeated it back to Fernando. "Liam is a proud man, a loner who doesn't like to take help from people, especially not women. It makes him feel weak, and he has to feel strong, to know others need him."

"*Bien*. Understand." Fernando smiled with that same grave mien. "He likes you, *señorita*. You like him."

That nonplussed Mac too much to summon an immediate response. If Fernando knew that much about Liam O'Shea, they must have been together a long time indeed.

"You are *mujer muy valiente*," Fernando said into the gap. "Like the *señor*." He put his two hands together, interlacing his fingers. "Good thing. But he needs more than he say."

Does he? Mac rolled these observations around in her mind, her heart beating a little harder than it should. After all, why should it matter to her?

"There is more, *señorita*."

Mac focused on Fernando again. "Yes?"

"You came here from very far."

She went still. "Yes."

"And you want to get back. But the way is not easy."

Shivers had begun racing up and down Mac's spine. "What do you mean?"

"I know the sacred place. I know *la llave*. The key. It has been broken. Only when it is *entero*, whole, can the way open again.

"Only then can you return."

CHAPTER EIGHT

★ ——————— ★

*Thus we play the fools with
the time, and the spirits
of the wise sit in the
clouds and mock us.*

—WILLIAM SHAKESPEARE

"RETURN?" MAC CROAKED.

"By the path through Xibalba. The way you came."

Xibalba. The Maya Otherworld, which the ancient Maya had believed could be reached through the mouths of caves—or the entrances to the temples they had built to their gods.

And broken keys. Mac remembered to breathe again. *Keys*—the two halves of the pendant. The ones she'd lost coming through, on the other side. The keys that had opened a tunnel through time.

And on *this* side of time, Liam wore one around his neck, while the other . . .

The other was Peregrine Sinclair's. In San Francisco. The one Homer would bequeath to her with stories of a curse that must be appeased.

"You know," she said dazedly. "Who I am. All of it."

He only gazed at her. "The key must return. The danger is great. You must bring it back, for you and for the people." Without warning he turned to go.

"Wait! Fernando, I need to know—"

But he had vanished as he seemed so prone to do, leaving her thoughts muddled and her legs weak with shock. She just managed to make them carry her back to her palmetto shelter. She sat down on the ground as the implications raced through her mind.

Fernando had told her that the two halves of the pendant were a key. A key to the temple—to the tunnel that had carried her across time. That she must have both halves, both pendants to make the tunnel work again.

It didn't matter how he knew how she had come here. She knew he was right. She'd unknowingly held both halves of the key to the wall in the tunnel, and activated whatever mechanism opened the path through time.

Now she had only one pendant—or access to only one. Liam's, which he wore around his neck. Only half of the key. And that meant . . .

That meant she was trapped in the past until she found the other one. *"You must bring it back, for you and for the people,"* Fernando had said. His people? The Maya? And why? Did they understand the full wonder of the miracle inside that temple?

They would, if anyone could. The ancient Maya'd had an obsession with time. They'd calculated back thousands of years before their civilization began, and centuries beyond its death. Who better to build a time machine?

But how did such a machine work, if machine it was? Did it pass through some other dimension between past and future?

And what about the consequences of her traveling through time—of saving Liam's life? He could marry, have children, impact other lives. Yet surely Liam O'Shea couldn't be so crucial in the grand scheme of things that his living would alter the course of history.

So maybe . . . she sat up. Maybe she was making entirely too much out of this. She knew what she had to do. She had to get back to her own time. She had to find the key that would open the time-gate. And that meant . . .

The palmetto wall sagged as she leaned against it. That meant getting the other pendant, assuming she could beg, borrow, or steal Liam's. And that meant traveling over a thousand miles away to a certain famous City by the Bay. In the year 1884.

How could she hope to accomplish that? There had to be another way. Maybe one half of the pendant alone would work.

It was worth a try.

One step at a time. The first was getting Liam's pendant. She'd wondered why he was wearing the symbol of a severed friendship, but now she was grateful. At least she knew where it was. *If* he hadn't taken it off when he'd dressed, maybe she could steal it while he was out. *If* the pills had worked the way they always had with her.

First things first. She'd have to make sure Liam was asleep before searching for the pendant. Another hour should do it. The less she saw of him between now and her next attempt to time-travel, the better.

She climbed awkwardly into the hammock and fell gratefully into an exhausted sleep.

The sun was angled low in the sky when she woke. She rubbed her eyes and rolled out of the hammock, guessing at the time. Blast Liam for stealing her watch.

Then she remembered the antique watch she'd shoved in her pocket following the attack.

It was still working, though it looked as though it had been on at least one hardy trip through the jungle. She'd slept longer than she'd intended, but with luck the pills would have kept Liam under. She tucked the watch back in her pocket and left the *champas*.

Fernando was, naturally, nowhere to be seen. She crept toward the tent, preparing herself. She didn't want to see Liam. She didn't want to be around him. She wanted to get the hell out of this place, before something worse happened. Before she became . . . attached.

But when she opened the tent flap and found Liam lying asleep, one arm dangling over the side of the cot and the other draped loosely across his chest, her heart crashed right through the walls of sense and logic. As if it were the first time she'd seen him in the flesh. Or when she'd realized who he really was. The feelings were the same, and overwhelming.

No. Not the same—stronger. She felt a sudden urge to touch him, to make sure he was still alive.

She walked into the tent and stood over the cot. His features were so relaxed in sleep, almost gentle, the deeper lines smoothed out and the sardonic smile relaxed. His lips were slightly parted. She remembered the feel of them, the strength in them, their unapologetic boldness by the lake. The feelings they'd aroused in her.

This was someone who might need someone else, who might feel . . .

"Liam?" she whispered.

He didn't stir, didn't so much as twitch.

"Does this mean I can say something without a sarcastic answer from you? That's good. Because if what I hope is true, this may be the last time I see you."

Or touch you.

Slowly she raised her hand, let it hover over his mouth. That was far too great a danger. She shifted her attention to the bandage around his head. No new blood leakage that she could see; the wound must have been superficial.

His hair was sleek and pale brown, streaked with gold, flowing back like a lion's mane. It was so beautiful, so unlike her own unremarkable straight dark brown hair. He surely wouldn't feel it if she just let her hand rest there for the briefest of moments.

"I know you aren't going to miss me," she said wryly. "I'm just a major annoyance to you—you've made that pretty clear. And you're the worst kind of judgmental chauvinist. But—" She gave in to temptation. Her hand moved of its own accord, stroking back the thick strands of his hair. "I don't think I'm going to forget you."

She could have sworn his lips twitched, but his breathing remained deep and steady.

"Just don't let that go to your already considerable ego, O'Shea. That was what the kiss was about, right? Trying to prove you had one up on me."

She studied his clean-shaven jaw. There was a ghost of a bruise there, but she didn't know if she'd given it to him. "I'm not apologizing for the punch. You had it coming. I just hope some woman's going to come along and teach you the rest of the lesson."

Yeah. Lucky woman with a job like that. As if he'd let any woman with a brain or a will of her own get near him.

His pulse beat, rich with life, in the warm hollow of his throat. His shirt was half open, revealing the impressive swell of his chest, crisp with curly blond hair. God, but he was so strange and beautiful, like some precious relic too rare to hold. . . .

Her attention snapped back to his neck as her mind

registered what she had just seen. A thin strip of leather lay across his collarbones, disappearing into his shirt. He was still wearing the pendant. She was in luck.

"This is it," she said. "At least I hope it is." *And when I get home, it'll be something to remind me of an adventure I had once, a long time ago.*

With utmost care she peeled the edge of his collar back from his skin and snagged the thong between two fingernails. She felt the weight at the end of it and began to reel it in like a fish on a line.

There was no mistaking the shape and design. It was the very chip of carved stone that Liam's bones had worn in the tunnel. When it was safely in her hand, she spread the thong into a wide loop and pulled the leather cord, inch by inch, up and over his head. It slipped free of his hair, and she began to relax.

"Looking for something?"

Liam was gazing at her through hooded eyes. She shoved the pendant into her pocket, on top of the watch. "I . . . was just checking up on you."

"Sure you were." His voice was leisurely and deep, the words drawled and deliberate. Effects of the medication, no doubt. She remembered how she'd felt the first time she'd taken the stuff: Good. Relaxed. Almost intoxicated.

"Should I be gra'ful for such so . . . licitous care?" he asked.

"I wouldn't dream of expecting anything like gratitude from you, Mr. O'Shea."

"Because I'm not a . . . gentleman?"

Considering the state he was in, Mac was surprised that he managed to inject so much challenge into a single sentence.

"I didn't come here to argue. You need to rest."

"Ha." He grinned crookedly. "You're right. I'm not a gentleman. Prob'ly never will be."

Not derisive, not the way she would have expected. There was an almost caressing note that made her stomach quiver.

"If I was, I'd never've kissed you, Mac. Not right. Don' know why I did it. Sorry."

Apologizing? Now that was something she'd never have expected. But instead of satisfaction she felt a sting of humiliation—that he was telling her what she'd already suspected. He hadn't kissed her because he . . . because he . . .

Found me desirable. Oh, hell, Mac. Get a grip. What does that matter now? Why would you want it, anyway?

"And I didn't—protect you," he went on. His gaze darkened to a smoky half-light. "You . . . could've taken a bullet yourself."

There was a strange intensity in him, a kind of little-boy earnestness that caught her attention and held her rapt.

"Believe me, Mac," he said. "I would die first."

"Listen," she said awkwardly. "It was my choice—"

"A . . . damnfool act of idiocy."

"Funny you should say that, O'Shea, given your reputation."

The corner of his mouth tilted lazily, dispelling the strange mood. "And what do you know about my reputation? Is it . . . written in your history books?"

"Not as much as you'd like, I'm sure." This was ground she was sure of—bantering with an edge of challenge. "Let's just say I know you've taken plenty of damnfool chances yourself."

He chuckled, husky and low. "They don' call me 'Lucky Liam' for nothing. I take chances. And I get what I want."

She didn't expect his next move, the way his hand reached out for hers in slow motion and captured it before she could think to pull away. "I'm beginnin' to wonder, darlin', if you aren't . . . part of my luck."

Darlin'? Mac swallowed. He was looking at her that way again, the way he had down by the lake—as if he could actually find her attractive.

Her fingers felt claustrophobic in his hold. Her lips felt very full and tender and none too capable of forming the right response. "I wouldn't bet on it. I . . . uh, I wouldn't say that I'm a particularly lucky person to be around."

An easy tug pulled her closer to the cot. "Humility, Mac? That does surprise me."

"I don't imagine it would be a trait you're familiar with."

"Touché." His thumb moved in an arc over the palm of her hand, and she flinched in surprise. The caress reversed itself, repeated. Sharp tingles shot from her hand straight to suddenly sensitive parts of her body. "But I owe you. I always pay my debts."

"Forget it."

"I don't forget." His thumb made another circuit of her palm. "But I wonder . . . why you did it."

Like a snake with its prey, Liam held her captive. Her mind couldn't come up with anything even remotely intelligent in response. "I would have done the same thing for anyone."

"Brave Mac." No ridicule, only a solemn gravity. Then he chuckled, a deep vibration she felt through her hand. "And so soon after you gave me that gentle little tap."

"I should have knocked you out."

"Ah, yes. I . . . had it coming."

Mac jerked. Those had been *her* words, spoken when he'd supposedly been asleep. If he'd heard that, if he'd heard the things she'd said . . . She worked her fingers in his grip. "Maybe there's hope for you yet."

"And what other . . . lessons do I need to learn, darlin'?"

Damn. He *had* heard. He'd been faking sleep the whole time, and she'd been too stupid to realize it. "Okay," she said. "You've had your fun. Let me go."

"Or you'll hit me again?" He tugged on her hand, and she was hard-pressed not to fall right on top of him. "Is that how women in your time . . . persuade their men?"

"You're not my—" She bit off the sentence. "O'Shea—"

"Call me Liam. We've braved death together, haven't we?"

This wasn't possible. She couldn't be feeling what she was feeling, letting herself be affected by the things he said and his gaze and touch. She wasn't a total idiot. Her hormones weren't supposed to control her mind.

But down by the lake it hadn't been her mind that responded to his kiss, that made her lash out. Her mind hadn't even been remotely involved.

This was desire. Reckless, crazy desire. Something she'd only felt glimmers of in her own time.

His fingers had worked their way up past her wrist and under the rolled-up sleeve of her borrowed shirt. "Maybe you need a lesson or two, Mac. We made a good start by the lake this morning."

"You've . . . got to be kidding."

"One lesson for another." Feather touches dipped into the soft hollow of her elbow. "Fair trade."

"You'd be a lousy student."

Gradually he was pushing up from the cot, revealing no signs of pain. "Are you afraid?"

"Of what? You? I thought we'd been through—"

"That a woman has nothing to teach me."

She grabbed his wrist and detached his hand from her arm. "I'm not *your* idea of a woman, thank God."

He propped himself on his elbows without so much as a wince. "You're right. I've never met a woman like you."

His straight face and steady stare made it seem almost like a compliment. He was damned good at that, making you trust him. Making you forget you'd ever had any common sense whatsoever.

The tent's exit was only a few feet behind her. She had the pendant. All she had to do was walk out. He wouldn't try to stop her. It wouldn't be worth his effort to continue the game. Not to a man like him.

She turned quickly, before she could change her mind.

"A woman," he drawled behind her, "who isn't afraid of bullets but hides her body in men's clothes. Who claims equality with men and runs away when they come within spitting distance. Do I have that right . . . Miss MacKenzie?"

She came to a dead stop. "It's just possible that a woman might not be interested."

The cot creaked. In self-defense she turned to face him again. He was on his feet, legs apart, unexpectedly steady.

"No," he said. "Not you. You have too much passion in you."

"Uh, I have to . . . get back to my own time," she said, fumbling over the non sequitur. "I don't belong here."

"You've discovered how to return?"

There had to be something certain, something she could hang on to. She pushed her hand into the pocket of her borrowed pants, clutching the pendant. "I . . . think so."

"Then I'll escort you—to make certain you reach your destination."

"I think it would be better if we just said good-bye

here." She thrust out her hand. "It was . . . nice to have met you."

"Nice?" He ignored her hand. "That isn't the way I'd describe either one of us, Mac."

There must be a way to end this conversation and distract him from his dangerous—yes, that *was* the term—focus on her.

Of course. The watch she found at the site of the attack; she'd meant to show it to him anyway. She fished the chain from her pocket, careful not to pull out the Maya pendant along with it.

"I picked this up off a bush right after you were shot at," she said. "One of the guerrillas, or whatever they were, must have lost it. I thought maybe—"

He'd snatched the watch from her hand before she could complete her sentence. "You found this where we were attacked?"

"Yes. It must have snagged—"

But he wasn't listening. He backed away and sat down on the cot, hard, his knuckles white as he gripped the watch.

"Perry," he said. "Was this what you wanted?"

Mac crossed the tent and knelt beside Liam. He looked stricken—tormented in a way that scared her, that drained him of his potency and life more surely than any injury.

"What is it? Liam, what's wrong?"

"This is Perry's watch," he rasped. "The one I gave to him five years ago." He opened the cover that protected the crystal.

The inscription inside was fine and small but readable. *Faithful are the wounds of a friend.*

Words of friendship. Words of trust, of gratitude. Words Liam had given to a man he'd considered a close and loyal companion.

A companion who'd abandoned him in the jungle, and then—

"Oh, God," Mac said. "One of the guerrillas had it."

"As payment, perhaps?" The shock was gone from Liam's voice, and his eyes held only a blank acceptance—a silver shield erected between him and the rest of the world.

Mac didn't have to ask him what he thought. She'd seen Perry's letter, his guilt . . . and then a damning piece of evidence left on the scene of the crime.

"No," she said aloud. "Maybe he lost it, or it was stolen."

Liam stood and grabbed a bottle on the desk. The watch and its chain fell with a dull rattle and thump to the earthen floor.

Mac stared at the abandoned timepiece. "What happened between the two of you?"

He lifted the bottle to his lips and drank. Mac caught the whiff of potent liquor and shot to her feet.

"Hey, you shouldn't mix alcohol with those pills—"

"No?" He drank again, long and deliberately. "Could it kill me?"

"Stop it!" She grabbed his arm and hung on, trying to pull the bottle out of his fingers. "Whatever you may think about your friend, I saved your life, and I'm not going to see my efforts go to waste!"

He laughed. There was a chilling indifference in the sound. "Like Perry's did?"

He let go of the bottle. Mac glanced around the tent, trying to decide what she should do with it. Pour it out somewhere . . .

A large, warm hand drifted across her cheek, wiping all thought from her mind.

"You did save my life, Mac. And you brought me the watch."

"I guess that . . . sort of proves I wasn't working for Perry, doesn't it?"

"It must prove something." Callused fingers cupped her chin. His touch was turning her legs into something out of a Jell-O mold.

She met his gaze. The cold metal barrier had begun to give way, soften, become molten again. Was it possible to drown in liquid silver, or would you burn to death first?

"Uh . . . if those guerrillas are still around, maybe you should set up a guard or something—don't you think?"

"I'm not worried." His thumb hooked her lip, moved on. "You wouldn't betray me, would you, Mac?"

Betray him? She couldn't even move, not when his knuckles were making a survey of her jawline with such tenderness.

"We hardly know each other," she said. "Don't you have to know someone well to, um, betray them?"

His hand slipped to the nape of her neck. "We could know each other much better, darlin'."

That crazy endearment again. "I was on my way out of here."

"And you were going to leave without saying good-bye."

"I *did* say—"

"When I was sleeping." He caressed the short hairs behind her ear. "You were going to leave then. But you talked to me, didn't you? And you touched me."

Mac was certain any reply would come out as an undignified squeak. Or a moan.

"Admit it. You were touching me. When you thought I was asleep."

"I was just making sure you were—"

"—and you want to touch me again."

Her mouth went dry. "No."

"There's no need to fight it."

"I'm not fighting anything."

He chuckled, low and quiet. "You're a fighter by nature, darlin'."

Somehow or other she'd gotten very close to him. Somewhere along the line the liquor bottle had fallen from her hand. She could smell the spilled alcohol. Liam's gaze was locked on hers, pulling her in, sucking her into a whirlpool of desire.

Panic shot through her. She jerked away. Liam tried to keep his hold and failed. She retreated and he followed, his boots sliding in newly-formed mud. As the back of Mac's knees hit the cot, Liam lost his balance, careening forward.

She barely caught him in time, pushed backward by his solid bulk. The cot's thin mattress sank under their combined weights. Mac worked her body sideways to avoid being crushed and found herself entangled with him—limb with limb, chest to chest.

She came to rest on top of a warm, hard-contoured, breathing male body. Every inch of him burned through her thin clothing, fever-hot. Hooded gray eyes made a study of her face. His lips curled in something like triumph.

Heat pooled between her legs, in her breasts, filling up the space where her brain ought to be. She planted her hands on the cot and pushed up. "Your shoulder—"

"No pain," he said. He worked his arm between their bodies, brushing her oversensitive breasts. "I think I've found the cure."

Where's your snappy comeback now? Mac asked herself. But it wouldn't come. Her mind had detached itself from her body.

"Mac," he said, caressing her name. "You know

what it's like to be close to death—feel it brush by you and leave you untouched."

"Yes," she whispered.

"Something always happens then, darlin'. It's when you know you're most alive."

Yes. The admission hummed through her, a first inevitable surrender. She felt more alive now than she had in years.

His mouth was so close, his body so unapologetically masculine. Right down to the unmistakable thrust of his pelvis under hers. She felt . . . womanly. Soft. Almost beautiful, all the things she'd never been and never could be. Didn't want to be. Except he made her want it.

He made her want *him.*

He cupped her cheeks in his hands. "We're alive, Mac. Now more than ever. Life calls to life. It demands repayment."

Secret shivers racked her from head to toe. Why fight it? She was independent, mature; she could choose what she wanted. She could prove that not all Sinclairs were alike, that they could save instead of betray, give as well as take.

She could choose to give herself.

His hips lifted, probed, demanded. "Prove what you said by the lake," he said. "Prove you're a match for me. Teach me."

She heard the challenge and knew it must be met without fear. The old MacKenzie Sinclair fell away like a snake's molted skin.

She braced herself over him, closed her eyes, and gave him his answer.

CHAPTER NINE

This time is out of joint;
O cursed spite,
That ever I was born to
set it right!

—WILLIAM SHAKESPEARE

SHE WAS EVERYTHING she'd been by the lake and a hundred times more. Her mouth descended on his with an abandon that startled him before he gave himself up to the exultation of victory.

For he'd been right. She was like a banked fire, a tempest locked in an improbable body. And now that tempest descended on him with unanticipated fury.

A fury in which he could lose himself, a flame to consume the rage and the pain he'd sworn never to feel again, the anguish that was nothing but impotence and weakness.

Mac was burning life to remind him that Perry hadn't succeeded. That loss and betrayal were not all that existed in the world. . . .

There was no hesitation in Mac's kiss, though it

lacked the finesse of experience. Her tongue darted out to brush his lips and ventured no further. She acted now in half-fearful defiance, to prove herself his equal.

But she was a woman. He could bury himself in her, and forget for a while. There was nothing between them but desire. Nothing to make him weak again.

He had wanted her, not understanding why. He admitted that now. But now it didn't matter, because the wanting was all there was. In this moment out of time he was free, liberated from every chain of reality. He wanted to pour his seed into the hot core of her body, to feel the swell of life in every nerve and let his blood shout defiance to very death itself.

And she wanted *him*. He was certain of that. She'd saved his life and come close to losing her own. The need in her was as strong as it was within him.

His mouth held hers with flicks and forays of his tongue as he maneuvered her about, rolled with her on the narrow cot until they lay side by side. Her slender thighs were trapped under his, her breasts puckered against his chest. He felt her try to speak, but he trapped her words with a deeper kiss and worked her beneath his body.

Soft. She was so much softer than he'd realized. He kissed her chin, her jaw, the hollow of her cheekbone, the slight arch of her dark brow. She gasped a little when he lifted himself and pulled the buttons of her shirt open with one hand.

"Liam," she cried. His name from her lips was urgent and sweet. But this was no time for talking. He wanted none of it—only feeling, sensation, *taking*. Her breast fit perfectly in the palm of his hand. He teased her nipple into a delicate knot and stroked it with his fingertip. Her back arched, pushing the hollow between her thighs against his groin.

It was hot, like the rest of her. He knew she'd be wet,

ready for him when he took her. No thinking. No questions. Only this.

The pulse in her neck throbbed under his tongue. He licked the little hollows under her slender collarbones and inched his way down to the exquisite treasures of her breasts. She made little sounds as he tasted one and then the other, lingering until each nipple puckered under the laving of his tongue.

Black, thick lashes shaded her gaze, but he knew she watched him, watched everything he did with fascination. Her breath was rapid and hoarse with excitement, her fingers worked into the cloth of his shirt. Grasping, urging him on.

She was his, completely his, holding nothing back, innocent and wild in a combination like to drive him to madness. Her body was supple as a sleek and exotic animal, taut under silky skin. He pushed her shirt aside and laid his palm on the flatness of her belly. It quivered like the velvet coat of a highbred horse.

The bones of her hips were distinct, but there was a sweet curve to them. He learned her body with his hands, and then with his lips. He unbuttoned her trousers—so loose and oversized around her waist—and eased them down. She helped him, wriggling her body until he thought he would burst the seams of his own pants.

She wore nothing under the trousers. And she was wet. He slid his fingers through the snugly curled hair at the base of her stomach, lower still. Her fingers clenched and unclenched in his shirt like the claws of a sensuous cat being stroked. He accommodated her. She arched again and shuddered under his caresses. And when he tested her with a finger, pushing gently inward . . .

He stopped. She must be all but a virgin. He could feel her tightness, the subtle resistance. Ready as she was, she had no skill at seduction, or the ease of a woman who'd taken many men into her body.

She had nothing to teach him. *He* was guide, and master, and teacher.

And protector. She was no innocent, not out here alone in the jungle, but there was an inexperience, an uncertainty that called to the last dwindling spark of reason trapped within his desire. *She's only a woman, and you're using her, just as they used Siobhan. . . .*

No thinking. With fumbling haste he worked open the buttons of his trousers. The release of imprisoned flesh was an ecstasy in itself. He slid against her slick thighs, higher, probing and eager. She'd spread herself for him. Her skin was flushed, her lips parted and glistening. He watched her as he made the first foray, heard her moan in pleasure.

Then he saw her eyes. Wide open now, fixed on him. And under the glaze of excitement and pleasure was something else. It was nothing so simple as fear. It was sudden, overwhelming knowledge of a threshold to be crossed, of life forever changed.

The knowledge Siobhan must have held in her heart when she'd taken her first lover and sold her honor for survival.

The knowledge Liam would see in Caroline's eyes on their wedding night.

He tensed, holding himself rigid above the woman he had resolved to take with so little thought. The past was there in bed with him, and the future stood watching, ready to condemn.

Condemn Liam O'Shea.

Mac's face held no condemnation. It was real, warm, trusting, wanting. Asking more than he could ever give.

Because he'd been wrong. He couldn't take Mac and feel nothing, take nothing, pay nothing.

He heaved himself off of her, the muscles in his arms

shaking with knotted tension. In his hunger and need to forget, he could put a child in her body, become responsible for her. Responsible for a woman who could have no place in his future or in his life. A woman whose recklessness and bold nature—the very nature that inexplicably drew him—would make it impossible for him to protect her.

And as those thoughts crystallized in his mind, the chill of them worked through his body and doused his lust to ashes.

Mac's gaze, blank with bewilderment and desire, followed him as he rolled away on the cot. He grabbed the edges of her shirt and closed them across her chest, covering her thighs with the long shirttail. With an awkward motion he tucked himself back into his trousers and buttoned them again. Only then did he reach over the side of the cot and grab the whiskey bottle Mac had dropped. There was still one sip left.

The silence was profound. Mac didn't move for many long minutes.

"Well?" he said harshly. "The lesson's over, Mac."

"What?"

He rolled to his feet and sauntered to the desk, slamming down the bottle with deliberate force. "Please forgive me if I let it go a little too far."

"The lesson, or the joke?" She paused, clutching her shirt to her chest. "It *was* a joke to you, wasn't it?"

Strange. Her voice was subdued and flat, not angry or hurt. Not Mac's usual spirit at all. He wiped his mouth with the back of his hand and watched her, severing any emotion except indifference. The empty bottle taunted him.

"Call it what you like."

Her fingers were steady as she knelt on the edge of the cot and buttoned her shirt. As if nothing had happened. As if he hadn't been about to take her with her full cooperation.

She was pale and composed, revealing no emotion. Just like that her passion was snuffed out. Instead of relief he felt an emptiness in his belly that was more than unsatisfied hunger, a flare of consternation that she'd pushed him away so easily.

More easily than he'd pushed *her* away.

"It was pleasant enough," he said, turning back to her, "but I got a little . . . carried away." That was all he would concede, all he could admit.

Mac had drawn her knees up under the tails of the shirt so that all of her but her feet was covered. "You never had anything to learn, did you?" she said.

Poker-faced. Not the Mac he knew. A stab of guilt thrust at him. "Ah, well, darlin'," he said. "No hard feelings."

A flicker of something in her eyes. Anger? Humiliation? But she rose from the cot and quietly retrieved the trousers he'd thrown on the ground.

"Turn around," she said.

He did, trying to remember the retort he'd been about to make. *Damn.*

"Well," he said, shrugging into his shirt, "you did say you thought you had a way back to . . . where you came from. I'll have Fernando prepare a meal, and then we'll go to the tunnel, or wherever you choose."

She stood where she was, her back still turned. "Wherever I choose?" she repeated. "How generous."

Flat. Cold. He ran his hand through his damp hair, wincing at the returning pain in his shoulder, and walked to the tent flap. "I pay my debts."

"Oh, yeah." The shirt pulled against her shoulders as she hugged herself. "That's what really counts."

He didn't pause at the entrance to exchange another barbed sally. Just outside the tent he waited, his mind gone blank, for any sounds of rage or weeping. None came. He tried to remember the last time he'd felt so much the blackguard. And for what, damn it? He was doing the girl a favor. She was still as pure—or not—as she'd been before.

If she *was* working for Perry—and Liam no longer knew what to believe—she was no worse off. And neither was he.

Liam slammed his fist into his palm. The pain of realization was still sharp, but now it was overlaid by deep and bitter rage. If Perry had tried to have him killed, the betrayal was beyond comprehension. Nothing would stop Liam from returning to San Francisco now.

He found Fernando with the single mule, speaking to her softly in an ancient Maya tongue; he looked at Liam as if he knew everything that had happened in the tent. Damn him, he probably did.

"We're leaving before dawn tomorrow for Champerico," Liam said in Spanish. "Did you get extra food from the village?"

Fernando nodded as he examined the jenny's hoof. "And the *señorita*?"

"Leave her to me."

The corner of Fernando's mouth twitched, but he offered no further comment. Liam felt the muleteer's gaze on his back as he walked away. Walking was what he needed to do; a long, hard walk now that the sun was lowering and the worst of the day's heat was past. That or a good soak in the lake—but he wouldn't go there again.

He grabbed a machete and got a few yards into the jungle before the pain in his shoulder returned. More punishment for his sins. He scowled and forced himself to keep going, pausing only to scrape sweat from his brows. For a time he imagined Perry's face in every

hapless tree or bush he attacked. It was almost satisfy-
ing—until his thoughts drifted, inevitably, back to Mac.

What was she doing now? Probably blasting him up
one side of the Petén and down the other. She wasn't
the sort to accept an indignity quietly. He could imagine the little hellion charging into the jungle with her
strange collection of devices, getting herself lost or
worse.

He was *not* responsible for her.

Damn it. Damn it. And damn it all to hell.

He turned and started back.

WHAT A FOOL she'd been.

Mac paced the length of the tent and back again,
trying to determine where to begin her search. Her
watch had to be somewhere in this tent, and by God she
was going to find it and be out of here before Liam
decided to come back.

She paused in her furious strides to survey Liam's
shaving supplies, laid out on the folding camp desk.
Razor, antique bottles filled with pungent lotion, a
comb and scissors. No wristwatch. She would *not* think
of the way Liam had looked with the sun on his hair,
shaving down by the lake.

Or remember how he'd reacted when she'd given him
Perry's watch. She hadn't imagined his vulnerability
then—or his need.

When he'd kissed and caressed her, she'd lost herself,
felt the borders between two bodies melt and merge.
She'd felt his need as something limitless, becoming part
of her own.

His body was no more capable of lying than hers
was. For a time he *had* truly wanted her. For a while
the vast gulf between them had ceased to exist.

Now it was as wide as the Grand Canyon. Or time itself.

She had to get back. Now. Tonight. As soon as she'd found her wristwatch; she didn't intend to leave any part of herself behind.

She dropped to her knees beside the trunk that contained his clothing; the lid had been closed over the trailing arm of a shirtsleeve, and the contents were in disarray. She didn't bother to be neat in her exploration. Shirts, trousers, a belt, socks . . . underwear . . . she tossed those aside sharply, hoping they landed someplace where stinging insects would make a nest in them.

No plastic waterproof wristwatch. Only a flat paper folder at the very bottom of the trunk, buried under everything else.

Inside was an envelope, neatly printed with Liam's name and a San Francisco address. Postmarked 1884. She couldn't resist opening it.

A swirl of perfumed scent rose from a sheet of fine stationery. Elegant lines of script flowed across the page; a woman's hand, delicate and feminine.

Dear Liam, the letter began.

Mac's gaze drifted to the bottom of the page, to the demure signature so perfectly placed.

Caroline Gresham, it said. *Caroline.* The name was extremely familiar. In fact, it made her think of . . .

Her blood seemed to drain from her fingers and toes and head all at once, leaving her giddy and dazed.

She began to read again.

Dear Liam,

I write this letter in haste, because I know that you and Peregrine are shortly to leave for the jungles

*again. Oh, how I wish I could go with you! Peregrine
says that someday I will have just such an adventure.*

*Peregrine has also promised to bring me a trinket. I
shall wait to see which of you brings me the better
one. Until you return, I shall keep you both in my
prayers.*

Your affectionate friend,
Caroline Gresham

For a moment Mac simply held the letter. *Good Lord.*
Caroline Gresham was the woman Perry had married—
Mac's own great-great-grandmother—the daughter,
Mac remembered, of a wealthy San Francisco business-
man.

Mac looked inside the envelope again and found
what she'd missed the first time. A photograph, new
enough looking to have been recently taken. A photograph of a beautiful young woman with pale curling
hair and flawless features and limpid eyes. She was almost too perfect to be real. And this was Liam's "affectionate friend." . . .

"What are you doing?"

Mac scooted around to face Liam, the letter and
photo still in her hand.

"Who's Caroline?" she demanded.

He stopped in his charge across the tent. "Caroline,"
he said between his teeth, "is the woman I'm going to
marry."

Mac stared at him as the ramifications slid into place
in her mind.

"Give me the letter," Liam commanded.

Her hand was shaking when she complied. "So that's
why you fought," she said unsteadily, "—why your
friend left you here. It was over *her.*"

The delicate paper crackled in his grip. "Don't play

innocent, Mac. It's a little too late for that." His voice was deadly calm. "What were you looking for? Any money I'd left lying around? Or was it simple spying this time?"

She shook her head. "Two men in love with the same woman," she said, trying to keep control of her rising alarm. "They fight, and one . . ." *Tries to kill his rival. Oh shit.* "One leaves the other with almost no supplies and goes home to his girlfriend."

"Perry, in love with her?" he said harshly. "He's in love with her inheritance. He's a damned fortune hunter. But you know that, don't you? As long as she's my ward, he'll get his hands on her over my dead body."

His words were grotesquely appropriate. Caroline, Liam's ward?

Oh, Homer, what did you get me into?

"He didn't succeed in getting me out of the way," Liam continued, oblivious to her shock. "And he'll pay for his blunder."

Mac felt for the camp stool beside the desk and sat down, weak-kneed. Maybe Perry *had* tried to kill him. And would have succeeded if not for Mac's intervention.

Liam was alive when he should have been dead. He was alive to return to San Francisco and marry Caroline Gresham.

But Caroline and Perry were Mac's great-great grandparents. If they didn't marry, would Mac cease to exist? And what about Homer, who'd inspired so many young minds and uncovered secrets of the past; her father, who'd save an entire platoon of comrades in Vietnam—even Jason, who had made such promising discoveries in his search for new cancer treatments?

And would this mess even end with her family?

Greater changes might come from each smaller one, until all of history itself was affected.

Mac trembled. She'd saved Liam's life, and she couldn't regret it. But now that she knew the dire consequences of her act . . .

Only she could set things right again.

She bent over, sickened. There was no going home anymore. Even if she tried, she might never make it. She might simply disappear, never having existed. Leaving the screwup she'd made still intact.

If she couldn't go home, what was she going to do?

The answer to that was obvious. She had to stop Liam from marrying Caroline. Impossible as it seemed, she didn't have any choice.

The strength flooded back into her body, and she sat up. One by one the implications of her decision raced through her mind. To stop Liam meant being with him. Going with him back to 1884 San Francisco, where his ward-bride awaited him. Going without a plan, without knowing what she faced, alone and out of her own time.

"You're going back to San Francisco to marry Caroline," she said to Liam suddenly. "And to take revenge on your former partner."

Crouched by his crates of supplies, he looked at her over his shoulder. "What's it to you, Mac?" he said with a cynical twist of his mouth.

"Do you love your ward?" she asked flatly.

"I know what's best for her—" Liam paused, gaze unfocused. "She's a lady. She was meant to be protected all her life."

"Not only from Perry?" Mac prodded.

He rose, walked halfway across the tent, and swung around again. "From him, and from all the harshness of the world."

There was something in his expression along with

that fierce determination, something that touched on the vulnerability she'd seen in him once before.

But he hadn't said he loved Caroline. If there was something other than love behind Liam's relationship with his ward, it was something Mac had to understand.

"If your curiosity is satisfied," Liam said, "I suggest you pack your things. It'll be dark soon."

"Pack?"

"So I can escort you back to the ruins."

Ah, yes. *Now* he was willing to believe she had somewhere to go.

She clutched the pendant in her pocket. "No."

"What?"

"No. I'm not leaving."

"You said you knew your way back."

"I was wrong. My theory isn't going to work."

"What the hell does that mean?"

Here goes. "I can't go back to my own time. Not from here. I . . . have to go to San Francisco to find what I need to make it possible."

He was very, very still. "When did you discover this, Mac? After I almost had you, or after you read the letter?"

Her breath caught at the bluntness of his words. "It doesn't matter. You owe me. And you said you'd take me anywhere I choose to go."

His gaze could have burned through a lead wall. "Do you think I'm so easily hoodwinked? You may have saved my life, but you won't further Perry's schemes by going with me."

"Even if I told you that I needed your help?" She swallowed her completely irrelevant pride. "Would you leave a lone woman out here in the jungle with nowhere to go? Because that's exactly my situation. And without you, I probably won't survive this place." She held his gaze. "I need you, O'Shea."

He stared at her, angry and perplexed. Finally, he gave her a bitter, mocking salute. "You're right. I wouldn't leave a woman out here alone, not even one like you. If it's money you want, a boat to hire, I can get them for you. But going with me to San Francisco is—"

"It's where I have to go," she said, struggling for a remotely plausible explanation. "At least it's a city I know better than any other. I won't be so . . . lost there." She touched his arm. "Please take me with you. I won't cause any trouble." *Except, if I'm lucky, keep you from marrying Caroline and killing Perry*, she silently amended.

"No trouble?" He snorted. "I don't understand what you hope to accomplish, or how you mean to survive, but if it's what you want—" He shrugged. "I'll get you to San Francisco. I owe you that much."

He turned to the crates of provisions in the corner of the tent. "It's three hundred miles on bad roads, or none at all, to the port of Champerico. A hard trip for a man at any pace, and I'm going to make it a fast one. For a woman—"

"At least I won't be alone."

Canvas rustled as he pulled the covering from the crates and checked the contents. "You'll sleep on the ground, in whatever shelter Fernando can devise."

"I think I'll survive."

"You'll be lucky to get a cramped cabin on a steamer, once we get to Champerico."

"I don't take up much space."

"No. And you won't complain or hold us back, because if you do, I'll—"

"I can imagine. Don't worry. You shouldn't have any trouble pretending I'm not even there."

Liam tossed the canvas over the crates again with

somewhat excessive force. "You'd better get some food from Fernando, and then sleep."

She hesitated and decided to try one more time. "You know, I wasn't snooping through your things to spy. I was looking for my watch. The one you stole."

"*You* have something of mine."

The pendant. He knew she'd taken it.

"Does Perry want it back?" he asked with an indifference that seemed a little too marked to be convincing.

"*I* want it. Call it a souvenir," she said. "If you let me keep it, you can have the watch." She was going to need the pendant eventually—at least she hoped so.

He dismissed her with a shrug. "We'll be leaving at dawn. No more delays."

"I'll be ready." She held out her hand. "Shall we let bygones be bygones, O'Shea? Until we reach San Francisco?"

His laugh was caustic and brief. He grabbed her hand, the calluses on his palms and fingertips rough on her skin, enveloping her in warmth and strength.

"Peace," he said. "Until San Francisco."

And then, my friend, Mac thought, *all bets are off.*

PART TWO

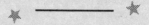

Love, all alike,
no season knows, nor clime,
Nor hours, days, months,
which are the rags of time.

—JOHN DONNE

✦ ———— ✦

CHAPTER TEN

It was the best of times,
it was the worst of times.

—CHARLES DICKENS

T
San Francisco,
mid-September, 1884

HE DAY WAS incredibly, brilliantly clear. No trace of fog lingered over the Bay; Mac could see everything, every detail of the city she'd lived in all her life.

Except that it wasn't *her* city.

Enfolded in a dark woolen cloak Liam had bought from a fellow passenger, Mac stood on the deck of the steamer as it passed through the Golden Gate.

There was no red-painted span stretched between the Marin Headlands and the Presidio. No TransAmerica pyramid to mark the skyline, no Coit tower, no Bank of America building, no skyscrapers. The silhouette of the city was strangely squat, frighteningly alien. And as the ship rounded the promontory, the vastness of the Bay itself spread before her: Alcatraz island rising bare and rocky out of the choppy waves, the hills of Berkeley and Oakland golden brown and almost unmarked by man, steamers and barges and ferries and great-masted clipper ships plying the unbridged water.

It could still shake her, the knowledge that all this was real. She'd had proof enough during the journey here—in the Guatemalan port where she and Liam had caught the steamer, aboard the steamer itself. But this surpassed everything else. *This* she felt like an adrenaline rush through her body, so that she had to grab the railing on the deck to hold herself upright.

This was San Francisco, and the year was 1884.

Mac leaned over the rail and watched the water rushing alongside the hull of the boat. At least she hadn't been seasick. Considering the length of the voyage and the journey before that, by foot and mule through the jungles and mountains of Guatemala to the port of Champerico, she had done pretty well.

Especially considering that Liam O'Shea had been as good as his word. He'd brought her, all right, but he'd kept his distance, which had been just fine with her.

Fernando had been enough company until they'd left him behind at Champerico, and she'd proved to Liam that she could keep up. In the end, he'd given her grudging respect.

But no more, except to provide her with this cloak to cover her peculiar clothing, and securing her a tiny cabin to herself on the steamer bound for San Francisco. They'd been in luck that one had been due in port only a few days after their arrival, and that they'd been able to get cabins. The steamer had limited room for passengers on its voyage up from South America. It was only later Mac learned that Liam was part-owner of the shipping company, and he could command more than any mere passenger.

Just a first indication that they were coming into Liam's world—a world where he was a wealthy man. A world where he knew the rules and she didn't. In the jungle they'd been equals, two people in a vast wilderness. But here . . .

"Miss?"

She turned. The captain's lieutenant, a pleasant young man with a darkly tanned face, touched the brim of his cap. "We'll be docking soon. Mr. O'Shea wishes to speak with you."

He looked at her expectantly. He wasn't the only one to do so on those few occasions that she'd left her cabin; she'd nearly gone stir-crazy with confinement, but she thought it better not to raise too many questions in such close quarters as the ship allowed.

They were all curious about her, the crew and small complement of passengers. Well they might be. Liam had put out some sort of story about her being the daughter of an explorer friend, and that she'd been ill and needed quiet and privacy. The only times he'd come near her were when he brought meals or other necessities to her cabin.

But *now* he wanted to see her. She nodded at the lieutenant and pulled the cloak more snugly across her chest. "Lead on, Mr. Harvey."

"He's coming, miss." Mr. Harvey touched his cap again and discreetly retreated just as Liam came into view.

Strange. It must be a measure of how disoriented she was, this slight wobble in her legs, this leap of her heart when she saw him. Standing on the deck, legs braced and tawny hair whipped by the wind, he was magnificent. Magnificent in the way a pirate is: dangerous, undomesticated, and with a heart as implacable as a machete blade.

She gave him her coolest smile. "Well, Mr. O'Shea. Long time no see. I'm honored by your presence."

His return smile was biting. "Was the voyage not to

your liking? Perhaps you'd have preferred to stay in Guatemala?"

She studied what passed for the San Francisco sky-line. "Not at all. It was very much to my liking."

"And how does it feel to be home?"

"It's not the city I left," she admitted.

"In what way?"

"The full account would take quite a while. Let's just say that my San Francisco is considerably more vertical and a lot less roomy. And that's only from a distance."

Voices rose among the ship's crew as they prepared for docking. Wood creaked and water slapped. Liam leaned against the railing in a pose about as easy as that of a jaguar waiting to spring. "You did well on the journey, Mac. Better than I expected."

Interesting. Such a compliment must have taken con-siderable effort on his part. "Your expectations were never very high," she said, "but thank you, anyway."

"You survived the jungle," he went on, ignoring her sally, "but civilization can be a far deadlier place. God knows where you'd end up if you were left to fend for yourself. That is—" He looked back, gray eyes pinning her like a specimen on a board. "That is unless you have someone to go to."

He meant Perry. Mac casually joined him at the rail. "I don't know anyone in this San Francisco."

The corner of his mouth lifted. "Of course not. So you'll be entirely alone in a strange city." He put his back to the railing, gaze hooded. "I find I can't just leave you here as we agreed. If something happened to you, Mac, I doubt I could live with myself. I do owe you my life, after all."

His words were merely badinage, and yet her heart-beat insisted on responding to the rough purr of his voice. "What did you have in mind?" she asked cau-tiously.

"Nothing improper, I assure you. The least I can do is see you settled comfortably so that you have all you need to . . . find your way home."

"You'll find me a place to stay?"

"More than that, Mac. Money, clothing—whatever you need. You'll be well taken care of."

"And what's the catch?" she blurted out.

"No catch at all."

That Mac seriously doubted, but she thought better of pressing him. *Play it by ear.* That was all she could do, and at the moment things were going as much her way as she dared to hope.

She and Liam stood side by side, within touching distance yet miles apart, and watched the ship glide among other steamers and great sailing vessels, lumber schooners and hay scows and swarms of smaller boats. Masts rose like a forest of small, bare trees. The wharf was chaotic with wagons and carriages and piles of crates and barrels and shouting stevedores.

Mac's tension drained away as she took in the exotic sights and sounds. It was better than a movie, better than the best book. And she was right in the middle of it. San Francisco, greatest port city on the Pacific Coast. Born of the Gold Rush, fed by the Nevada silver strikes, made exotic by the Barbary Coast and Chinatown and over two hundred thousand souls of every race and heritage.

Out of the corner of her eye she saw the ship's captain appear, and she heard Liam consult with him about dealing with customs and baggage and other details related to his shipping business. But her attention was wholly caught up in the miracle of the past. A past that was now her present, one which she'd soon become an actual, improbable part of.

A much bigger part than she wanted. If only she

could figure out how to go about putting history back on course, maybe she could relax and enjoy it. . . .

"Your bag, miss." Mr. Harvey thumbed the brim of his cap and set the carpetbag down on the deck.

It held all she owned in this time: her backpack, the spare set of Liam's oversized clothes, a pair of boots Liam had bought for her, along with the bag itself, during a brief stop in Guatemala City. Her jeans already had holes in them, obtained during the trek amid endless jungles, over mountains and through wild and largely unpopulated country. They weren't going to last much longer.

With any luck they wouldn't have to.

"We've arrived, Mac," Liam said, disconcertingly close to her ear. "Unless you prefer to stay on board."

"I'm coming." She swept up her bag and followed him down the gangplank to the bustling pier. The wood under her feet was anchored on landfill, packed down over the skeletons of Gold Rush vessels abandoned by gold-hungry crews; the pier was lined with rickety wooden offices and warehouses, signed with faded paint and crusted with salt spray.

Beyond the pier the wharf was thick with carriages and drays and wagons, sailors and passengers disembarking from vessels up and down the wharf. Pigs and dogs scurried between the legs of men shouting the names of hotels, boardinghouses, and restaurants eager for the business of new arrivals. Mac nearly tripped twice over the hem of her cloak as she tried to take it all in.

Liam caught her elbow. "One would think you hadn't seen an American city before."

"Not like this." Not blessed with women in gowns that brushed the cobbles and pinched the waist to an impossible circumference, men in bowlers and top hats, steaming deposits of equine leavings, and a sky that reached much too close to the ground.

He tugged her toward a line of carriages waiting along the wharf like horse-drawn taxis. "Then pay attention," he snapped. "And pull up your hood."

"I'd like to see you in *my* city."

He grunted something both impatient and unintelligible and signaled to the carriage first in line, a boxlike affair on large wheels. The dark-coated and bowler-hatted driver, perched on a seat above and behind his two horses, looked them over with an indifferent air that became considerably more alert when Liam showed him a handful of silver coins. He grinned and jumped down, took possession of Liam's single trunk and Mac's bag, and opened the carriage door with an ostentatious flourish.

Even with Liam's assistance Mac's cloak insisted on tangling up around her ankles. She twitched the material aside, giving the carriage driver a glimpse of jeans-clad leg as Liam half pushed, half lifted her into the carriage.

Liam settled onto the seat beside her and rattled off an address to the driver, whose curious gaze lingered until Liam firmly shut the door in his face. Liam's features had taken on a grim cast, and there was a glint of expectation in his eyes and a tautness to his body that hinted that something significant was about to happen.

She ran her hand along the patched leather of the seat. "What kind of carriage is this?"

"A brougham. Surely you've ridden in a carriage before?"

"Only the horseless kind."

Interest sparked in his eyes, though his set expression didn't crack by so much as a hairline. "And when will these . . . 'horseless carriages' be invented?"

"Oh, the next year or so, if I remember correctly."

He adjusted his hat low over his nose. "Perhaps I should set you up as a fortune-teller."

"I can think of worse professions." She leaned forward to get a better view out the window. "Where should I put up shop? The Barbary Coast?"

He looked at her sharply. "What do you know of the Coast?"

"What I've read in books. Colorful place. Wasn't it supposed to be the biggest den of iniquity on the—"

His hand shot out to close around her wrist. "I didn't bring you this far to see you throw yourself into ruin, or worse."

She was momentarily subdued by his vehement response. It almost did seem that he cared what became of her, which was more or less what he'd claimed on the ship. And that was something Mac still couldn't figure, though the possibility did something warm and fuzzy and unsettling to her insides.

Liam released her with a low grunt and sank back in his seat, arms crossed. "Put thoughts like that out of your head, Mac," he said. "That's not where you're going."

"And where exactly did you say we *are* going?" she asked.

"We'll be there soon enough."

Definitely ominous. Mac had a brief, uneasy notion and quickly dismissed it. Even Liam wouldn't be that rash—would he?

She steadied herself and searched for street signs as the carriage lurched into motion. No smoothly curved Embarcadero here, only a stairstep succession of jutting piers. Nothing was immediately recognizable. After a few bumpy minutes the driver turned onto a wide thoroughfare, and the wharf area gave way to the city proper.

Market Street. Mac pressed her nose to the smudged

glass. In her own time Market was the central artery of San Francisco, dividing the financial and residential districts from the southern industrial area. So it was now. That was almost the only similarity.

Questions bubbled in her mind like an overflowing pot, but she couldn't get them out. She couldn't even worry much about Liam and his secretive, contradictory attitude or what she was going to do when this ride was over. All her mind would accept was observation, a mute cataloging of everything that passed within her view.

Buildings no higher than four or five stories, if that, square and somber and pierced with rows of identical windows. Quaint signs advertising apothecary shops and ship's chandleries and steamship lines. Telegraph offices and cigar stores and buggy companies. Carts and hacks and gigs bumping over the cobbled street, alongside horsecars and cable cars running on rails.

And people. Barefoot urchins hawking newspapers, sober businessmen tipping hats, laborers making deliveries. As the carriage moved away from the Bay, the traffic grew heavier and more women appeared on the streets. Women in dresses that could double as cruel and unusual punishment, complete with bustles that made shelves of their posteriors.

It looked like something out of Masterpiece Theatre. Only those were usually British productions, except for that Edith Wharton adaptation. The one about the American girls who'd gone to England to find husbands. About the right time period, too. . . .

"Damn it," Liam snapped. "What's taking him so bloody long?" He pounded on the side of the coach. "Come on, man!"

The carriage moved no faster. Vehicular traffic had thickened, and Mac found herself fascinated by the aftermath of a minor mishap between a produce cart and a carriage driven by a nattily dressed man. A crowd had gathered in the middle of the street to witness flying curses and vegetables.

At least in this era, caught between the "wild west" and the twentieth century, no one was likely to pull out a gun to solve the argument.

No, this kind of confrontation would probably be more dangerous a hundred years from now, in the middle of a modern city. Or in the jungle, where no rules applied.

Victorian San Francisco, on the surface, was civilized.

The carriage lurched to a stop at the curb a few blocks farther down the street. Liam jumped out before the driver left his seat.

"Wait here," Liam commanded.

"Hold it. Where are you—"

But he was already striding away toward a building of nondescript brick and wood, three stories high and studded with rows of plain windows. A sign on the ground floor, neatly lettered, proclaimed "Rooms and Suites Available." Was this where Liam intended to put her up?

She didn't have long to wait. After a few minutes Liam came charging back, his expression more grim and forbidding than ever.

"The Palace," he rapped to the driver, who was impressed into swift obedience by Liam's glare.

"Didn't they have any rooms available?" Mac asked as he sat down beside her.

He gave a narrow-eyed look. "I think you'll prefer the Palace Hotel. You have heard of it, haven't you?"

She nodded. The Palace Hotel of Liam's day was an extravagant marvel in a city of extravagance. It had been home to the moneyed elite, wealthy travelers, and diplomats. It was also extremely expensive. "Is that where you live?"

"Hardly. But it should do well enough for you—for the time being."

It would have to. Mac turned to the window again and watched for the first sight of the Palace.

The wait was brief. Only a few blocks away rose a building taller than any other Mac had seen—seven stories plus a mansard roof, square and imposing and lined with row upon row of bay windows. It dominated the block like an emperor among genuflecting subjects.

She'd seen pre-earthquake photos of it, but they didn't do it justice. Nothing short of reality could.

"It's incredible," she said.

"I'm glad you approve. I wouldn't have wanted to disappoint you."

His faint derision couldn't rob Mac of her wonder. She noted the sign for New Montgomery Street as the coachman drove under a great arch to the side of the building and on through a gated entrance big enough for two carriages side by side.

The sunlight dimmed. Hoofbeats echoed in the vast space of an open court within the hotel itself, a glass-domed rotunda overlooked by seven balconied and columned galleries. A line of carriages waited in the circular drive to take on or deposit passengers; men and women and children looked down on the courtyard, their voices drifting disembodied from the heights.

Mac angled her head for a better view of the glass dome high above. "This is—"

"I know. Incredible." Liam jerked her hood up and fastened a button under her jaw. "Keep this up. I don't want gossipmongers prying into my business."

She pushed the hood back. "Afraid people will wonder who you're smuggling in here?"

He tugged the hood forward again and didn't bother to reply. Mac had a good idea what he was thinking. The Palace was a social center in the city, and it wouldn't do for people to see him bringing one woman into a hotel when he was planning to marry another.

That was the curious part of all this, that he'd keep her around at all. But she'd play along while she could, hoping she'd learn enough in the meantime to form a better plan.

Mac's preoccupation melted away when the carriage door swung open. The strangeness of it all came crashing down like old buildings in an earthquake. The smell of smoke and horses and perfume laced the air. Pairs and groups and crowds of people in period costume moved in stately patterns among columns and potted palms, decorative fish in a vast and antique aquarium. Muted voices became a roar as overwhelming as a storm-tossed ocean.

This was undeniably real, and she was as alien as if she'd dropped out of the sky in a flying saucer.

"Oh, boy," she whispered, feeling dizzy. "Oh boy, oh boy."

At least Liam was otherwise engaged and not a witness to her distress. He spoke briefly to the coachman and turned to consult with a uniformed bellhop. The employee produced a sheet of paper, on which Liam scribbled a note, folded it, and returned it to the other man. Mac watched the figures fade in and out of focus.

Stay on your feet, Mac. That was all she had to do. Stay upright until she could get to someplace quiet, where she could sink into a nice, peaceful faint. Or at least have a minor fit of hysterics.

Right. Probably acceptable behavior for a Victorian female, but not for MacKenzie Sinclair. She could just imagine herself swooning artistically over a sofa or settee, handkerchief draped from languid fingers . . .

"Are you all right, Mac?" Liam asked, rejoining her.

"Fine," she said, pitching much like Liam's steamer had done on rough seas off the coast of Baja California a few days ago. She tried desperately to focus on Liam—the one familiar face, the single link between her time and his.

He took her arm. "You're pale as a ghost. You're not about to swoon on me, are you?"

"Me?" She chuckled weakly. "Not hardly."

"Good. The last thing I need now is a fainting female." *And a public scene,* Mac added silently. But the rough disdain of his tone was belied by the firm, gentle hold he kept on her arm, lending her the support she needed to stay on her feet.

The bellhop already had her pathetically small carpetbag. "The room is ready, sir," he said. "If you'll follow me . . ."

Liam swept Mac into motion, muffling her against his chest so thoroughly that virtually all she could see was the cloth of her hood and his coat. She was uninterested in offering the faintest protest. His strong, masculine scent was almost soothing. She closed her eyes and let herself be carried along, past knots and eddies of chattering guests and out of the echoing space of the Grand Court.

When Mac risked another glimpse of their surroundings, they were in a pillared hallway punctuated by gaslights and potted palms. The bellhop led them through a door and into a richly upholstered, windowless room. The room lurched and began to move, and Mac realized they were in an elevator. The thing was carpeted, mirrored, ornate, and empty of other passengers except for the bellhop with her bag and the operator in the corner.

It was certainly no modern express elevator, but at length they reached whatever floor Liam had requested. He hustled her out and into another hall with a gallery along one side, undoubtedly one of those Mac had seen overlooking the rotunda. She heard the bellhop's low-

voiced comment, and there was the sound of a key turning in a lock.

Liam got rid of the bellhop with a jingle of coins and
a terse dismissal. The door slammed. Mac felt herself
set down on a bed—a large one, from the feel of it. A
heavy weight pulled the mattress down beside her; she
could feel the heat of Liam's body through her cloak.

He pushed the hood away from her face, calloused
fingers brushing her cheek. "How are you feeling now,
Mac?"

She propped herself up on her elbows, testing her
dizziness. It was fading rapidly. Liam's arm supported
the small of her back, warm and strong.

"A lot better, thanks," she said. "I guess it was the
strangeness hitting me all at once."

"Too much grandeur for you?" he asked, tucking layers of pillows around her until she could hardly move.
"I warned you that civilization could be dangerous."
He vanished for a moment and returned with a crystal
glass of water, which she was glad enough to have. Her
mouth had gone dry as a bone.

The place was a showpiece of Victorian excess, re-
plete with richly polished woods, sumptuous fabrics
and lavish decoration. It was big, high-ceilinged, and
worthy of royalty. Mac knew she didn't belong *here*.

The walls were painted a delicate peach, with wall-
paper ticked in tiny flowers. That was the single conces-
sion to subtlety. The floor was sleek-grained wood,
covered by an Oriental carpet that looked too expensive to walk on. The bed on which she sat was a carved
mahogany Eastlake half-tester, made up with a quilted
satin bedcover and piled with gaudy fringed pillows,
more than enough to suffocate under.

Against one of the two plainer walls stood a mahogany wardrobe and matching dressing table complete
with a gilt mirror and a delicate cushioned chair. A

rolltop desk was positioned at the other wall, and an additional cheval mirror stood in the corner. Two more overstuffed chairs upholstered in burgundy and brown were arranged in front of a marble fireplace, already occupied by a crackling fire. Heavy drapes swept down in graceful arcs from wide bay windows.

There was even an electric clock on the mantel. Mac had almost forgotten how to tell time, she'd been so long without her watch. The clock was comfortingly ordinary.

"I don't suppose," she said, "that there's a bathroom in here too. Er—a water closet?"

Liam pointed toward the rear of the room.

Sure enough, there was a half-open door she hadn't noticed. They had toilets by 1884, didn't they? She hadn't seen any in Guatemala, but then again Liam hadn't paused in any populated area long enough for her to find out. And there would surely be a bathtub— good Lord, a soak would be paradise after weeks on shipboard and traveling through the wilderness, snatching quick and modest baths in rivers or settling for a hasty sponging.

"I trust you find the accommodations satisfactory?" Liam asked.

"It's beautiful. Thank you."

"Then I must go."

She was startled into full attention. This was happening too fast. If he was planning to leave her already . . .

"Where?" she demanded, pushing forward on the bed. "I thought you said—" She broke off at the look on his face.

Whatever gentleness he'd shown her a few moments ago was gone. He was all grim determination again, from the stony bleakness of his gray eyes to the hard set of his jaw. "I have business that's been awaiting my attention since we left Tikal."

And she knew, then. She knew what business was so important that he wouldn't wait one minute longer than necessary to see to it. The business he'd never forgotten during their journey, no matter how little he'd revealed his preoccupation to his unwanted companion.

"Perry," she said. "You're going for Perry, aren't you?"

The full force of his attention fell on her like a physical blow. "Worried, Mac? For me, or for him?"

She planted her feet on the floor and stood. "You still have no proof that he tried to—"

"I'll have it, soon enough," he said. He jammed on his hat and turned on his heel. "Make yourself comfortable. A meal will be sent up to you shortly."

Mac had sworn to herself that she wasn't going to beg, but all of a sudden her pride didn't seem quite so important anymore. "Then you're just going to abandon me here—"

He stopped with his hand on the knob. "Don't worry. I'll be back soon enough. Oh, and I wouldn't advise that you think of leaving. It's a dangerous city out there."

The door rattled as it slammed shut.

Mac stood very still long after he'd gone, listening to the echoing hollow of her thoughts. She walked carefully to the bed and sat down again. Thinking on her feet wasn't such a hot idea when her knees were shaking so much.

Okay, Mac. What now?

Liam was out of reach, undoubtedly on his way to do something rash and hazardous. And now she wasn't with him to . . . what? Stop him? Protect him?

She pushed to her feet and marched to the window. Old San Francisco spread out before her in an undulating surface of square rooftops, punctuated by the occasional church spire or belching smokestack. It ran northward from the flats of the Financial District, up and over the hills and all the way to the Bay. From here the view of sparkling water was unimpeded and magnificent and utterly terrifying.

As she'd done so many times before, Mac pulled the Maya pendant from beneath her shirt and held the cool stone in her hand. This was it. Either she'd collapse in a useless heap or take up the gauntlet and find a way to do what she had to do.

Somewhere out there Peregrine Sinclair, her own great-great-grandfather, was going about the business of courting Caroline Gresham. Was he a murderer who'd kill a good friend for the sake of a woman—or her fortune? It seemed too incredible, but Liam believed it. And so, it seemed, had Homer.

If it were true, Perry wouldn't be expecting Liam's return. There was no telling what he might do once he realized his attempt had failed—or what Liam would do to *him*.

She turned from the window and went to the bathroom. It had a toilet and bathtub and sink, everything antique and fancy but recognizable and presumably functional. She turned on the faucet in the wood and marble washstand and splashed two palmfuls of cold water over her face.

Think, Mac. You've got to come up with something. . . .

A discreet tapping came at the main door. Mac snatched a towel hung beside the sink and rushed across the room, remembering to assume a little dignity before she answered the knock.

But it wasn't Liam. It was a young man in a dark suit with a wheeled cart spread with covered platters, cut crystal goblets, and ornate silver. Room service of a degree Mac had never seen in her life.

As *she* was something the young man hadn't seen often. His gaze took in her jeans and shirt and traveled to her flushed skin and tousled hair.

"Your dinner, ma'am," he said. "As ordered. Will there be anything else?"

The young man's expression told Mac all she needed to know about her appearance. It was a shame she didn't have anything in her possession that resembled the local currency, but she doubted the banks of 1884 would accept traveler's checks so she could go out and buy herself a dress.

"Thanks," she said slowly. "As a matter of fact, I think there is something you could help me with. I need to find out where someone lives. My, uh, cousin—Peregrine Sinclair."

Ah. The waiter obviously recognized the name, though his face didn't exactly light up at the mention of it. "May I ask why, ma'am?"

Strange question from a hotel employee, but she'd have to play along. "Well, I'm a . . . stranger in town, and I was hoping to pay him a visit this evening. I seem to have lost his address."

Abruptly the young man pushed the food cart into the room and backed away, casting an uneasy glance over his shoulder. "I'm sorry, ma'am," he muttered. "I can't help you."

She squeezed past the cart and started to follow him out the door. "Maybe you could find someone who can—"

But he was already retreating, and another person had stepped into his vacant place. Mac looked up—and up—at a rather large man in a gray suit who blocked her path as effectively as a locked door.

"Who are you?" she demanded.

The bruiser removed his hat. "I'm sorry, miss," he said. "Mr. O'Shea said you were to remain in your room."

Two and two came together fairly quickly in Mac's brain. "There must be some mistake."

He looked her up and down, much as the waiter had done, and his expression was just as dubious. "I have orders. Mr. O'Shea said you'd be safer here, until he comes back."

Mr. O'Shea *said*, and apparently his word was law. This was Liam's city, and she didn't have the slightest idea how far his wealth—and his influence—might reach.

Far enough, evidently, to hire a thug to guard her door and make sure she didn't escape. "So Mr. O'Shea wants to keep me safe, does he?" she muttered.

The guard shrugged and replaced his hat. "You're to be comfortable, miss. You can have anything else you want."

Anything but freedom. So much for Liam's generous impulses. "I don't suppose you have any Coke machines, do you?"

But any petty satisfaction at the guard's momentary confusion didn't make her feel better. He stepped forward, herding her back into the room, and gripped the doorknob.

"If you need anything, miss, I'll be right outside. Enjoy your meal." He closed the door firmly, if gently, in her face.

Mac turned from the door and bumped into the food cart. Her stomach rumbled, reminding her that her last meal had been scanty and many hours ago. Well, she had to eat, if only to keep up her strength.

The dishes under their silver covers were recognizable enough: some kind of meat in a rich sauce, a salad, soup, potatoes, vegetables, shellfish, and a small decanter of what smelled like wine. The latter was particularly tempting, but she passed on it. A clear head was what she needed now.

The one thing she was sure of was that Liam was coming back. And when he did, there was going to be a reckoning.

CHAPTER ELEVEN

The strongest of all warriors
are these two—
Time and Patience.

—LEO TOLSTOI

THE LATE AFTERNOON air was clear and crisp, with no hint of fog: a perfect autumn day, and still quiet on Nob Hill while its inhabitants completed their business in bank and office and began the serious pursuit of drink and pleasure in the bars and hotels along the Cocktail Route.

Liam hardly noticed. The beauty of the evening meant nothing to him; he was not thinking of the business colleagues and acquaintances he might have joined in their endless rounds of libations.

He was trying not to think of Mac, who was safely sequestered in her room at the Palace and, unless he missed his guess, was even now realizing she couldn't leave. There'd be time enough to attend to her when Perry was dealt with.

Perry, who at this very moment was courting Caroline. Liam had been a fool to think Perry would be lounging about in his rooms on Market for a single precious second.

Liam leaned forward in his seat as the brougham rounded the corner onto California Street. He'd been waiting for this ever since Mac had given him the proof of Perry's treachery. For weeks he'd been patient; the sea voyage had been worst, for he'd had little to occupy his mind but thoughts of the coming confrontation and what he was going to do with Mac.

Now the waiting was over. By day's end he'd have the truth, if he had to beat it out of Perry's blue-blooded hide.

The brougham came to a stop beside the wrought-iron gates of the Gresham mansion. Like Hopkins's monstrosity at the crown of Nob Hill, it had been built with wealth earned in the past thirty years by a man who'd started from virtual obscurity. Edward Gresham had earned his money in the gold fields of the '50s by providing the miners with necessities, and then built on those riches with canny investments and stubborn persistence.

Gresham was gone, but his daughter remained behind those grandiose Italianate walls. Caroline, the girl for whose sake Gresham had demanded from Liam a solemn deathbed oath: to protect her all her days, to see that none of life's harshness ever touched her delicately shod feet or the hem of her Paris gowns.

To Liam had been granted Caroline's legal guardianship—Liam O'Shea, former street urchin, who'd worked his way west on the building of the railroad and made his own fortune on the Comstock. "Lucky Liam," who'd once saved Edward Gresham's life and had known his daughter since her childhood.

At almost eighteen Caroline was no longer a child. In

almost every respect she was the lady Gresham had wanted her to be. The lady Liam expected her to be.

But she was flawed with the weakness of her female nature, vulnerable enough to respond to the under-handed charms of the son of an English viscount, a man with little money but a very impressive pedigree. Liam was the only one who could save her. And, infatuated or not, Caroline must be spared the sordid details of Perry's betrayal.

Liam jumped out of the carriage, ordered the driver to wait, and strode through the gates. His sharp knock on the vast mahogany double doors was answered by the Gresham butler, a stiff-rumped Englishman who'd been lured away from some New York nabob. A very useful stiff-rumped Englishman, and one who had a definite taste for silver.

The butler looked somewhat startled to see Liam, which was understandable enough. Liam had sent word only to Chen that he was home, and he'd never turned up at the Gresham door directly from an expedition.

But there were exceptions to every rule. If Biggs's surprise had a more malign explanation, Liam would know soon enough.

"Ah, Mr. O'Shea," the butler said belatedly. "What a pleasure to see you returned."

Liam pushed through the door. "Didn't expect me, Biggs?"

The butler looked uncomfortable. "When Mr. Sin-clair arrived before you, we were told your return might be somewhat delayed."

Somewhat delayed. Liam smiled grimly enough to send Biggs gliding back a step. "Perry is here now," he said.

"He is, sir." Biggs took Liam's hat, staying well out of his way. "I kept your man Chen informed, but I fear I was unable to do anything to prevent—"

The sound of a lilting piano melody drifted along the hall. Caroline; there was no mistaking that finesse. "Sounds as if they're having a nice little party. I think I'll join them. No need to announce me, Biggs—it's a surprise."

He paused long enough to drop a sizable bribe into the hat Biggs held and started down the hall. He could have found his way to the music room blind. And when he entered it, he was invisible just long enough to take in the cozy little picture of romantic felicity.

Caroline sat at the grand piano, her skirts draped with perfect elegance, her golden hair gathered in curls and ringlets. Her sweet, unaffected voice accompanied the ballad she played. Her performance was all for the man who leaned attentively over the instrument.

Peregrine Wallace Sinclair, youngest son of the Viscount Holdridge. Dark-haired and handsome, flawlessly aristocratic in his fine suit and polished shoes, the ideal scion of England's peerage. That he had no wealth of his own didn't make him any less welcome in San Francisco's highest social circles. Or any less interesting to Caroline's naive and unsophisticated imagination.

Liam plunged his hand into his coat pocket and gripped Perry's watch in a stranglehold. Until now his rage had been reined in by necessity and some small hope that he might be wrong.

Belief came easily when he saw Caroline and Perry together, and with it came fury and grinding pain.

He stepped farther into the room. Two heads, blond and dark, swung toward him.

"Good evening, Caroline," he said. "Perry."

Caroline's fingers found the first sour note on the keys. "Liam?" she whispered. The piano bench scraped back. "Liam! You're home!"

She gathered her skirts and rushed across the polished parquet floor. Halfway to him she must have seen the look on his face; her impetuous rush slackened to a walk. She closed the remaining space with ladylike decorum, her hands clutched in the folds of her skirt.

"Oh, Liam," she stammered. "I thought . . . I feared you might be lost."

Liam well knew his first responsibility; he didn't indulge his desire to look at Perry's face, to see the dawning alarm in the Englishman's eyes.

Instead he kept deliberately mute, examining Caroline from dainty feet to the crown of her golden head. Not a hair out of place. He could see her blushing under his inspection and struggling to hold her dignified pose, but there was no sign that any real damage had been done by Perry's early return.

No damage to Caroline, in any case.

He smiled faintly. "Who gave you the idea that I might not return, my dear?"

She uttered a nervous laugh and began to offer some inane witticism she'd undoubtedly learned in finishing school, but he was hardly listening. His initial concern was satisfied, and there was far more urgent business at hand than playing at pointless social rituals of welcome.

Perhaps she deserved some reassurance; she had, after all, been worried about him. But he was in no mood for gallantry. Caroline was his ward, and she'd obey, niceties or not.

"As you see," he said impatiently, "I'm well. I've only just returned, and I have important matters to discuss with Perry. Elsewhere." He glanced around the room. "Where is your aunt?"

"Oh, upstairs having one of her headaches." There was distinct petulance in Caroline's tone, umbrage at Liam's failure to pay her proper homage. Perry had surely been giving her plenty of that.

"Then I suggest you go find her and ask her if she

needs anything, since she's too indisposed to carry out her responsibilities as chaperon," Liam said. "I won't be staying for tea."

"I should hope not, coming here in all your dirt," a light, cultured voice interposed. "Though I suppose I ought to welcome you home, old man."

For the first time Liam looked up to meet Perry's gaze.

He didn't know what he'd expected: instant fireworks, perhaps, or fear and trembling on the traitor's part as he realized his schemes had been foiled.

But Perry wasn't trembling. He was regarding Liam from across the room with a faint half-smile, devoid of even a trace of shame. He strolled away from the piano to join Liam's ward. "Caroline was worried about you," he said. "I tried to assure her that nothing in the world could do you in without your permission. I'm delighted to have you prove me right."

Good God. The man's gall was incredible, his coolness beyond belief. The rage Liam had kept in check began to boil over. If he didn't get out of here quickly, dragging Perry with him, there'd be a very nasty scene Caroline could not be allowed to witness.

Perry knew it. Sudden wariness flickered in the Englishman's gaze.

"Perry's right," Caroline said, ignoring Liam's command as easily as she recovered her air of insouciant feminine charm. She inserted herself between the men with a muted hiss of satin and petticoats and took Liam's arm. "I was so worried, and I haven't welcomed you home properly. If I'd known you were back, I would have arranged a dinner, at least. And you *can't* go until you've told me everything that happened on your journey. You did bring something back for me, didn't you?" She fluttered golden eyelashes in a practiced gesture of flirtation. "Look what Perry brought me from the jungle!"

She put a hand to her bodice. Just below the high neck of her gown, on a golden chain, hung a piece of carved and polished jade.

"Isn't it lovely? Perry found it in a Maya tomb. He told me wonderful stories about—"

"How thoughtful of Perry," Liam interrupted. "Unfortunately, I'm not staying." He freed his arm from Caroline's hold. "I'll be back tomorrow. In the meantime, Perry will be coming with me, and I want you to go upstairs to your aunt. Is that clear?"

She pouted. She was very good at it; it would have worked on most men. "But Perry has only just arrived—"

"His visit is at an end," Liam said. He strode back to the door and signaled to Biggs, who waited just outside. "Biggs, see that Miss Gresham goes upstairs and remains there."

The butler bowed to Caroline. She cast Liam a look halfway between tears and outrage and flounced away, Biggs at her heels.

"That wasn't well done of you, old man," Perry remarked. "Somewhat boorish, at best, considering your abrupt entrance."

Liam turned and met Perry's gaze. "Worried?" he asked, advancing on the Englishman. "Can't hide behind her skirts now, can you?" He wanted to charge at Perry, wipe the smirk off that pale, handsome face. But there were better ways of going about this—much better ways.

Perry retreated a step and stopped, raising his hands in appeasement. "I'm not hiding. I know why you're here. But this is hardly the place to . . . hold the discussion you have in mind."

"You're right. That's why you're coming with me.

There's someone I want you to meet. Someone I found in the jungle."

Perry didn't react beyond the lifting of one well-groomed brow. "In your present mood, old man, I doubt you'll do well at introductions."

"In my present mood I have very little patience for your games. Either you come with me now, or I go upstairs and tell Caroline how you betrayed me in the jungle."

"You wouldn't do that."

"No? You made certain to be with Caroline, alone, when I wasn't here to prevent it. Unfortunately for you, I've returned, and *I* decide whether you ever see Caroline again."

The easy indifference left Perry's expression. "You don't have that much power. She's not your property—"

"Don't underestimate me, Perry. You failed the last time."

"Did I, old man?"

Liam bared his teeth. "The proof stands before you."

But Perry didn't take the bait. He was utterly cold-blooded, relaxed, and elegant in his movements as he retrieved his hat and cane from the hall stand. He let Liam maneuver him out the front door and to the waiting brougham, revealing not so much as a single uneasy gesture to betray his guilt.

The air in the carriage was as thick with tension as the Bay with fog in high summer. Liam directed the driver back to the Palace, mollifying his banked rage with a long, hard stare at Perry's impassive face. It was Perry who broke the silence first.

"If it's an apology you want, old man, I'll be happy to give it," he said, shifting his cane between his hands. "I admit what I did in the jungle was hardly honorable."

Hardly honorable? Liam almost laughed aloud. Was it so easy for Perry to dismiss an attempted murder? Or was it possible he thought Liam didn't know who was behind it?

"I should never have abandoned you as I did," Perry went on slowly. "I was angry, and not thinking clearly. I knew you could reach the nearest village with the provisions I left you, but—"

"Save your apologies," Liam snapped, "until you've met my friend. You may find that things turned out a little differently than you expected."

The carriage door opened. "The Palace Hotel, gentlemen," the driver announced. Perry hesitated, gazing up at the towering bay windows.

"No need to be afraid, Perry," Liam said behind him. "If I wanted you shanghaied, I wouldn't have brought you here."

Perry alighted, and Liam took his arm as companionably as if they were still the close friends they'd once been. They walked through the Grand Court and to the elevators; Perry hid it well, but Liam felt his tension.

Liam's own tension mounted as they stopped before the door to Mac's room.

Now he would know. Now he'd be sure how much Mac was tangled up in all this. He wondered why he wanted her exoneration.

But the hell of it was that he did.

He nodded to the hotel employee he'd set to guard Mac's door, gesturing the man discreetly out of the way, and knocked.

The door cracked open an inch. A familiar brown eye peered through the slit, blinked, and vanished. The door swung wide to reveal Mac in her shirt and trousers, her expression caught between a foolish grin and the threat of an imminent tirade.

But Liam wasn't watching Mac. He examined Perry's face, waiting for the first shock of recognition.

"Miss MacKenzie," Liam said, "may I present my colleague and partner in adventure, Mr. Peregrine Sinclair."

★ ★

MAC HADN'T KNOWN what to expect, but this had been pretty far down on her list of likely occurrences.

She should have seen it coming. Liam had kept her prisoner here, making sure she didn't run away if she, Perry's partner in crime, decided that she'd be better off gone than stuck waiting for the inevitable confrontation.

The confrontation that was about to take place.

Perry walked in first, giving Mac an all-too-brief moment to study the man who stood at the eye of the coming storm.

Peregrine Sinclair.

Mac locked her knees and ordered herself to stay firmly on her feet. She would have liked nothing better than to indulge in a few blessed seconds of incredulity, awe, and general stupefaction. She was standing in a hotel room in 1884 with her own great-great-grandfather, for God's sake. She had known this moment would come, but the reality was a little more overwhelming than she'd anticipated.

Perry's thin, handsome features were marked with the unmistakable Sinclair stamp. He was young and alert and bore all the elegance of born-and-bred aristocracy, from his neat tie and flawlessly trimmed mustache to his highly polished shoes and brass-headed walking cane. He was, in fact, the perfect image of a Victorian gentleman.

He was also either a man without a heart, utterly

unscrupulous and ruthless in pursuit of his goals—or a relatively innocent party to a nasty misunderstanding. And Liam, just behind him, was watching Mac's face keenly.

"Miss MacKenzie," Perry said, doffing his hat. His hair, like Mac's, was nearly black, and his brown eyes were watchful. "I haven't had the pleasure."

His accent was properly British and softly precise. He looked Mac over, taking in her jeans and shirt and short hair with a calculation that left nothing unremarked.

"I'm, uh, pleased to meet you," Mac said, offering her hand. Perry took it, his clasp warm and firm.

Liam pushed passed him into the room and shut the door. "Not quite the tender reunion I'd expected," he said caustically.

Perry released her hand and looked at Liam. "Now that we're here, may I ask what this is all about?"

Liam's eyes were dark as slate, and the muscles in his jaw bunched and released. "So the game continues, Perry?"

"Perhaps if you'd clarify the rules," Perry said. "I gather I'm supposed to know this young lady?"

"Then you deny it."

"Meaning no disrespect," Perry said, casting a swift glance at Mac, "but I'd remember such an acquaintance."

"And you, Mac?" Liam said. Suddenly he was close behind her. "You haven't met Mr. Sinclair before?"

Mac turned to face him. "Unfortunately, I've never met your friend in my life, and he's certainly never met me."

The mockery faded from Liam's gaze. "Don't play his game, Mac. I only want the truth. Whatever it is, I won't hold it against you."

"Unusual attitude on your part, old man," Perry said. Liam wheeled on him, fists clenched.

"Hold it!" Mac wedged herself between them. "I'm not exactly thrilled at being a pawn in this little chess match. So let's get this straight, shall we?" She glared at Liam. "I don't suppose you've told him why you brought him here, have you?" She turned an equally fierce gaze on Perry. "And you have absolutely nothing to feel guilty about—except for the fact that you left Liam in the jungle. Is that right?"

The two men looked at each other, one convincingly puzzled and the other close to explosion. Perry's expression cleared. "Liam said he met someone in the jungle," he said to Mac. "He gave no details. Apparently you know about our unfortunate argument. But I don't understand how you are involved—"

"Don't you?" Liam interrupted. "She was the one who found this."

He pushed his hand into his coat pocket and brought it up holding something round and silver and trailing a broken chain. Perry's watch, which Mac had last seen lying in the dust in Liam's tent. He hadn't forgotten it.

Liam stared at Perry; Perry gazed at the watch, and glanced from Mac to Liam with drawn brows.

"I'd wondered where I lost that," he said.

"Lost it. Careless of you—old friend." Liam dangled the watch from its chain, swinging it back and forth like a hypnotist's prop. He spoke to Mac without taking his eyes from Perry's face. "I never told you the history of this watch. I gave it to Perry years ago, when we returned from our first expedition together. It was in the Himalayas, and he was wounded pushing me out of the path of a boulder." He smiled. "It was always an unlikely friendship. I was the American provincial with no taste and money to burn, and he was the fine Englishman with little more than an excellent education and a long list of blue-blooded ancestors behind him. Can you imagine it, Mac?"

"I regret the loss of that friendship far more than any watch," Perry said. "It was never my intention, Liam, no matter what you—"

Liam turned and hurled the watch across the room, striking the overstuffed chair by the fireplace with deadly accuracy. "No," he said softly. "It was only your intention to kill me."

Mac held her breath. Perry's face went white, and then he choked out a laugh.

"What?"

"It didn't work, Perry," Liam said, his voice a rasp. "Your guerrillas didn't do their job. And whatever hold you had on Mac wasn't enough. She saved my life, and she brought me the proof I needed."

"Proof?" Perry stabbed the tip of his cane into the carpet. "What in God's name are you saying?"

"All's fair in love and war, isn't it, Perry?" Liam said. "It wasn't enough to abandon me. You had to make certain I never returned, so you'd have Caroline's fortune uncontested."

Perry's face lost its shock. "My God," he said. "You Irish bastard—"

The tension in the air stretched to the breaking point, and suddenly Mac knew she was the only rational being in the room. God knew *someone* had to be. Her body felt like a fragile barrier between two angry men, but it was the only weapon she had. Along with simple desperation.

"Listen to me," she said. "I'm just as interested in getting to the bottom of this as either of you—"

"Stay out of it, Mac," Liam growled.

"It's a little late for that." She met Liam's glower and turned to Perry. "Let me lay it out for you, Mr. Sinclair. Liam thinks you used the watch to pay guerrillas to attack him in the jungle, and that I was working for you as well. He brought me here as a trap for you, expecting us to betray each other."

"She turned up in the jungle, alone, just after you disappeared with the bearers and supplies," Liam added. "And she had the photograph."

Perry either thought Liam had gone mad, or he was doing an excellent approximation of confounded disbelief. "What photograph?"

"You know bloody well. Were the crazy stories of traveling through time her idea, or yours? Did you expect me to swallow such blarney? Oh, she played the damsel in distress well enough, but I didn't think even you could stoop so low as to put a woman in danger to serve your ends."

Perry's lean frame was as taut as a strung bow. "This is preposterous," he said. "Trust me, old man. If I wanted you dead, I'd go about it in a much more efficient fashion."

The bluntness of his speech was as effective as a bucket of cold water. Perry straightened his waistcoat and stroked the tips of his mustache with precise, deliberate motions. "Let me make myself clear. I do not know Miss MacKenzie, and I did not hire anyone to kill you." He held Liam's gaze. "Yes, I left you in the jungle, knowing you'd be delayed in returning. I wanted to get to Caroline before you. You simply wouldn't listen to reason—"

"Reason!"

"But I ask you to listen now. For God's sake, we've saved each other's lives more than once. Think, Liam. If you know me at all, you *know* I wouldn't do this."

Liam made a sound of disgust and strode away, then turned suddenly and looked straight into Mac's eyes. "Well, Mac?" he asked with unexpected gentleness. "Do you believe him?"

She couldn't read Liam's expression, or the strange light in his steady gaze. "I've never met Mr. Sinclair before," she said, "but I believe he's telling the truth." She swallowed. "If I thought he'd tried to kill you, he'd be my enemy as much as yours."

He came to her then, holding her more surely with his unwavering regard than with any physical restraint. "Would he?" He raised his hand; she shivered as his fingers brushed her cheek. "And what is it they say about the enemy of my enemy?"

"I'm not your enemy, old man," Perry interposed coolly. He looked at Mac. "Liam's life was never in any danger from me."

Liam dropped his hand, his expression hardening. "Then you can prove your good faith," he said to the Englishman. "Stay away from Caroline."

Perry walked to the window, leaning on his cane as he gazed out on the city. "You know that's impossible."

"I know that nothing has changed, whatever happened in the jungle." Liam smiled without a trace of humor. "There are less than two weeks left until her birthday, and you won't be getting any more chances to deceive her with your flattery and corrupt her innocence."

"Corrupt her?" Perry spun around, cane raised like a weapon. "You're deceiving yourself. You don't care about her happiness. You don't love her. Why are you so afraid to let her make her own decisions?" His eyes narrowed. "Or is there something else you fear—"

Liam strode to the door and flung it open. "Get out of here, Perry, before I decide you're a bloody liar."

Perry took up his cane and sauntered unhurriedly across the room. "This isn't finished, old man."

"You're right." Liam all but shouldered Perry out the door. "I'll be watching you. Keep that in mind—old friend." He glanced back at Mac. "Don't worry. I'm persuaded of your innocence. I keep my promises."

"Wait," Mac said. "We haven't—"

Without another word Liam followed Perry and shut the door behind them.

For a painful stretch of time all Mac could hear was her own pounding heart. She backed up until her legs hit the bed, and sat down.

Great. Just wonderful. Liam had walked out on her again, and nothing was resolved. She laughed weakly and rubbed at her forehead. Maybe she should be grateful for a little peace and quiet to think, because she seemed to be back at square one.

What should she say when Liam came back? She could tell him straight out why he couldn't marry Caroline. But of course that was ridiculous. He'd only think her even more crazy.

Or she could appeal to Perry. She'd been honest with Liam; she didn't believe Perry was a murderer. Maybe if she could meet Caroline as well, some incredibly effective plan would pop into her head. . . .

She'd be damned if she'd wait around for that to happen. She jumped up, strode to the door and opened it. Liam wasn't there, of course, to receive a piece of her mind.

But neither was the bruiser he'd left on guard. She took a cautious step into the hallway. No one by the balustrade, or—

"Miss MacKenzie?"

She started, turned sharply and found herself looking into a pair of keen brown eyes. Peregrine Sinclair stood beside her door, hat in hand, his demeanor as unruffled as if he'd just arrived on a social call.

Or as if he'd read her mind.

CHAPTER TWELVE

*Time is that wherein there
is opportunity, And opportunity
is that wherein there is
no great time.*

—HIPPOCRATES

"WHERE'S LIAM?" MAC demanded.

"He'll be gone for some time, I believe," Perry said, swinging his cane with perfect nonchalance. "When I was waiting for a hack I saw him receive what appeared to be an urgent message. He left several minutes ago."

"But *you* didn't leave," she said.

"As far as Liam is concerned, I did," he said. "I made certain of it. And as for the guard Liam placed on your room, he's also otherwise engaged. I don't expect him to return for an hour, at least."

Otherwise engaged? Mac peered over Perry's shoulder. "Why did you come back?"

He shrugged. "Call it a hunch, Miss MacKenzie. A hunch that we might perhaps be useful to one another in some small capacity."

Interesting. Sinclairs, it seemed, thought alike.

She held open the door. "Come in."

He smiled, a faint quirk of his lips, and complied. After an awkward moment she realized he was waiting for an invitation to sit, and she gestured him toward the two chairs by the fireplace. He waited for her to seat herself first, then set his hat in his lap and hung the cane on the chair's arm.

"Where shall we begin, Miss MacKenzie?" he asked. "We've had little more than an introduction, and that under less than pleasant circumstances."

Mac did her best to match his composure. "Liam mentioned you . . . a few times in the jungle."

"And not favorably," he said. "How awkward it must have been for you to be drawn into the net of his suspicion." He leaned forward, studying her face. "It's clear you know each other rather well."

Mac fortified herself with a deep breath. *Here goes.* "Yes. We met in the jungle, as he said. And we traveled together from the Péten to San Francisco."

He raised a brow. "Were you his prisoner, Miss Mac-Kenzie?"

"No. I didn't even realize how little he trusted me until we arrived here."

"Ah. I confess to being very interested in what happened in the jungle to convince Liam I tried to have him killed—and what part you played in it. Not to mention how you came to be in the jungle alone when Liam was there. It must be a fascinating tale."

Fascinating, yes. But not one she was prepared to let him in on just yet.

"I'll try to be brief," she said, inventing quickly. "My name is Rose MacKenzie. I'm the daughter of Hector MacKenzie, an explorer and missionary in Central America. My father recently died, and I was left with little money in a small village in Guatemala. I was trying to make my way to the port when Liam found me."

"An explorer's daughter," he repeated. "Liam does have a certain rough gallantry that would lead him to rescue a maiden in distress."

Rough gallantry. That was one way of putting it. "Yes. But there was some rather bad timing involved. You see . . ."

And she proceeded to explain, in calm, efficient words that she hoped were convincing, how she'd been with Liam less than a day when the guerrillas had attacked, how he'd been wounded, and how he'd behaved when she found the watch at the site of the assault.

"My loss of that watch caused a good deal of trouble," Perry said. "But there's one thing I still do not understand. Your presence did prevent his death, and you brought him the watch. This hardly accounts for his suspicion." He searched her eyes. "He did mention a photograph."

So Perry hadn't missed that. "Um, I did have a photograph. Of you and Liam."

His gaze sharpened. "Indeed."

"Well, before my father died, we did a great deal of traveling. We'd heard, of course, of the famous exploring team of Sinclair and O'Shea, and, um, we ran across a native who had this photograph. . . ."

Perry leaned back, tapping the brim of his hat. "A native. How very interesting. Go on, Miss MacKenzie."

"I, um, asked Father to buy it. I had it with me when Liam found me, and he was sure it was the same one you had in San Francisco."

"May I see this photograph?"

In for a penny, in for a pound. Mac went to the dressing table and pulled out her backpack, keeping her body between it and Great-great-grandpa. When she put the photo in Perry's hand, he sat up very straight.

"I begin to understand," he said, turning the battered photograph in his hands. "I remember when this was taken, and to my knowledge only one was made. It appears I was wrong." He returned the photo to her with obvious reluctance. "So when he found you with this following our argument, and then the business with the guerrilla attack and the watch—ah, Liam." He shook his head, swift speculation moving behind his eyes. "Even he has enough sense to realize now that his suspicions were unfounded."

I hope you're right, Great-great-grandpa. Mac put the photo away, pausing by the dressing table to breathe out a long sigh of relief. Perry seemed to accept her story, however improbable it was. Maybe this was going to go her way—

"Nevertheless, Miss MacKenzie," Perry said, "there's something you aren't telling me."

Mac braced herself and turned. "Oh?"

"You must be quite a remarkable woman to arouse such strong feelings in Liam. That he suspects any female capable of working against him is amazing, yet you made him believe it. You traveled with him and apparently held your own. How was that possible?"

What she needed now was sheer bravado. "Do you also think women are such ineffectual creatures, Mr. Sinclair?"

"To the contrary." He got to his feet, setting his hat behind him. "But I know Liam. I can think of only one situation that might account for your peculiar relationship, Miss MacKenzie. How long have you and Liam been lovers?"

★ ★

IF SHE WAS startled by his frankness, she didn't show it.

Indeed, Perry doubted he would have been surprised by anything Miss MacKenzie did or said. He had learned long ago to be a swift judge of people, and his first glimpse of her told him just how unusual a woman she must be.

The girl was an oddity. She wore pants that molded her slender legs, an oversized shirt, and boots like a man from a mining camp. She was pretty in an unpolished way, but not exactly beautiful, and certainly no lady. Her dark hair was cropped short and uncurled. Her wide, dark eyes were those of an innocent, but her very presence here made such innocence impossible.

Perry had seldom seen Liam fraternizing with women of any sort, even on expedition, though he knew Liam was no celibate. Liam was always courteous with the ladies, in his rough way, but his deeper feelings for the gentler sex remained a mystery.

All that had changed, if what Perry suspected was true. For some reason this Miss MacKenzie, with her unlikely stories, had a profound effect on Liam. Perry had seen them together only for a few moments, but that had been enough. The girl aroused Liam's strong protective instincts—instincts he had heretofore focused almost entirely on Caroline.

Very promising, indeed.

"Well, Miss MacKenzie?" Perry prompted softly.

She sat down, her face a little paler than it had been a moment before. "Yes," she said. "We were lovers." There was that slight hitch in her voice, a hesitation that Perry suspected had little to do with any maidenly modesty.

"And yet he didn't entirely trust you," Perry mused. "You said you were not his prisoner. You came here voluntarily, did you not?"

"Yes."

"And was this because he offered to help you, or for some more personal reason?"

She looked up. Oh, yes, she understood him.

"I needed his help," she said. "But it became more than that. For both of us."

"And yet, lovers or not, he deceived you when he brought you here as a trap for me."

"He believed he had his reasons."

The stiffness of her words didn't disguise her emotions. Perry sat down again, studying her face. "You may be justifiably annoyed, Miss MacKenzie. But you still have . . . some affection for Liam."

Only the expression in her eyes confirmed his guess, but it was enough. "I see," he said. "And what does Liam intend now? He set a guard on your door. What are his plans for you?"

"I don't know," she admitted. "There's a lot about Liam that I don't understand yet. He told me very little about Caroline when we were together, but he did make his plans very clear. You accused Liam of not caring about her, and he accused you of being a fortune hunter." Her gaze held quiet challenge. "Maybe you can explain this relationship to me, Mr. Sinclair."

"It's simple enough. Miss Gresham is Liam's ward, and has been since her father's death. He gave Gresham an oath to protect and care for her."

"Did he promise to marry her as well?"

"I don't know." Perry stared down at his hands. "He is determined to shelter her from the world, even if he drives all the joy from her life and crushes her spirit."

"Because he wants to protect her from you?"

"It was he who introduced Caroline to me shortly after she returned from her European finishing school six months ago. But when I began to care for her, his attitude toward me changed. During this last expedition . . ."

"*Are* you a fortune hunter, Mr. Sinclair?"

He laughed at the bluntness of her question. "I am not. But I'm unlikely to convince Liam otherwise."

"But you're certain he doesn't love her."

"I have never been so sure of anything in my life."

"And *you* do."

"Yes. I know how terrible marriage is without love. I can't let that happen to Caroline, Miss MacKenzie."

"And how does Caroline feel? Does she love Liam?"

Perry deliberately unfolded his hands. "She has known him since childhood, years before her father died. Her habit of obedience to him is strong. She is too young, too naive to understand how Liam could destroy her chances of happiness."

"But she feels something for you."

"I believe she does. And she needs time to make the right decision. Time Liam doesn't intend to give her."

Miss MacKenzie stood and paced to the door and back again, gnawing her lower lip. "You came here hinting that we might assist one another, Mr. Sinclair. I know what you want, and maybe I can help you."

Perry rose to meet her. "The question is what *you* want, Miss MacKenzie, and what you'll do to get it."

"I want Liam."

"Why?"

"I . . . think I understand at least one thing about him," she said slowly. "I'm not the kind of woman who needs to be sheltered and protected, and Liam isn't the kind of man who can live that way."

"I see that you do know him, Miss MacKenzie. You must also be aware that he is very rich."

The girl did have pride. She glowered at him. "Are you accusing *me* of being a fortune hunter? Maybe you should give me the same benefit of the doubt I'm giving you."

"Ah. Then you love him."

The uneasy flicker of her eyes prepared him for prevarication, but in the end she surprised him yet again. "I also need time, Mr. Sinclair."

"And time is the crux of the matter, is it not?"

She gave him an odd look and shook her head, as if to clear it. "Liam said something about two weeks."

"Caroline's birthday. I believe Liam has deliberately been waiting to ask her to marry him until that day— the day when her fortune becomes her own."

"Isn't that a bit risky with another suitor in the wings?"

"It would seem so, wouldn't it? Why would he put it off, Miss MacKenzie? The possible answer to that question gives me hope that we have a fighting chance."

"Why didn't you simply ask Caroline to marry you before all this happened?"

"I have my reasons, but they are somewhat moot under the circumstances. Liam is interested in you, of that I have no doubt. How interested will be the measure of our success or failure."

They looked at each other in perfect understanding, and Perry wondered how it was that he felt he'd known Miss MacKenzie before—as if he'd always suspected her existence somewhere in the world.

The existence of a woman who would be Liam's match.

"Then all we need is a plan," Miss MacKenzie said. "Frankly, that's what I don't have. This isn't my . . . city."

"But it is mine," Perry said. "We must see to it that Liam doesn't dismiss you. You must remain in his sight, his consciousness. He must be compelled to admit he wants you, and not Caroline."

"That's a pretty big job," she said in a small voice.

"Losing your confidence already?" he chided.

"Come. You are clearly a woman of courage. If you fail in your conviction—"

Her chin jerked up. "I won't fail. I have more commitment to this than you can possibly understand."

More of Miss MacKenzie's mysteries, it seemed. But Perry was content to let those mysteries stand—for now.

"Very well," he said. "The matter seems simple enough. In order to be near Liam, you must be introduced to the social circle of which Caroline is a part." He looked Miss MacKenzie over, frowning thoughtfully. "If I'm not mistaken, you have not spent a great deal of time in society, have you?"

"There isn't too much of that in the jungle," she said. "I have no illusions. I don't pretend to be the high-society type. In fact, I don't even own a dress. But I can learn to get around here, with your help."

Perry nodded. "I shall present you as my American cousin from some lost branch of the family. Backward missionary's daughter deprived of the benefits of society, thrown on the mercy of a distant relative, and only now making her debut. That ought to account for a few peculiarities of behavior, don't you think?"

"But how do you propose to get us near Caroline?" she asked. "Liam won't let you just resume your courtship."

"You may leave that to me."

"I guess I'll have to." She squared her shoulders. "All right. Let's do it."

"Then it seems we are allies, Miss MacKenzie. Shall we shake to seal our partnership?"

He waited, as was proper, for her to offer her hand first. "We might as well drop the formality," she said. "You can call me—" He would have sworn a grimace crossed her face. "Call me Rose."

Rose, indeed. A most unlikely name—and he suspected this Rose had thorns. "My friends call me Perry," he said.

"What next, Perry?" she asked, releasing his hand.

"I have a plan to set in motion, but I'll be in contact shortly." He reached into his waistcoat pocket for a card and went to the desk in search of a pen. "This is my address, should you need to reach me. Have you funds?"

"Not a dime."

He emptied his pockets of coins and laid several on the dressing table. "This should provide for any necessities for the time being."

She opened her mouth as if to ask for details and then thought better of it. "I hope you know what you're doing."

"Always, Rose. Have no fear of that."

He left her with a handful of reassurances and walked out the door feeling considerably better than when he'd first arrived in Liam's company.

Who would have thought it? The trap Liam had set had turned to Perry's advantage. An advantage Perry could not have imagined in his wildest dreams.

Liam had found himself a woman in the jungle. A woman utterly unlike Caroline. And therein lay the chance of victory.

Perry met Liam's guard in the hallway as he paused by the elevator. A few quiet words brought a nod and sly grin from the man, who found another excuse to leave his post.

The sky was growing dark when Perry emerged onto Market Street. He swung his cane as he walked the short distance to his boardinghouse, tipping his hat to the ladies he passed.

The ladies. Rose MacKenzie might not be one of them, but she had something most of them didn't have. Something an ordinary man might not appreciate.

As Liam did not appreciate Caroline.

Perry started up the stairs to his second-floor apartments, staring at the worn carpet runner under his feet. Strange how untroubled he felt, considering the day's startling events. The shock of Liam's abrupt return, followed by the guilt—an emotional weakness Perry thought had passed the Sinclairs by long ago. Guilt was a thoroughly useless burden.

But perhaps love had made him vulnerable. If so, it was the least price he would pay to save Caroline.

Friendship he had already sacrificed. Yet he recalled the good days Liam had invoked in the Palace Hotel room. Two men from vastly different backgrounds had fallen together in their search for something intangible: Liam, never satisfied with what he had, for a purpose beyond his accumulated wealth and hard-won success; Perry, aimless and jaded after too long in a business that leeched the life from anyone it touched, for some reason to live.

It had been Liam who'd made Perry *feel* again, rediscover the challenge in living itself. And Perry had forced Liam from his shell of isolation and hidden bitterness. They'd found common ground in jungle mud and desert sands, in ancient ruins and the thrill of discovery. Their partnership had taken them halfway around the world and back again. Danger had bound them as brothers.

Until Liam brought Perry back to San Francisco to meet his young ward. Caroline Gresham, fresh, vibrant, passionate.

And no more than a duty to Liam, a valuable object he'd sworn to protect, a child he would never recognize as the budding woman she was becoming. Just as he had not *seen* her today, when she'd tried so hard and with so little success to make Liam notice her.

But Perry saw what Liam did not. He found in Caroline the youth and careless joy so long missing from his life, a joy remarkable in a girl who'd known so little love of the kind she deserved.

Love. What a very odd thing it was. Perry paused to sift his pocket for the keys to his suite, remembering. He'd certainly never expected to discover that tender emotion so late in his checkered career. Love had been rare enough in his ancient, cold, patrician family.

But what had begun as mild flirtation with a young woman eager to hear his tales of adventure had blossomed into something far deeper. And it was Liam's doing. He'd given Perry an immeasurable gift, and now he obliged his friend to betray him. For Caroline's sake.

For she needed room to grow, to explore, to know what she wanted of life—all the freedoms Liam would never permit her.

Perry reached his door, shaking his head. *Ah, Liam, you blind fool.* Love was what Caroline needed, what she must have—the one thing her father's money could never provide.

God help him, Caroline believed that what she wanted was Liam's love—that he would love her as a woman. Value her for herself, not an oath fulfilled or some cardboard figurine of a perfect lady. She was too naive to see that was something Liam could never give.

Perry turned the key in the door and walked into his suite. He dropped his gloves on the sideboard in the front sitting room and tossed his hat behind them, nearly covering the photograph that he'd been meaning to put away.

The photograph. Taken in better days, four years ago: two men in the jungle, content in their freedom. The same photograph Rose inexplicably had in her possession.

No. Not the same. And the explanation hardly mattered now. Perry's attempts to make Liam see reason had failed, but he'd been given another chance. There would be no more room for sentiment. Or clemency.

Perry retrieved a glass and decanter from the sideboard and poured himself a drink, lifting it in a toast.

"To you, Rose MacKenzie, friend of my enemy. May you save Liam O'Shea before it's too late."

CHAPTER THIRTEEN

Build thee more stately mansions,
O my soul,
As the swift seasons roll!
Leave thy low-vaulted past!

—OLIVER WENDELL HOLMES

H OME.

Liam paused on the flagstone walk just within the fancy ironwork gates and wondered why the word still rang so hollow.

Once it had meant something—a dream and memory to his mother: a prosperous farm in Ireland, security, hope. Then hope had died, and "home" had become a filthy tenement in a new land that didn't deserve to be called anything but Hell.

Liam was the only one left to keep his mother's dream. And now "home" was before him, a Queen Anne mansion equal to the city's best, rising in splendor amid a gated garden handsome enough to shelter and protect a bloom such as Caroline Gresham.

In that it would serve its purpose.

Liam walked to the door and gripped the highly pol-ished brass doorknob, feeling the solidity of it under his palm. If it hadn't been for Chen's urgent message, he'd be with Caroline now, attempting to reverse the dam-age Perry had done during his absence. Caroline would be upset enough when he told her she wouldn't be see-ing Perry before her birthday ball.

If Perry wasn't a murderer—and Liam had seen and heard enough to seriously doubt it—the Englishman had still betrayed him with his designs on Caroline.

As for Mac . . . Liam smiled crookedly. She was probably cursing a blue streak at this moment. Not that he could blame her. He'd used her as bait for a trap, and she'd come out of the affair smelling like a rose.

He'd judged her unfairly, photograph or no photo-graph. Mad she might be, but she was not a traitress. He owed her for that misjudgment, and he intended to repay the debt.

Of course she could not stay in San Francisco. Liam had already given the matter careful consideration, and he knew where to send her. Somewhere she'd be safe, and could live her life as she wished. Once he made his offer, he knew she'd see the benefits of it. His ranch in Napa would suit her far better than the jungle.

In the meantime she was secure at the Palace—guarded, of course, because he knew how rash she could be. He couldn't have her running about the city, for her sake as well as his own.

Dealing with Mac would have to wait until morning. And there would be no seeing Caroline tonight, what-ever the urgency. He'd spoken with the man Chen had mentioned in the message, and plans for the raid had already begun. Such opportunities had to be seized as they came. They waited on no man's convenience, least of all Liam O'Shea's.

At least he could do his work tonight free of the certainty of Perry's guilt. Or Mac's.

He turned the knob and pushed open the door. Almost at once a barrage of barking, both high-pitched and low, echoed through the entrance hall. Norton was first to arrive, his long ropey tail beating the air. Bummer the Second scrambled in pursuit, claws skittering on the parquet floor and displacing the carpet runner.

Liam caught Norton's enormous paws halfway to his shoulders. "Well, boy, I see you still haven't learned your manners."

The Irish wolfhound answered with a wet slap of his tongue across Liam's jaw. Bummer danced around his legs, his terrier's eyes bright with a plea for attention. Liam eased Norton back to the ground, crouched, and braced himself as Bummer jumped into his lap with a joyful yip.

"And you, imp of hell. Have you been driving Chen mad with your antics?"

Bummer wriggled, and Norton rolled over majestically to present his lean belly for rubbing. Liam stroked the wiry coat. "And well you're named," he told the wolfhound. "The emperor would have approved."

Norton yawned. Bummer launched himself from Liam's arms and dashed full speed at the man entering the hall from the rear of the house.

"Mr. O'Shea." Chen had only a moment to nod before Bummer began performing fantastic acrobatic leaps about his soft-shod feet. "Welcome home."

Liam rose, nudging Norton gently with the toe of his boot. "Thanks, Chen." He watched Chen scold the terrier in quiet Cantonese, earning rare obedience from the dog. "I went to see our contact, as you advised. Everything is set for tonight."

Chen was accustomed to Liam's lack of ceremony. His serene expression didn't change, but Liam saw the concern in his eyes. "And the matter of your expedition with Mr. Sinclair?"

"That's a long story. You knew something was wrong when I didn't return with Perry?"

"Indeed. When I observed that some aspect of your plan had gone amiss, I alerted our friend in the Gresham household to be particularly watchful. I knew you would want a full report of all unusual activities when you returned."

Liam relaxed. Chen had been as efficient as always; *he'd* expected Liam to come home. "I've seen Miss Gresham, briefly. What do you have to report?"

"During the week since Mr. Sinclair's return," Chen said, "Miss Gresham has been to two parties, one ball, and one outing to the park, each in the company of Mr. Sinclair."

No less than Liam had expected. "And Mrs. Hunter?"

"Has apparently been present, though indisposed, during all meetings in the Gresham home. There has been no activity or conversation worthy of undue concern, according to the reports I received."

So Perry had made good use of Liam's absence, but he hadn't pushed too far. Apparently he hadn't felt ready to press his suit. Time had run out for Perry sooner than he expected.

"Very good," Liam said. "I'll take care of the rest." He turned his thoughts to the more pressing problem. "As for the raid, send a message to our friends in Chinatown. We'll meet in the usual place at midnight, and be ready to move by one."

"I will begin immediately." Chen stepped over Bummer and took Liam's hat, turning to signal down the hall as he did. A petite and pretty Chinese girl in a silk tunic emerged from the servants' quarters, smiling shyly.

"You remember my niece Mei Ling, Mr. O'Shea," Chen said. "She has done well in her work as maid since she came to replace Mary. Her English is already becoming very good."

"I'm glad to hear it." Liam returned the girl's smile. "You're comfortable here, Mei Ling? Not afraid?"

She ducked her head. "Not afraid. Safe . . . here."

Probably safer than she had been even in the hidden sanctuary where the other rescued slave girls boarded until they could find new homes far from their erstwhile masters. The tongs still found ways to trick some of the girls back into their clutches, but they'd been less and less successful of late. Liam knew how to deal with corrupt lawyers and bought policemen.

"Yes," he said. "You're safe here. Let your uncle know if you need anything."

The girl gave a self-conscious nod and retreated back down the hall. Liam's smile faded as he thought of the countless children like her who had been far less fortunate. But if all went well tonight, a dozen of her sisters would have a second chance at freedom in their new country.

There was just enough time for a few hours' rest. Fastidious Chen was probably near to swooning at the sight of his employer; Liam hadn't shaved or bathed in two days. On expedition that was common enough, but tonight he couldn't afford to be less than sharp and alert.

"I'm going to clean up, Chen," he said. "Don't bother with a meal—a sandwich will do." Liam patted the top of Norton's shaggy, massive skull and started toward the staircase. "One more thing. If you receive any messages from Mr. Bauer, bring them immediately. He's doing some work for me."

Not by the twitch of a brow did Chen reveal a hint of curiosity. He might assume that Liam had engaged the private investigator to help with the raid against the tongs, as he'd done in the past. But Liam had set Bauer a far more personal task.

With a bow Chen withdrew, Bummer at his heels. Norton bounded up the stairs ahead of Liam. Thick, richly patterned carpet muffled the footsteps of man and beast. The sound of the clock in the parlor filled the echoing quiet. Handsome, expensive paintings on each wall flowed one into another as Liam passed by.

Home. It should feel more welcoming after three years and all the money he'd put into the place. Nothing had changed; why should it? He'd wanted the beauty and grandeur for Caroline, not himself.

He'd be happy with a hut in the jungle, with lakes and streams for washing and flowers for decoration. A place without high walls that closed the world into a pretty little box.

In less than two weeks those days of freedom would be behind him.

He paused on the upstairs landing and turned toward the chamber that would be Caroline's. It had been decorated in her favorite colors, with no expense spared: a queen's quarters, connected to his rooms by a wide pass closet. When they were married she could retire there—when she was not sharing his bed.

Restlessness twitched through him as he entered his own room. He glanced at the great walnut bedstead, imagining Caroline in it, her golden hair spread across the pillows. He censored the notion before it could fully form.

But another image filled the vacant place in his mind: snubbed nose, smudged face, dark hair cropped short as a boy's, snapping dark eyes, bold mouth, and outthrust jaw.

Mac. Mac in his bed, challenging him to join her.

Mac with her lean firm body twisting catlike around his own. Mac dueling wits with him, winner take all. . . .

Liam strode into the bathroom and snapped on the bathtub faucets, letting the tub fill with cold water.

Devil take it, what was wrong with him? He hadn't touched Mac in nearly a month, though they'd traveled side by side in the jungles and mountains and slept within a few feet of each other.

But this afternoon, at the Palace, when she'd faced him down so bravely . . .

He strode to his dresser and tossed his coat over the back of a chair. No—he tugged his limp tie loose and threw it likewise on the desk—there was no good reason to think of Mac at all. Not when his thoughts should be only of his future wife.

He began to unbutton his shirt, building a mental picture of Caroline. Petite, with dainty ankles and rounded arms; face as flawless as an angel's, as lovely as any English aristocrat's; china-blue eyes. . . .

Dark eyes. Short hair. Long legs and tanned skin and parted lips.

Liam slapped the shirt over the chair, glaring at his unshaven reflection in the mirror. He'd been too long away from his obligations. Once Mac was safely in Napa, he'd have no more of this baffling and troublesome temptation.

He'd make himself into the stable, respectable husband Caroline needed, here in this house, within these walls, confined to a simple domestic life. Tonight's raid would be his last. No more taking chances, no more adventures, no more meetings with bold, pestiferous, distracting females in the jungle. . . .

His reflection stared back at him, grim and stolid. Liam turned away from the mirror and the man he was to become.

★ ★

THE CHINATOWN ALLEY stank of human refuse and the stale odors of cooking. From where he crouched behind a stack of crates, Liam had an unobstructed view of the gated and barred house that was the object of tonight's raid.

Almost no moonlight reached the alley, and the nearest streetlamp was far away. There were places of concealment everywhere—enough to hide the motley group of raiders: Chen and three other Chinese men like him, who'd lost relatives or friends to the slave trade or to tong bullets; a few policemen who'd come to agree with Liam that there was too much corruption to work within the law; even Irishmen like Liam himself, once known as the principal enemies of the Chinese in San Francisco.

Now they were scattered in a wide arc around the house, each man within signaling distance of the rest. Waiting for the instant when the tong hatchetmen guarding the entrance would be distracted, and the raid could begin.

The girls had arrived on a steamer late that afternoon, twelve of them, some no older than thirteen, each and every one bound for a life of slavery and prostitution in Chinatown or communities in the countryside.

Since the Exclusion Act two years before, it hadn't been so easy for the tongs and their bribed allies to bring the girls into San Francisco. Not so easy, but far from impossible. At least four of this group had arrived smuggled in crates as freight; others had been carefully coached to convince immigration inspectors that they were native Californians returning from a trip to the land of their ancestors.

There were always men—officials and police—who

would take bribes from the wealthy tongs and profit heavily by it. Men who had no pity for the girls and the terrible life of degradation that awaited them.

Two years ago Liam had assembled this little group. What they did was technically illegal, but Liam had no faith in the law to protect these innocents.

He nodded to Chen across the alley. In a minute or two Chen's niece would make the daunting walk across the street, in full view of the hatchetmen. The chance of seizing another Chinese girl in a town that never had enough of them would be too great a temptation for the tong men to resist.

Liam ground his teeth together and touched the butt of his pistol. Using Mei Ling had been completely against every principle he lived by, but it had been getting increasingly difficult to catch the tong off guard. They didn't know who carried out the raids—Liam and his men always went masked—but they were more careful than they'd once been. The two heavily armed hatchetmen at the house were proof enough of that.

Only this once, Liam had told Chen. But the girl had insisted with remarkable courage, having at one time been destined for the bagnios herself. And it might be the only way to save the other twelve.

Liam's thoughts drifted inevitably from Mei Ling to the other two women who had succeeded in plundering his peace of mind.

Hell. He shifted his crouch, stretching a cramped muscle. Every time he swore to himself he wouldn't think of Mac again, he broke his own oath. What was she doing now? Was she sleeping, or wide awake still cursing him for today's little drama?

Or worse . . . was she feeling forsaken, afraid, alone in that hotel room with no idea of her fate, abandoned by the man who'd promised her safety? Liam scowled. He should have taken the time to explain, but

Chen's message couldn't wait. And after the confrontation with Perry, Liam hadn't trusted himself to maintain the necessary control.

Mac would test the control of a saint. Liam's scowl became an edged grin. Mac, afraid? Ridiculous. She might want to kill him, but she wouldn't be frightened even if she were here beside him, about to throw herself into danger. She'd march into the street, oblivious to her peril, and spit right in the eye of the *boo how doy*. . . .

"Mr. O'Shea! Mei Ling is ready!"

He turned quickly to acknowledge Chen's whisper. Mac wasn't here, thank God, and there was no more time for thinking. Liam tugged his mask over his face. Either he'd come out of this with twelve young girls on their way to freedom, or he'd die in the attempt.

Fierce joy swept through him—the joy of challenging fate itself. There was no deception in this. No posturing to prove himself a gentleman worthy of Caroline Gresham. Only the rush of blood, the racing heart, the bunching of muscles preparing for action.

A lone, timid figure draped in a silk robe and hood crept into the street in front of the guarded house, looking about fearfully. One of the hatchetmen noticed and signaled to his partner. They straightened from their gambling and moved to the gate.

Liam raised his hand. Chen followed suit. All around the house the raiders tensed.

And then the waiting was over.

IT SHOULD HAVE been a day for celebration.

The raid had gone perfectly. All the girls had been rescued, spirited away to the hidden safe house where the tong would never find them.

Liam abandoned his tie, heedless of the uneven knot, and walked to his bedroom window. The morning was beautiful and clear, perfect for traveling. If matters had gone as intended he would have made the necessary visit to Caroline, keeping his promise to her and providing the required explanations, and then he'd have gone to the Palace for Mac. A bit of reasoning and persuasion, and he and Mac would have been on their way to Napa by ferry and rail. Liam had expected to return by tomorrow evening at the latest, leaving Mac safely bestowed on the ranch.

But the new information from Bauer, received less than an hour ago, had overturned Liam's best-laid plans. Biggs's note had arrived only a few minutes later, carried by the Gresham stableman.

Both had conveyed the same message: *Come at once.* Only Bauer's had mentioned Perry, but that was more than enough.

Liam tugged on his black cutaway coat, swearing under his breath. Had he underestimated Perry's capacity for guile yet again—and his powerful desire for Caroline's fortune?

Liam gave Chen a few terse instructions and strode to the stables to the rear of the house. Forster had the phaeton waiting. Liam took up the reins and turned the carriage toward California Street, driving blindly past neatly-kept houses basking in the hazy glow of the early autumn sun. His thoughts were as fouled as a fisherman's net caught on a sunken ship.

He arrived at the Gresham residence in less than ten minutes. The stableman who took charge of the phaeton had the good sense not to offer a cheery greeting.

Biggs answered Liam's knock so quickly that he must have been hovering very close indeed. His ordinarily stolid countenance was clearly being put to the test.

"Where are they?" Liam demanded without preamble.

The butler coughed discreetly. "In Miss Gresham's sitting room. Mrs. Hunter is, as usual, indisposed and laid up in her bed. Another young lady is with them—"

Liam stiffened. "Another young lady?"

"She came with Mr. Sinclair. One Miss MacKenzie." He noted Liam's expression and arched a brow. "Ah, you know of her, Mr. O'Shea? I didn't realize—"

Apparently neither had Bauer, who hadn't mentioned a second visitor. And apparently Mac's guard at the Palace had been bought—or tricked.

Liam brushed past Biggs and strode for the stairs. The sitting room door was open, and Liam paused in the hall to regain his composure.

Perry saw him first. The Englishman turned, his face as bland and cool as ever.

The tableau Liam had walked into didn't change for several seconds. Caroline and Mac stood side by side before a cheval mirror, the former in the process of fussing with some fastening on Mac's dress.

Mac's *dress*. Good lord. She was wearing a dress with long, sweeping skirts and an ill-fitting basque bodice. Her expression was one of discomfort and quickly hidden unease.

And Caroline—she turned her head and froze, just long enough for him to see a fleeting uncertainty in her gaze.

"Liam!" she cried, sweeping toward him. "I am so glad you are here. You will never guess what has happened!"

"No?" he said grimly.

If she noticed his mood she chose to ignore it. "Perry came first thing this morning with the most remarkable story. Did you know about his little cousin?" She gestured toward Mac and rushed on without waiting for an answer. "To think this poor girl has been denied the benefits of society for so long! When I heard about her, I knew I had to help. She only arrived an hour ago, but I've already found one of my old dresses that almost fits. . . ."

Liam heard no more than one word in ten of her chatter. He was staring at Mac, struggling to decide whether he was more amazed at her vaguely ridiculous appearance or enraged at her unexpected and very un-welcome presence.

Perry was behind it, of course. But Mac, whom Liam had absolved of any treachery in the jungle, had come with him. Willingly, to all appearances, however Perry had convinced her. Liam damned himself for a thrice-cursed fool.

"I was not told about Perry's . . . cousin," he said, interrupting Caroline's monologue.

She took his arm. "I am certain you will pity her as I do. Her father was a missionary in South America—he recently passed away, and she was left with no re-sources except Perry himself. She came all the way to San Francisco on her own." Caroline's words were shaded with unmistakable excitement and something dangerously like admiration.

"She did, did she," he said.

"Yes. She only just arrived yesterday. Is it not an amazing coincidence that she came to San Francisco the same day you did?" Caroline prattled, tugging Liam's arm to regain his attention. "Perhaps you were even on the same ship."

"I'm afraid I didn't have the pleasure of meeting the young lady," he said with a tight smile.

"Then you must allow me to introduce you!"

The damage was done. He couldn't remove either Mac or Perry without causing a scene, and Caroline was very deeply caught. "By all means," he said.

Caroline drew him farther into the room. "Miss MacKenzie, I have the great pleasure of introducing you to my . . . old friend, Mr. O'Shea."

Mac looked at him, her dark eyes bold as ever. She dropped an awkward curtsey and offered her hand.

"Mr. O'Shea. I'm very pleased to meet you."

He took her hand. It was strong for a woman's, but he could have crushed it with little effort. He exerted just enough pressure to make a point. "The honor is all mine," he said. "Perry's cousin, I'm told? I didn't hear him mention you before."

"I'm afraid I . . . come from a rather obscure branch of the family," she said. "I don't expect Mr. Sinclair and I would ever have met, except"—her mouth gave a very convincing tremble—"except that Papa died."

"You have my very great sympathy, Miss MacKenzie," he said. "I hear you came all the way from South America alone. It must have been a very difficult journey. Not one for a woman."

"But you must know all about such difficulties, Mr. O'Shea," she said. "Miss Gresham—Caroline—has already told me what great adventurers you and my cousin are. I'm sure you've braved far greater perils than my poor papa and I."

"Some adventures are riskier than others," he said. "It takes excellent judgment to recognize when one has gone too far."

"Oh? I'm sure you would know all about that, Mr. O'Shea." She simpered with a flutter of dark lashes.

"What I don't know, I learn quickly," he said.

Caroline carefully positioned herself between them. She had a vaguely sheepish air about her, as if she were preparing to present Liam with another unwelcome surprise.

"We— Liam, I have told Miss MacKenzie . . ." She

gave him her most beguiling smile. "I was hoping to take her out to the shops. She cannot be expected to get by on my hand-me-downs. I think my dressmaker might do something with her."

"She must be a miracle worker," Liam muttered. Caroline was thrilled at the prospect of playing benefactress to a woman several years her senior—and one so pathetically in need of exposure to the essentials of life. Her eyes glowed with the fervor of a missionary bent on saving souls.

"I cannot imagine what might have become of her without our help," Caroline went on obliviously, as if Mac were not even there. "But now there is hope. She is a little uncertain, and so inexperienced—"

Liam choked.

"—in the ways of society, but it's only a matter of the proper instruction. She must be respectable, since she is a missionary's daughter—"

Liam looked heavenward.

"—and I have been thinking how best to bring her out—"

"Bring her out?"

Caroline faltered. "Well, perhaps not as much as that. But surely there is no harm in taking her about and helping her get settled here. She has no connections other than Perry."

"Quite right," Perry said. "With our assistance she may at least find decent employment."

Liam turned slowly to confront the Englishman, who merely arched a brow in unspoken challenge.

"There. You see?" Bolstered by Perry's support, Caroline all but danced under her layers of expensive velvet and satin skirt. "Oh, Liam, it's almost like being part of one of your adventures."

Instead of rage he felt the mad desire to laugh. Saints above, did Caroline think she could transform a sow's ear into a silk purse? Not that Mac had ever been remotely like a sow. In that dress, ill-fitting as it was, she struck him as . . . quite appealing. Bloody hell.

"Please . . . don't be so stern, Liam," Caroline whispered. "Rose doesn't know you—"

"Rose?"

"Miss MacKenzie. Surely there's nothing wrong in calling her—"

"*Rose?*"

"It's a lovely name. Perhaps . . ." Caroline's expression grew dreamy. "Perhaps she is a wild rose in need of cultivating."

"We'll talk about this later, Caroline. I have business with Perry."

"And we *women* have important things to discuss." She returned to Mac's side, a perfect, ideal picture of budding womanhood. Everything Liam had sworn to protect.

But it was Mac's dark head rising above Caroline's golden curls that Liam noticed, and Mac's gaze he met before he turned away.

Perry was leaning indolently against the wall, watching the proceedings with cool detachment.

"Well, Perry," Liam said, moving to join him. "This is an unexpected surprise. It seems you've come to know Miss MacKenzie in a remarkably short time."

"I was most impressed with her when you introduced us yesterday," Perry said, pitching his voice for Liam's ears alone. "She seemed a very bright girl. Not the sort you should keep prisoner, old man."

"I won't even ask you how you got past my guard," Liam said, lowering his voice to match Perry's. "I'll get right to the point. What do you think you're going to accomplish with this little charade? What did you do to gain Mac's cooperation?"

"It should be obvious. I'm simply aiding an unfortunate young woman in need. You did misjudge the poor girl, assuming she was working for me in the jungle—and to kill you, no less." He looked up, brown eyes sharp in an impassive face. "You used and abandoned her, Liam. If you don't see fit to atone for your mistakes, it behooves me as a gentleman to make up for your lapse. Certainly Caroline would be quick to agree. And considering your behavior in the jungle—your close relationship with Miss MacKenzie . . ." He shrugged.

Liam came very close to grabbing Perry around his pristinely starched collar. "Is that what she told you? I didn't abandon her. I had plans for her—"

"Can you blame her for doubting your intentions? When I offered my help in this strange city, she had no recourse but to accept. And of course I knew Caroline would be the perfect mentor to take her in hand." He smiled a blandly infuriating smile. "Don't worry, old man. When I asked for Caroline's help, I didn't reveal your previous . . . knowledge of Miss MacKenzie. That might be rather awkward, don't you think?"

Blackmail, Liam thought. *But blackmail can work two ways, my friend.*

"I don't know what you plan to gain by this, but you won't succeed," Liam said softly. "Do you seriously believe San Francisco will accept your story of a long-lost cousin and missionary's daughter?"

"With my sponsorship and Caroline's, I've no doubt of it." He cast Caroline a frankly indulgent glance. "And I know you won't make it difficult for us. It would hardly be in your best interests."

"And Caroline's interests? Your devotion has a certain imperfection if you'd put her in company with an adventuress."

"It's you who've defined Miss MacKenzie so uncharitably, not I. I'm not worried about Caroline."

"Worried about what?" Caroline came up beside them, glancing from one man to the other. She took Perry's arm. "I hope you gentlemen are done with your business. Rose and I are nearly ready for our outing."

"Outing?" Liam repeated.

"To Cliff House," Perry said. "Caroline told me you'd promised it to her before we left for the jungle. She's most anxious to begin showing Rose the sights of the city."

"I know it's soon after her arrival, but she does *so* want to go," Caroline put in. "All those days on the ship were so tedious. No society at all! And I've been waiting such a long time for your return." She cast Liam an imploring look. "You did promise we could go whenever I liked."

Yes, Perry had worked on Caroline well. Liam could object, certainly, but it was better to keep Perry clearly in sight until a more permanent solution could be found.

"If it's too much trouble for you to escort them," Perry said smoothly, "I'd be more than happy to do the honors."

"That won't be necessary." Liam turned to Caroline. "Please take Miss MacKenzie upstairs while I see to the carriage."

He waited until Caroline and Mac were well out of earshot before he addressed Perry again.

"Enjoy this while you can, old friend," he said. "After today Caroline will be . . . otherwise engaged."

Perry drew a pair of driving gloves from his pocket. "Oh, I intend to make the most of it. I advise you to do the same."

CHAPTER FOURTEEN

★ —————— ★

Time travels in divers paces
with divers persons.
I'll tell you who Time ambles withal,
who Time trots withal,
who Time gallops withal,
and who he stands still withal.

—WILLIAM SHAKESPEARE

"Now, THIS ISN'T nearly enough, of course," Caroline said, waving the corset in front of Mac's nose. "You'll need gowns for morning and evening and walking and carriage rides, at least five pairs of shoes and boots, three sets of gloves, several chemises—" She counted off on her plump fingers. "And hats, bustles, redingotes and wraps, a pocketbook, fans and parasols and jewelry and hairpieces . . ."

Mac groaned silently and wiggled cramped feet in her borrowed, one-size-too-small, high-heeled, narrow-toed walking boots. Her back already ached from carrying around numerous pounds' worth of skirt for the past two hours. She had yet to try on the corset Caroline insisted she wear—or the newest figure enhancer, the bust improver. Caroline had assured her that it would do wonders for her figure.

Trekking through the jungle and over mountains with Liam had been nothing compared to this. So much for the frailty of Victorian women. Mac thought about all the elegant fashion plates she'd seen in the streets and the Grand Court of the Palace. It must take Amazonian strength to walk around all day wearing this sort of getup; Mac was already desperate for her jeans and T-shirts.

Caroline didn't seem to mind. She thrived on the restrictive intricacies of Victorian fashion—as she loved being the center of attention, no matter what form it took.

"I know what I've lent you isn't nearly enough," Caroline said, "but it's only to see you through the day. Tomorrow I will arrange to have my dressmaker fit you for evening gowns, and we shall go shopping at the City of Paris. Oh—" She clapped her hands like a child. "It will be such fun."

Fun. About as much fun as Mac had had this morning, unexpectedly meeting Great-great-grandma for the very first time. Perry hadn't told her where they were going until they were halfway to the impressive Gresham mansion. He hadn't given Mac much warning of his scheme to introduce her to Caroline.

But the initial awkwardness of the introduction and Mac's role-playing as backward provincial had kept her from giving way to the astonishment of being in the same room with both her great-great-grandparents. There was no time for shock.

Perry had been correct—Caroline was fascinated by Mac's supposed origins. And Liam's ward had proved to be more beautiful than her photograph, with flawless skin, golden hair, and china-blue eyes.

At first she'd seemed the quintessential Victorian lady—or what Mac imagined to be the quintessential Victorian lady: dressed to the nines, pinched and padded into an hourglass figure, feminine, sweet and willing to help—even if she hadn't bothered to hide a certain condescension toward a plain, disadvantaged girl from uncivilized climes.

But that first impression had soon given way to another. Because Caroline was *young*. Younger than Mac realized. Young enough to be trembling on the brink of womanhood: wanting her way and not knowing what she wanted, achingly curious, malleable and stubborn, bold and uncertain, just like any other teenager in the history of time.

Exactly the right age to be totally messed up by men who thought they knew it all. At twenty-five Mac felt positively ancient by comparison. Compared to her own *great-great-grandmother*, for pity's sake.

There hadn't been much time to get to know Caroline in the two hours since Mac's arrival. She'd made a point of watching Caroline and Perry together; the girl basked in Perry's attention, comfortable in his presence. If the two of them had been left alone to go their merry way, Mac wouldn't have had a care in the world.

All that changed, however, when Liam arrived.

Mac had expected him to react badly when he found her here. If he'd been convinced before that she and Perry weren't working together—and she wasn't sure he *had* been—he'd have every reason to suspect her now. And wonder what the hell she was up to.

But for the first time Mac had seen Liam with his ward—his bride-to-be. Their meeting hadn't been what Mac anticipated. With Liam Caroline's body language changed, became tense and wary and focused in spite of her facade of grace and charm. Mac had observed the girl's constant awareness of Liam, as if everything she did was performed somehow for his benefit, every word carefully chosen.

Performed: that was the term. An act designed to win Liam's approval. To make him *notice* her.

"You aren't listening, Rose," Caroline said, her voice suddenly much louder in Mac's ear. "But I must be overwhelming you. You had no such necessities in the jungles."

Mac looked behind her for Caroline's plush half-tester bed and plopped down heavily, grateful for the respite for her feet and back. She ran her hand along the satiny floral bedcover. Caroline's bedroom, like the sitting room, was even more ostentatious, if possible, than Mac's room at the Palace.

Caroline came to stand over her, lips pursed in disapproval. "I know things were very different in your former life, but now you must take my advice. It would never do to be seen . . . carrying yourself so negligently. You shall never win society's approval that way." She patted her golden curls. "I can only imagine what your cousin and Liam would say."

I know what Liam would say. Suppressing a sigh, Mac straightened. "Is it always so important what they think?"

The frothy coquettishness Caroline had shown with Liam and Perry was completely gone from her manner. "Of course. You must realize, Rose, that to win a man's regard you must learn to be a true lady. Composed, compliant, and agreeable."

Mac pricked up her ears. Caroline's tone was definitely condescending, yet there was a hint of wistfulness in her voice—even a touch of carefully veiled sarcasm. As if she were playing a role she accepted with unacknowledged reluctance.

"So you'd consider yourself an expert in . . . proper feminine behavior?" Mac asked.

Caroline looked at Mac sharply, and her limpid blue eyes narrowed for a fraction of a second. If she recognized irony, she wasn't the airhead she appeared—or *wanted* to appear.

She moved to the small fireplace across the room and sat upright in one of the chairs, arranging her skirts around her feet. "Oh, yes," she said with false lightness. "I venture to say that I am an expert in the art of being a perfect lady."

"I'm sure," Mac began cautiously, "that Li—your guardian appreciates that."

"Liam?" Caroline pleated the material of her skirt. "He has the same . . . exacting tastes that my papa had. He paid for my finishing school after Papa died, when I was fourteen."

"He seems to be a man of very . . . strong opinions," Mac prodded.

Now Caroline was all airy indifference. "Sometimes he can be quite trying. But Liam is very strong. He's traveled all over the world." She gave Mac a patronizing smile. "You needn't be afraid of him, Rose—he will come to like you. I'm sure he will."

Thanks for the reassurance. "I'm grateful. But I'm . . . rather curious about Mr. O'Shea. What kind of background does he come from?"

Caroline stared at her folded hands. "Mr. O'Shea's people came from Ireland," she said. She paused awkwardly and hurried on. "He was in the mining business, and the railroads, just like Papa. He's very rich and admired by everyone in San Francisco."

Mac remembered Homer saying that Gresham had worked his way up to wealth as Liam had, but from much more prosperous beginnings. Liam had been dirt poor. Either Caroline didn't know that, or chose not to mention it. Maybe she was the kind who wanted to pretend that she, and everyone she knew, had always been rich and respectable.

Could Caroline be ashamed of Liam's past, or her own?

"So," Mac said, "Mr. O'Shea enjoys his place in society? He seems—I don't know him well, but it almost seems as if he wouldn't quite fit in with the . . . elegance of your world."

"You're quite mistaken," Caroline said quickly. "He may be . . . rough at times, but that is the way with strong men. My papa was often like that. Of course my papa gave me everything I wanted. There was nothing he would not do for me."

"While Mr. O'Shea is less accommodating."

"He is always protective. A woman feels safe with him." Caroline stood, brushing her skirts with her hands. "You haven't yet told me about your journey here," she said brightly. "You must have seen some very uncivilized places in your travels. How did you get on? Perry's stories can make them sound almost fascinating."

Perry's stories. Not Liam's. "They can be," Mac said. "Hasn't . . . Mr. O'Shea ever suggested that you accompany him on one of his adventures?"

"Certainly not." Caroline took an agitated turn about the room. "He would never take a lady into such peril."

"No," Mac said dryly, "I can't imagine Mr. O'Shea sharing that willingly with any woman."

Caroline came to a sudden stop. "Only see what happened to you. You were deprived of every refinement and advantage. Think what might have become of you if not for Perry! And in any case, Liam has no more need to leave San Francisco. Everything he wants is here."

"And what do *you* want, Caroline?"

"I want—" she began, biting her lip. "I want—"

But if she were tempted to confide in Mac, the incentive was obviously not strong enough. "I want to help you, Rose," she said abruptly. "You must be guided by me, and by Perry, if you wish to get on here."

"Mr. Sinclair is a real gentleman," Mac said, scooting off the bed. "He's the son of a lord, isn't he?" She sighed. "If he weren't my cousin—"

"Mr. Sinclair is everything a gentleman should be," Caroline interrupted. "He is quite the favorite of our society."

"I can't imagine a man more different from Mr. O'Shea."

"No," Caroline murmured. "Completely different. . . ." She shook her head. "Do you like the ocean?"

"I—"

"You'll see it when we go to Cliff House." She smiled. "And tomorrow we shall shop all day. I have great hopes for you, Rose. With luck we may even find you a husband."

Mac had no chance to comment on that peculiar notion. The door swung open and Liam walked into the room.

"A word with you, Caroline," he said. He barely glanced at Mac before taking his ward's arm and escorting her out. Through the half-closed door Mac heard most of the conversation that followed.

"I hope you remember to carry yourself with decorum this afternoon, Caroline," Liam said, his words stiffly formal. "Your new . . . friend will ride with her cousin, and you with me."

"But I had promised Perry—"

"Miss MacKenzie hardly knows me, Caroline. She will be more comfortable with Perry."

Silence. After a moment Caroline spoke again, her voice taking on a faintly wheedling tone. "Will you let me drive the carriage today? Perry said it's not difficult, and I've been thinking I should like to try—"

"Out of the question. You don't have the slightest idea how to handle a team."

"I could learn."

"It's far too dangerous—not to mention fast."

"But other ladies—"

"You aren't other ladies." He paused. "How go the arrangements for the ball?"

Only a touch of sullenness lingered in Caroline's voice. "Perfectly. It will be the grandest event of the year. Everyone will envy me. And I shall save the very best dances for you and Perry."

Liam cleared his throat. "Perry may not be able to attend."

"What?"

"He has other commitments."

"I cannot believe that. He has given his word, and Perry is a true gentleman. He would never disappoint a lady."

"Perhaps you don't know Mr. Sinclair as well as you think you do."

"I know he is a good friend," she retorted. "I thought he was yours."

"Your judgment—" He stopped himself. "Caroline, look at me. Everything I do is for your own good. You must trust me. I know more of the world than you ever can."

Then Mac didn't hear anything but the ticking of Caroline's clock. Driven by the need to know what was happening, she cracked the door open and peered into the hall.

Caroline was standing very close to Liam, leaning

toward him, her breathing deep and her gaze locked on his.

"What I don't know," Caroline murmured, "I can learn."

Liam averted his eyes and stepped back. "You've learned everything a young lady requires," he said. "Kindly finish your preparations. I'll be waiting downstairs with the surrey." He turned and walked quickly away.

Mac closed the door and regained the bed just before Caroline charged into the room. Liam's ward touched her own cheek as if to check for a flush and paused to examine herself in front of a large mirror. "I must ask a favor of you, Rose."

"A favor?"

"Yes. Liam will expect me to ride with him, but I would much prefer your cousin's company."

Mac slid off the bed, her skirts bunching up around her hips. "How can I help you?"

"By playing a little game." Caroline turned, her mouth quirked in a sly smile. "When we go down, you shall wear my fur cloak and I shall wear my second-hand, the one I would have given you. And I will give you my favorite carriage bonnet. If we both wear veils, Liam won't realize what we've done until it's too late."

"I don't think we can pass for each other," Mac cautioned. "Our heights—"

"Never mind that. It need only be for a few moments."

"Mr. O'Shea will be angry."

"Let him," Caroline said, tossing her head. "I'm not afraid." She sized Mac up with a provocative glance. "But perhaps Liam frightens *you*."

Mac suppressed a reckless laugh. "I'll help you. You and Perry do seem to get along so well."

Caroline studied her a moment longer and shrugged.

"Good." She frowned, walking a slow circle around Mac. "Yes. I do think you look quite presentable enough for your first appearance on the town. Just one more little adjustment . . ."

She poked a straight pin into the heavy fabric at Mac's waist.

Mac rolled her eyes heavenward. *So why didn't you just set me an easier task, Homer—like preventing the sinking of the* Titanic?

But there was no answer, and no going back.

MAC WAS ALMOST ready to face Liam again when he arrived with the surrey.

It was "the shiny little surrey with the fringe on top," as the old song went, with two sets of long, roomy seats. Mac studied it as she stood with Caroline in the shadow of the front entryway, each of them wrapped in their respective coverings from top to toe.

Mac's bonnet was smothering, heavy and dripping with plumes. The veil enabled her to watch Liam jump down from his seat behind the horses and stop to exchange a few words with Perry, who waited at the curb with a much lighter, two-passenger carriage that Caroline had called a "gig."

A moment later Liam was stalking toward Mac and Caroline, his expression set. Perry picked up his pace and came flush with Liam as they reached the door.

"It must be now," Caroline whispered to Mac. "You wait here for Liam, and I will go with Perry."

Perry knew exactly what he was doing. He planted himself next to the disguised Caroline and took her arm, greeting her as Rose. The two of them were already to the gig when Liam addressed Mac, who had pretended to be busy with the hem of Caroline's fancy cloak.

"Are you ready, Caroline?" he asked impatiently.

She nodded, head down, and accepted his offered arm. She sensed him looking at her, perhaps wondering at her silence, but still he said nothing as he handed her into the carriage. It wasn't until she stumbled over her skirts getting into the front seat that he stiffened with realization. Out of the corner of her eye she saw him look toward the gig. He breathed a curse.

So the game was up, but Caroline had achieved her goal. She was in the gig with Perry, ready to leave at a moment's notice.

The bonnet was snatched from Mac's head before she could remove it.

"Was this your idea, or Perry's?" Liam growled.

"Caroline's, actually." Mac met his gaze with more self-assurance than she felt. "She wanted to ride with Perry. I think she was a little upset with you."

Liam stared at her, clearly preparing to read Mac the riot act, but Perry chose that opportune moment to drive the gig past the surrey.

"Mustn't keep the horses standing, old man," Perry said, checking the restive animals with a steady hand on the reins. "Caroline and I shall meet you at Golden Gate Park." His horses broke into a trot.

Liam hopped up into the driver's seat beside Mac, jaw set, and slapped the reins over the backs of his own team.

"Golden Gate Park," Mac said nervously. "I really am looking forward to seeing it. Must be pretty different now, compared to my time. They haven't even landscaped it yet, have they? Is it still all sand dunes?"

She thought he wasn't going to reply until he looked at her, brows lifted in amazement—and suddenly began to laugh.

★ ★

MAC, PRETENDING TO be Caroline. If the attempt hadn't been so ludicrously successful, it would have been unthinkable.

It was, in fact, a very good joke.

Liam's laugh faded to a rueful smile. *He* was the fool not to have seen it immediately. Of course, by the time he'd realized what had happened, only a public commotion would have corrected the situation.

Perhaps if he hadn't been so bloody distracted. Distracted by Mac in the Gresham house—distracted by her now, in that borrowed carriage dress that made her look disturbingly—

Feminine. That was the word. Feminine in the way Liam had always maintained a woman should be and had never expected to see in Mac.

There was something to be said for the change. The bodice of her dress gave her a surprisingly interesting shape; beneath the snug, high-collared fit of the basque, her bosom had taken on unexpected prominence. Her waist was minuscule, her hips emphasized by the bunched fabric and bustle of her skirt—a far cry from her denim trousers or the thin cotton pants and shirt she'd borrowed from him once upon a time.

She almost looked like a lady. But she didn't look like *Mac,* and he wondered why the thought unsettled him. He had the unexpected notion that Mac didn't need such trappings to be utterly female—and he remembered, with shocking clarity, that day she'd stood in the jungle lake with water gleaming on her naked skin. Or lying on top of him, small breasts bare against his chest, kissing him with wanton passion.

He snapped away from that image. Hell—the problem was that Mac was pretending to be something she wasn't. It had to be part of whatever scheme Perry had planned, however he'd dragged Mac into it.

It wasn't going to work on Liam O'Shea.

So now Mac sat stiffly in her seat, toying with the plumes on the ridiculous bonnet and trying to distract him with nonsensical questions. She wouldn't get off so easily. He set the horses to a faster gait in order to keep Perry and Caroline in sight—where he intended to be every step of the way to Cliff House.

"So, Mac," he said, "it was Caroline's idea to make you my guest on this expedition." He shook his head. "It's no wonder I was confused." He guided the horses down the hill and onto Market. "I would hardly have recognized you dressed as a woman."

"Oh, you mean this?" she said, plucking at her skirt. "Caroline was very generous in lending it to me."

"Ah, yes. My ward. She seemed anxious to help you, and you were amenable enough to her little trick. So eager for my company—Rose?"

A stain of red darkened her ears. "I never did tell you my first name," she said. "You never asked."

"I prefer Mac. It suits you far better." He steered the surrey along the vast cobbled river of Market Street, dodging other carriages, horsecars, hacks, wagons, pedestrians, and even the rare lopsided bicycle. Perry's gig was still in clear view.

"And now," he said, "perhaps you'll explain to me what you were doing with Perry and Caroline."

She clasped her gloved hands in her lap. "It's simple. Perry offered his help, to enable me to make my way in the city. I took him up on his offer. He suggested that Caroline would help me find clothes and other things I needed."

"And so you simply went with him. Without consulting me, without—"

"I didn't know where you'd gone!" She turned in her

seat to glare at him. "I knew you and Perry were rivals, but you didn't leave me any choice. I wasn't going to sit in that room and wait for you to decide my fate."

Liam took a firmer grip on the reins. "I had plans for you, Mac. Plans to take care of you—"

"You never consulted *me*," she interrupted. "You just left."

"And you expect me to believe that was your only motive for coming here with Perry."

"By now I know better than to *expect* you to believe anything."

He remembered her stories of time travel back in the jungle, and his anger began to dissolve, softened by unanticipated worry. He kept forgetting that Mac was more than a little mad. Not able to look after herself in a place like this. A man like Perry would find it easy to take advantage of her.

It gave Liam surprisingly little pleasure to be at odds with her now. In the jungle it had been different, with just the two of them, but here . . . Something had changed.

He didn't analyze the thought further. "Do you like animals, Mac?" he asked.

She started at his about-face. "Of course I like animals. If you mean the seals—"

"Not quite." Liam whistled. A basso bark was the only warning of Norton's flying leap from the floorboard onto the rear seat of the carriage. The vehicle rocked with the force of the wolfhound's landing.

Liam reached back one-handed and undid the latch of the special traveling basket on the back seat. Bummer the Second squirmed out and began to bark, scrambling from one end of the seat to the other. Norton thrust his shaggy muzzle across Mac's shoulder and gave her a great sweeping lick that caught her right across the cheek.

All at once the strained atmosphere of anger and suspicion was gone. Mac was laughing—not a quiet, feminine titter but a full-throated sound of genuine
amusement.

"Friends of yours?" she asked. "I didn't know you
kept such good company." She caught Bummer and
lifted the terrier over the back of the seat and into her
lap. Sometime in the last minute she'd managed to pull
off her gloves; now she held the terrier down with one
hand and patted Norton's muzzle with the other.
"What are their names?"

Of course *she* wouldn't be discomposed, even with a
pair of boisterous canines shedding and slobbering all
over her carriage dress. Caroline would be outraged at
the affront to her toilette, and he wouldn't hear the end
of her complaints that he'd brought the dogs along.

"How remiss of me not to offer introductions," he
said. "This is Bummer the Second, and"—he jerked his
thumb toward the rear seat—"that's Norton."

"Norton—as in Emperor Norton? He just died a few
years ago, didn't he? And Bummer was one of his dogs.
Did you name yours for his?"

"You seem to know a great deal about the emperor."

She grinned. "He *is* in all the San Francisco history
books."

Not giving up on her crazy story even now. Liam
eased the carriage past a cable car rattling along in its
tracks as they passed the unfinished hulk of the city hall
dome and turned onto Fell. "Eventually I'll call your
bluff, Mac."

She gazed at the cable car while Bummer barked at a
mongrel on the sidewalk. "What's going to happen
when someone calls yours?"

Liam snorted and directed the surrey onto the broad
gravel paths of Avenue Park. Other carriages and their
occupants were taking the air on this fine autumn day:

victorias and landaus, rockaways and gigs and buggies. Children and dogs played on the patches of groomed lawn to either side of the lane.

And just ahead were Perry and Caroline in Perry's rented gig. Caroline's head was very close to Perry's as they chatted with a society matron in her landau.

Liam ordered Norton out of the carriage and coaxed the horses alongside the gig. Mac set Bummer on the back seat.

Perry looked up. "What kept you?" he asked. "Liam, you do know Mrs. Wyndham."

Liam made the slightest of bows. He knew her, all right; she was one of the social arbiters who determined when one had become rich or fashionable enough to be part of the Nob Hill set—the society Liam had exerted himself to join for Caroline's sake.

Perry, however, had his uses for Mrs. Wyndham and her ilk. They had the money he lacked; he had the culture they desperately aspired to. He knew how to make the most of his aristocratic heritage.

At the moment he clearly wished to present his supposed "cousin" to San Francisco society. He made introduction of Miss Rose MacKenzie to Mrs. Wyndham, relating the outrageous story of Mac's fabricated origins.

Mrs. Wyndham, rotund and severe in a dark brown carriage dress, examined Mac with considerable interest but didn't question Perry's story. She gave Perry a regal nod.

"I trust you will take good care of your cousin while she is with us, Mr. Sinclair," she said. "And Miss Gresham, I shall be delighted to attend your ball. I hope to see your new protégée there. Mr. O'Shea, Miss Mac-Kenzie." With a lift of her beringed hand she waved her coachman on.

"I knew you would be found acceptable with a little

help," Caroline said, beaming at Mac. "The ball will be so much fun."

"Um—ball?" Mac echoed.

Caroline's brow wrinkled. "Surely you've been in mourning for your poor father long enough?" She turned to Perry. "Hasn't she, Perry? The ball will not be too early?"

Perry patted Caroline's hand. "I think it best if Rose is encouraged to put her losses behind her rather than dwell on them."

Liam coughed. Three sets of eyes focused on him. Caroline shifted in her seat.

"I knew you could not object, Liam," Caroline said, her tone deceptively humble. "I thought it only right that Rose should be invited to my birthday ball." She turned to Mac without waiting for Liam's response. "You will adore it, Rose. I shall present you to all my friends. And it will be your first. . . ."

Mac listened, bemused, as Caroline outlined her plans for the ball. Liam set the surrey in motion alongside Perry's gig, keeping his expression carefully neutral.

Caroline had manipulated things to her liking once more. Perry's doing, of course. The ball was an unavoidable nuisance, but now it had become another setting for Perry's game.

Not that Mac would enjoy it. She would be as much as home at a formal society ball as Liam was.

The four of them drove on without speaking, bypassing the park proper with its conservatory and largely undeveloped dunes. A turn north on Stanyan carried them past the cemeteries that dotted the Outside Lands beyond the city limits. Within minutes they reached the long straight lane that led through the countryside to Point Lobos, Cliff House, and the Pacific Ocean.

"Well, Mac," Liam said when Perry and Caroline

had fallen a little behind, "I'll give you credit. You seem to know how to survive in this city."

She chuckled. "I wouldn't want to go through that kind of inspection too often." She looked sideways at Liam. "I'm sure Caroline can't wait to be the next Mrs. Wyndham, laying down the law for the rich and famous. How thrilling."

A feminine squeal interrupted Liam's belated response. Several seconds passed before he recognized the voice as Caroline's—and the carriage, passing them at a rapid clip, as Perry's gig.

Perry's gig, driven by a girl. A girl with blond hair. Caroline, urging Perry's team to a reckless pace on the old speeding drive that ran alongside the main avenue to the ocean.

Caroline squealed again as the gig hit a rut in the road and her hat went flying. The speeding drive had once been the province of young bucks anxious to test their teams against each other, but it hadn't been kept up. It was uneven, furrowed by weather, dangerous . . .

And Caroline didn't know a bloody thing about driving.

CHAPTER FIFTEEN

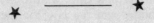

Were it good
To set the exact wealth
of all our states
All at one cast?
to set so rich a main
On the nice hazard
of one doubtful hour?

—WILLIAM SHAKESPEARE

THE GIG WAS well ahead before Liam slapped his own team from their easy trot into a rolling canter. Even that wasn't fast enough; Caroline had her horses at the gallop.

Liam cursed and exhorted his team to greater speed. He had only an instant to spare for Mac; he started to warn her, but she was already prepared. She caught the edge of the seat as they burst into flight.

The surrey bumped over uneven patches on the pitted clay surface and swayed with the speed, but Mac was sitting up, her face into the wind, grinning from ear to ear.

"Can you go any faster?" she shouted. Bummer echoed her plea with a bark from the rear, and Norton passed them by, tongue lolling.

By all the saints, Mac had never looked more alive, more attractive than she did now, with the wind ruddying her skin and her short hair in windblown tangles. It was as if she might spread wings and fly of her own accord.

Liam knew that feeling. It was the very soul of existence. Adventure, risk, the reckless need to dare the limits of life itself: Mac felt their seductive power just as he did. And Liam was caught in a rush of desire as powerful as it was unexpected.

Desire he had tried to ignore ever since their brief time together in the jungle. Desire he shouldn't be feeling, born of the excitement of the moment and of his anger and his wayward thoughts.

The surrey was almost even with the gig as they started up the curved, ascending lane to the jutting headland on which Cliff House perched. Both carriages slowed, and Liam could see Perry's steadying hands over Caroline's. Guiding her, encouraging her to defy her guardian.

Caroline was breathless with laughter. Like Mac, and totally unlike. All Liam felt as he watched Caroline laugh was rage.

And fear. Gut deep, coming out of a past long gone—fear of failure. And loss, and death.

He drove that madness away and pulled the surrey alongside the gig with a sharp jerk of the reins.

They looked at him, Perry and Caroline—her smile fading, his gaze cool, united in their mutiny. Reins slackened, and the horses came to a stop.

"You see, Liam," Caroline said triumphantly. "I *can* drive."

Liam pushed the reins into Mac's hands and jumped down from the surrey. "Get out of the gig, Caroline," he ordered.

She tightened her fingers on the gig's reins and lifted her chin. "No. Perry and I were only—"

"Get out. Now." Liam reached up and snatched the reins from her hands.

"See here, old man," Perry said. "There was never any danger. I'd advise you to calm yourself."

Liam turned on Perry. "You blackguard." He helped Caroline down. "Go inside and wait for me."

She feigned a sob. "Liam, please—"

But he wouldn't be moved by her tricks. "Miss Mac-Kenzie," he said between his teeth, "would you be so kind as to accompany Miss Gresham into Cliff House?"

Mac scrambled down from her seat. "Get a grip, O'Shea," she hissed as she passed him. She gently took Caroline's arm, and the two women moved off.

Liam turned back to Perry, clutching the carriage wheel in his hand. The rim cut into his palm. "Get out of here before I lose my temper."

"A terrifying prospect indeed." Perry gathered up the reins. "Take my advice, old man, and consider the nature of your audience before you do something you'll regret. You're not hurting me."

"*Go.*"

Perry went, though not without a certain leisurely insolence. He clicked to his team and sent them off down the lane, his unflappable demeanor completely intact.

Liam strode back to the surrey. The horses were in need of cooling off after their run, and Liam himself felt near the point of explosion. He drove to the hitching racks beside the long white building at the top of the road and paid a loitering young man to walk the horses.

His gut was churning with a snarl of emotions. He wasn't thinking as he stepped through the doors of Cliff House. The place was all but empty. A few families, groups, and couples were scattered amongst the tables in the main dining room. Caroline and Mac were the only visitors standing before the large windows that framed an impressive view of Seal Rock and the ocean.

But it wasn't the view Liam noticed. He stared at the two women, deeply conscious of the vivid contrast between them. Against the window they were only shapes, but he thought he could see something more: a glow, a burning that was like a candle's flicker in Caroline and a roaring furnace in Mac.

Mac glanced over her shoulder, meeting his gaze. Meeting and holding, challenging, promising . . .

Liam broke free and strode across the distance between them. He grasped Caroline's hand, pulling her away from the window and Mac.

Caroline didn't resist. Her bootheels clicked on the floor in a rapid, uneven beat as she struggled to keep up with him.

He found a secluded hallway leading off the dining room. As good a place as any; this wouldn't be any delicate wooing. He'd been putting off the inevitable far too long.

He released her hand. "We have something to discuss, Caroline."

Her eyes were very blue and very wide, just as they'd been when she was a child. Only then they'd been filled with trust and admiration. "Discuss?" she said. "Like the way you . . . chastised me in front of Perry and Rose?"

"Caroline," he said, more evenly. "You deliberately ignored my warnings. You could have been hurt."

"Perry was with me. I was safe."

"Safe?" He laughed. "What was the point of that little performance, Caroline? Did Perry put you up to it?"

Her hands twisted in the folds of her skirt. "I . . . it was my idea."

She looked up at him, as pretty and exquisite as a china doll. Perfect. Beautiful. An ornament easily broken, to be unwrapped only with the greatest of care—never to be handled with strong emotion. Or passion.

There was no danger of that, no stirring within him, nothing to spark between a man and woman. The lack of that spark was an emptiness, a hollow yearning he could not remember feeling before he'd gone to the jungle.

Before Mac.

He clenched his jaw. "You're nearly eighteen, Caroline," he said.

Her attention was fixed on him. Her lips parted; the delicate lashes of an angel fluttered against her cheeks. "Yes."

"Your father gave your care into my hands."

"You are not my father." She averted her face. "You don't care about me."

The words twisted deep into the emptiness inside him. "I do care," he said hoarsely. He caught her chin and turned her face toward him again. "Caroline—"

He caught her shoulders and lowered his mouth to hers. The kiss was no more than a brush of lips, though Caroline shivered at his touch. Liam felt nothing. He had expected a sense of rightness, of relief in doing what must be done. But the coldness in his belly only grew more chill, more fathomless, as if all his vows to Gresham and to himself meant nothing at all.

There was only one answer to that nothingness. He lifted Caroline against him, taking her lips more fully, seeking life itself.

The life he'd sensed when he'd held Mac in his arms, hot and bright and pulsing as the jungle sun. The wash of ocean waves and barking of seals became the beat of rain and shrieking of parrots, another place and another heart pounding close to his, a radiance that knew no limits.

But it wasn't Mac he was holding, and the light within Caroline was not bright enough, not strong enough to pierce the darkness, to make him feel . . .

The wrongness of it shocked him back to himself as surely as the sound of purposeful footsteps rounding the corner into the hall.

Mac stopped in a swirl of skirts, her ears red as summer roses. Liam released Caroline; she put her hands to her lips and backed away to lean against the wall, trembling and mute.

The darkness in Liam spilled over, a bedlam in his mind that left him numb to any feeling. He took Caroline's hand and pulled her out of the hall and across the dining room to the door. The fresh ocean air let him breathe again; he paused on the steps and searched the line of carriages waiting at the hitching racks.

A respectable-looking hack driver was leaning against his brougham, smoking a cigarette and blowing smoke circles lazily into the air. Liam strode up to him, Caroline in tow.

"Are you for hire?" he demanded.

The driver dropped his cigarette and crushed it under his heel. "I'm waiting for my fare. . . ."

"I'll double what they're paying if you take this lady home directly and see that she is put into the keeping of her chaperon. Tell Mrs. Hunter that no one is to see the young lady until I return. If I hear you've done exactly as I tell you, I'll triple the fee. Liam O'Shea's the name."

The driver straightened. "I know you, Mr. O'Shea."

"Good. Then you know I don't tolerate incompetence. She's to go directly, and safely, to her home. Can you guarantee that?"

"Sure. I'm the best driver in the city."

Liam snorted and counted out a handful of coins. "Send another driver to pick up your fare and come to my house for the rest of the money when the job's complete. You'll find the Gresham home on California Street."

"I know it, sir." The driver pocketed the coins and tipped his hat. "She'll be home safe and sound in a jiffy."

Caroline made no protest as Liam handed her into the brougham. She peered at him through the window, pale against the glass. Soon the carriage was down the lane and rounding the headland, out of sight.

He walked to the surrey to retrieve the dogs. Both were gone—probably down at the beach for their run. Grimly he went back into Cliff House, but Mac was nowhere to be found.

She was not outside, nor on the descending road to the ocean. It wasn't until he looked over the railing along the rocks and down to the beach below that he saw her.

She was walking close to the surf, her skirts caught up in one hand. The dogs were with her—Norton bounding ahead and doubling back again, Bummer chasing the waves at her feet.

Liam strode along the curved lane and onto the sand, ignoring the coarse grains that worked into his shoes and destroyed their fine polish. All he could see was Mac.

Her walking boots, stockings, and hat lay in a heap

just out of the water's reach. He stopped to gather them up. Her footprints melted into wet sand as he followed them.

The sand also muffled the sounds of his approach, allowing him to observe uninterrupted. The hem of her gown was soaked five inches up, and her hair was tangled with salt spray. She didn't mind displaying her ankles for all to see. Once she'd revealed a great deal more, only for him.

She was a bloody siren, bent on dragging a man to his doom under the icy waves.

No. She was a sea nymph, unselfconscious in her immodesty, unaware of its effect on mortal men who came too near.

His body stirred, betraying him. With a final long stride he caught up to her.

"Well, Mac," he said harshly. "I see you've found a way to amuse yourself."

She turned without surprise, pushing her spray-wet bangs from her forehead. "It's a hell of a lot better than watching your little soap opera up there. I can get that at home for free." She whistled sharply and Norton came running up to her, beating her skirts with his sandy tail. "Is it finally over?"

"It's over." He snatched up a piece of driftwood. "Why did you run, Mac?"

"I didn't—"

"Of course," he said with a fierce edge of triumph. "You're jealous. You couldn't bear to see me with anyone else."

Her stillness was sudden and profound. Mac's fingers pushed deep into Norton's rough coat. "You think I'd want to be in Caroline's shoes after what you did up there? Humiliating her, treating her like a baby—"

He felt heat under his skin. "I know what Caroline needs."

"Sure. That's really the way to show it, all right. You have it down pat. Congratulations."

"You wouldn't know a bloody thing about how a lady should be treated. You're little better than a tramp, *Miss* MacKenzie."

"Tsk, tsk. You're forgetting to be a gentleman, Mr. O'Shea. But that's all right. Go on just as you've been doing, and you'll make things easy for everyone."

"And what do you mean by that?"

But she seemed to have thought better of what she'd said, for she turned her back and walked away along the surf's edge. Liam tossed the driftwood aside with a savage jerk, and Norton set out in pursuit with a joyful bark.

"Damn it," he said, lengthening his stride to catch up to her. "I warned you, Mac—"

"The way you warned Caroline and Perry?" she said, trailing her sodden skirts. "You're good at that. Always need to be on top, huh?"

"You'd like that, wouldn't you?" He finally caught her arm and swung her around. "You'd like me on top in a very different situation."

"Pardon me?"

He pulled her closer. "You can fool the others, Mac, but not me. You'll always be what you are, no matter how many Mrs. Wyndhams approve or how many gowns you wear. It's all paint over dross."

She tried to jerk free. "You should know."

The blood was pounding in his ears. "Should I?"

"You think you've figured me out, Liam, but I can play the same game. You're a man who's had to fight all his life for everything he has." Her voice dropped so low that he almost couldn't hear it over the surf. "You had a hard childhood, no privileges or gentleness, only stark poverty and struggle. Now you're rich, but you haven't left that childhood behind, have you? Is that why you want to marry Caroline, because she's like some pretty toy you didn't have as a kid? Because she means you've finally succeeded?"

He let her go as if her flesh had turned to fire. "Lucky guesses, Mac?" he rasped. "Or is this Perry's opinion?"

"Perry has nothing to do with it. But Caroline does. You don't know when to stop, Liam. You're trying to make Caroline into something— Damn it, what's going to happen when she *really* proves she has a mind of her own?"

Liam felt cold through to the center of his heart. "You don't need to be concerned about that, Mac. Soon it'll be over, and you'll be out of this city. That's how it will be. How it has to be."

She only gazed at him, looking almost lost. Conceding the last word to him, granting him victory.

A victory that felt utterly hollow.

He turned and called the dogs. They came running, Bummer dancing around and around his feet and Norton leaning companionably against his side. True friends, incapable of using human speech to wound and rend and betray.

"I'll take you back to the Palace now, Miss MacKenzie," he said tonelessly.

"And Caroline?"

"I've sent her home."

"I think I'd rather walk."

He wouldn't have been surprised if she tried it. "Will you come willingly, or shall I throw you over my shoulder?"

"Someday," she said, sitting down in the sand to pull on her soiled boots, "you might learn there are better ways to get what you want than brute strength and intimidation."

He didn't answer her. They walked stiffly, Mac in the lead, back to the road.

The carriage ride to the Palace was made without conversation. Mac, somber and unyielding, was ready to speak only when he let her off in the Grand Court.

"Ask yourself one thing, Liam," she said quietly as he prepared to drive away. "Why are you so anxious to be rid of me now? Why are you so afraid?"

And she turned away before he could summon a reply.

Liam kept his mind blank as he drove home. Even the dogs were unusually quiet. Only on the last stretch of Sacramento Street did he set the horses in one last, reckless run to the gates of his great, empty house.

It was at those gates that the world lurched violently and threw Liam forward against the dashboard of the surrey. The horses screamed and reared. A hard grip on the seat kept him from falling out; the effort wrenched his arm and slammed his head against the roof. He heard a yelp and a whimper and struggled to right himself.

The carriage had collapsed on one side, front and rear wheels tilted at an impossible angle. Bummer lay very still on the ground a few feet away, Norton licking him with worried nudges of his muzzle. Ignoring the pain in his arm and head, Liam scrambled out of the surrey. He gave the horses a swift check and found them trembling and white-eyed but whole. He moved quickly to crouch beside the dogs.

"Bummer," he said. "Can you hear me, boy?"

The terrier's visible eye opened and then shut again. His whimper was barely audible. Liam ran his hand over Bummer's side, careful not to exert any pressure. One of the dog's legs was bleeding badly, and he flinched when Liam brushed his ribs. Pushing Norton gently out of the way, Liam gathered the terrier in his arms and strode for the gates.

Chen met him before he reached the front door. "Mr. O'Shea, what—"

"We've had an accident, Chen. Send for the veterinarian immediately. And clean up Bummer's leg. I think his ribs are broken."

With utmost care Chen took the dog, murmuring assurances into the terrier's limp triangular ear. "I will take good care of him."

"I know you will. When Bummer's safe, send a message to Mr. Bauer that I'll need to see him right away. I'll be in front speaking with Forster."

"At once, Mr. O'Shea." Chen vanished into the house, Norton trotting anxiously behind.

Liam knew Bummer couldn't be in better hands until the veterinarian arrived. His next most pressing business wouldn't wait. He went out into the garden and was taking the path toward the carriage house when he saw Forster by the surrey, bent over one of the ruined wheels.

"Well?" he said, joining the other man. "What caused it?"

Forster straightened. "I can't account for it, Mr. O'Shea, except that it looks like someone sawed halfway through the front axle. A few good runs and it was bound to give way." He clucked his tongue. "It's a miracle the horses weren't hurt."

"Yes." Liam remembered how he'd raced the surrey not once but twice, how Mac had been in the carriage only minutes before.

She could have been badly hurt.

She . . . could have died.

This had been no accident. No accident that Caroline had been safe with Perry in the gig.

He unbuttoned the collar of his shirt and ripped off his tie. "See to the horses, Forster. The veterinarian's on his way—have him examine them carefully, and give them an extra measure of grain tonight. The poor beasts have earned it."

"I'll do that, Mr. O'Shea. Are you all right?"

"Perfectly."

Forster gave him a dubious glance and went to calm the horses, unbuckling their harness. "There, now," he soothed. "You'll be fine, my beauties. No one will hurt you again."

Liam stood by the surrey as Forster led the team away. No, no one would hurt the horses or Bummer or anyone else again. His bitter thoughts turned toward the center of town, toward Market and a certain suite of boardinghouse rooms.

This time I'll kill you, Perry.

THE ROOM WAS heavy with the scent of incense, a scent that didn't quite cover the more acrid smell of opium from the adjoining chamber. Perry was grateful for the low light and heavy shadows; he'd been careful to wear a hat that gave him some anonymity so that the man he was to meet would have trouble identifying him later.

When everything was finished.

While he waited under the impassive scrutiny of the tong guards, he thought back to the news he'd had from Forster a few days before. The news that had led him here to this alien place, to ally himself to men with whom he had nothing in common. Men who would probably see a sawed-through carriage axle as a warning rather than a murder attempt.

An attempt which had not succeeded.

Perry smoothed his mustache. It had been quite a shock at first, but he'd gotten over it quickly enough. He hadn't even waited to discover Liam's reaction. He knew he'd operate more smoothly without having to contend with Liam's rather violent mistrust.

The contrary Irishman had no doubt already fixed the blame for his "accident." But if he'd gone in pursuit of Perry, he wouldn't have found him.

Perry knew how to disappear.

There was a stirring from one side of the room, the hiss of a sliding panel being drawn back. A man walked in, wrapped in dignity, his dark silk suit dull in the dimness. Two hatchetmen followed, and a smaller individual with wire spectacles and a humble air.

The boss seated himself in the carved mahogany chair and regarded Perry for a length of time undoubtedly meant to intimidate. Perry met his dark gaze unflinchingly. Inspection apparently completed, the boss signaled to one of his men and spoke swiftly in another language.

The bespectacled man moved up, bowing. "The master wishes to know if you will have tea, sir."

"I'm afraid I haven't time for pleasantries. I'm here on a matter of business. To our mutual benefit."

The interpreter repeated some approximation of Perry's words to his master with much humble posturing. The boss was either bored or annoyed; he uttered a few terse comments and waited for his man to render them in English.

"The master wishes to know what you want with him."

Perry leaned back in his chair. "You may tell your master that I know what you're planning to do about Mr. O'Shea, and I think I can be of help to you."

The interpreter was a little less efficient in his work this time, and his boss less happy. "And what," he said, "makes you so certain you can be of use to us, Mr. Sinclair? We have many outsiders working for us already."

"Because I know O'Shea very well. I'm his closest friend, as it happens."

The boss leaned back, stroking the expensive silk of his jacket. "And so?"

"I also know about his secret operations," Perry said. "The ones that have been so inconvenient to your business. I have reason to believe he's organizing another raid, and I may be able to provide you with details."

"I see."

"And if that's not enough, I may be able to get rid of him for you. I'm well aware that you can't afford to go about your . . . attempts on Mr. O'Shea too obviously unless you want the police down on your head. Some of them do remain uncorrupted and only require a good reason to put an end to your very profitable transactions." Perry smiled coldly. "I can take care of O'Shea without any risk to you. But only if you leave it to me and don't interfere."

"And what do you expect for this . . . service?"

"As I said, you run a very profitable business. I need money. I'm sure we can work out a mutually satisfactory agreement."

When the translation was done the boss sat very still in his chair while the hatchetmen shifted and looked as if they'd like nothing better than to make use of the weapons for which they'd been so aptly named. One of them even leaned down to speak into the ear of his boss, making a chopping motion with his hand.

But Perry knew he'd succeeded when the boss signaled again and the interpreter scurried out to return with an exquisite tea service on a delicate enameled tray.

"Perhaps we may be of aid to each other," the boss said. His servant presented a steaming cup to Perry and returned to his master. "Now we shall seal our bargain."

Perry took the fragile cup, inhaling the subtle fragrance. And waited.

The boss sipped his tea. Perry did the same without further hesitation.

If the tong leader had decided not to trust him, he could easily have poisoned the tea. No one knew Perry had come here; few would ever miss him. But the risk was worth taking. The stakes had gone too high.

There was absolutely nothing left to lose.

★ ────── ★

Tell her the joyous time
will not be stayed
Unless she do him by
the forelock take.

—EDMUND SPENSER

S HE'D BLOWN IT but good.

Mac felt a trickle of sweat run down the front of her bodice as she watched the masked and costumed society couples perform a quadrille on the Gresham's elegant parquet ballroom floor. She plucked at her elbow-length gloves, longing to peel them off. In spite of open windows and the late hour, so fashionable for nine-teenth-century balls, the room was stifling. Ten pounds more or less of ball gown didn't help—even though it left the upper part of her arms bare and plunged in front a little too low for comfort.

At least she'd put her foot down at the idea of a full costume. The half-mask she wore had the advantage of making her feel a little more anonymous. Caroline's in-struction during the past two weeks hadn't appreciably improved Mac's talent for dancing, so Mac was relegated to the status of wallflower for every dance but the waltz.

Thank God. Six weeks in the past and she still felt as if she were on a movie set.

The movie set of a historical farce, at that. A farce in which she, the heroine, had messed up history and couldn't seem to put it right again.

Everything had gone downhill after Caroline's rebellion at Cliff House and Mac's confrontation with Liam on the beach. She'd hardly had two words from Liam since, even though she'd been at the Gresham home so often she might as well have moved in.

And she hadn't seen Perry at all. It was as if her great-great-grandfather had literally disappeared—a circumstance that made Mac extremely uneasy. Her careful questions to Liam had been ignored, and Caroline had clammed up and looked on the verge of tears when Perry's name was mentioned.

It had been a thoroughly *lovely* fortnight. Liam hadn't let Caroline out of the Gresham mansion. The big surprise was that Liam not only allowed Mac to see Caroline, but had actually encouraged long visits. And those visits were almost always in his presence, since he'd made himself a part of the furniture from dawn to midnight every day. Mac suspected he'd decided she was the lesser of two evils—though given their last conversation, she was amazed that he'd let her within spitting distance of his precious ward.

Or maybe he thought he'd rather have Mac underfoot than out conspiring somewhere with Perry. He permitted Caroline Mac's company because he wouldn't let her have anyone else's until the ball, except a few girlfriends for occasional tea or a brief gossip. And, of course, the indispensable dressmaker.

Mac had learned more than she ever wanted to know about Victorian female gossip, fashion, and etiquette. Caroline had seesawed between "perfect ladyship" and moody silences, treating Mac either as a long-lost friend or a hopeless rustic who didn't know Spanish lace from Irish.

She might not win an Oscar for "Best Modern Woman Impersonating a Victorian Lady in a Historical Drama," but at least Mac wasn't giving herself away badly enough to be thought anything but eccentric by Caroline's friends.

That's me. Eccentric Mac, who knows damned well she doesn't belong here. And she also knew damned well that time was ticking away. Literally. She was treading water pretending to be what she wasn't in a society that wasn't hers. And until she found a way out of this mess, she was stuck here.

It wasn't just her heart she'd be leaving in nineteenth-century San Francisco. *If* she could leave. . . .

She pushed that thought away and snapped open her fan. No point in thinking about how she was supposed to get home until she had a reason to.

There was one *good* thing to think about. Liam may have been ignoring her, at best being frigidly polite—but he wasn't conceding much more to his bride-to-be. Mac hadn't seen any sign that he'd asked Caroline to marry him. He certainly hadn't tried to reprise his kiss at Cliff House. To the contrary: he seemed bent on making himself as much a living example of menacing and omnipresent implacability as was humanly possible. If there was love on Liam's part, Mac hadn't observed it.

She flexed her feet in their dancing slippers, longing for her sneakers—or even her worn-out hiking boots. Damn it, where was Perry? Caroline had been confident that he would never miss her birthday ball, no matter what had caused his long absence.

Mac was reasonably sure Caroline was right. If Perry were able to come.

Good grief.

The quadrille ended, and the hired orchestra struck up a waltz. Mac faded back against the wall, determined not to be dragged out again by some well-meaning, tailcoated male who would grab a peek down her décolletage.

Her vigilance was rewarded. She was left alone to watch Liam walk onto the ballroom floor—Liam, leading Caroline to the center of the room. A Liam who had never looked so elegant—or so much like a cat among pigeons. Or a tiger pretending to be a house cat.

He wore his black and white, perfectly cut evening clothes as well as he'd worn khaki and canvas in the jungle. This was not his milieu, but when he stalked forward crowds parted for him like the Red Sea before Charlton Heston. He was the ideal blend of danger and elegance: Tarzan visiting his estates in England, James Bond in the rough, a fair-haired god of Adventure. A woman would have to be blind not to notice.

Caroline wasn't blind. And you'd never know from watching them dance that Liam had been cold and Caroline sullen for most of the past two weeks. Liam's dancing wasn't elegant—it was powerful, sweeping Caroline about the room like a feather in a hurricane. And Caroline was an exotic bird in her costume gown of brilliant green silk and burgundy satin ribbons.

At the moment they were very much a couple, though Liam was almost twice Caroline's age. Both fair-haired and pale-eyed, both gorgeous, both from the same century.

And Caroline gazed at Liam, flushed and laughing, as

if she were transfixed by the wild stare of a frightening and fascinating predator. . . .

Damn, Mac thought with feeling. *Damn damn damn damn da—*

"You aren't dancing, Rose?" someone asked from the general direction of a nearby potted plant.

She knew the voice, though the man who came up beside her was wearing a black cape and a mask that covered most of his face.

"Perry?"

He raised a gloved finger to his lips. "Quietly, my dear. I doubt Liam would be pleased to see me here."

Mac eased farther back against the wall and pretended not to notice him. "Where have you been?" she demanded in a whisper.

"Ah. I'd wondered if my absence would be noted."

"Noted? That's putting it mildly. Liam's been grim as death, Caroline's been sulking, I haven't been able to get an explanation out of anyone, and now you turn up in disguise—"

"All with good reason, I assure you."

"Such as? Maybe the fact that Liam was pretty mad at you following that stunt you pulled at Cliff House? I'd say that backfired for sure."

"It was hardly a 'stunt,' as you put it. There is a purpose in everything I do."

I wonder, Mac thought. "In that case, seeing as we're allies, maybe you could fill me in. Liam has virtually locked Caroline away. You've left him a completely clear field."

"I've been well aware what goes on in the Gresham and O'Shea households," he said coolly, "including your lack of progress with Liam. It *was* your intention to attract his interest, was it not?" He smoothed his immaculate white waistcoat. "You assured me you'd do anything to win him from Caroline."

"I don't see how I could have done much of anything, with Liam stuck to Caroline like glue. I've only seen him in Caroline's house—Hey, wait a minute. What do you mean, you know everything that goes on?"

"I have my methods. And kindly don't gape, Rose."

She looked back toward the dancers. "Somehow I don't like the sound of that."

He shrugged. "One of us has to look out for our mutual concerns. I'd hoped that in my absence you might find it easier to deal with Liam. Plainly that was not the case."

"So what did you want me to do? Kidnap him?"

"That might not be a bad idea," he muttered.

The small hairs rose on the back of her neck. "Excuse me?"

Even from several feet away Mac could feel Perry's intensity—an almost palpable aura she usually associated only with Liam.

Determination. Tenacity. Ruthlessness.

"You didn't disappear just to make it easier on me," Mac said. "We were supposed to work together on this. If I don't know what you have in mind—"

"I have in mind to stop Caroline from marrying Liam," he said. "And I'm afraid it has become necessary to take more drastic measures to assure it doesn't happen."

There was a flat certainty in his words that chilled Mac through the layers of stifling gown, though she'd been thinking along the exact same lines. "Why now?" she asked.

He touched his upper lip, and Mac realized with a shock that he'd shaved his mustache. "I told you that Liam was planning to propose on her birthday. After tonight he'll no longer have control over her fortune, but he wields enough authority and influence over Caroline that I fear she will accept him."

"Then why didn't you take the risk of asking her yourself?"

"She isn't ready." Perry paused to observe Liam and Caroline dancing—watching with an almost frightening concentration, as if he could reach out and pluck Caroline from Liam's arms by sheer force of will. "The situation is delicately balanced. To push the issue now would play into Liam's hands. She needs time."

"Which we don't have."

"The carriage accident complicated matters considerably—"

"Carriage accident?" Mac interrupted. "What are you talking about?"

"The Beautiful Blue Danube" rolled by uninterrupted for several excruciating seconds.

"Then Liam didn't tell you?" Perry said. "I shouldn't be surprised. I knew you weren't in the surrey when the accident occurred, but—"

Mac closed the space between them in a few awkward strides and barely restrained herself from grabbing the satin edges of his cape. "What the hell are you talking about?"

He told her in so many dry, colorless words. Mac searched his eyes.

"How did it happen?"

"My sources tell me the axle was sawed halfway through."

She went very still. "Then you're saying it was deliberate. Someone wanted the carriage to crash."

And it must have happened after he dropped me off. Damn it, Liam, why didn't you give me some clue. . . .

"Someone," she said coldly, "wanted to kill Liam."

"So it would seem. And judging by your expression,

Rose, you're remembering Liam's accusations at the Palace, and wondering if I had anything to do with it."

Her eyes narrowed. "You disappeared after this so-called accident—"

"Given Liam's earlier suspicion and our recent contretemps, it wasn't difficult to guess where he'd assign the blame for the latest mishap." He held her gaze steadily. "Come, Rose. If I bore Liam such fatal ill will, why would I volunteer this information and earn your suspicion as well as his?"

He had a very good point, and yet— "How can I be sure? I hardly know you."

"But you of all people should understand what it is to be falsely accused of a crime. If I wanted him dead, I would have found a far more efficient means of committing the deed. Either you trust me, or we are both in very hot water."

What he said made a grim kind of sense. Somehow she couldn't see Perry trying to kill someone and making a mess of it not once, but twice.

"Even if I take your word," she said, "Liam won't."

"All the more reason for me to remain incognito—for the time being. That is in your hands, Rose. Do you trust me?"

"I don't have much choice. But I warn you, Perry—" She stared him down with fierce determination. "If you try to hurt Liam in any way, you'll regret it."

The corner of his mouth twitched. "I wonder if Liam appreciates what a vigilant protector he has in you, Rose. You would make a formidable enemy. But have no fear. There is no need to kill Liam to secure Caroline's happiness." He glanced quickly about the room. "You must be prepared to act quickly and do whatever is necessary if we're to keep this marriage from taking place."

"And what do you think will be necessary?"

"The dance has almost ended. I can't linger here. I have my own work to do." He was distracted as the music finished in a grand Viennese flourish. "I hope you were not exaggerating the attraction between you and Liam. You may have a chance to put it to the test very soon."

"What—"

"Be ready for my message."

"Wait! If you had nothing to do with the accident, then who—"

But he was already gone. The waltz was ended, and Liam and Caroline had left the floor. Mac spotted Caroline gossiping with a group of girls her own age, fully absorbed in the activity.

And Liam—Liam was crossing the room at a brisk pace, headed for the wide double doors to the rear of the chamber. The Gresham butler, Biggs, was waiting for him. The two men slipped out of the room with a definite air of secrecy.

Mac's mind was full of Perry's news of the carriage accident, his claims of innocence, and the frightening implications that arose from those assumptions.

Regardless of what had happened in the jungle, someone had acted against Liam here in San Francisco. Someone had tried to kill Liam in the guise of an accident. He wasn't a subtle man; she wouldn't be surprised if he'd made a number of enemies throughout his life.

If Perry was innocent, then someone *else* had a motive. That person could, at this very moment, be arranging another attempt.

And it was entirely beyond Mac's control to interfere. Unless . . .

She didn't hesitate further. She had to find Liam—irrational, perhaps, but she had to make sure he was all right. She retraced the way Liam and Biggs had gone, hugging the wall and hoping no one noticed.

There was something to be said for being a wallflower. Her departure went unremarked. She got the heavy ballroom doors open without undue difficulty and closed them behind her. A dark wood-paneled hallway ran along the side of the ballroom; all Mac could hear was the echoing sound from the ballroom itself.

Until she caught the unmistakable timbre of Liam's voice from somewhere down the hall. The sound started a hum in her body just below where her snug bodice ended.

She pressed a hand to her belly and walked toward the origin of Liam's voice. It came from behind a closed door—and there was another voice in the room with it, faintly accented.

The door was thick, but it was not impermeable. It was also open a very convenient crack. *Another chance to develop my newfound skills at eavesdropping,* Mac thought wryly. She did a quick scan of the hall to make sure it was empty and pressed herself as close to the door as she could.

"If it weren't for the urgency of this, Chen, I couldn't risk it. You know I was to propose to Miss Gresham tonight."

"I understand, Mr. O'Shea," said the accented voice. "Do you wish me to tell the others—"

"No. If the tongs expect us to act tomorrow night, then we'll have to do it now, before they get new information. Only you and I know about the change. By the time we tell the others, whoever we can gather at this short notice, there won't be any time for the informant to betray us."

"Are you certain it is a matter of betrayal, Mr. O'Shea?"

A pause. "I'll find out. But it's a sign that we'll have to change our methods." He sighed. "Tonight will be my last raid. When this is over we'll meet with the others and decide who should take over the leadership."

"As you say. I shall set things in motion. I have messengers waiting."

"Good. I'll join you as soon as I can. I have another matter to take care of."

"And may I wish you luck, Mr. O'Shea?"

Liam's answer was long in coming. "Thank you, Chen."

There was the muffled scraping of feet. Mac had just time enough to flatten herself against the wall before the door opened and someone emerged from the room. Mac caught a glimpse of book-lined walls before the door hid her view again.

The man whose back she saw retreating down the hall was definitely not Liam. He was shorter, dressed in a different kind of suit, and his hair was very black. Chen, she surmised. She was certain Liam had mentioned his name before.

A sense of self-preservation ended her speculation. Best to get back to the ballroom before she was missed—or before Liam caught her. What she'd heard gave her plenty to think about.

The tongs, raids, informants, betrayal—it sounded ominous indeed. And dangerous. She remembered something about the tongs—powerful criminal associations that had ruled Chinatown with an iron fist for most of the late nineteenth and early twentieth centuries.

What kind of raid would Liam be making on them? Something he wanted kept secret. Something that might be likely to win him enemies.

And just as ominous was his confirmation that he planned a certain proposal tonight. . . .

Footsteps sounded inside the room. Mac lifted her skirts and jogged down the hallway toward the ballroom doors. She reached them and had just slipped through when Liam came striding after, the light of battle in his eyes.

He came to a stop when he saw her. "Well, Mac. You look a little distracted. Have you been dancing?"

She sucked in a steadying breath before she thought to wonder if she might pop out of her low-cut bodice. This was almost as much as he'd said to her in a week, and she felt oddly giddy.

"Actually," she said, bluffing her way, "I've been up to no good. Isn't that what you'd rather hear?"

"I'd certainly be more inclined to believe it."

"Well, I haven't been dancing." She grimaced. "I'm not exactly great at it, I'll admit. It's probably a good thing for the gentlemen's toes that I've been bowing out."

"What? Caroline hasn't succeeded in her transformation of you? She'll be distressed."

"Oh, I doubt that. She's keeping herself busy. I'd say this is her perfect milieu."

Liam scanned the room. Mac could tell when he located Caroline—still gossiping, still flitting about like a brilliant butterfly, the center of attention and loving every minute.

"So I see," Liam said, with no smile to spare for his ward's antics. But when he turned back to Mac the smile came, edged with the usual mockery. "Do you know, Mac, that when I first came to San Francisco I wasn't much of a dancer myself."

It took her a moment to absorb the fact that Liam had just admitted to an imperfection in himself, and for no other apparent reason than to make her feel better. *Nah.* He must have an ulterior motive. But the very notion made Mac's heart fill to overflowing and her throat catch.

"You can dance," she said. "I was watching."

"And were you now?"

Her ears caught fire. "There isn't much else to do around here. Except maybe contemplate how profitable it would be to introduce the local ladies to the virtues of high-top sneakers." She pointed to her slippered feet. "These shoes are killing me."

"Perhaps you'd prefer to dance barefooted. That should suit you better and provide entertainment for everyone."

"Hmmm. Maybe you're right, at that. Might put a little life into this party. I don't know about you, but I'd rather be back in the jungle, climbing pyramids and slogging through the mud and battling mosquitos and scorpions. That's the life—"

He didn't respond. He was searching the room again as the musicians came back from their break and began to tune up. Mac followed his look and did a double take.

Good grief. That masked man with the cape, crossing the room directly to Caroline, was Perry. He was going to ask Caroline to dance. She was still laughing as she turned to him; she stopped and went very still.

Liam was watching. Liam was clearly wondering, and he was getting ready to—

"Liam!" Mac said brightly. "Since you're talking to me again, why don't you ask me to dance?"

He glanced at her, distracted, and slowly focused on her face. "I thought you didn't dance."

"This is a waltz, isn't it? *That* I can do, more or less. And since you've been there, maybe you can teach me a thing or two."

His grin was startling. "You tempt me, Mac." He flashed one last look across the room, but the dance had begun and Caroline and Perry were lost in a crowd of couples. He held out his hand. "Will you do me the honor, Miss MacKenzie?"

She gripped his fingers. "Of course, Mr. O'Shea. Wouldn't want to disappoint you."

Liam maneuvered them into the dance with surprising grace. Mac concentrated on keeping pace with him until she got the rhythm.

"You're not as bad as you claimed, Mac," he said.

But after the first few steps Mac wasn't thinking about her feet. She was thinking about other parts of her body, and his: the heat of his hand at her waist, burning through the layers of cloth as if they were nothing; the strength of his fingers joined with hers, cradling them as if they were fragile; the breadth of his chest brushing her breasts, the flex of muscles beneath his trousers, the width of his shoulder under her palm.

"You seem preoccupied," Liam said, his tone oddly husky. "Nothing to say, for once?"

"I . . . I'm trying not to step on your feet."

Liam whirled her about so that they danced at the very edge of the crowd. "Come, Mac. This will be our last dance together. We should make the most of it."

"Last dance" didn't sound very good at all. "It's also our first," she quipped. "Can't expect to be Fred Astaire and Ginger Rogers."

"Another of your strange jests? I may not be this Astaire, but perhaps I can make up for the lapse."

And he did, with a vengeance. As the next phrase of the waltz began he pulled her into a ferocious embrace that carried her like a whirlwind about the room.

No formality here, holding her at arm's length; not for Mac the swirling, floating waltz of a Scarlett O'Hara in her crinolines. The bustle required a more sedate, boxlike motion, but Liam pushed well beyond anything sedate. Mac didn't have to concentrate on her steps; Liam controlled every move. He made the waltz the devil's dance people had once named it.

The air left Mac's lungs and never quite returned. Liam's breath sighed against her temple, her cheek, her lips. His arm was like a vise around her waist.

"Are you enjoying yourself now, Mac?" he asked.

"I'm still trying to decide if you're breaking a social rule."

"By dancing with a scapegrace vixen?"

"No. By trying to see if we can occupy the same space at the same time."

His chuckle held an edge. "Ah. You mean this." He pulled her impossibly closer, so that she could feel every bump and plane on his body from knee to chest. "We know each other, Mac. Why should we be formal?"

"Does that mean you finally think of me as a friend?"

"Friend?" His mouth was very close to her ear. "I don't make friends with women."

"What a thing to say to a lady," she said. "But then again, you've pointed out that I'm not a lady."

"Admitting the truth at last? I could almost admire your honesty."

"That's a start. I'll bet you could find something else to admire if you worked at it."

"You may even be right, Mac." His voice had gone lower still, almost caressing. Shivers raced from the nape of Mac's neck to the base of her spine. An area Liam was rubbing with the palm of his hand. . . .

"This is much nicer," she said quickly, "than the silent treatment you've been giving me. Formality puts up so many barriers between people, doesn't it?"

"Rather like a corset," he said, "which you are not wearing."

His hand flexed on her waist in emphasis. Damn it,

she was blushing, and it had been *her* choice to dump the torture device—without telling Caroline, of course. No one would know the difference, unless they were holding her the way Liam was. . . .

"You're right," she said. "I'm not. Where I come from, we don't need that kind of armor to protect ourselves."

"You speak as if you had something to protect."

She flashed her teeth. "Not anything I can't defend on my own."

Liam held her eyes so long and intently that she almost lost her footing. Good grief, he wasn't making it easy for her to work up the nerve for what she was preparing to do.

"Do you expect to be defending it soon, Mac?" he asked.

"I guess that depends, doesn't it?" She threw herself into the image of what she must try to be from now on—the shameless hussy he'd always claimed she was. "I can't think of too many temptations. There are only so many good men in the world."

"And less who'd fall for your wiles."

"You think so? But then again, you never did finish what you started in the jungle, so you'll probably never know."

His steps faltered and he caught himself, muttering an apology to the couple they'd nearly collided with. Mac felt real hope then—hope that she'd awakened something in him, if only uncertainty—enough uncertainty to set him off course, to delay his plans for one more day. . . .

But his mouth hardened. "It won't matter," he said. "Not when this dance is over."

"Wrong, Liam," she said softly. "I think you need a bit of reminding."

With a tug and a wrench she took the lead, turning

them toward the edge of the ballroom. There was a convenient row of decorative pillars close to one wall. Mac maneuvered Liam behind one of them and shoved him against it.

"As I said," she purred, "it's time for a few reminders."

And she kissed him for all she was worth, hard, pulling his head down to hers. He was stiff for about half a second, then crushed the breath out of her as if he were a human corset. His lips ground on hers, and his tongue pushed inside with potent force.

It was just as it had been in the jungle—as wild, as crazy, as overwhelming. It was challenge given and accepted, a battle royal between two people determined to claim victory. Until something changed. Mac almost lost the memory of her purpose, almost melted, almost let the kiss last far too long.

But she heard the music stop somewhere very far away, and that was enough. She pulled back, meeting his unguarded gaze with naked triumph.

"Was it like that with Caroline? Can you live the rest of your life married to a girl who'll never give you what I just did?"

He grabbed for her, intent on prolonging their tête-à-tête. "You brazen—"

"There you are!"

Mac and Liam snapped apart like two halves of a wishbone. Caroline was standing beside the column, a fixed smile on her lovely face. "I have been searching all over for you, Rose. You keep disappearing . . . it is really too bad of you!" She flashed a bright glance at Liam. "How lucky you are to have Liam take care of you."

Mac did her best to appear nonchalant. Maybe Caroline hadn't seen anything. Maybe she wasn't actually glaring at Mac behind that pretty smile. . . .

Liam quickly offered his arm to Caroline, who hesitated just an instant before taking it. "I'm sure there are others who would be happy to dance with you, Rose," she said sweetly.

"Thank you," Mac murmured. But Caroline had already dismissed her with a toss of her head.

"Won't you ask me to dance, Liam?" she cooed.

"With pleasure," Liam said—for Mac's benefit, she felt sure. But as he led Caroline away he threw Mac a look of hot challenge that made her glad she had skirts to cover her wobbly knees.

The music was beginning again, and Liam was with Caroline as if nothing had happened between him and Mac. He could be getting ready to make his proposal at this very moment. Mac watched the couples take their positions on the dance floor; Liam's features were unreadable as he gazed down at his ward.

His expression remained so when Biggs suddenly materialized at his elbow, conveying some message that stole his attention from Caroline. Mac saw Biggs retreat, Liam speak to Caroline as the other couples began to dance, Caroline's angry response. Liam took her hand and she snatched it free.

Liam said a final brief sentence, bowed and turned away, following in Biggs's wake. Caroline's stare pursued him until an attractive young man took Liam's place. With overstated cheerfulness she accepted his partnership, and they began to dance.

Mac tracked Liam's progress across the ballroom and out of it. Through the back doors again; she caught a glimpse of another man standing with him—Chen, she recognized, before the door closed.

It didn't take much guesswork to figure out where Liam was headed, given his earlier conversation with Chen, and Mac was determined to find out what was going on. At the very least it had stopped him from proposing to Caroline; at worst it could expose Liam to dangers she didn't understand.

But she fully intended to.

Praying that Caroline was well occupied and not watching the doors, Mac sneaked out of the ballroom. She'd gone no more than a few paces into the hall when she ran right into someone, who caught her arms and quickly let her go.

"Mr.—Chen, isn't it?" she said, flustered.

He bowed. "And you are Miss MacKenzie. Mr. O'Shea told me to expect you."

"He did?" She tried to see over Chen's shoulder. "I mean . . . where did he go?"

"He has important business to attend to, Miss Mac-Kenzie. He asked me to request that you not attempt to follow him."

"Follow him where, Mr. Chen?" She looked beyond him again, wondering if she could get past. "He's doing something dangerous, isn't he?" *Something that could get him killed. . . .*

She made an exploratory feint to the left, and Chen smoothly intercepted her without appearing to move at all. "It would be difficult to kill Mr. O'Shea, Miss. Very difficult. I know—he saved my life once."

That arrested Mac's attention. "He did?"

"And more than mine. The work he does now is very important to those who would suffer otherwise. I beg you not to make it more difficult."

"What work? At least tell me that much."

"I regret that I cannot, except that it helps many who are innocent."

She bit down hard on her lip. "Mr. Chen—I'm afraid Liam is in more danger than—whatever it is he's doing. I'm afraid someone may be trying to kill him."

"Mr. O'Shea is aware of that. But I will watch him,

Miss MacKenzie. Please do not worry or attempt to pursue. It will only distress Mr. O'Shea."

Distress him? Distressed about her worrying, or her interfering? But Mac stifled her laugh and thought about Liam getting farther and farther away as Chen delayed her.

"I regret to be asking such a thing of you, Miss MacKenzie," Chen said solemnly, "but I must have your promise that you will not follow. Until then I cannot go with Mr. O'Shea and watch him."

Blackmail. Everyone was good at that around here. She had an idea that Chen was dead serious; he wasn't going to let her past. "Okay," she said with great reluctance. "My word. But please—"

"Miss MacKenzie, I would die before I let Mr. O'Shea come to harm."

There was no doubting his absolute sincerity. Mac was startled by the power of her immediate, gut-level response.

So would I, Chen. So would I.

But Chen was already running down the hall, the opposite way from the library. Mac fought an inner battle and kept herself from going after him. She had given her word.

Damn. But there *was* someone who might be able to shed some light on all this. If anyone had answers, it would be Perry.

She went back into the ballroom cautiously. The dance was winding down again, the couples scattering to the perimeter of the room. There were plenty of men, but none with swirling black capes as part of their costumes. Perry, it seemed, had made his escape.

What he'd said to Caroline during their dance remained a mystery, but Mac assumed he'd been working on her. His talk about "drastic measures" kept ringing in Mac's mind. If he didn't contact her again soon . . .

If Liam didn't show up safe and sound tomorrow morning . . .

Her troubled line of thought wasn't eased when she saw Caroline watching her from across the room—keenly and with uncharacteristic absorption. Mac had a feeling it was not a friendly examination. Her brief period of intimacy with Miss Gresham was probably at an end.

You've definitely blown it, Mac. But at least the ball was drawing to a close, and she wouldn't have to be standing here making nice when she wanted to be pacing in her hotel room, tearing her hair out and swearing a blue streak.

That was the best she could hope for tonight. She was damned sure she wasn't going to get any sleep.

MAC JERKED AWAKE in the chair by the fireplace. Someone was knocking on the door.

She glanced at the mantel clock. Ten A.M. So she had slept—for about an hour. Far too long, at that. She struggled to her feet and went hastily to answer the knock.

The bellman was not one she recognized. "Miss Mac-Kenzie?" he said with something like relief. "I have a letter for you." He passed an envelope into her hands and backed away.

"Wait a minute. Who is this fro—"

He wasn't hanging around to answer. In five seconds flat he was out of sight. Mac shut the door and tore at the flap of the envelope with shaking fingers. Her gaze went to the bottom of the single sheet of paper.

Perry. She blew out her breath and sat on the edge of the bed.

Rose, the note began:

You are perhaps aware that an emergency called Liam from the ball last night before he was able to propose to Caroline. He was not present at the close of the ball, and did not arrive home until the wee hours of the morning.

Thank God. Liam was all right. Mac read on:

However, this past hour I have confirmed that he has issued an invitation to Miss Gresham to join him this evening at the Poodle Dog for an intimate supper. Her chaperon, Mrs. Hunter, is to escort her. I have no doubt of his intentions.

The Poodle Dog? Mac remembered the name, though she wasn't sure if she'd heard it here or read it in a book. A fancy restaurant, if she recalled correctly.

This is your opportunity to make good on your hopes of renewing Liam's interest and showing him the intensity of your feelings. All you need do is follow my instructions carefully, and I will take care of the rest.

So. Perry probably didn't know about her little attempt last night. Damn.

I have already seen to it that Caroline will not receive Liam's invitation. I will send a carriage at 6 o'clock to deliver you to the Poodle Dog, earlier than the invitation specifies. A man will take you to a private room, and there you will wait for Liam's arrival.
I venture to presume that you understand what you

must do, and it may be your last chance. Drastic measures, Rose. But it is vital that I know if you are succeeding.

If your attempts have been insufficient to turn the tide, you must let me know at once so that I can be prepared to give any necessary aid. You will do this by summoning the waiter outside the room and asking him to bring in the wine. He is in my employ. You will drink and see that Liam does the same, and by that signal I will know our plan has failed.

Well, some of that didn't make a whole lot of sense. What was Perry going to do if she did fail? Burst in the room and come to her rescue?

As for the elaborate secret signals—it all sounded very underhanded and . . . sinister. But she did trust Perry. She had to.

She returned to the last paragraph of the letter.

If you succeed, however, I will declare myself openly to Caroline. I should have done so long ago. We are both taking great risks, Rose, but we are doing what is right.

Mac set down the letter and closed her eyes. If only she knew what "right" was. She certainly no longer knew her own heart.

CHAPTER SEVENTEEN

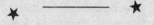

Come, fill the Cup,
and in the fire of Spring
The Winter garment of Repentance
  fling:
The Bird of Time has but a little way
To flye—and Lo! the Bird is on the
  Wing.

—OMAR KHAYYÁM

HE WAS EARLY, which was just the way he wanted it.

Liam took the stairs to the doors of the Old Poodle Dog two at a time. All day he'd kept himself busy: running with Norton and looking in on Bummer—who was recovering nicely, thanks to Chen's and the veterinarian's quick attention; consulting with Mr. Bauer, who as yet had not found a definite trace of Perry; seeing to his various neglected business interests and fulfilling long-delayed obligations to his associates and investors in San Francisco.

And mopping up the aftereffects of last night's disastrous raid. Only two of the seven girls had been rescued, and those almost by sheer luck; the rest had been spirited away before the group could find them, vanished into the very bowels of Chinatown where they might never surface again except as downtrodden prostitutes.

There had to have been an informant. Someone had known their objective and had given the tongs enough warning that the slave traders had taken extra and early precautions. It hadn't done any good to move the raid up by one day. None at all.

Liam's jaw tightened as he walked into the restaurant lobby. No use in repeating last night's attempt; the raiders must completely change their methods of operation if they were to get the tongs off guard again. And Liam could not be the one to make those changes. Not after tonight. All of that must be put behind him.

Because, after tonight, his oath to Edward Gresham would be fulfilled. The thought brought him little satisfaction.

After tonight Mac would be out of his life.

"M'sieur? May I be of service?"

The Poodle Dog's maître d' approached him with a diffident step, recognized him, and asked him to make himself comfortable while a waiter was summoned to show him to his room.

The first-floor dining room, always popular, was crowded with respectable couples and families; far too public a place for a proposal.

Liam's room was on the second floor. More private, but still eminently respectable. He'd be waiting when Amelia Hunter delivered Caroline, all proper and correct.

Caroline would certainly not know what went on in the rooms on the upper two floors—floors reserved for

. . . less reputable assignations between men of wealth and their paramours. She would be fully occupied in his. There would be a quiet dinner by candlelight, the proposal free of interruption, and then . . .

A waiter, circumspect as all Poodle Dog employees, arrived to lead Liam to the elevator. The man made no comment as the contraption made a rattling ascent to the second floor—and beyond, to the third. Even then it did not stop.

"There must be some mistake, my man," Liam said impatiently. "I am to meet a lady—"

The waiter's face remained impassive, but his eyes held a glint of knowing amusement. "Yes, sir. A lady, on the fourth floor."

If Caroline had been brought to the fourth floor, there certainly had been a mistake. The elevator doors opened on a plush, carpeted corridor. Gas lamps were turned very low. The place stank of genteel decadence.

The waiter led him down the hall to the room at the end. Liam knocked once, opened the door, and stepped inside.

A woman rose from the velvet couch where she'd been sitting and turned to him. A woman taller than Caroline, more slender, her hair the wrong color . . .

"Mac! What the hell are you doing here?"

The door closed discreetly behind them.

"Caroline asked me to come," Mac said, a little too quickly. "She said the three of us would be having dinner together."

A coldness washed through Liam, followed by raging heat. "Perry," he growled.

Mac didn't flinch, didn't show any sign of guilt. "What's going on?" she asked. "Have you finally seen Perry? Where did he go?"

He ignored her question. "Let me understand you,"

he said, moving farther into the room. "You claim that Caroline asked you to come here."

"That's what her note said."

For the first time Liam noticed Mac's gown: it displayed more décolletage than anything he'd seen on her before, and it hugged her figure like a second skin.

"Caroline," he said, "would not have asked you to accompany her. Not after last night."

They stared at each other, a lightning-flare of purely physical awareness arcing between them.

Her skirt rustled as she came toward him. "I didn't intend to hurt Caroline—if she did see us."

He snorted. "Have you been in a place like this before, Mac?"

She blinked at his change of subject. "Not exactly."

"Do you know what people do in this room?"

"Eat, I suppose— It is a dining room, isn't it?"

"A very private one." He circled the room until he was almost behind her.

"I figured," she said, turning to keep him in view.

"But this wasn't the room I reserved for tonight."

No. This parlor was a regular love nest. He'd been in rooms much like this one, here and in far less elegant locations. Dining—on food, in any case—was only one of the lesser attractions. There was probably a bed behind those red curtains if the wide settee didn't suffice for the purpose at hand.

He inspected the table of hors d'oeuvres that had been laid out beside the fireplace. Wineglasses, but no wine—an odd omission under the circumstances.

"Come now, Mac. You must know that the Poodle Dog is renowned in San Francisco. For its cuisine, its elegance, and the rooms above the second floor." He picked up a delicate appetizer and crushed it between his fingers. "Rooms like this one."

Mac glanced around, fidgeting, and suddenly joined

him by the table. She selected a cracker and put it down again. Nervous, his Mac—beginning to think she'd gotten herself in a little too deep.

"Such rooms are well known to the powerful men of our fair city," he drawled, "and to a certain class of women."

She picked up one of the wineglasses. "I guess they showed us to the wrong room."

"Did they?" His anger was fading, replaced by speculation and some other emotion less vehement but equally acute. Her nearness was reminding him of last night—and of the jungle. Heat. And passion.

"Mac, Mac," he said, shaking his head. "What do you want?"

She rolled the stem of the wineglass between her fingers. "Actually," she said, "I was rather hoping for a good French dinner."

"Are you . . . hungry?"

She set down the wineglass, provoking him with the deep brown warmth of her eyes. "Ravenous," she whispered. But she looked away again, and he took a moment to study her: the slenderness of her figure in the gown, the thrust of her breasts above the bodice, the pulse beating so intriguingly at the hollow of her throat, the paleness of her skin.

Damnation. Had Perry put her up to seducing him, making him forget all about Caroline and the proposal? Liam knew Mac hadn't met the Englishman at the Palace; Liam's contacts there had assured him of that. And he'd kept her close at the Gresham residence, with Caroline, since Perry's disappearance.

But Perry obviously wasn't gone from the city, fled after a botched murder attempt. He'd found out about Liam's invitation to Caroline. And now, one way or another, he was using Mac to stop the proposal.

"We both know Caroline's not coming," Liam said.

He found himself lifting his hand, touching Mac's cheek, brushing his fingers across her soft skin.

She was very still under his caress. For a seductress she was remarkably restrained. Except for the dress, which had clearly been chosen to display her charms. She hadn't been very adept at the business in the jungle, either.

But it *had* been good between them. Damn it to hell.

"It's not too late, Mac," he said.

"I'm glad you feel—"

"Not too late for you to leave." He dropped his hand, sucked in a lungful of air and let it out again. "Go," he rasped. "Go now, and we'll forget this happened."

"The way we forgot about the jungle?"

"How *did* it happen in the jungle?"

She jerked up her chin. "I was too much for you then, and I still am. That's why it's all words with you. That's what you fall back on when you can't do anything else."

"Why, you harridan—"

"I said it before. I scare you, Liam. Isn't that why you didn't finish that day in the jungle? Couldn't keep it up . . . the macho facade, I mean?"

His mouth dropped open. Did she actually think . . . The blood rushed into his face and, at the same time, to another place entirely.

The devil. Incredible as it seemed, her defiance and insults aroused him even as she derided his manhood. She had that much inexplicable power over him.

He remembered her passion in the jungle, that mingling of boldness and innocence that had puzzled and inflamed him, the catlike strength of her slender figure. He remembered the eagerness and wetness of her opening to him without maidenly modesty, no reluctance, wanting as he wanted.

And then her kiss in the ballroom, bringing it all back into sharp focus.

His trousers pulled tight over his groin. Words, was it? Did she think that was all he had to prove himself? He scanned the room behind Mac, noted the position of the wide velvet settee with its mounds of pillows. Part of his mind was coolly planning even as his body was hot and hard with desire.

Very well. He'd teach Mac a lesson—the one he'd never completed in the jungle. And this was a lesson he'd enjoy to the fullest.

"You doubt my manhood?" he challenged.

"There's little about you I don't doubt, O'Shea."

He moved toward her. She took a step back, paused, and retreated another step when he kept coming. Right toward the settee—right where he wanted her.

"Then you need proof, my thorny Rose," he said. The proof he intended to give her throbbed and ached for release.

Her smile was a little shaky. "And what would that be?"

A few more steps. She wasn't watching where she was going. "No mere words, Mac. Something you can touch. Something you can hold in your hands."

Her gaze flickered down. His erection strained under her inspection like a restive stallion. "I've, uh, always been a skeptic," she murmured.

"But not for much longer, I promise you."

At that moment the backs of her legs bumped the settee. With a soft grunt of surprise she sat down on her bustle. Liam wasted no time. He sprang the remaining few feet and pinned her down among the pillows.

Her first instinct was to fight. He could feel the tension in her body—a tension that relaxed all at once, as if she had commanded her wayward muscles to obey. Her eyes were wide, but not with fear.

Her eyes. He'd forgotten what beautiful eyes she had. A man could drown in them, dark and fathomless as they were, and lose himself forever.

But he wasn't here to lose himself. Carefully he began to unbutton her gloves, peeling them inch by inch away from her hands. When he had bared both of them, he kissed the undersides of her wrists.

"Proof, Mac," he said. He clasped her hand and guided it down between their bodies. She stiffened again.

"Surely *you're* not afraid?" he taunted.

Only her chin twitched as he helped her fingers find their mark. That hesitant contact was sweet agony. He felt her mold the cloth of his trousers to the shape of him, trace his length hesitantly and then with greater boldness.

"Okay," she said. "I'm beginning to be convinced."

"Of what?" He hissed as she touched him again, more boldly still. "Tell me, Mac."

"That, uh . . . you're not all talk."

"What else?"

"You're definitely of the masculine persuasion."

She was teasing him, the minx. He pressed her hand down harder and held it there. "And?"

"You must not find me too unattractive."

This time he had to stifle a laugh. She had turned the tables on him again. "You're right," he admitted. "Even I have to accept the proof of that." He let his free hand slide down from her wrist to settle just below the swell of her bodice. "You might even find more ways to encourage me."

"And what exactly . . . did you have in mind?"

He nuzzled the side of her neck. She smelled clean and brisk, like sea air. "You have an imagination, Mac." His fingers negotiated the gentle slope of her breasts. "Use it."

Her back arched beneath him. "You might not like some of the ways I've been using i—"

But she broke off on a gasp as he kissed the place where her breasts met the edge of her bodice. Her skin was tender and thoroughly feminine here, unmarked by sun or weather. She made a muted little sound—encouragement or protest, he couldn't tell and didn't care—as he unfastened the top button of her bodice, and then the next. She wore no corset, no bust improver, nothing but a chemise underneath. It was a simple matter for him to ease her breasts from their scanty confinement.

They were sweet and ripe for kissing, lifted and supported by the bodice that no longer protected them. The dark areolas of her nipples tightened as if in anticipation.

"You threw down the gauntlet last night," he said, cupping her breasts. He kissed the angle of her jaw. "You've been doing it ever since I brought you back to San Francisco. And now I think I'm going to take it up."

Her nipples puckered under his hands. He kissed her throat, her shoulder, the last level plain of fair skin above her breasts. And then he took what he wanted so badly to taste. He covered one breast with his mouth and suckled, rolling her nipple against his tongue, licking and teasing until Mac's head was tossing against the pillows.

When he'd had his fill of one breast he moved to the other, savored it, made her shudder and squirm and thrust up against him.

He wanted very badly to undress her, to feel her naked body writhing under his, to make her vulnerable, to possess her completely. But this was not the place, or the time. There was no need to go so far. Not to get what he must have.

He continued to kiss and nip her neck, her chin, the corners of her lips while he reached down to gather the bunched hem of her skirt in his free hand.

She didn't protest. Even Mac was helpless at a man's touch. At *his* touch. He had her skirt up to her knees and his hand underneath before her body recognized his intrusion.

"That's . . . not a gauntlet you're taking up," she said hoarsely.

"Isn't this what you wanted, Mac?" he said, catching her lower lip between his teeth.

He found the ties of her underdrawers, parted the delicate fabric and found moist skin. More than moist; she was wet, hot and wet and ready. He fumbled urgently with the buttons of his trousers.

"I warned you, Mac. You started this fire. Now you're going to put it out."

Her eyes closed as he pushed her legs apart and positioned himself between them. Acres of heavy skirt and a lacy froth of muslin were no impediment; he had her where he wanted her. The mere anticipation of taking her like this, so unexpectedly, so hard and fast, excited him almost beyond endurance. It could never be like this with Caroline. Would never be.

"Tell me you made a mistake," he taunted. "Admit you're no match for me, and I'll let you go."

He waited, breath suspended, for her answer. But he hadn't read her wrong. Nothing had changed since the jungle. His memory hadn't played tricks on him, hard as he'd tried to forget. She grinned like a she-cat and grabbed a handful of his shirt.

"Forget it, O'Shea. You'll never hear me say uncle."

A wild, triumphant joy seared through him then, almost euphoric, as if he'd discovered some fantastic ruin never seen by civilized man. That elation beat in his blood, drove his body in a primal dance of hunger and

victory. Mac arched against him, spurring him on. In.
One stroke, one long, deep stroke. . . .

"Liam?"

Through a fog of lust he heard his name. Mac had
gone very still, clutching his shirt in both hands, her
gaze fixed past his shoulder.

Toward the door.

"Oh . . ." The faint, disembodied voice trailed off
into a whimper. Liam almost ignored it, almost flouted
the barrier of Mac's suddenly rigid body. He *wanted*,
and he always took what he wanted—

Mac planted both hands against his chest and
shoved. In his startlement he jerked back, watched in
blank confusion as she grabbed at her skirts and pulled
them down over her legs.

"Oh, my," another, older feminine voice said behind
them.

Liam turned his head. The door was open. Two people stood on the threshold. The younger woman's
pretty face was pale except for two vivid spots of color
in her cheeks. The elder looked like a cat who'd gotten
into the cream.

The elder was Mrs. Hunter, Caroline's chaperon.

And the girl who stared at Liam with horror in her
eyes was Caroline.

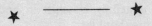

CHAPTER EIGHTEEN

Times go by turns,
and chances change by course,
From foul to fair,
from better hap to worse.

—ROBERT SOUTHWELL

ICE DOUSED THE fire in Liam's blood. He turned his back to the couple and buttoned his trousers with unsteady fingers.

This was a farce, a nightmare, a joke. It must be. Mac scooted off the other side of the settee, ears crimson, trying to smooth her hopelessly creased gown. Liam turned with as much dignity as he could muster.

"Caroline," he began.

Caroline had gone from flushed to white. Her little fists were clenched as she pushed away from her aunt's offered comfort.

"You . . . you scoundrel," she said with quiet, astonishing ferocity. And then she whirled and swept out the door, Mrs. Hunter at her heels.

The resulting quiet lasted all of an instant before it

was broken by yet another intruder. The waiter who'd shown Liam to the room poked his head cautiously through the door and walked in, bearing a silver tray with a chilled bottle of wine.

"Your wine, madam," he said.

"Get out," Liam growled.

The man set the tray down on the table and obeyed with alacrity. Liam strode to the table and picked up the bottle. It was already uncorked. He splashed a liberal portion into one of the wineglasses.

He hardly heard Mac come up behind him. Her hand was shaking as she reached for the bottle and a glass and followed his example.

He lifted his glass to her. "Congratulations, Mac."

But she gave him no answer. No smile of victory, of triumph complete. He tilted the glass to his mouth and prepared to drown himself in the contents.

The first taste told him something was wrong. The second assured him of it. He spat into the glass and was slamming it down when he saw Mac preparing to drink.

The wine never made it to her lips. Most of it soaked the front of her bodice as he swatted the glass away, and the rest stained the fine imported carpet at her feet.

She stared at him in shock. Genuine shock, not in the least feigned. She hadn't known the wine was drugged.

With frigid, bitter calm he handed her an embroidered napkin.

"Get yourself cleaned up, Mac," he commanded. "It's over."

OVER.

His brain was pounding to that infernal word, just as it had all night. It was limned in blinding light that burned through his lids. He opened his eyes a crack, winced, and tried to roll over. The solid bulk of an Irish wolfhound trapped him in place.

"Norton," he groaned. "Get off the bed."

A tail thumped against his arm with enough impact to encourage a more rapid recovery. His mouth tasted abominable. He couldn't remember a bloody thing since last night . . . had it been last night? Since Caroline had walked in on him and Mac.

Liam groaned again and cursed into his whiskey-scented pillow.

"Mr. O'Shea?"

Even Chen's soft speech rang like a struck anvil in Liam's ears. He propped himself up on his elbows and glared at his servant. "What time is it?"

Chen bowed and set the tray with tea and morning paper on the table beside the bed. "Three o'clock in the afternoon, Mr. O'Shea."

Liam massaged the skin between his brows. Hell, he'd lost most of a day. He was wearing the same clothes he'd had on last night at the Poodle Dog—everything but his shoes, which Chen had probably removed.

"When did I come in?" he asked.

"Just before dawn." Chen lifted his sleeve and poured a cup of hot tea. The smell of it—green tea with herbs, which Chen insisted was good for a hangover—was already beginning to clear Liam's head.

Before dawn. It was starting to come back. The fiasco at the Poodle Dog, the way he'd numbly flagged down a hack for Mac and watched her drive off, his determination to go in exactly the opposite direction. A night of riotous dissipation along the Barbary Coast—the details of the latter remained blessedly obscure. It'd been some time since he'd gone down to the dives and hells of the Coast.

Chen cleared his throat discreetly. "Mrs. O'Shea, you asked me when you first returned to inquire as to Miss Gresham's well being."

Liam didn't remember, but he was glad he'd had that much sense. He paused to fight off a wave of dizziness and threw his legs over the bed. "And?"

"Miss Gresham is receiving no callers. Mrs. Hunter was quite adamant. I told Mr. Biggs to make certain that Mr. Sinclair has no access, should he reappear."

Thank God for Chen. "You think of everything when I can't think at all. Thank you."

"You honor me, Mr. O'Shea. There is more. Mrs. Hunter gave me this note to deliver to you."

Liam recognized the perfume and the fine paper. Caroline. He shook his head to clear it and tore open the envelope.

The delicate, careful hand was indeed Caroline's, but the note was brief and almost lacking in feminine flourish.

The meaning, however, was manifest. She wanted him to come to her house, tonight. She wanted to resolve matters between them. She was giving him another chance.

A strange, heavy feeling settled in the pit of his stomach. It felt like disappointment, and that was sheer madness. He had to set things right.

But as he rose from the bed he felt as if he were about to march to his death on the gallows, to be hung on a rope made of lace and blond curls and acres of petticoat.

He drove the phaeton to the Gresham's in a state of complete mental blankness.

Mrs. Hunter answered the door. Biggs was nowhere in evidence.

"I've come to see Caroline," Liam said tersely.

"I know." She pursed her lips and let him into the

house with obvious reluctance. Her attitude struck
Liam as ironic; she'd done a poor enough job of watching over her charge.

If she hadn't been in on last night's fiasco with Perry.
She would have to be questioned, but now was not the
time.

"Where is she?" he asked.

Mrs. Hunter tilted her chin toward the stairway. Her
disapproval burned into his back as he climbed the
stairs. The house was eerily hushed. He reached Caroline's sitting room door and knocked, expecting to find
her waiting. There was no answer.

"Liam?"

He turned to face the open door of Caroline's bedroom.

She was waiting for him, sure enough. Waiting in a
sheer wrap that barely concealed the lacy white chemise
she wore beneath. A chemise that revealed the thrust of
her breasts, the roundness of her thigh sliding under
satin. Her feet were bare, and her hair hung loose
around her shoulders.

"Good God," he choked. "What the hell are you doing?"

Her voice was low—too low, forced into a register
that made it sound like a parody of Mac's husky alto.
"Waiting for you."

Liam felt his face flame, but his body was chilled
through. "Cover yourself," he rasped.

"Why? Don't you think I'm beautiful?"

Oh, yes, she was beautiful. Perfect. Any man would
want her.

Any man but the one with her now. In the dim light
he thought he saw the shape of a phantom standing
behind his ward; taller, red-haired, tragic in spite of her
gaiety. Siobhan.

They were not alike. Nothing alike. But Caroline

might have been his sister standing there, ready to give herself to a man, with no idea of the consequences, because it seemed daring and grown-up and . . . no, not a way out of poverty. Not for Caroline. She'd never known want, and never would.

"I know you—want me," Caroline said, stumbling over the word, as if she only vaguely guessed what it meant. "You were going to ask me to marry you."

Yes. He was going to ask her for the sake of his oath. Never thinking beyond the ceremony because his mind refused to dwell on what must follow.

"Liam," she whispered. "Look at me. *Look* at me."

He couldn't. There were ghosts in his way, the ghosts of defeat and those he had lost, phantoms of all the things he'd thought he wanted.

But Caroline was not among them. He did not want her. He couldn't. He knew it with a certainty beyond any he'd known in his life. He could protect her, cherish her, care for her. He could fulfill his vow. But he could never love her.

She wanted something he had forgotten the meaning of, had lost years ago in the tenements of New York.

Caroline moved closer. She put her hands on his chest before he could walk away.

"Kiss me," she said. "Kiss me like you did at Cliff House."

He caught her wrists. "No." It was the only word that would come. "No—"

"You want *her*." Her chest rose and fell rapidly. "You want her, not me."

He held her shaking shoulders gently and set her back. He stroked her hair once, only the ghost of a touch, and left her.

He could hear her sobs as he descended the stairs.

Mrs. Hunter was waiting, perched on the settee in the music room. "Go to her, Amelia," he said tonelessly.

"She needs you." She started for the stairs and he stayed her with a gesture. "Keep Caroline inside and admit no one. Do I make myself clear?"

He didn't wait for her answer. He walked the length of the hall, paused at the door, and slowly opened it.

The sun was beginning to set. Soon it would be dark—a time of oblivion, if he chose it to be. He could go back to the Coast and drink himself insensible, or take his riding horse and Norton and go racing along the beach until they could run no more.

But tomorrow everything would still be as it was.

He started toward the carriage house and had gone only a few steps when a man emerged from the garden shrubbery.

"Mr. O'Shea," he said.

Liam stopped, instantly wary. "Bauer. What are you doing here?"

The investigator was coolly professional as always. "Your man Chen told me you might be here," he said. "I have news that might interest you."

"Out with it, then."

"I've located Mr. Sinclair."

Liam took a sharp step forward. "Where is he?"

"I tracked him to Chinatown. He was incognito, but once I recognized him I was able to follow him to one of the primary tong houses."

A cold chill numbed Liam's body. "And?"

"He apparently met with Yung Po. I don't know the nature of the conversation, but Sinclair seemed satisfied with the meeting."

Yung Po. One of the most powerful tong lords, a man who controlled a quarter of Chinatown, who dealt in bribery and opium and, most especially, girls to fill the houses of prostitution. Girls Liam's group had often been able to rescue—until the last raid, which had ended in near disaster.

A raid that had been foiled by an informant. Until now Liam had suspected one of the group, or someone closely connected.

Perry had never been one of the group, but he'd been close to Liam. Close enough to learn of the raids if he'd been interested enough.

San Francisco was filled with city officials and police more than willing to be bribed to overlook laws broken by men like Yung Po. Some of them profited even more directly by the trade in opium and slaves. Perry was no official, but he had friends all throughout the city. If he had special knowledge he could sell to the tongs for a cut of their income—if he were working for the tongs and had promised to get a certain troublesome Irishman out of the way once and for all, it would doubly serve his purpose.

"When did you see him?" Liam demanded.

"Only last night. I couldn't find you until now. But I talked to a few men in Chinatown, and Sinclair's met with Po before. He was first seen at the tong house less than a week ago."

Liam closed his eyes. Only a few days before the raid.

"I've had men trailing Sinclair," Bauer said, "but he went underground somewhere in Chinatown. It's very easy to get lost there if you want to disappear. The minute he surfaces again I'll send word."

As if that could undo anything that had happened. Perry was more than a would-be murderer, more than a man who'd callously court an innocent girl for her fortune. He'd used Mac and then set her out as bait, indifferent to the harm that might come to her as a result. And he'd set himself to profit by the sale of children into lives of sexual slavery.

"Listen to me, Bauer," he said coldly. "I want you to have men watching this house twenty-four hours a day. I don't care how much money you spend or what steps you take, but I want Miss Gresham safe from him. I've given orders that Caroline is not to leave the house. If Mrs. Hunter goes out she's to be followed."

"As you wish. And when I find Sinclair?"

Liam stared blindly into the garden. "He's my problem. I'll deal with him."

"He's a dangerous man, Mr. O'Shea."

"So am I, Bauer. So am I."

Bauer had the good sense to leave then, melting away without so much as the crunch of a footstep on the gravel path. The chill in Liam's belly remained long after Bauer was gone, long after Liam retrieved the phaeton from the Gresham groom and drove out the gates.

He knew, now, where he needed to go. He'd done all he could for Caroline, but he had a second responsibility. One he'd never asked for. A woman who'd been in danger three times for his sake, whom he had to make safe in spite of her conniving ways and dubious motives.

He drove into the Grand Court of the Palace and his icy numbness washed away on the fierce tide of an emotion he understood.

It was impossible to be numb in Mac's presence, impossible to forget he was alive. She flouted him, defied him, forced him to fight. And it was a fight he wanted now, a fight to make his blood beat hard and his wits regain their edge.

Not by a single shift in his expression did he reveal his purpose as he left his team in the care of hotel staff and went in search of the concierge. A quiet word and a sum of coin earned assurances of discretion and privacy.

Then he was taking the stairs two at a time, refusing the sluggish dignity of the elevator, and standing before Mac's door.

It was locked. He thought better of breaking it down and confined himself to an ordinary knock.

Mac opened the door, took one look at his face, and started to shut it again. He wedged his foot in the door and pushed through. She retreated a few steps and then held her ground, braced like a matador waiting for the charge of a particularly nasty bull.

Liam closed the door behind him and turned the key in the lock. He looked her up and down, taking in the lacy muslin chemise that was her sole garment. His body instantly tightened. He shrugged out of his coat and tossed it over a chair.

"Well, Mac," he said softly. "I see you're dressed to welcome me."

And if her gaze, brilliant and dark, was anything but welcoming, he knew that was about to change.

CHAPTER NINETEEN

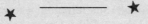

And the best of all ways
To lengthen our days
Is to steal a few hours
from the night, my dear.

—THOMAS MOORE

MAC KNEW SHE was in trouble. Her mind knew it, anyway; her body had an entirely different opinion.

She'd been expecting this sooner or later, but somehow Liam had still managed to take her by surprise. Here she was, wearing practically nothing and confronting around two hundred pounds of angry male.

Mac backed up toward the bed and felt behind her for the muslin wrapper she'd left there. She tugged it on without haste. He watched every move she made with a dark hunger—hunger made more potent by barely suppressed anger. Heat coiled and pooled low in her body.

"I guess you came here to . . . to talk about yesterday," she said.

"Talk, Mac? Is that what you think I want?" He

grabbed his tie and loosened it with a yank that spoke
volumes.

Okay, Mac. You can handle this. She moved to the
other side of the bed. "I don't suppose it'll do much
good to tell you that I didn't expect Caroline to walk in
on us last night."

"No." He hurled his tie to the floor and began to
work on the buttons of his shirt. "But we do have some
unfinished business."

Mac watched his undressing with unwilling fascination. "All I wanted was . . . um . . . to distract
you—"

"You succeeded." He unfastened his left shirt cuff.

Only too well, it seemed. Perry had set things up very
carefully. Without telling Mac the full extent of his
plans.

"I'm sorry it happened that way," she said.
"Whether or not you can accept it."

He continued undressing with slow, jerky motions.
"Did you know about the wine?"

"The wine?"

"That it was drugged," Liam said.

"Drugged?" She felt a little dizzy and reached for the
mahogany bedpost. The wine had been meant as a signal that she wasn't succeeding—a signal she'd never
given, botched when the waiter had walked in without
being summoned.

"The wine was drugged?" she repeated.

He looked up at her, his shirttail loose at his waist.
"You didn't know," he said. "You tried to drink it after
I did."

Good grief. Mac had a vague memory of pouring
herself some wine, so confused by her own emotions
that she'd only wanted to drown them. Liam had
smacked the glass from her hand.

And she'd thought it was out of anger.

"Perry," Liam said, striding to the window. "He masterminded it all. It wasn't enough for him that Caroline saw us together. He wanted me out of the way, and he didn't care if you were hurt in the doing of it." He stared out at the city. "I know you met me at the Poodle Dog on his advice.

"But you didn't know about the wine. Or the carriage. The axle could have broken anytime once we started to race." His fingers worked into fists on the windowsill. "You could have been killed."

"I . . . heard of the accident," Mac said, still struggling with shock. "You weren't hurt—" She moved toward Liam and stopped herself. "You think that Perry set up the accident and this drugged wine, and I was working with him?"

"Damn it, Mac!" He swung to face her. "He's used you, deceived you just as he did me. You were a handy tool, no more." He made a low, bitter sound. "I had him investigated before our last expedition, when he began to show interest in Caroline. He wasn't merely a younger son cut off from his family's fortune, as I first suspected. He worked for the British government before I met him. As a spy—probably an assassin. He had no scruples. I went to Guatemala to warn him away from Caroline."

Mac shivered and sat down on the bed. A spy? It certainly explained Perry's ability to get information and disappear so effectively. But an assassin . . .

"I don't believe it," she said, preparing herself for a hopeless argument. "I don't believe that he tried to kill you, whatever his past. Yes, I met him—at the ball. And he was the one who told me about the carriage accident. I don't know how he found out about it, but he didn't have to volunteer the information. Especially if he considered me disposable." She concentrated on keeping her words calm and level and logical. "He knew you'd consider the accident proof that he *was* behind the attempt in the jungle, and he predicted how you'd react. But I chose to trust him. I wish I could give you a better reason than gut feeling and instinct." She waited for the lash of Liam's scorn and disbelief. "If I thought for a moment that he really meant to hurt you—"

"You'd what?" He examined her face intently.

She swallowed and looked down at her lap. "Isn't there something else you should be worrying about— like who's really trying to kill you?"

His footsteps whispered on the carpet. "Do you mean the tongs, Mac? You overheard my meeting with Chen in the Gresham library."

"Yes. Enough to know you were on your way to do something dangerous." She sat up straighter, hoping for information. "I know the tongs are criminal organizations that practically run most of Chinatown, but—"

"They deal in human cargo, Mac. Girls brought illegally from China, bribed and coerced into leaving their homes, too young to fight or to know what they're getting into." He strode across the room and back again with brittle anger. "Children ruined by men who see them as commodities, whores to be used until they die of disease or violence or despair. A very profitable enterprise."

The passion in his voice was more eloquent than any mere explanation could have been. Mac was almost humbled by it. This was a part of himself he kept hidden, a part that had revealed itself only in his obsessive desire to protect Caroline—and sometimes Mac. A part she still didn't understand.

"Then . . . that's what you were doing the night of the ball, wasn't it?" she asked. "Something to do with these girls. Raids. Saving them—"

"From their masters and from the corrupt outsiders

who'd take their own cut of this obscenity. The law is all but useless in stopping it. For a year the band's been successful. Until the night of the ball, when the raid went sour. When someone betrayed us to the tongs."

The informant. "Then you do have other enemies. These tong people—"

"And their ally," he said. "Peregrine Sinclair."

Oh, God. "Was he part of your group?"

"He wasn't involved. He didn't have to be." Liam's mouth set in a harsh smile. "I've had him watched since I returned to San Francisco. He was clever, but not clever enough. My men saw him with one of the foremost tong bosses. He was the one who undermined the last raid. He's doing the tong's dirty work for them and for himself at the same time."

Mac closed her eyes. Impossible. That Perry was so utterly villainous, so heartless, so capable of deceiving her. . . .

But even if he wasn't, Liam's danger had been real, and deadly. He could have died in that carriage accident, or on one of these raids. Cold lightning raced along her nerves.

"Are you finally convinced that your ally is a blackguard?" Liam demanded.

She couldn't lose faith now. "No."

He slammed his fist against the wall, shaking the light fixture overhead. "He could have killed you without a second thought. You played Perry's game and helped rob a girl of her innocence—"

"I *what*?" Mac jumped to her feet. This conversation was moving almost too fast for her to follow, but she refused to be left behind. "You mean Caroline? You never let me get close enough. What happened? Did she finally shatter your image of the delicate, naive Miss Gresham? Did it finally get into your head that no one can protect anyone from life the way you wanted to protect her?"

She regretted her words as soon as she saw his stricken expression.

"I'm sorry, Liam," she said. "Truly sorry. I never wanted to cause you pain—"

Even if she'd been listening she couldn't have heard his footsteps, so quietly did he move. She looked up just as he reached her, as he caught her chin in his hand.

"Don't worry, Mac," he said. "You'll make it up to me."

She felt the heat reborn in him, burning away that all-too-brief insecurity, the doubt he couldn't allow himself.

"Were you afraid I'd abandoned you?" he asked, stroking her cheek with startling tenderness. "I'd never have done that. I had plans to see you settled in a safe place, where you could live as you wished. You didn't give me a chance to tell you. But now it doesn't matter, does it?" He touched her lips with a calloused finger while his other hand began to work at the waistband of his trousers. "I don't give a damn anymore who you are or what you've done. I don't care if you worked for Perry or even if you're crazy. You succeeded, Mac. You made me want you."

The top button of his trousers popped free of the buttonhole. He let them fall, giving Mac an eyeful of magnificently aroused male. She remembered the way that sleek hardness had felt under her hand, and against her—

"No need to stare, darlin'. You'll see plenty and get a lot more before we're through."

Darlin'. How long had it been since he'd called her that? Back in the jungle, when he'd played *her* for a fool. . . .

"It works better when you don't try to woo a woman

with intimidation," she said, managing a semblance of sarcastic bravado.

"You didn't need wooing yesterday," he said, trailing his finger to the hollow of her throat. "Pretty speeches are wasted on you. It's something a little rougher that excites you, isn't it?" He'd returned to that deep purr that made his blunt words unbearably erotic, lethally carnal. "Last night you were ready for me, wet for me." He rested his palm on the swell of her breast. "You were right when you said it was good between us. It'll be better this time. This time we won't stop."

Her mouth went dry, robbing her of a retort.

"Shall we find out if I'm right?" he said, kicking his trousers free.

Still she couldn't move, frozen in an agony of terror and desire. Terror, not of him, but of herself. Of the wild feelings he aroused in her as he aroused her body, spinning her out of control. Of how desperately she *did* want him. Wanted him to make love to her, all the way.

"You think you've won," Liam taunted, herding her back to the bed. "But there's always a price for victory, darlin'. Take it from me."

Yes, there was a price. Mac had only begun to understand in the Poodle Dog, when he'd almost taken her there on the settee.

It was hunger: a physical, aching need—the woman she'd never fully recognized within herself, coming to painful life inside her awakened body. Liam had done that. He had that power over her, a power too terrible to give to a man she should never have known.

"It'll be good, Mac," Liam murmured. She felt the play of muscles in his thighs as he carried her with him onto the bed. He stretched out beside her, his hand resting on her hip in masculine possessiveness.

She lay still while he ran his hand down her muslin-clad thigh and under the hem of the chemise. *Well,*

Mac, she told herself, trying to maintain her calm, *look at this rationally. You do want him. You can enjoy this for what it is. Exactly as he will.*

Her thoughts fragmented as Liam's fingers worked along bare skin. She bit the inside of her lip as he found what he was looking for and stroked her—once, again, a third time. His fingers found no resistance, no friction. He withdrew, but she felt no relief.

"Ah, darlin'," he said, "you don't have to say a thing." He waited until she met his gaze and then deliberately licked her wetness from his fingers.

The gesture almost undid her.

"You want me inside you," he murmured. "You want me to take you hard and fast, the way I would have done it last night. Admit it." He pinned her down, his erection pressed to her inner thighs, his breath hot on her ear. "The woman in you wants to be tamed, and there's only one way and one man to do it."

He began to stroke her again, pushing her chemise up over her thighs, her hips, to her waist. "You took from me. Now I'll do the taking. But you'll enjoy it, darlin', I promise you."

His touch was expert. It couldn't have been more effective. In spite of all his threats of "hard and fast," he didn't hurry. His finger slipped inside her, moving with a rhythmic omen of what was to come. She jerked and arched against him.

"That's it, darlin'. Give in." He pushed her chemise higher still, and then it was over her head and she was naked. Defenseless. His mouth found her breast, nipping and suckling. A moan betrayed her, and then there was no more point in pretending.

And no more passively lying there like a frightened virgin—even if the latter designation was almost true. She'd be damned before she gave him all the advantages in this affair. There'd be two to tango, and she wasn't going to let him forget the experience.

With a heave and a lift of one knee she encouraged him to shift position. While he was still off-balance she rolled, carrying him with her, until she was on top and straddling him.

He didn't know what'd hit him. She reached down between them and found his prominence. No confusion there. She had him where she wanted him.

"Since we're on the subject of confessions," she said softly, "I think it's your turn."

She smothered his retort with a kiss designed to get his attention. She was a very fast learner; he looked almost dazed when she came up for air.

"Admit it," she said. "Admit that you wanted me in the jungle as much as you want me now."

She closed her hand around him, worked her fingers up and down his length until he shuddered as she had shuddered at his caresses. "Admit," she said fearlessly, recklessly bold, "that you want me the way you've never wanted any woman before."

She waited. An eternity passed.

"Yes," he said. He trapped her arms and pulled her down flat on top of him. "Yes, damn you."

And he proved it with his kiss.

CHAPTER TWENTY

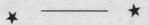

*One crowded hour of glorious life
Is worth an age without a name.*

—THOMAS OSBERT MORDAUNT

THEY DANCED.

No decorous waltz this time, but a wild and primitive duet that began with a kiss and followed only one inescapable rhythm.

It didn't matter that he was experienced and Mac had almost none. She knew her instincts were good when he groaned at her touch, at the stroke of her tongue on his neck and chest and belly. She gloried in the power of her newfound womanhood.

But Liam wasn't quite prepared to surrender his traditional masculine prerogatives. When matters had progressed to the greatest extremity he rolled Mac beneath him again, parted her legs, and entered with a deep, bold stroke.

He'd been right. She wanted him hard and fast. There was no pain, though she'd been celibate for more years than she wanted to count. He made her forget there was such a thing as celibacy. He made her forget there was anything beyond this rapture, this completion, this unbearable joy of taking and being taken.

But it was more than that. A shifting had begun inside her, and she almost grasped the meaning of it before Liam drove it from her mind again.

Plain, skinny Mac was gone, reborn like a phoenix out of the fires of passion, from the conflagration that consumed them both and left them weary and tangled in each other's arms.

For a moment suspended out of all time they were in harmony, all conflict forgotten, content beyond joy. Mac took that moment and built a box around it within her mind, a case of velvet and satin and clouds and dreams. Wherever, *when*ever she went, it would go with her, protected and eternal.

She didn't mind when Liam slept afterward. She studied his face, so unguarded in sleep. Almost gentle. Almost innocent. She could see the boy he'd been, the boy who had existed before the school of hard knocks got hold of him. A boy who'd fought all his life and didn't know how to stop.

But there was so much she didn't know about him. So much she badly wanted to know. *Who* that boy had been. What he had suffered. How that suffering had built his obsessions and his need to save and protect those he thought incapable of caring for themselves.

Like Caroline. Like the slave girls. Irrational in one obsession, noble in the other.

Wanting even to protect *her*. Mac, who'd never had anyone but Homer try to protect her from anything.

Liam had called her jealous. She was—jealous of the secrets Liam kept so firmly locked within himself.

She brushed Liam's hair from his forehead and immediately flashed back to that time in the jungle when he'd come so close to death.

God.

Her hand trembled, and she snatched it away before she woke him. Suddenly, so suddenly, she understood what had changed in her heart even as Liam had filled her body.

It was impossible. It was crazy. It was true.

She rocked back and closed her eyes. When had it happened? How? Had it been during one of their numerous verbal battles? At Cliff House, when she first began to understand him, or at the ball, when she'd found the nerve to make her move and felt the depth of his response?

Or had it begun the first time she saw him in the rain, a photograph come to life—a man she would never have met if not for a fluke of time and fate? A man who drove her crazy, a dyed-in-the-wool male chauvinist, arrogant as all get-out and totally oblivious to the feelings of any other human being. . . .

No. Not every human being. Just the girl who'd been his ward and the woman who loved him.

Mac got up, pulled on her chemise, and wandered to the bay windows. The sky was patterned with scudding clouds against the darkness, as unquiet as her thoughts. The city was likewise dark except for the streetlamps and houses beyond the commercial district. Dark and alien. Not her city. Never her city.

The room was chilly. She wrapped her arms around herself. Already the magic she and Liam had created was fading, bowing to reality. Was this what other women had to deal with . . . this clutching terror, this unfathomable sadness?

Those hypothetical other women had choices she didn't have. Because sometime in the near future, once a few remaining complicated matters were cleared up, she wouldn't be needed here any longer. Her task would be complete.

She could go home. Back to the place she belonged, just as Liam belonged here.

Damn it. She *wouldn't* feel sorry for herself. She'd gone into this with her eyes wide open. So had Liam.

The gulf of a hundred years separated them, and that was the least of the barriers between them. She'd done the best she could to foul things up for Liam. He could never accept the full truth of her reasons, intellectually or emotionally. His future would always be her past.

But there was *now*. She could make the most of now. Liam had stamina—a heroic amount of it, and the night was still young. For an egocentric scoundrel he was a surprisingly considerate lover.

If it were only sex she'd have nothing to regret.

She started back toward the bed, slipping the chemise from her shoulders. She would wake Liam in the best way she knew how, and do a little more forgetting in his arms. . . .

But she found him staring at the rosette on the ceiling, the bedsheets tangled around his hips.

"You're awake," she said awkwardly.

"Always the keen observer." He stretched, a flex and crack of muscles that Mac watched with fascination. Yes, where he was concerned she was a very keen observer. Not that she wanted to be too obvious about it.

She sat down on the opposite edge of the bed, unexpectedly shy. He resumed his rapt study of the ceiling fixture.

"I've been thinking, Mac," he said.

She pulled her muslin wrapper over herself like a blanket. "Oh?"

"Yes. About what's to be done with you after I deal with Perry."

"Deal with Perry," she echoed warily.

"I want you out of the way, where you can't be hurt. I've already made certain that he can't get anywhere near Caroline. But you . . ." He rolled onto his side and propped himself on his elbow, frowning. "You'll have to leave town, Mac."

"While you kill Perry?"

He flinched almost imperceptibly, and that gave her hope. "You know I can't let him go," he said.

His words effectively banished any hope of renewing their physical communion. The atmosphere in the room distinctly favored war, not love.

"You can't do it, Liam," she said, holding his gaze.

He sat up against the headboard and folded his arms across his chest. "Did you think that because I slept with you I'd be taking your orders?"

"No. But I had hoped maybe . . ." She twisted a handful of sheet in her fingers. "I thought you might finally be willing to consider me a friend."

His silence made the laugh that followed all the more cutting. "A *friend*? That's a conversation we've had before. I've a much better use in mind for you."

" 'Use' is the operative term, isn't it?" she said bleakly.

He wasn't angry. To the contrary, he had become absorbed in studying her anatomy. "I think you enjoyed my use of you. As I enjoyed yours of me."

She couldn't deny it, or the way her body responded to the growing heat in his stare. Her long hesitation must have encouraged him. He reached across the bed for her, almost lazily, so sure of himself and his sensual power.

"Come, darlin'," he said. "It's not a fight I'm after. You're not my enemy."

She let go of the sheet and slid off the bed and out of his reach. "That's reassuring. I'm not your friend and I'm not your enemy. What does that make me, Liam?"

For a time he lay stretched across the bed, unmoving,

as if he were giving her question due consideration. "It makes you a woman. Isn't that enough for you?"

"Not by your definition." She fought her anger even as she felt it filling the places in her heart that were so easily hurt by his scorn.

He rolled off the bed, magnificently naked and not in the least self-conscious about it. He strolled toward her. "And I thought taking you to bed would tame you."

"Like a good little Victorian woman?" she asked sweetly. "Like Caroline?"

He stopped. "Caroline is different. I swore an oath to watch over her. Gresham trusted me." He laughed. "Trust is a very rare commodity, Mac. I trusted Perry once."

"But you don't trust Caroline."

"She can't be trusted. She has a dangerous wildness in her makes her an easy victim of men like Perry."

There was a shift in his tone, the faintest crack in his implacability. Mac got up and walked toward him, step by hesitant step.

"You sound as if . . . you've seen this happen before."

At first she thought he wouldn't answer. But he turned his head toward the window, and she saw his profile: it made her think of stone that appeared impregnable but could be shattered with a single well-placed blow.

"I know," he said, as if he were speaking to someone only he could see. "She'd put herself into their hands, and they'd use her, destroy her, until she ended her life on some street corner selling her body. . . ."

He was no longer talking about Caroline. He no longer seemed to be in the room at all, but somewhere far away in time and space.

"It was someone . . . close to you, wasn't it?" she asked.

No reaction. No questioning of her meaning, no anger, no mockery. Only a flat, frigid harshness that covered something unbearable.

"Siobhan," he said at last.

"That's a beautiful name."

"She was beautiful once. It was beaten out of her."

"By . . . a man?"

"By life."

"Who was she?"

He looked over his shoulder, the familiar cynicism back in his eyes. "You want my life story, Mac? It's a sad, sad tale. Before the English landlords took our farm in Ireland we were prosperous people. They left us with nothing."

"Liam—"

"Da said 'Go to America.' He had great plans to make us comfortable again. But he wasn't a man. He broke his promises. He left Ma and me and Siobhan in a New York tenement. He took what money he'd earned and went his own way."

Abandoned, Mac thought. "Then Siobhan was your sister," she said softly. "How old were you?"

"Old enough. I was eleven. Siobhan was fourteen."

Mac took another step, commanding her hands to stay at her sides. "What happened?"

His gaze had grown unfocused. "We had no money. No food. I worked where I could, but it wasn't enough. I wasn't Da. Ma was sickly. She could never accept what had happened. She wouldn't accept my—" He fell mute, and it was several moments before he spoke again. "She went mad, I think. She never left the tenement. But Siobhan wanted more. She wanted what we'd had in Ireland, and she was beautiful. There was always a wildness in her. She met a man who told her he'd give her all that and more in exchange for her virginity."

Even with so little said Mac knew where the story

was going. She was already beginning to understand the source of Liam's fixation. A young woman barely out of childhood, a girl with a reckless streak who didn't know what she wanted, perched on the edge of freedom—or ruination. . . .

"I tried to watch her," Liam continued, flat and distant. "I tried to stop her, but she always had her own way. And I wasn't Da. So she went with this man and he kept her until he tired of her, and then she went to another. And when one of them made her sick enough that no one wanted her, she took to the streets." His hand flexed against the wall, grabbing at nothing. "I couldn't stop her."

Her heart clenched. "You were a boy."

"I tried to bring her home," he said, "but when Ma saw her it was too much. Siobhan ran and when I came back from work the next morning Ma had used my knife on her wrists."

Good God. He'd been a kid, watching his sister destroy herself and his mother . . .

"She killed herself," Mac whispered.

"I cared well for my dear old ma," he said harshly. "I took her to the church and then I went searching for Siobhan. I didn't find her for a week. She was already wasted from her disease. I couldn't stop it. She died."

It was all becoming terribly clear to Mac. *"I couldn't stop it,"* he'd said again and again. *"I tried."* A boy who'd tried so desperately to be the man, to make up for his father's betrayal, to protect his womenfolk against life's inevitable cruelties. And had lost the battle, because he was only a boy and his world was far too merciless a place.

"And then . . . ," she said, hugging herself to keep from hugging him, "and then you had no one."

All at once he looked at her—looked *at* her, not through her. "I didn't need anyone," he said. "I took care of myself. I made my own way. I have more money than Da ever dreamed of. I have everything."

Except freedom from the past, from your own perceived failure. Because you've never lived that down. Her eyes filled, and she fought to keep the tears behind her lids. *You've been trying to make it up ever since. With the slave girls. With Caroline. Trying to save the ones you can.*

Warm breath caressed her face. "Tears, Mac?" he asked, bitterness unconcealed. "Did my story move you so deeply?"

"Liam . . . I'm sorry—"

"Save your pity. I don't want it." He turned on his heel and went for his clothes.

"You think I don't know what it is to lose people you love?" she said, dogging his heels. "I do. I know how it feels when you're helpless to stop it."

He tugged on his pants and began to button his shirt, ignoring her. There was nothing to do but throw everything at him, whatever the risk.

"You don't love Caroline," she accused. "She was perfect for you because you *didn't* love her. She was safe. You could control everything she did, protect her for eternity, but she wasn't a risk to your heart, and you could still make up for the past. When you lost her you didn't lose love, you lost the chance to redeem yourself."

It was the wrong thing to say. He spun so fast that he almost knocked her down.

"To hell with you," he rasped. "You're not God to be knowing what's in my heart."

She summoned up every ounce of her courage and grabbed him by the front of his shirt. "For God's sake, Liam, let me be your friend." She brushed his unshaven chin with the back of her hand. "I care about you. I *care.*"

A bone-deep shudder went through him, passed into her own flesh and blood as if they were joined.

She reached for the top button of his shirt and slipped it from the buttonhole. "Don't run from me. *I* need you, Liam."

His answer held no words. He caught her hard in his arms, cupped her bottom in his hands, pressed her against the nearest wall.

And kissed her, with a stunning tenderness. He leaned into her as his mouth worked over hers, and she felt him melt through her wrap and chemise and burn straight into her heart.

She wouldn't let him take the lead this time. He *needed*. Needed to feel cared for, loved, without expectations or demands or judgment.

He didn't move as she slipped her hands under his shirt, baring his chest. He made only a single sharp sound when she peeled the shirt over his shoulders, trapping his arms.

She spread her palms against his chest, lacing her fingers through the crisp curls of pale hair. His heart thudded under her hand. She leaned into him and kissed his chin, his shoulder, the firm swell of his pectorals. Her tongue flicked his nipple, and he let out a rough sigh.

She was still kissing him as they moved to the bed. A moment later she was straddling his thighs, her kisses following the downward path of hair that stretched from chest to ribs to belly and disappeared into the waistband of his trousers.

He was very quiet while she undid the buttons and tugged his pants down around his hips. He was entirely at attention, practically leaping into her hand.

Sleek and smooth, hard and hot. She focused on the texture of him, stroking up and down, watching his face. He was letting her make love to *him*. A mark of trust that left her humbled and dizzy with quiet joy.

Only when she was sure he was lost did she bend low and take him in her mouth.

His breath sawed in his throat as she tasted him, suckled him as he'd suckled her, all sensation and compulsion. His fingers thrust into her hair, kneading and tugging. She went on until he was rigid and on the edge, and then she slid astride him. It was easy to accept him into her waiting body. Easy to move with his hands on her hips, letting her take him as he'd taken her. Letting her give in the only way he could allow.

But in the end he clasped her waist in his hands and rolled her beneath him, kissing her ears and chin and hair with each slow, deep thrust as she rose to meet it. Hip to hip, belly to belly, chest to breast. Equal. Complete. Together they made it last, drew it out to a pinnacle of uncomplicated, untainted joy. And it was Liam who sent her before him until her exaltation pulled him after.

When it was over she didn't let him go. He was caught in the afterglow of their lovemaking, and she was ruthless. She pulled him against her, tucked her head into the curve of his arm, stroked his hair. And he took her comfort. He held her with quiet desperation, as if he thought she would rise and vanish before his eyes.

Liam, she thought. The first tear escaped, and she tried not to let him see. *Oh, Liam. If only I could tell you the truth. If only you'd believe it.*

But for now, for this time out of time, maybe some part of him did.

CHAPTER TWENTY-ONE

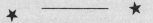

Not heaven itself upon
the past has power;
But what has been, has been,
and I have had my hour.

—JOHN DRYDEN

S HE SLEPT.

Liam watched her from beside the bed, holding his shirt in his fists. He'd thought she'd never sleep; she'd kept herself awake with a strange fierce adamancy, as if she couldn't trust him the minute her back was turned.

As if she could keep him here forever.

He wanted to caress her, to love her again. Her dark lashes were thick against her cheek, her hair tangled on her forehead, her lithe body sweetly curled on the bed in unconscious invitation. And she would have welcomed him.

But there was Perry to deal with. Nothing Mac could say, nothing she could do would divert him from his course.

Not even her devastating questions, the way she'd

probed and pushed until he was revealing things about himself he had never understood. Flaws even he had not recognized. Revelations she'd presented to him with pity in her eyes, having led him to bare his heart until he had nothing left of his manhood.

She had that power—to make him forget his strength and pride, to suck at his soul with a witch's talent for overcoming his resistance.

He had been more exposed than any mere nakedness displayed. She knew the full measure of his weakness. And still she'd pulled him down into her arms and he'd let himself be drawn into oblivion, unable to fight for what self-respect remained to him.

She had taken it all. She had made him *need*, when he'd never needed before. She'd given her comfort with such selfless nobility, generous in her victory.

Victory.

He reached down, his hand inches above her hair. No. He'd not be weak again. Mac was like a force of nature, a quiet storm he couldn't predict or control. But he didn't need her. She could give him nothing he couldn't live without. There were other willing women in the world, women who wouldn't steal his very soul.

Liam walked away from the bed, tugging on his shirt. *Damn her*. She'd said she needed him, but that was another of Heaven's little jests. Mac didn't need anyone, let alone Liam O'Shea.

But even she had her secrets.

Liam abandoned his buttons and went to the dresser against the wall. He examined the larger drawers one by one and found her pack pushed well into the back of the lowest.

Silently he pulled the pack from its hiding place and opened the toothed fastening—the zipper, as Mac had called it—and searched among the exotic contents for the one thing he needed to find.

The flat package of paper and cardboard was still there. He unwrapped it with unsteady fingers and found the photograph. Exactly as he'd last seen it in the jungle, dog-eared and creased and faded.

He stared at the photograph until it became a blur of gray shapes. He trusted Bauer's honesty implicitly. Bauer had seen this photograph, untouched and pristine in its frame, in Perry's rooms only days ago.

Liam took great care in rewrapping the photograph. He replaced the pack in the drawer and slid it closed.

Still Mac slept. He finished with his shirt and put on his coat, watching her. He wanted to remember the way she was now, when there weren't any words between them.

Once he'd dealt with Perry he might or might not survive the consequences. It didn't matter. He couldn't make Caroline safe by marrying her, but he could be certain she didn't fall into the hands of a murderer and slave dealer.

And Mac he didn't have to worry about. Not brave, stubborn, crazy Mac.

His hand was on the doorknob when the first knock struck wood. He opened the door before the next could fall.

A nervous young man stood at the door, his gaze flicking from Liam past his shoulder into the room. Liam recognized him as one of Bauer's assistants, the boys he hired to run messages and do minor work for his detective business.

"Mr. O'Shea?" the boy said. "Mr. Bauer said I might find you here—"

Liam wasn't surprised. There was very little Bauer didn't know or couldn't guess—about his clients as well as those he investigated. "He has a message for me?" Liam asked grimly.

"Yes." The boy screwed up his face in concentration.

"He said that Mei Ling has been kidnapped by the tongs. Chen's already gone to rescue her. Mr. Bauer said to tell you it's probably a trap, and to warn you—"

But Liam was already moving. He cast a glance at Mac—who hadn't been awakened by the racket, thank God—and picked up his hat. "I have something for you to deliver. Do you know the law offices of Gregg and Hern down Market Street?"

"Yes sir, but—"

Liam pulled two envelopes from his pocket and pressed them into the boy's hand. "See that one of these gets to Mr. Hern, and the other to Bauer. Tell Bauer my final instructions are there, in case I'm not able to give them myself. My lawyers will see he's paid well for carrying them out."

"But Mr. Bauer said—"

"You've done your job, boy. Now do mine." He gave the messenger a generous tip to mollify him. "If Bauer wants to know where I am, tell him I've gone to Chinatown. Go."

The boy knew better than to argue again. The moment he was out of sight Liam turned for a last look at Mac.

She'd never seemed more beautiful to him.

But his weakness was past. Perry had set a trap for him, and he was going to walk right into it.

He closed the door with no sound at all.

MAC'S BARE FEET hit the floor with a thump.

Five A.M., the electric clock on the mantel said. Five A.M., before dawn, and Liam was on his way to get himself killed.

He'd thought she was asleep, and that was the only good thing to be said about the situation. At least she knew where he was going. And she knew she was going to follow.

The air was cool on her skin as she stripped off her chemise. The cloth still smelled of Liam. She held it to her nose, memorizing his scent. The time out of time they'd shared was over, and no matter what happened today or in the days to come Mac knew they'd never get it back.

Her jeans and T-shirt, patches, holes, and all, were still packed away in the bottom of the wardrobe. They weren't going to last much longer, but she wasn't about to wear skirts into the fight that was sure to come. The butter-soft denim felt like heaven against her skin—familiar, safe, hers as nothing in this world could ever be. She put them on as she would put on armor, filling the pockets with all the courage she could find.

The T-shirt wasn't warm enough for a San Francisco autumn morning. A walking-suit jacket came out of the closet, ridiculously inappropriate with the jeans but warm enough to serve its purpose. Her jungle boots were pressed into service as well, though Mac mourned the sneakers she'd left so far behind.

Last came the pendant. She'd hidden it away as she'd put aside all thoughts of returning to her own time until her work in the past was done; now it seemed right to wear it.

To remind her how all this must end.

She had no weapon other than her Swiss Army knife, no particular skills to protect Liam from his own recklessness. But if he were walking into a trap, he wouldn't be doing it alone.

She slipped out into the hallway with instinctive caution. A man was leaning on the balustrade a few rooms away, his attention focused on the Grand Court below.

Mac went the other direction, crouching low to avoid his notice. Chen had stopped her from following Liam before; it wasn't going to happen again. She steered clear of the sluggish elevator and found the stairs. No one stopped her.

The Palace Hotel had more than one exit. The one she chose was as far from the Grand Court as possible, leading out to an alley that was peacefully dark and quiet. Market Street was empty except for a scattering of delivery wagons and a few preoccupied individuals on early morning errands. Mac broke into a jog under the flickering streetlamps and constructed a map in her mind.

She knew how to get to Chinatown. The location hadn't changed in over a century; it was still centered on Grant Avenue, though everything else had altered drastically since the 1800s. No famous pagoda-like arched gateway welcomed her arrival, but she knew when she'd come to the right place.

The buildings were different than the Chinatown she remembered from her own time: more crowded, closer together, built of wood and brick and surprisingly plain. This was not a place designed for tourists.

Streetlamps here were few and far between. The faint scents of fish and sandalwood mingled in the air along with less pleasant odors. On Grant itself there were ordinary little shops displaying silks and lacquered trays, dried fish and fresh poultry, herbs and medicines.

But what Mac sought wouldn't be in the open. She shivered and moderated her pace, every sense alert. The alleys branching off the main street were as narrow as canyons, pitch dark, with overhanging balconies almost touching to either side. They might hide anything, including an ambush. Or a certain Irishman who'd get himself killed trying to take on the world single-handedly.

Damn you, Liam, she thought desperately, *if you die after all the work I went to to save you—*

Someone bumped hard into her shoulder from behind. Mac spun around, the ridiculous little knife in her fist.

The attacker stumbled back, raising a gloved hand to ward Mac away. "Pardon me," the person whispered in a strained voice.

Mac looked into the pale eyes that peered from beneath the brim of an oversized hat. At a body muffled in a coat that nearly dragged on the ground and trousers rolled up to flap around slender ankles. And feet wearing dainty pale blue lace-up boots.

Her gaze snapped back to what she could see of the face.

Good grief. It was—

"Caroline!"

"Rose!"

They stared at each other, dumbfounded. Mac was the first to regain her senses. She grabbed Caroline's arm through the bulky coat and dragged her into the doorway of a closed shop.

"What in hell are you doing here?" Mac hissed.

Caroline tugged the muffling scarf from around her chin and thrust out her jaw. "I could ask the same of you. But I shouldn't be surprised. I knew you were part of this somehow—"

Mac prayed for patience. "I know a lot has happened in the past twenty-four hours, and even I don't know everything. You may think you have a good reason to hate me, Caroline, but this isn't the time to discuss it. Someone's life is at stake—more than one person's life—and—"

"It's Perry, isn't it?" Caroline clutched Mac's arm. "Is he in trouble? I knew it. I knew something was wrong, but he wouldn't tell me at the ball, and after Liam—" Her flush was visible even in the dim predawn light. "Liam has turned against him. I know he needs my help. Last night I found some of Papa's old clothes and snuck out to find him. There were men watching the house, but I got past them and—"

As if things couldn't get any worse. "Caroline, I can't talk to you now. You have to go home. It could get very dangerous here."

"I know." Suddenly she seemed like a much older woman, calm and competent and grave. "I was wrong about a great many things, but I'm not wrong about this. Everyone has told me what I must do and how I must behave. But now I'm old enough to make my own decisions." She hesitated. "I don't know who you really are, and I'm not sure I like you, but you're not afraid to do things, no matter the risk. Liam wouldn't stop you. Now he can't stop me. And you can't send me away."

Mac scrutinized the beautiful, feminine, obstinate features under the hat brim. The features weren't Sinclair, but the spirit was—a spirit Mac hadn't really perceived until now. Or maybe she hadn't known where to look.

Something had changed in Caroline almost overnight. This wasn't a spoiled child standing here, or a frivolous airhead, or a wild imprudent girl intent on ruining herself. This was a young woman who was finally figuring out what she really wanted.

Great-great-grandma was destined to become a reformer and suffragette—who was to say it wouldn't begin here? And Caroline wanted to help Perry, the man history said she was supposed to marry.

"If you're going to come with me," Mac said quickly, "you're going to have to stay down and be quiet. Don't do anything reckless, or you could endanger everyone even more. Stay with me. Agreed?"

Caroline grinned—no simpering smile but a fullblown flash of white teeth. "Agreed."

Mac peered up Grant Avenue. Already the sky was

beginning to brighten, and God only knew what had happened during the precious minutes they'd been standing here gabbing.

"We've got to find out where they went," she muttered. "They could be anywhere."

"I think I might know the direction Perry was going," Caroline volunteered. "I saw him in a closed carriage outside my house just as he was leaving. I followed him here, and I was beginning to—"

Mac didn't let her finish. She gave Caroline a little push in the direction of the street. "Show me! And don't do anything stupid. Go!"

Caroline began to run with surprising speed in her oversized men's clothes. Mac stayed on her heels, casting a small and desperate prayer heavenward.

If you've got a few extra Sinclair guardian angels up there, Homer, send 'em on down.

"RUN, CHEN! SAVE your niece while you can!"

Chen hesitated, and Liam knew the man was torn between his loyalty to Liam and fear for the girl shaking in his arms. Chen had never lacked for courage. But in the end he did what he had come to Chinatown to do—save Mei Ling. The man hadn't asked for Liam to get involved, but he had the sense to take help when it was offered.

"I'll hold them off here," Liam shouted. "Get her to safety!"

Chen ran, urging his niece along beside him. Liam steadied his pistol, turned back the way they had come, and waited for their pursuers.

The streets and alleys of Chinatown were still strangely quiet, even so soon before dawn. Its people knew there was trouble this bright autumn morning,

and they were going to avoid it—they, who usually suffered the most from the tongs' criminal activities.

But this time the tongs weren't hunting one of their
own. Mei Ling's kidnapping had been a ruse. Chen had
come alone to save her, refusing to involve his employer, and if it hadn't been for Bauer's watchfulness
the kidnappers might have had to wait some time before Liam walked into their trap.

Liam hadn't made them wait. He'd found Chen
quickly enough, and let the man know in no uncertain
terms that the problem was Liam's to rectify. Together
they'd found Mei Ling easily enough. The tongs had
wanted her to be found.

But the tongs hadn't counted on the ferocity of her
rescuers. Six hatchetmen hadn't been adequate to stop
Chen and Liam, and now two of the enforcers lay
wounded in the shadowed alley beside the house where
they'd held Mei Ling.

The other four had fallen for a ruse that had sent
them in the wrong direction—but only temporarily.
Just long enough for Chen to get Mei Ling out of Chinatown, where the hatchetmen would not dare follow
in the growing daylight.

Liam could hear the hoodlums coming now. He took
careful aim. At least one of them would go down before
they took him, and the rest would have one hell of a
fight. It was too damned bad Perry hadn't turned up, so
he could have put a bullet in him as well—

A heavy object smashed into the side of Liam's head.
He staggered, struggling to keep his hold on the pistol.
It was knocked from his hand. He didn't even have a
chance to see where it had fallen before the next blow
caught his temple, and then he couldn't see anything at
all.

The next thing he was aware of was a voice, a jumble
of meaningless sounds. His head throbbed as if some-

one were twisting a knife into his brain, but he concentrated in spite of the pain, and at length he began to understand.

And to recognize the voice.

"I told you to wait for me," Perry said. "It was all arranged. I have the carriage here. Your precipitous action could have ruined everything, and you would have had the police to deal with. They're probably coming now, thanks to your incompetence."

Someone answered—a gruff, angry voice heavily accented. "You were late. Why should we trust—"

"Because you haven't any choice. Your boss agreed to the plan. There's little enough time as it is. O'Shea walked into the trap as expected. I promised to deal with him, and I will. Your operations won't suffer from his interference beyond today. Now—" Liam heard a shuffling and someone took firm hold of his arms. "Kindly help me get him into the carriage, and then I suggest you hide yourselves before the police arrive."

Liam played senseless, keeping his body limp while they dragged him to his feet. He smelled the unmistakable odor of horses, heard their harness jingling as he was propped against the side of the carriage, supported by the one man he had so badly wanted to find.

The man he'd stop once and for all. . . .

"If you can hear me, Liam, don't show it," Perry hissed into his ear. "If we're to get out of this alive, they have to believe I intend to kill you."

Liam almost gave himself away at the shock of Perry's words. His first instinct was to grab Perry around the neck and force him to explain himself then and there. He didn't have a chance to so much as debate the possibilities, for Perry gave a low curse and grasped his arm.

"I may have misjudged the situation," he whispered.

"From the look of things it seems they're planning to eliminate both of us here and now—"

"Boss doesn't trust you," the accented voice said, uncomfortably close. "He said get rid of you now. Police won't come for us if you kill each other."

"Eminently logical," Perry murmured. "If you can hear me, Liam, I suggest—"

Liam didn't wait for his suggestion. He surged up, ignoring the fiery pain in his skull, and heaved himself toward the accented voice. His body connected, and the man grunted under his weight as they hit the ground. A flash of movement from the corner of his eye showed Perry struggling with another hoodlum.

Then someone found a gun and fired.

THE GUNSHOT ECHOED through the streets like an explosion. Mac skidded to a stop, panic clutching at her gut, and searched desperately for the source of the noise.

"This way!" she yelled, grabbing Caroline. They pelted around a corner and into a side street, stopped, and turned into an even narrower alley.

A dark closed carriage waited at the end of it, the horses lunging against their harness in panic. Men were fighting, one pair on the ground struggling for control of a pistol and another grappling against the side of the carriage.

One of the men on the ground was Liam.

Mac didn't think. She ran for the melee as if her life depended on it, Caroline right behind. They'd just reached the chaotic scene when another pair of men emerged from a maze of close-set buildings, men in dark shirts and loose trousers with distinctly threatening attitudes. One of them brandished a hatchet, the other a gun.

"Watch out!" Mac yelled. The new arrival with the gun stopped and took aim at her. The man with the hatchet shouted something to his partner, distracting him, and the two of them went directly for Liam.

"Perry!" Caroline cried.

Mac had exactly one second to take it all in. Liam was crouched over his erstwhile opponent, swaying, blood on his temple, preparing for the new men's attack. Perry was busy banging his adversary's head against the side of the carriage.

Caroline rushed for Perry. Mac raised her knife, screamed bloody murder at the top of her lungs, and charged the guy with the hatchet.

For an instant her gaze met Liam's, and then he was moving—straight between her and the hatchetman. The man with the gun was taking careful aim for Liam's skull.

With a maneuver that would have made Wonder Woman proud, Mac changed directions, bent double, and used her head for a battering ram, hitting the gunman square in the stomach. He grunted and staggered back. The gun went off. Fighting dizziness, Mac stuck her knife to the hilt in the man's hand. He wailed and dropped the gun.

It wasn't over yet. She was about ready to dive for the gun when she saw Liam squared off with the hatchetman. Unarmed, and still swaying on his feet as if he might keel over with the next stiff breeze.

Instinct warred with sense. She didn't know how to use the gun—but Liam did. She went for it, rolling, and grabbed it around the barrel. By the time she was on her feet again Liam was dodging the swing of the vicious axe and losing his balance.

Mac did the only thing she could think of. She swung the gun and clipped the hatchetman on the back of the skull with the butt just as he was ready to connect the blade of his axe with Liam's neck.

The man fell. Liam tried to get up. Mac was going to him when something hit her from behind, and she was lying under the weight of the forgotten gunman, who had a knife to her throat. His wounded hand dripped blood onto her jacket.

Everything slowed down to a snail's pace. Liam gave a cry Mac had never heard from any human being, made an aborted movement toward her and stopped when the tong enforcer pressed the knife blade against her skin.

She met Liam's gaze and forgot the rest of the world. Her own danger meant nothing next to the pain and terror in his eyes.

The hatchetman raised his knife. Liam leaped up with an animal roar. Mac saw the knife descend, felt an explosive rush of air close to her cheek, heard a deafening bang, and then there was a great deal of blood and a man screaming in pain.

Part of her registered the sight of Perry standing by the carriage with a pistol in his hand . . . and a view of the man who'd been holding her, flat on his back, groaning, with a substantially larger hole in his arm than her knife had made.

"Mac!" Liam rasped, very close to her ear. "Mac—"

"I'm all right," she gasped. "Perry— Oh, damn it, *Caroline—*"

She got Liam's attention just in time. Perry's first adversary had apparently recovered from the pounding Perry had given him, for he'd taken advantage of Perry's distraction and grabbed Caroline. Caroline was fighting her captor like a banshee, all feet and little clenched fists; Perry was aiming his gun, as helpless to save her as Liam had been with the hatchetman.

But Liam moved. He dove for the knife Mac's attacker had dropped, positioned himself, and threw it with deadly accuracy at the enforcer's leg. It hit with enough impact that the tong man thought better of further argument. He dropped Caroline, tried to run, and fell with the knife still protruding from his calf.

Four tong enforcers lay on the ground in various degrees of unconsciousness or debilitating pain. Perry had Caroline in his arms, and she was clinging to him for everything she was worth, all but ignoring her guardian.

Mac more than made up for that lapse. She found Liam still on his knees, sucking in air, his hair tangled around his face and glued to a nasty cut near his temple. She hardly had time to move; he was already at her side by the time she forced her muscles to react. His hands clutched at her shoulders and he examined her with a thoroughness bordering on frenzy.

"Mac," he said hoarsely. "Are you all right?"

"Yes, but—"

"*Damn* you," he snarled. "Why did you come here? I didn't need your help."

"That's not how it looked to me," she retorted thoughtlessly. "Liam—"

He tried to shake her, but his grip had remarkably little power. In fact, his skin was draining of color, his eyes darkening with pain . . .

"Liam?" She reached for him and tried to focus. He was moving back and forth in her line of vision, undulating like a ship on the ocean. But it wasn't because she was dizzy. He was the one doing the tilting—crumpling, falling, his coat sleeve awash in blood.

She thought she screamed, or maybe it was the sound of police whistles coming closer and voices calling out in warning. She felt the vibration of many footfalls through the ground beneath her, recognized Chen's distinctive accent above the others. Uniformed men with guns and nightsticks swam in her vision.

"Miss MacKenzie!"

She looked up at Chen. "Please . . . get help. Liam's hurt—"

After that she didn't hear Chen's reply, or any of the hubbub around her. She knelt in the sticky dirt, cradled Liam's head on her lap, and stroked his wet hair away from his forehead.

"This is the last time I'm going to come to your rescue, Liam O'Shea," she said, choking on tears that wouldn't stop. "You'd damn well better recover, or I'm never going to let you forget it."

For once he had no retort.

CHAPTER TWENTY-TWO

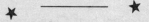

Time's glory is to calm
contending kings,
To unmask falsehood and
bring truth to light.

—WILLIAM SHAKESPEARE

"HE'LL BE FINE, Miss MacKenzie, I do assure you. They are only flesh wounds, and you did well to stop the bleeding so quickly."

The portly doctor closed his bag and gathered the other two watchers in with his gaze. "I'll grant you, if the knife had struck a little more to the right, it might have been far more tricky. But under the circumstances, I've stitched him up and all he'll need is a bit of rest."

Rest, ha, Perry thought. Liam would be on his feet within a day, if Perry knew anything about the Irishman.

And he did. He'd come to know more about many things in the past two weeks—more about Liam, and Caroline, and himself.

As for Miss MacKenzie . . . She was wan and pale,

a mere shadow of her usually robust self; she sagged in relief at the doctor's news. She'd hovered at Liam's side all the way back to his house, ignoring Chen's anxious presence and Caroline's questions and the police Chen had summoned.

Now the police were gone. Chen listened intently as Rose questioned the doctor at length; Caroline was downstairs with Mei Ling, comforting the girl as best she could.

Perry smiled softly. Caroline. She'd surprised even him today with her bravery and common sense. He'd been shocked to see her in Chinatown with Rose—and then not so shocked, knowing how much rebellion lurked under that lovely, delicate exterior.

But they'd both underestimated Caroline's stubbornness. She'd had the sense to stay out of the fight until the hatchetman came for her; then she'd fought tooth and nail instead of swooning or screaming.

Perry was proud of her. He knew she must have followed him when he'd stopped to watch her house for a few brief moments before facing the ordeal in Chinatown; she'd followed out of concern for *him*. She'd stayed by his side, obeyed his instructions like a woman with twice her experience. Even when Perry had been helpless to save her from the hatchetman and Liam had thrown his knife, she'd never lost her courage.

At the end of it all she'd run to Perry, not Liam.

He counted it a sign of hope. Hope that she was beginning to see him as more than merely a friend; hope that the pain he'd given her would fade quickly. Already she was thinking beyond herself, staying with Mei Ling and doing what she could for the dazed young woman. Perry's brief explanation of the fate that awaited girls like Mei Ling—a fate Caroline had been ignorant of—had roused her immediate indignation.

It was the first stirring of the woman Perry knew she

could be. *Would* be. He'd heard only a trace of bitterness in the last words she'd spoken to him: "*I know Liam has no need for me. Nothing can ever truly hurt him.*"

In that she was wrong, Perry thought with a twinge of sadness. It wasn't the physical wounds that mattered most. From those a man recovered. But that was not something she could yet understand; Liam had hurt her youthful pride, torn her admiration of him to tatters, and she would need time to.

Time to fully realize how wrong it would have been to marry her guardian, to see that things had worked out for the best. Time to recognize what love could be. That was all she needed now—time and love.

Perry knew how to be patient.

"Mr. Sinclair?"

He came back to himself. "Doctor?"

"Mr. O'Shea asked me to send you in. I advised him to rest, but—" The doctor shook his head. "I trust you won't tax him."

"You may trust me," Perry said gravely. He nodded to the doctor and glanced at Rose. She stood frozen against the wall, her face a mask to hide what Perry knew she must be feeling.

Liam hadn't asked to see *her*.

Perry went to Rose and clasped her shoulder. She looked at him with such desperation that he almost mouthed the platitudes he knew she had no use for.

Instead he squeezed her shoulder and turned to beard the lion in his den.

Liam lay on the bed, propped up against a bundle of pillows, his arm and chest swathed in bandages. He was as pale as Rose, the hollows under his eyes and cheekbones pronounced, the lines around his mouth deepened with pain. He opened his eyes as Perry shut the door.

"So," Liam said. "It seems you saved Mac's life. And mine."

Interesting, a part of Perry thought distantly, which action Liam mentioned first. "I know that surprises you, old man," he said. "But perhaps now you're prepared to believe I never wanted you dead."

Liam laughed and hissed as the motion wrung a protest from his body. "No. Just out of the way."

Perry pulled a chair close to the bed. "Do you mind if I sit down?"

"I'm not in any shape to stop you."

"Of that I wouldn't be too sure. But I do trust your common sense—now." He sat down and crossed his legs. "Where shall we begin?"

"I don't know." Liam passed his uninjured hand over his face. "I don't know what to believe anymore."

From Liam it was a shocking admission, especially to one he'd considered an enemy. "You want to know why it appeared that I was working with the tongs," Perry prompted. "You want to know what really happened with the carriage, and the drugged wine, and the ambush in Chinatown. Is that a place to start? Or do you perhaps still suspect I was behind the jungle attack?"

"Should I think what happened with the guerrillas was coincidence?" Liam said heavily.

"It seems to be the truth. Odd, isn't it? It was that coincidence that led you to assume I was responsible for the carriage accident as well. I learned of the sawed axle soon after it happened. I suspected you might hold me responsible for it even before I knew you had better reason than I'd supposed."

"And that's why you disappeared."

"Only in part." Perry uncrossed his legs and sat forward. "Hear me out, old man. You may have trouble believing what I tell you, and I don't ask for your trust. I knew you wouldn't listen before, but now . . ."

"I owe you," Liam said. "Mac—"

Ah, yes. "Mac." "As I owe you for Caroline's life. Hard as it may be for you to accept, I didn't go to the tongs hoping they would help me eliminate you, and then suddenly have a change of heart. A dramatic scenario, I grant you, but not accurate."

"Then why?"

"I don't deny that everything I did was to free Caroline from you—and save both of you from a disastrous alliance."

"Noble of you, old friend," Liam said bitterly.

"I also don't deny a selfish motive." He let silence fall until Liam was looking at him again. "I love Caroline. I want her happiness—and yours. I learned long ago that the end does sometimes justify the means."

"That sounds more like the Peregrine Sinclair I know."

"But how little we do know each other. How little we know ourselves." He forced himself to focus on the issue at hand. "Let me dispense with the tong business first. It was when I learned of the carriage mishap that I realized there was more going on than our disagreement over Caroline—"

Liam sat up against the pillows. "How *did* you learn about it? Only Chen and Forster knew—"

"And both are loyal to you. But I do have experience in getting information, old man, as you discovered when you investigated my past." He saluted Liam with two fingers to his temple. "You were good at unearthing matters I'd thought buried. But I was the best at what I did for the mother country."

"You were a damned spy and hired—"

"We're speaking of the present, not my past." He leaned back in the chair again, ignoring the sting of memories he'd put behind him. "Following the incident at Cliff House, I came to Sacramento Street fully intending to have it out with you. But the accident persuaded me it would not be the right time—and also convinced me that someone meant you ill. When Forster saw me on your grounds he advised me to leave, since he'd overheard you threaten to kill me. I thought it best to lie low and see what I could learn about the true villains of the piece."

"And made yourself the most conspicuous suspect."

Perry shrugged. "It was a risk I had to take. I'd already lost your trust. And I was reasonably certain at that point that you would not ask Caroline to marry you until her birthday, because I knew you did not truly wish to marry her at all. I had nearly two weeks in which to investigate."

Liam looked away. "Wiser than God himself, aren't you?"

"No," Perry said softly. "Not always wise. But I didn't want to see you dead, Liam. I already knew about your work with the slave girls—yes, I made it my business to know all you did, for Caroline's sake. It didn't take me long to realize that the tongs and their outside supporters had decided to risk . . . dealing with you. They'd lost too much business and too much money on the girls you'd rescued. They arranged the accident as a warning. If you died in the process, all the better."

"Your resignation from active service was a great loss to the queen."

"Thank you. Once I knew the nature of the threat, I set about contacting the tong lords in question and offering my services to them. As your friend, I had access to you that they did not. I offered to get rid of you for a portion of their profits in the slave trade. They saw the benefit of having one outsider take care of another; less risk of police interference that way. The boss couldn't pass up the opportunity. I told them they mustn't take any more action until I was ready."

"And they believed you."

Perry grimaced. "Apparently not enough, since they planned to kill us both in the end. In any event, I knew you would almost certainly propose to Caroline the night of the ball, so I came disguised and spoke to Rose about how we might prevent it. I'd learned of your raid for the following night, so I warned the tongs and then set an anonymous message to Chen that the tongs knew of it. As I hoped, you moved the raid to that very evening—"

"Damn you," Liam said, pushing forward as if to rise. Only physical weakness held him down. "*You* were the informant. They were ready for us when we went that night—"

"Yes. I'm not proud of that miscalculation. Apparently my warning put the tongs doubly on guard. I am sorry."

"Be sorry for the girls we couldn't save."

Shame was not an accustomed emotion to Perry, but it was one he'd begun to learn. Love did that to a man. "I shall make up for that," he said evenly, "in time. The next morning I learned of your expected rendezvous with Caroline at the Poodle Dog, and saw to it that the invitation she received was altered."

"You sent Mac in her place."

Liam's coldness belied the concern he'd shown earlier for Rose. Perry wondered how much he'd underestimated the threat to Liam's pride. "It was my idea, Liam—don't blame her. You see, she couldn't accept that I'd tried to kill you, however little her faith in me seems justified. But she was worried about you—deeply."

That gave Liam pause, enough that Perry felt a renewal of hope. If the man had his eyes opened to the chance he had right in front of him . . .

"You made sure Caroline walked in on us," Liam said.

"I did. But Rose didn't know that was part of my plan."

"And what about the drugged wine?"

Ah. There was no avoiding this confession. Perry wrapped indifference around himself and spoke without a trace of emotion. "That was an error—an overeager waiter in my employ. If Mac hadn't succeeded in winning your interest, I determined to get you out of harm's way. I could only delay the tongs for so long, and I knew they meant to kill you eventually, whatever the risks."

"You put Mac at risk. She almost drank it."

There was more dangerous anger in Liam now than at any time before. Another hopeful sign.

"The drug would only have rendered you both unconscious. I have connections in this city and beyond that you know nothing about. I could have spirited both you and Rose to a safe place, long enough to convince Caroline you were not truly interested in her, and the tongs that you were no longer a threat. I would never have harmed either one of you, Liam."

He only stared at Perry as if he wished he were on his feet and capable of knocking his former partner to the floor. "If Mac had been harmed—" But he caught himself and was satisfied to twist his sheets into tortured balls between his fingers.

"And was Mei Ling's kidnapping also your idea, Perry?"

"No. The tongs knew you'd come if they abducted her. I took full advantage of the trap. I told them I'd have a carriage to get you out of Chinatown when you

came to rescue Mei Ling, and all their problems would
be solved."

"And you thought you had everything so well controlled that no one would be hurt? Not Chen, not Mei
Ling?"

"It was a risk, but I did what I could to minimize it.
Did you wonder why it was so easy to free Mei Ling
and hold off the hatchetmen until she and her uncle
escaped? I did what I could without betraying myself.
When it was apparent they might kill you, it was necessary to hit you in order to assure them of my sincerity."

"And what if you had got me away?"

"I would have gone through with your 'disappearance,' at least until matters with the tongs had cooled.
Quite a moot point now, since they know I betrayed
them." Perry rose and walked halfway across the room.
"I doubt the tongs will feel comfortable making any
further attempts on either one of us, given the renewed
police interest in their activities. Nevertheless, I think a
change of scenery might be advisable for the players in
the game."

"Is that all it ever was to you, Perry? A game?"

Strangely enough, that accusation hurt more than
any of the others. "It was never a joy to me, Liam—not
here, and not in England. I would like nothing better
than to settle into a quite uneventful life with the
woman I love."

Liam's eyes were empty of emotion. "How can I trust
you with her?"

"Perhaps it would help to tell you that I'm not the
fortune hunter you feared. A rather large family breach
was recently healed, and I've been welcomed back to
the bosom of the Sinclairs. I came into a nice sum of
money, old man—enough to support Caroline comfortably without dipping into her funds in the foreseeable
future." He paused, smiling wryly. "It is something

your man—Mr. Bauer, is it not?—can confirm easily enough."

"How long have you known?"

"Only for a week, but by then there was little point in telling you of it. There were more pressing matters to deal with. Given the current situation, I wish to take Caroline—properly chaperoned, of course—to England to meet my brother. He was always the most decent of my immediate family, and she would enjoy the travel."

Liam was quiet for a long time. "Mac always trusted you," he said at last. "But you used her as well."

"I doubt anyone can use Miss MacKenzie without her cooperation. She's a very bright girl, though one might question her taste."

Liam's gaze locked on his with a strange, burning ferocity. "What do you mean?"

"Do you know what she told me when she first approached me? That she wanted to help me, and all she wanted in return was you. Not your money, but you. Now I'm inclined to think she was telling the truth all along."

"Truth? What is the *truth* in any of this?"

"I've learned one thing in my varied career, old man, and that's that there is no one truth. Each man must find his own."

"You missed your calling, Perry. You should have been a philosopher."

"Perhaps it's not too late."

But Liam didn't answer, didn't speak again until Perry had reached the door and was on his way out of the room.

"Perry."

He paused without looking back.

"You left something here that belongs to you. In the left upper drawer of the desk."

Perry went on his guard. He walked back to the desk and opened the indicated drawer.

His pocket watch lay inside. Battered, scratched, the chain broken in one place, it was both familiar and strange. The hands were frozen in a perpetual announcement of four o'clock.

"Take it," Liam said.

Perry did, knowing well what this meant. His throat was oddly taut. He held the watch in his palm, rereading the inscription, and then began to wind it, slowly and deliberately, until it hummed with life again.

"Go to Caroline," Liam said. "Make sure she's all right."

The tightness in Perry's throat made it damnably—and ridiculously—difficult to speak. "And Miss MacKenzie? Do you wish to—"

"The doctor told me she was well," Liam interrupted. "She can more than take care of herself."

So that was the way the wind blew.

Perry tucked the watch in his waistcoat pocket. He left the room, closed the door, and went to summon Rose.

CHAPTER TWENTY-THREE

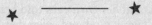

*Why meet we on the bridge of Time
to 'change one greeting and to part?*

—SIR RICHARD FRANCIS
BURTON

MAC WALKED UP the stairs with feet that dragged and legs that felt heavy as lead. Talking things out with Caroline during the past half-hour had been difficult, but she would have gone through it a thousand times rather than do what had to be done now. At least Caroline was young enough to be flexible, to change, to listen. And to bare her own heart.

Mac felt old. Too old to risk pouring out her soul to the man who waited upstairs. Too much aware of how little good it would do when she'd be here a matter of days. Or hours. She had only to ask Perry for his pendant, and then . . .

She didn't knock on the door. Norton lay sprawled at the foot of the bed; his head and ears came up, and he was on top of Mac almost before she could prepare herself for his affectionate onslaught.

As she accepted the dog's enthusiastic greeting she watched Liam become aware of her, returning from some faraway place within his own mind. He straightened on the bed, suppressing a wince of pain. He was well bandaged, and her own eyes told her he was going to be all right. Thank God and every deity that had ever existed in the history of time.

"Don't even think of standing up," she ordered.

Oh, yes. She'd read him right. The hard set of his shadowed jaw and the bleakness in his gaze told her how much he hated to be helpless this way in front of her. It reminded him of Chinatown, and the failure he saw within himself—the self-contempt, the terror she'd seen so vividly when they'd both been close to death.

"Well, Mac?" His breathing was harsh. "Are you here to play nursemaid to the invalid?"

The attack wasn't aimed at her. It was all for himself. "You're too cantankerous to need nursing, O'Shea. I felt more sorry for the doctor."

"It seems I'm to be talked to death instead."

Mac dragged a chair close to the bedside. "There are things I need to explain—"

"Like Perry?"

"You . . . know he didn't try to kill you."

His muscles bunched, and she knew he wanted very badly to rise and pace the room like a caged jaguar. "If you've only come to talk about Perry—" he rasped.

"No." She reached out to him, unable to help herself. "What I need to tell you Perry doesn't even know. I—"

Her hand was seized in a firm but remarkably careful grip. "Good God," Liam said. "You *are* hurt."

She followed his anxious look. The modest bandage around her hand was hardly like Liam's; she'd almost forgotten the cut was there. "Just a scratch," she said, giving him a lopsided grin. "I'm not too handy with a knife—not fighting with it, anyway. It's nothing, really. I've had worse mosquito bites in the jungle—"

"You little idiot. Did you mean to get both yourself and Caroline killed?"

Gently she worked her hand from his grasp. "I can't take credit for bringing Caroline along. She came on her own. And it so happened I heard your conversation with the messenger at the Palace." She chuckled thickly. "Couldn't let you go and get yourself killed, considering the trouble I took to save your life in the jungle."

The corner of his lips twitched. "You'll never let me forget that, will you?"

I hope in time we're both able to forget. She shook her head. "I have something to tell you about that. If you're ready to listen. If you can accept the truth this time, I'll give to you. I told you part of it before, when you couldn't accept it. Maybe enough's happened that now you can."

He folded his arms across his chest and leaned back. "Go ahead. I'm entirely at your mercy."

"The day I pushed you out of the way of that bullet in the jungle, I changed the course of history. You . . . you were supposed to die, Liam O'Shea, in the Péten in August of 1884."

That pronouncement caught his full attention. "Of course," he drawled. "Your time travel again. That's why you refused to tell me my future."

So he remembered that conversation. "Yes," she admitted. "I knew it could happen any time."

"And you just happened to be there, my savior, when my fate came upon me."

"You were the reason I came to the jungle in the first place, in my own time. That was why I had the photograph, why I recognized you." She braced herself. "You see, I was in the ruins to . . . make amends for something one of my own ancestors was supposed to have done. To apologize to the . . . spirit of the man he was supposed to have murdered."

She could see the progression of thoughts behind Liam's mask of indifference, the gradual realization as he began to catch on.

"I don't expect you to understand theories even I can't make sense of," she said. "When I found myself in the past—when I saved your life—everything changed. Because you were alive when you were supposed to be dead, you could go back to San Franciso and marry Caroline. I couldn't let that happen."

He stared at her with eyes as opaque as silver coins. "Why couldn't you, Mac?"

Her heart thumped painfully against the wall of her ribs. "Because my name isn't Rose MacKenzie. It's MacKenzie Rose Sinclair. Perry is my great-great-grandfather, Caroline is my great-great-grandmother, and if they didn't marry, my family and everything they'd ever done would cease to exist."

It took a moment for her to realize that the sound Liam was making was a laugh—deep, low, wrenched from his gut. "So everything you did was to save the future of the Sinclairs. But there's one thing I still don't understand. It would have been so much easier to let me die as I was meant to." He leaned forward, ignoring his wounds and the pain they must have caused. "Why did you save my life?"

"Because damn it, I—" She lifted her chin. "I couldn't just stand there knowing a man was about to die and not try to stop it."

Liam settled back slowly. His eyes closed—in pain, she thought. She'd pushed him too hard.

But he smiled. "The Sinclairs are such a noble breed. Where would the world be without them? It seems I have only to thank you for your devoted care. I couldn't have survived without it, let alone ordered my own life, which you tell me shouldn't have continued beyond that day in the jungle." He snorted. "How heavy a responsibility I must have been for you, Mac. You sacrificed even yourself in the pursuit of it. My apologies."

She curled her fingers around the arms of the chair until her knuckles hurt. "It wasn't a sacrifice, Liam," she whispered.

"You did get some pleasure out of our . . . friendship," he said. "A pity I'm flat on my back, or we could give it a go one last time. For old times' sake, eh, Mac?"

They stared at each other. Liam's breathing was ragged. She stood, pushing the chair back. "You need to rest now, Liam. I'm . . . sorry—"

"You gave me my life. I told you I always pay my debts. Have I paid this one sufficiently, Mac?"

"More than . . . sufficiently."

"I'm relieved to hear it. I wouldn't want to leave anything undone. I'll be going out of town as soon as I can get out of this bloody bed."

It didn't matter that she was going away herself; his announcement made her blood ice over like water in the Arctic. "You're leaving?"

"The tongs have made San Francisco too hot for Chen and his niece. I can't be sure of protecting them any longer. But I have property in Napa, and I'm taking Chen to look it over."

"You're giving them a new place to live?"

"Land that's lying fallow. Maybe they can make use of it."

"That's very kind of you." She meant it with all her heart.

"I'm the very soul of kindness."

"What will you do . . . after that?"

His muscles tensed under their bandages and covering of sheets and blankets. "Sooner or later you'll have to give up your position as my guardian angel, Mac," he said. "It might as well be now." He turned his head away, dismissing her. "Do me one last service when you go downstairs and ask Chen to bring me a whiskey. My happiness will be complete."

There was nothing more to be said. He shut her out completely, as once he'd rejected her in a tent in the steaming jungles of the Petén. Mac fled, trying desperately not to think or feel. She realized halfway down the stairs that Norton had remained at her side, as if sensing her distress; she buried her fingers in the wiry fur of his back as if it were a lifeline to sanity.

Sanity was what she needed now. Sanity to carry out the very practical steps she needed to get home. Talk to Perry, get his pendant from him, arrange transportation back to Guatemala.

Mac touched her jacket over the place where Liam's pendant rested between her breasts. The stone was always cold, not warm as hers had been in the jungle, just before the tunnel through time had sucked her through.

If things went as she hoped, the pendant would warm again when she walked back into the tunnel. Once she had Perry's pendant, she'd have the tools she needed to make it work. *If* Fernando had told the truth. *If* the pendants were what had made the tunnel function. *If* it took her back to her own time.

It had to. Once she left San Francisco for Guatemala, she couldn't look back. On the other side from Liam O'Shea she might have some hope of forgetting.

Anything rather than stay here one instant longer than necessary.

Norton trotted along beside her as she walked into the library where she'd left Perry and Caroline. Caroline was gone; Perry was absorbed in a book, a glass of butterscotch-colored liquid in one hand. He set down his drink as she entered.

"Rose," he said. "What—"

He jumped up and caught her by the arms as she lost her balance, leading her to the heavy high-backed chair nearest the fireplace. "Are you ill?"

"No." *Good grief, what a time to learn to swoon in grand old Victorian fashion.* "I'm fine, really."

"Indeed?" He hovered over her until she convinced him by sitting up and meeting his eyes.

Dark Sinclair eyes. Not the eyes of a killer. That at least was resolved. Homer could rest in peace.

"Yes," she assured Homer's grandfather, smiling wryly. "Let's just say it's been a very interesting day. I know it's a little early for a nightcap, but whatever you're drinking, I wouldn't mind having a sip of it myself."

He was long past any surprise at her bluntness. He walked to a sideboard laden with glasses and bottles, poured her a small measure of amber liquid, and refilled his own glass.

"Thank you." She took the glass, sniffed it, wrinkled her nose, and took a sip. When her fit of coughing had subsided, she cradled the glass between her hands, resolved not to try again but needing something to hold on to.

"It's just not the same as a Dr Pepper," she said. "I have something to tell you. And something to ask." She glanced around the room. "Is Caroline all right?"

"She's in the guest bedroom with Mei Ling." Perry settled back in his chair, crossing his legs. "She's found a cause of her own."

"I have a feeling that she'll be good at whatever she decides to do with her life. And you— You'll let her make those decisions, won't you?"

He laid his hand over his heart. "Your concern for Caroline touches me." There was not irony but warmth in his tone. "I swear to you that Caroline will have all the freedom I can grant her once we're married."

Mac rubbed her foot along an intricate pattern in the carpet with great concentration. "You've talked to Liam."

"There seems hope for a renewal of our friendship," he said. He reached into his waistcoat pocket and pulled out a watch. A silver watch, battered and dented, that Mac recognized at once. "He insisted I take this back."

The lump that hadn't left her throat for the past several hours made it difficult to speak. "I'm so glad. I . . . wish I had time to get to know you and Caroline better. I wish I could stick around for your wedding, just to see it all through to the end."

He stilled with his glass to his lips. "Are you leaving us?"

"Yes. I have to."

"Why?"

"I've . . . come to see that I don't belong here," she said. "This is not my world, Perry. It never was. I can't tell you more than that."

Perry got up and strode to the sideboard. "It's Liam, isn't it? He blames you for all that's happened. The fool. I'll speak to him—"

"No. Please. There's nothing you can do."

His gaze was fixed on the row of bottles and glasses. "Then I was wrong to believe you loved him."

So smooth and aristocratic, his voice, and so devastating his words.

"I told you it wasn't something I can explain."

He muttered something about damnable pride and idiocy. "I see. And what will become of Liam?"

"He doesn't need a keeper. He certainly doesn't need me to babysit him." The glass in her hands was shaking, and she had to set it down. "I've done quite enough for him, don't you think?"

Perry lifted his glass to her in ironic salute. "You would have made an admirable colleague in my old profession, Rose. I confess I don't understand you."

"You don't have to. But if you feel I've done anything for you and Caroline, there's something I'd ask in return. It isn't much." She grasped the leather thong around her neck and pulled the chip of Maya stone from under her jacket and T-shirt. "You have a pendant like this one."

A flicker of surprise crossed his face. "That's Liam's. One of those we—"

"One of the two pendants you and Liam made four years ago," she said. "I want yours as well, Perry."

"May I ask why?"

She cupped the cool stone in her hand. "Call it a souvenir. You do have it, don't you?"

"Yes. In my rooms."

"Will you give it to me?"

He inspected her as if he could wring the full story out of her by sheer concentration. "Very well, Rose."

Thank God. "Then I have one more thing to ask. I need your help to arrange transportation back to the jungle as soon as possible."

"Back to the jungle? Surely—"

"I know what I'm doing, Perry." She stood up, testing her legs. They were prepared to hold her up now that the worst was past. "Liam has told me he plans to be out of town as soon as he's recovered enough to travel. I want to be gone by the time he gets back, whatever it takes." Her throat was aching, and she went on more briskly, "I'll need to borrow a little money. Just what I need to get back to Guatemala."

Perry steepled his fingers under his chin. "I suppose I can't convince you not to go ahead with this madness."

"No."

"Then I'll do what I can to help, of course."

"Thank you." She started for the door and paused. "I am glad to have known you, Perry. And Caroline."

"It isn't farewell just yet," he said.

But it would be very soon. In a matter of days she'd be beyond anyone's reach. Safe. With nothing more challenging before her than enduring a two-week sea voyage, tramping a couple hundred miles through the jungles, and trying to make a Maya time tunnel take her back to 1997.

Simple.

"I'll wait to hear from you," she said.

She walked down the echoing hall to the great front doors, Norton loyally by her side. At the threshold she knelt before the wolfhound, rubbing his ears between her fingers.

"Well, fella, this is it. I probably won't be seeing you again."

The dog thumped his tail against the polished floor. Mac fought to keep the tears in check just a little longer.

"I can tell you what I'm not going to miss about this time," she joked. "Long heavy dresses and corsets and institutionalized male chauvinism, to name a few. I can't wait to get back to Coke and feminism and nice, safe air travel and . . . Oh, hell." She flung her arms around the massive, shaggy neck. "I'm going to miss you, Norton."

And your master most of all, her heart whispered. She gave the dog a final caress and left him looking after her as she closed the door between them.

His bark reached her through the door. It became a howl as she strode away from the house, blindly following the route she knew would take her back to the Palace. Afternoon fog was beginning to roll in off the ocean, wreathing her in a chill that matched the lump of ice under her ribs.

Soon—she had to keep believing it—life would be back to normal. No more crazy excursions for MacKenzie R. Sinclair. There was a small apartment, a quiet life, and a job waiting for her back home.

And memories—more than enough to last her a lifetime.

CHAPTER TWENTY-FOUR

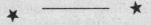

Ye Gods! annihilate
but space and time,
And make two lovers happy.

—ALEXANDER POPE

THE DAILY DOWNPOUR was nearly over. It was smack in the middle of the rainy season, but Mac was almost grateful for the hard going. It had kept her from thinking.

She leaned on her improvised walking stick and caught her breath. The mules stamped and shifted in the mud behind her, jingling their harnesses. Fernando soothed them with a quiet endearment and waited for Mac to signal them forward again.

Thank God for Fernando. She glanced back at the Maya muleteer. Somehow she hadn't been surprised to see him show up at the door of her grungy hotel room in Champerico. It hadn't been mere luck that she'd been able to hire the one person in Guatemala she knew to guide her back to the ruins: Fernando had been waiting for her.

Waiting for the pendants, the *keys,* he had asked her to return to the jungle. The keys he'd said would open the way back to the future. She'd shown the pendants to him, and he'd nodded and smiled and said nothing more, as if he'd always had utter faith in her ability to obtain them.

He hadn't asked about Liam. Mac had the feeling he knew Liam wasn't going to turn up. Fernando had simply minded his own business and set about his job of getting Mac to the ruins in one piece.

The Maya had done his job well. Their tiny expedition—Fernando, another muleteer, herself, and three mules—were nearly to the ruins. They'd passed through Tikal less than an hour before. Mac knew where they were; she didn't think she'd forget as long as she lived. It had all started here.

And here it would end.

The trail Liam had cut through the jungle had already become overgrown, almost indistinguishable from the rest of the forest. Mac batted at the slight indentation with her walking stick. It was still the path of least resistance, and she knew exactly where it led.

She hitched up her loose cotton pants and adjusted her headband. No point in putting it off; in an hour she'd know. In an hour she'd either be back to her own time or . . .

Forget that. There wasn't any "or." There was only forging on into the unknown. She straightened, lifted her chin, and waved Fernando ahead.

The ancient, vine-covered buildings waited for her, tranquil and unchanged, as if they had known she would return. There were a few more leaves covering the crumbling walls, a little more undergrowth to wade through. But she was there.

She went to the mules and began to untie the bundle that contained her backpack, a packet of food, and her faithful flashlight. She'd come to the past with so little; she was taking almost as little back. She had her old worn jeans and T-shirt packed into a roll hung to the backpack. She had the odds and ends she'd once used to try to convince Liam of her origins.

All but the watch. She'd never gotten it back, and now it was too late. Hell, she could always buy another. And Liam couldn't change history with a single waterproof watch. She'd had enough thinking about time to last her an eternity.

An eternity without Liam O'Shea.

"*Bueno, señorita.*"

She turned to Fernando, who regarded her with solemn attention. "*Si.* This is it," she said. She tugged the two pendants from under her loose shirt. Fernando's gaze rested on them a moment and returned to her face.

"*Vuelve a su casa.*"

"*Si,* Fernando. I am going home." The pieces clicked as they touched each other, still nothing but cold stone under her hand. "If I understood you correctly, I need these to go there. I know you wanted them back—"

He shook his head. "*No las necesito, señorita.* I ask one thing. When you are on the other side, you give *las llaves* back to the people."

The people. *His* people, she thought. Like the guide who had led her to the ruins in the first place.

Crazy thought. But if she couldn't find someone to return them to, she'd leave them in the temple. God knew she didn't want to mess with them ever again. There were too many questions, and her heart was too heavy to contain even a single answer.

"I will," she said gravely. She pulled a leather pouch from her pocket and put it into his hand. "*Gracias por su ayuda.* I wish I could give you more."

He didn't even weigh the contents or check the number of coins but simply held the bag and stared at her with something like sadness. Mac offered her hand and found his return grip firm and warm.

She almost mentioned Liam, almost asked Fernando to tell him, if he ever came back to the jungle . . .

No. It was over.

"Well," she said, giving Fernando's hand a final shake. "*Adiós,* then."

Abruptly he caught her hand again and put the pouch in her upturned palm. "*Vaya con Dios.*"

He gestured to his fellow muleteer, caught the bridle of the lead mule, and never looked back as he vanished through the green wall of undergrowth.

Only then did Mac notice he'd left his machete beside her backpack. She picked it up and called after him, but if he heard he wasn't coming back. She thrust the blade into the soft earth at her feet. Maybe he thought she'd need it to protect herself from roving explorers.

Like Liam O'Shea.

To hell with it. No more procrastination. She tossed the pouch of coins into her backpack and hitched the pack over her shoulders. The flashlight was solid and real in her hand. Once she was home she'd learn to deal with reality again. No more mysteries. No more curses. No more crazy and debilitating emotions.

The tunnel was very dark, just as it had been before. She knew she should be afraid. She was blundering into another great unknown; anyone in her right mind would be scared stiff. But she'd left her right mind, as well as her heart, somewhere back in San Francisco. That was a definite advantage; she was numb now, numb and almost indifferent as she made her way to the end of the stone-lined hall.

The wall, too, was as it had been before, carved with a hundred inscrutable designs. Mac held up the flashlight to study it one final time, knowing it had nothing else to reveal. Nothing she wouldn't learn by taking the next and final step.

So this is it. Dr Pepper, here I come. She sucked in a lungful of air and closed her eyes. "Good-bye, Liam. You gave me the adventure of my life, and I wouldn't change that for the world. Be well, and be happy." She laughed through an unanticipated onslaught of tears. "Just try not to alter history too much and undo all my work, okay?"

She propped the flashlight against the wall. The stone chips were still cool as she looped them from her neck. They had to work, cold or not; there was no going back.

She clutched one in each hand, squared her shoulders, and walked right into a firm, warm, masculine shape. Powerful hands caught her arms.

"You've led me on a merry chase, MacKenzie Rose Sinclair," Liam growled, "but I can safely make that promise."

★ ★

HE WASN'T TOO LATE. By the saints, he wasn't too late.

He saw her now, in the dim lantern-light, just as he'd seen her that first time: wide-eyed, boyishly slim, her body taut with readiness to fight or run.

She trembled in his embrace like a wild thing expecting imminent death. Which might not be too far off the mark.

"So you thought it would be so easy to escape me, Mac?" he asked, giving her a little shake. "Make Liam O'Shea look like a fool and be on your merry way. Only it didn't quite work, did it?"

"How did you get here?" she stammered.

"The usual way. I chartered one of my own ships to bring me down. Strangely enough, I couldn't find Fernando in Champerico. Heard he'd gone off with a *gringa*. But when I got here, who did I find leaving the ruins?" He grinned. "Remarkable coincidence, eh, Mac?"

She pulled away with a jerk. "Perry," she said. "Perry told you."

"Yes, he told me."

"Then—"

"I'm not holding this conversation in a bloody tunnel. Come on." He grabbed her arm again and this time she went without resistance, stumbling and awkward, into the sunshine of the jungle afternoon. She blinked, disoriented, fists clenched at her sides.

"If I let you go, swear you won't run," he said.

Her head jerked up. "I'm not running from you, Liam O'Shea."

He dropped her arm and planted his hands on his hips, gazing his fill of her. She was beautiful in her trousers and shirt and ragged hair. Beautiful the way the jungle was beautiful, the way no tame, ordinary woman could ever be.

"You already ran," he said with a lazy drawl. "Pretty damned far. And with no intention of coming back, according to Perry. Ha." He scowled. "I told Perry to keep watch over you while I was in Napa with Chen. And he let you go."

"You told him—"

"Oh, he claimed to have misunderstood me, damn his English hide."

She swallowed, though she tried to hide that little betrayal of vulnerability. "Why did you follow me?"

He leaned against the nearest stone wall and crossed his feet. "You left something behind, Mac. You were in such an all-fired hurry to escape, you didn't give me a chance to return it."

He dipped into the pocket of his pants and pulled out

her watch. The strange, slick black surface felt alien in his hand, but when he passed it to her he touched something far warmer. Her fingers trembled as she snatched them away.

"Thank you," she said. "But it wasn't necessary to come all the way here—"

"I don't steal from friends."

Her eyes revealed more than her stiff expression; they focused on his face and warmed to the color of rich coffee. "It wasn't necessary," she repeated. "I'm sorry you went to all that trouble."

Her voice held a tremor, infusing everything she said with painful uncertainty. He couldn't tell if she were asking him an unspoken question, or expressing regret because she didn't want him here at all.

In a few minutes he would know, one way or the other.

"You still have something of mine, Mac," he said.

Her fingers wrapped more securely around the pendants in her hands. "I . . . I'm sorry, Liam," she said. "I can't return it. I need—" She lifted her chin a notch. "I need them both to get home. Back to my own time."

"So you did discover the way to get back."

"You *do* finally believe me. Don't you?"

He pushed away from the wall and circled her slowly. "I see you got Perry's pendant as well. Did you tell him the story of your remarkable travels?"

"I didn't have to. He gave it to me without question."

"Good old Perry. He knew you were leaving and didn't bother to tell me until you were on the ship."

"He wasn't supposed to tell you anything."

"Were you that afraid of me?" He stepped closer to her, so that she had to look up to meet his gaze. "Afraid I'd extract some terrible revenge for your revelations at my sickbed?"

"I wasn't afraid," she said, jaw set.

"Then why did you go?"

Mac was silent, as distant as if she'd wrapped a transparent cocoon about herself.

"Why, Mac?" He moved closer still, forcing her by sheer will to return from her inner seclusion. "Why did you leave while I was gone?"

"I . . . couldn't risk tampering with history beyond what I'd already done," she said. "And you'd made it pretty clear that you wanted me gone. There wasn't any point to having a scene like this one, was there?"

Liam knew she was right. He'd been angry—angrier than he'd ever been in his life. He'd let her feel the full brunt of his icy rage. It had taken him a few days to realize the anger wasn't at her.

And then a few more days to accept the real cause of his anger, overcome the shame and self-contempt that had overwhelmed him. He'd been able to think in the wilds of Napa. Think clearly for the first time since he'd met MacKenzie Rose Sinclair.

But he hadn't recognized the truth until he returned and found Mac gone. The memory of that terrible realization still clutched at his heart.

"So you were afraid of changing the future," he said. "What would you have done, Mac? Led a feminine revolution and become the first female mayor of San Francisco? Browbeat the entire male population into giving women the vote?" His tone dropped to an intimate near-whisper. "Become an advocate of free love, perhaps?"

She looked away. "Love is never free."

"But you gave it willingly enough when it served your purpose."

"I gave you my reasons for what I did. What I *had* to do. I can't undo it and I wouldn't if I could—"

"Not even if you could have stopped yourself from coming to the jungle?"

"No. I swore to Homer—my grandfather—that I'd come. I just hope he's satisfied."

"Promises can be terrible things, Mac."

She understood him perfectly. "It's hard to see," she murmured, "when a promise shouldn't be kept."

"You freed me of one that would have ruined at least three lives. You also saved my life not once, but twice." He smiled crookedly. "I won't thank you for that, Mac. You can't expect a man to be grateful for that kind of disgrace."

She stumbled back a step. "Why did I think for a second that you might have changed?"

His grin widened. "I fibbed a little before, darlin'. I didn't come just to return your watch. I came to find the other thing you'd stolen from me."

"What—"

"All the way here I wondered if I'd ever get it back." He strolled another tight arc around her.

Above the loose collar of her peasant shirt, the tanned column of her neck quivered. "I don't think I understand."

"You will." He took her chin in his hand. "What I need won't take much time. You see, Mac? I'm admitting I need something from you. You should be pleased." He trailed his fingers along her arm, grazing her breast. Her nipple puckered under the shirt, and he felt his body responding.

"Damn it!" She snapped out of her stillness and spun away, stomping across the overgrown clearing and nearly tripping over a buried stele. "No more. You're not going to win this game, O'Shea. I know what you're trying to prove, and it's not going to work. The war's over, and I'm going home—"

A few of his longer strides made up for ten of hers.

He caught up and grabbed one wildy flailing hand. With a sharp, swift motion he swung her around. She opened her mouth and he kissed her—a thoroughly earnest kiss befitting the situation. Her palms slammed into his chest, and the pendants fell to the ground. She pushed him violently away, but he had what he wanted.

It took her all of an instant to realize that he had both the pendants in his hand.

"Give those back!"

He pushed the pendants deep into his pocket. "Not until I have what I came for."

"And to think I felt sorry for you," she spat, all wild Mac again. "I thought I'd hurt you, but you're still an arrogant, impossible, reckless . . . If ever a man deserved a good kick in the seat, it's you!"

Liam listened to her enumeration of his faults and felt immense pleasure. It wasn't indifference she was showing him, but something far warmer.

"I wouldn't know what to do without you here to insult me," he said.

"You don't know a damned thing about insults. I know a whole catalog of them that haven't even been invented yet!"

"In that future of yours?" He backed away and set his feet wide apart on the verdant earth. "I think I'd like to hear them for myself." He made a show of thinking it over. "Yes, I think you'll take me with you to . . . 1997, was it?"

"So you *do* believe about the tunnel!" She glared at him.

"I'm willing to risk that you're finally telling the truth. With you gone I'd find life entirely too tame here. I'd resigned myself to a quiet life in San Francisco, and you took that away."

"So now I'm supposed to provide you with a new life? Just because I saved your hide—"

"Twice."

"—doesn't mean . . . *You* were the one who said I had to stop being your guardian angel."

"Ah, yes. My prickly angel." He cocked his head at her. "I've always wondered why the tunnel carried you back to the year and day I was in this jungle. Almost the very day I was to die. Can you tell me the reason for that, Mac?"

The martial light went out of her eyes. "I . . . don't know. I've never known why."

"It was something of a miracle, wasn't it? Sent from heaven above, perhaps."

"You aren't the kind of man who puts faith in miracles."

"I wasn't. I'm beginning to wonder if I was wrong."

She folded her arms across her chest and turned away.

"I think you are afraid, darlin'," he said, laying his hands on her shoulders. "Afraid of giving me power over you by admitting what you couldn't admit to me after Chinatown."

"I don't know what you're talking about."

"I think you do." He rubbed her arms gently from shoulder to elbow. "I'll strike a bargain with you. Give me the truth and I'll let you go. All debts will be squared once and for all."

She made a soft, helpless sound. He leaned close to her ear, fitting his body against hers. "It was more than wanting with you, wasn't it?" he said. "It's why you made me talk about my past. The real reason you followed me to Chinatown, not just to protect your hard work."

"I . . ."

"You owe me the truth. Spit it out, Mac, and I'll let you go home."

She fought it. Her body went rigid under his hands,

tensed to reject him, and he wondered if Perry had been wrong. She would refuse to answer, simply to deny him one last victory in their endless battle.

But at last she sagged in his arms. "You stupid Irishman," she said hoarsely, "I think I've loved you from the first moment Homer gave me that blasted photograph. Now are you satisfied?"

Liam felt his muscles turn as watery as jungle mud. It was all he could do to keep them both on their feet, but he turned her to face him.

"You little witch. Why didn't you tell me?"

She was crying, though she tried not to let him see. Her breathing was ragged, laced with little hiccups. "You made it abundantly evident that you didn't want any more to do with me. You said you were leaving. . . ."

"You're right." His quiet agreement brought her up short, made her freeze again in preparation for his worst. "I thought it would cure me if I went away. But it didn't. And then when Perry told me you'd left me, I went a little mad. I scared Perry out of his wits. He deserved it, the blackguard."

He grinned, but Mac was in no mood for levity. She slipped free, her expression still and wary.

Liam kicked the ground with the toe of his boot. "Ah, to the devil with it. I guess you won't be satisfied until I give you the words. Just like any woman." He gazed into her eyes. "I love you, Rose—MacKenzie—whatever the hell you want to call yourself. I may not be much good at it, and I may be all the things you said, but nothing can change that. Not even your history and your future and all your time travel. I love you."

There. By the saints, it was done, and it hadn't even killed him. But she only stared, lips parted.

"Why?"

"Why? Isn't that just like a woman." He found him-

self as tongue-tied as a schoolboy. There was only one
way to answer her. "I see you need more proof, darlin'."

And he proceeded to give that proof, pulling her
close, kissing her for everything he was worth, until she
wasn't stiff in his arms but soft and flowing against
him, her arms locked at his waist, her lips urgent under
his. Giving and taking equally.

"Satisfied?" he asked when they were finished, kissing her hair and temple and chin.

"I guess I'll have to be," she sniffled. "For now."

"That has an ominous ring to it." He pulled her
down beside him on a convenient block of stone and
held her close, stroking her cropped hair and taking in
the clean, healthy scent of her. No perfumes or preten-
sions. Not his Mac. She was just the way he wanted
her.

She curled up to his chest, her head against his heart.
"This doesn't feel quite real," she said.

"I can't say I blame you. I was a fool." He lifted her
chin on his fist. "You scared the devil out of me. You
were too bloody competent. You didn't need me. And
on those rare occasions that you did, I wasn't able to
protect you."

"Liam—"

"Hear me out. It's hard enough saying it as it is." He
gave her a lopsided smile. "I think I already loved you
the first time I met you, here in the jungle. Maybe it
happened when you slugged me down by the lake—"

She chuckled. "I did make your life a living hell,
didn't I?"

"And after Chinatown," he said softly, "I knew I
wasn't worthy of you. You'd seen the worst in me. You
said you'd done everything to save history and the Sinclairs—"

She jerked up. "It wasn't only that—"

"I know." He pulled her back down. "But you ran before I came to my senses, and if Perry hadn't told me I'd have never found you before—" His voice was in deep danger of turning wobbly, so he shut his mouth. Mac was gazing at him with such warmth that he wondered if he could ever speak again.

"Then you came knowing I might really go back to my own time," she said.

"You did have those strange inventions. But it suited me to think you were merely crazy. Until I learned that Perry's photograph was still in his rooms, undisturbed. It didn't take much more to convince me when I was already losing the battle." He kissed her nose. "You and I, Mac—you and I—we're like the two halves of that Maya stone. This was meant to happen. There isn't any other explanation."

"You're turning into a poet, Liam. I don't know if I can handle it."

"You'll learn, darlin'."

She was quiet for a long time, and when she broke the silence she broke away from him as well.

"There's only one problem," she said huskily. "I can't go back with you, Liam. I don't belong here, and I could change—"

"Who said anything about going back?" He got to his feet and folded his arms, readying for another argument with the little termagant. "I thought we'd established that I was going forward with you."

A chain of emotions crossed her face, settling on cautious hope. "But . . . It's not that simple . . . Do you have any idea what you'd be getting into, Liam?"

He shrugged. "I'm sure you'll explain it to me."

"Do you realize what it will mean to you? A world you know nothing about, completely different from your own?"

"I doubt," he said dryly, "that it could be more of a challenge than loving you."

She shook her head. "You don't know. The future is a scary place. You can't possibly be prepared. . . ."

He advanced on her, swinging the confiscated pendants from his hand. "Look at it this way, darlin'. I won't give you back your pendants unless you take me with you."

She gaped at him, and then her lips curved and her eyes narrowed and the laughter returned. "Blackmail, O'Shea?"

"It has its uses."

"If you do go with me, there are some things you aren't going to like. You'll have to let me be your guide, Liam. Me, a woman. And you'll have to listen to me."

"When have I ever had any other choice?"

She snorted. "You won't be anybody in the future. You won't even exist, not until we make you a new identity. You won't have a job, and my job doesn't pay much. I have a little apartment in Berkeley, not a mansion. No one will know how far you've come. You won't be rich—"

"There you're wrong, darlin'. I arranged a few matters before I left San Francisco. Perry is going to see that most of my fortune and property is held in trust for a certain MacKenzie Rose Sinclair, in perpetuity, until she claims it. I assume it'll only increase in value over the years?"

"Oh, my God." She sat down hard on the ground, not even bothering to find a rock. "Then you worked things out with Perry—"

"We came to an understanding," he said. "He was quite a schemer, but he does love Caroline. I'll . . . miss him."

"So will I. And Caroline?"

"Caroline," he said slowly, "will be happy with Perry. He loves her, and she'll come to love him."

"Yes," Mac said. "And she's found a cause for herself. I never told you she was destined to be a reformer and suffragette, did I?"

He rolled his eyes. "Why am I not surprised?" He offered his hands and pulled her to her feet. "If all that's settled, let's be on our way. I don't want you saving the life of any other rogues who happen by."

"Believe me," she said, wrapping her arms around his waist, "I have all the rogue I can handle."

"Ah—I did forget to tell you that there's someone else coming with us."

Her smile faltered. "Someone else?"

He whistled. A great gray shape hurled out of the foliage, swift and strong. With a joyful bark Norton flung himself on Mac.

"Norton!" she cried. "You brought Norton to the jungle?"

"He wouldn't be parted from me, the galoot, and I think he was pining for you. Bummer is staying with Mei Ling and Chen. He's got a new home in the Napa Valley and plenty of mischief to get into, I'm sure."

Mac's face was wet with Norton's enthusiastic kisses. "I guess bringing a dog isn't too likely to mess up history. But—" She frowned. "Isn't there anything else you want to bring?"

"I have all I need here." He looped his arm around her and rubbed Norton's ears with his other hand.

"There's still a possibility the time tunnel won't work."

He gave her the pendants and folded her fingers around them. "The sooner we go in, the sooner we'll find out."

She looked at the stones in her hand. "They're warm," she murmured.

"So they are."

They gazed at each other, kissed tenderly, and plunged into the darkness of the tunnel, Norton at their heels. When they reached the wall Mac picked up her electric torch, switched it off, and stuffed it into her backpack. "Don't want to leave this behind," she said. "You never know who might find it."

"God forbid," Liam muttered.

Mac whispered a similar invocation. "Well, here goes nothing." She took one pendant in each hand and held them before the wall. "Grab onto me and keep a good hold on Norton. And pray." She breathed another prayer of her own, waited for Liam to take a firm grip on her waist, and touched her folded hands to the wall.

MAC KNEW IT had worked when the nausea subsided, the numbing disorientation faded, and her first footstep forward hit something light but definitely solid.

The stones were already losing the fierce heat that had come uncomfortably close to burning her palms. She transferred them to one hand and reached down with the other. Her fingers closed on stiff fabric. The distinctive shape told her what it was: Homer's baseball cap. She lifted it to her lips and gave the dirty bill a resounding kiss.

One thing, however, was definitely missing. Liam's bones. Because Liam had never died and left them for her to find in 1997.

She sagged back, and Liam caught her. Norton licked her hand.

"It worked," she said dazedly. "It worked."

Liam was shaking a bit himself. "And did we come to the right . . . time?"

"I think so." She smiled weakly, though she doubted

he could see her expression in the dark. "When I went through the first time, I lost my grandfather's cap. But I guess we can't be sure until we get out of the tunnel completely." She unfolded her clenched fingers from the pendants. "Here. You take one of these until we're out, just in case."

He took the pendant with unsteady fingers. "I confess I'll be glad to see daylight again."

"So will I." She shrugged out of her pack and felt for the flashlight. "Let's get out of here."

Norton, who apparently liked the darkness no better than they did, had bounded ahead, and his barks echoed from an increasing distance as he ran down the tunnel. He kept up his canine communication until Mac and Liam could see the faint illumination of the entrance, and then Norton's lanky silhouette against the brightness of day.

The jungle was not the one they had left behind. The clearing was no longer completely overgrown, there were subtle changes in the buildings, and . . .

There was a welcoming committee waiting for them. A small group of Maya men and women in the simple clothing of farmers and woodsmen, whose features were the same as those on the ancient steles and temples. Norton's hackles lifted, and he growled a warning.

Liam's hand was at the knife on his belt. "Who are they?"

Mac covered his hand with her own. "We're home," she said. "The young man in the front . . . I know him. He was the guide who brought me here."

The guide who had led her to the ruins and then left her. His features were the same, but now they were grave and still. He turned to his companions and spoke in a language Mac didn't recognize.

"What do they want?" Liam said. He took a step

forward, shielding Mac, and called out a greeting in Spanish.

The young man's gaze dropped to Liam's fist—the one that still held half of the pendant—and he began to speak in Spanish too swift for Mac to follow.

Liam listened, head cocked, and translated. "He says: 'You have the keys. We have waited. Now you return them.' "

It took a moment to penetrate, and then Mac remembered. Fernando's final words to her, in halting English: "*You give the keys to the people.*"

She opened her own fist. The Maya murmured among themselves as she held her pendant on her upturned palm.

"The keys," she said. "The keys to the time tunnel."

Liam gave her a quizzical glance and let his own piece dangle from its leather thong. "This is what they want?"

"I think so." She took Liam's pendant and laid it beside her own—two unremarkable chips of carved stone against the pale skin of her hand. "I don't understand, but . . ." She looked at Liam with swift excitement. "I'd thought once that the Maya were probably the best people in the world to come up with time travel. They were obsessed with time. And their great civilization all but vanished over a thousand years ago. Do you think that maybe . . ."

Crazy idea. But no crazier than what she herself had done. And now the modern Maya guide and his people waited for her to restore something that belonged to them. The keys to an ancient tunnel through time.

"Ask them what they'll do with the stones," she said.

Liam did so. The guide answered with measured solemnity.

"He says they'll put them back in the temple," Liam

said, scratching his chin. "Bury them and return to their
. . . watching."

"Watching? For what?"

Liam hesitated. In the stillness a parrot called. A
warm wind dried the perspiration on Mac's forehead.

"He says that the keys are held in sacred trust from
the time of their ancient grandfathers," Liam said. "Until the day comes when they are called to the . . .
other place."

They looked at each other, wordless. Mac was almost
tempted to hold the pendants a little longer, to explore
all the possibilities revealed at this final hour of her
great adventure. The things she could learn, the wonders she could reveal, like the greatest of the Sinclairs . . .

She closed her fist around the stone chips, and nearly
dropped them when they flared with a renewed heat
that burned into her palm. The charred remains of two
leather thongs fell to the ground. She gasped and
opened her hand.

The pendants were gone. In their place was a single
square of carved stone, whole and complete.

"By all the saints," Liam said.

"You said it," Mac said fervently. "I think I get the
picture."

The guide and his companions still waited—waited
for her to do the right thing. She lifted her chin and
walked across the small, infinite space between them.

"I think this belongs to you," she said, and placed
the stone in the guide's extended hand.

The jungle hushed with a preternatural stillness. The
guide turned to the others, cradling the stone like the
most precious of gems. An older Maya took the stone
carefully, wrapping it in a length of cloth.

"Well, I'll be damned," Liam said, tilting his hat
back.

"It was never ours to begin with. But it gave us something wonderful."

Before he could answer, the guide moved on Mac with startling swiftness and grabbed her hand, turning it palm-up. Liam lunged and stopped in the same instant.

"Look at your hand," he said.

She looked. In the curve of her palm was branded a pattern, Maya glyphs and symbols that exactly matched those on the fused stone key. Burned there by an unearthly heat and an ancient unknown magic.

The guide spoke. Liam's translation was halting. "He says you are marked. He says . . . the Old Ones will always be with you."

"That's nice to know," Mac said, her knees a little wobbly. "I think."

Without ceremony the guide dropped her hand and stepped back. "Now you go," he said in heavily accented English. "It is time."

The other Maya began to drift in a semicircle, herding Mac, Liam, and Norton away from the tunnel and toward the wall of jungle at the edge of the clearing. Liam planted himself as if he would resist.

"No one pushes Liam O'Shea," he growled.

Mac almost laughed. *This* was something completely familiar. "What's wrong, Iggy?" she challenged. "Scared to face the great unknown? Maybe the jungle seems safer than what's waiting for you in my world."

He rounded on her. "Scared?" He grabbed her hand and charged in the direction the Maya wanted them to go.

There was an opening in the foliage—a machete-cut path Mac recognized. It was the one the guide had made for her, unaltered from the day he'd led her to the temple. She hadn't lost any time at all.

But she'd gained more than she'd ever dreamed.

"This is it," she said, squeezing his hand. "On the other side of this path is Tikal. The Tikal of my time. And then . . ." She turned for one last glance at the ruins that had changed her life, and the people who, in some strange way, had made it possible.

They were gone—vanished into the jungle or the temple without so much as a rustle of leaves or any sign that they had been there.

"Well, that takes care of that," she said ruefully. "It's a good thing we won't need a guide to get back."

"You'd better let me go first," Liam said.

"You'd better get used to me doing some of the leading, Liam O'Shea," she retorted. "But maybe we can start by going together."

He gave her a long look, and grinned. "I like the sound of that, darlin'."

She let out a long breath and flexed her hand, testing the burn marks patterned into her palm. They didn't hurt, almost as if she'd had them for years. "I may not have the pendant anymore, but I'm not likely to forget this adventure soon."

"You have a better souvenir than that." He took her in his arms, lifting her off her feet and matching action to words. The kiss was long, heated, and designed to prove that Liam wasn't about to change in fundamentals, no matter how far he'd come in time.

"We're not done adventuring yet, darlin'. But when we settle down, we're going to make up for all the O'Sheas that weren't born in the last century."

Her ears burned as she caught his meaning. "Hey, I'm only one woman, you know."

"Ah, but what a woman." Suddenly he grew serious, setting her down with his hands firm on her shoulders. "You're going to marry me, Mac, and I won't take no for an answer."

"Me say no to Liam O'Shea?"

"I won't let you forget you said that, darlin'."

Norton added his two cents with a ringing bark. Mac leaned back in Liam's arms to pat the wolfhound's shaggy head. "Then I guess the sooner we're back in civilization, the better. And anyway"—she slapped at her arm—"the mosquitoes are getting a little too friendly."

"They recognize one of their own—a troublesome, annoying, persistent little—"

She covered his mouth. "Watch it, Liam. Remember, I know your middle name."

"And I know yours." He cupped her cheeks in his big hands, devastating tenderness in his eyes. "My thorny Rose."

They gazed at each other like lovestruck teenagers until Norton nudged his muzzle under Mac's hand. She laughed. "We may have left Victorian times behind, but we still have a chaperon."

"And we still have the greatest adventure before us," he said. "Shall we go find it?"

"Just a minute." She shrugged out of her backpack and pulled out the photograph she had carried so long and so far. She walked back to the temple and propped it against the ancient wall, close to the dark entrance.

Liam came up behind her. "You're leaving it here?"

"Yes. It feels . . . right, somehow. I don't need it anymore. Not when I have the real thing." She took his outstretched hand.

Thank you, Homer, for sending me out to break the family curse. Even if it never existed.

You forced me to find my own life, and I'm grateful. I'll try to live up to the Sinclair tradition.

And I'll never be alone again.

The slap of skin on skin startled her from her wordless prayer. Liam frowned at the remains of the mosquito in his free hand.

"I think your modern mosquitoes have taken a liking to me," he said. "I trust there's more to your fantastic world than this."

"Oh, yeah," she said, kissing his knuckles. "And I can't wait to show you."

He grinned, tucking her arm through his. "Then lead on, Mac. The future awaits."

About the Author

Susan Krinard graduated from the California College of Arts and Crafts with a BFA, and worked as an artist and freelance illustrator before turning to writing. An admirer of both Romance and Fantasy, Susan enjoys combining these elements in her books. She also loves to get out into nature as frequently as possible. A native Californian, Susan lives in the San Francisco Bay Area with her French-Canadian husband, Serge, a dog, and a cat.

Susan loves to hear from her readers. She can be reached at:

P.O. Box 272545
Concord, CA 94527

A self-addressed stamped envelope is much appreciated. Susan's e-mail address is:

Krinard@ccnet.com

If you enjoyed *Twice a Hero,* watch for Susan Krinard's next electrifying novel in the summer of 1998.

"Susan Krinard was born to write romance."
—bestselling author Amanda Quick

"Susan Krinard . . . is the yardstick against which all other supernatural romances should be judged."
—*Affaire de Coeur*

"A truly fresh and innovative writer, Ms. Krinard takes easy command of the futuristic romance format to bring us breathtaking excitement and unmitigated reading pleasure."
—*Romantic Times*